Heather and Velvet

Teresa Medeiros

Heather
and Velvet

LOVESWEPT®
DOUBLEDAY
New York • London • Toronto • Sydney • Auckland

Loveswept ®

PUBLISHED BY DOUBLEDAY
a division of Bantam Doubleday Dell Publishing Group, Inc.
666 Fifth Avenue, New York, New York 10103

Doubleday and the portrayal of an anchor with a dolphin
and the word Loveswept and the portrayal of the wave device
are trademarks of Doubleday, a division of
Bantam Doubleday Dell Publishing Group, Inc.

Library of Congress Cataloging-in-Publication Data
Medeiros, Teresa, 1962–
    Heather and velvet / Teresa Medeiros.—1st ed.
        p.   cm.
    I. Title.
PS3563.E2386H43   1991
813'.54—dc20   91-12077
                                          CIP

ISBN 0-385-42147-8

First Edition

Dedication

To the Romance Writers of America and all my sisters and brothers-in-arms who have spilled their hearts, ink and tears to keep me sane: Emily Alward, Elizabeth Bevarly, Melissa Bregenzer, Norma Brown, Gwen Duzenberry, Elizabeth Lynn Gray, Kristin Hannah, Karen Harper, Mary Hooper, Lori and Tony Karayianni, Rebecca Lee, Stephanie Spearman, Shirley Turner and Jean Marie Willett.

For Andrea, who reminded me that some things were worth fighting for.

And for Michael, always.

Prologue

Scotland, The Highlands
1773

The bastard looked dead. Sebastian nudged him with his foot, waiting for the callused paw to reach out and jerk his thin leg out from under him, bracing himself for a roar of laughter. Ale trickled from the corner of his mouth. Sebastian dared to poke him harder, digging his bare toe into the fleshy abdomen. Nothing. Not even a drunken snore. The bastard *was* dead.

Sebastian squatted beside him. How had he gone so quietly? Sebastian had always imagined him going out in a bellowing, raging frenzy, the livid veins in his temple pulsing to a final snap. It hadn't been like that at all. Just a slump and a thump and he was gone.

Sebastian brushed a dirty hank of hair from his brow, and his gaze flicked upward to the carved rafters of the hall. He held his breath in the silence. It was as if all the bells in the world had stopped ringing at once, leaving only their echoes hanging in the air. Other sounds came to him then, untarnished by the smashing of pottery or the thud of a fist against his ear: the whisper of the swallows in the rafters, the rustle of a pine, the blurred hum of the wind across the moor. He bowed his head. It was the silence of a cathedral and it made him want to weep.

There was no time for weeping, though. MacKay would come for him now. His father's enemy would come to take Dunkirk as his father had always warned he would. Sebastian's lips tightened. MacKay might take the castle, but he would never take him.

He hooked his hands under his father's boots. Brendan Kerr didn't smell any worse dead than alive, but that would soon change if he was left long in the summer heat. Sebastian tugged. His gangly arms hadn't caught up with the growing breadth of his shoulders, but through sheer determination he soon had his father's body scooting through the pheasant bones that littered the stone floor.

When he reached the grass, Sebastian stopped, shaking with exertion, his stomach a hard knot of hunger. Sweat sifted through his long, dark eyelashes. He wiped it away.

Ye've the eyes of a lass, boy, and the puny spirit of one as well.

Sebastian stumbled backward, flinching from long habit. His thin legs sprawled beneath him, and he bit back a cry. But his father did not rise. Brendan Kerr lay humped on the grass; a fly buzzed around his temple.

The boy's teeth clenched against a savage urge to shove his father's body over the cliff, to send it tumbling and spinning to the moor below. But no. His mama would not have wanted that. He would give his father a proper Christian burial. He would bury him so deep and pile so many stones on him that his voice would never rise to haunt him again.

The afternoon sun was sinking when Sebastian cast the last rock on his father's grave. The clack echoed in the silence. A cooling breeze ruffled his hair and stiffened his sweat-drenched tunic against his skin. The moment seemed to call for something more. Awkwardly, his dirt-encrusted fingers signed the cross against his breast. It was his mother's symbol, his mother's religion, only half remembered and fuzzy from disuse.

A golden eagle soared over the moor, buffeting Sebastian with a giddy sense of freedom. He bounded up the stairs of Dunkirk to its tower. It took him only minutes to stuff his meager belongings into a knapsack—a ragged tunic, two shriveled potatoes, a silver filigree brooch that had belonged to his mother. He turned to go, then paused, standing motionless for a moment in a slant of sunlight.

Slipping to his knees beside the bed, he threw a guilty glance over his shoulder. The last time he had dared touch his father's coffer, he had received a cuffing that left his ears ringing for days.

Sebastian's hands trembled as he lifted the lid. The rich tartan lay as he remembered it, folded by his father's hands with a tenderness that had made Sebastian's heart ache with jealousy. The plaid was the last memory of a past when the Kerrs and the MacKays had fought side by side, united under one chieftain, one clan. He ran a grubby finger over the green and black squares, dreaming of a time when claymores had clashed and the skirl of bagpipes had haunted the misty hills.

Sebastian stood, draping the plaid around him. The luxuriant wool enveloped his thin body and tried to slide away. He pawed through his knapsack, digging out his mother's brooch to pin the garment at his shoulder.

The setting sun flushed the sky to orange as Sebastian scaled the low, crumbling wall and clambered down the cliff.

As the wind rippled the grasses of the moor into a patchwork of fading gold, Sebastian ran, exulting in the clean bend and stretch of his young muscles, the richness of the earth beneath his toughened soles. The plaid whipped around his thighs.

Midway across the moor he stumbled to a halt and turned to see Dunkirk silhouetted against the darkening sky.

He would return someday, he vowed. Not to skulk away like a thief in the night, but to ride up his own road in a fine carriage with a full purse and a fuller stomach. He would be so powerful, no one and nothing would dare stop him. Not the law. Not MacKay. Not even the taunting echo of his father's voice.

He would stand on that hill, arrayed in finery, and spit on his father's grave.

Someday.

Sebastian tightened his knapsack with a jerk and loped into the deepening night without another backward glance.

Part One

A gaudy dress and gentle air
May slightly touch the heart;
But it's innocence and modesty
That polishes the dart.
            Robert Burns

One

Northumberland, England
1791

Prudence plunged through the slick underbrush. The coil of hair at the nape of her neck unrolled and fell around her shoulders in sodden ropes. She paused in her mad flight to pluck out pearl-tipped hairpins with methodical fingers. She tucked them in her deep pocket with a tidy pat so none would be lost, though she suspected the caution was unwarranted. Although her aunt would never admit it, she would not waste genuine pearls on her homely niece.

Prudence wrung out her velvet skirts before pushing on. Wet leaves slapped at her face. Lightning flooded the night sky, and stark boughs whipped against that canvas of white. Prudence opened her mouth to yell again, but the sound was snatched by a gust of wind, then drowned by a jarring crack of thunder. Torrents of rain drenched the forest, rendering even the cone-laden pine trees an ineffectual umbrella against the wind-lashed deluge. Prudence wrapped her arm around a tree and cocked her head, straining to hear any hint of a desperate cry over the steady roar of the storm.

Turning her face up to the rain, she longed to give herself over to the exhilaration of the night—the pounding of thunder, the flash of lightning, the pelting of the summer rain against her skin. How different it was from being curled in the cozy cushions of her window seat, book in hand, watching raindrops stream down the leaded glass window. A primitive thirst opened her mouth wide to catch the rain on her tongue. This was no time for musing, though. Her hesitation could mean the death of one who was dear to her.

Her heavy skirts clung to her legs as she burst out of the thicket on the edge of a steep hill. Wind howled around her, whipping her gown away from her body. A heavy clap boomed through the forest. Prudence thought it was thunder, but a flash of lightning illuminated the road below, proving her wrong. The sky went dark again. She braced herself against the muddy hillside and squinted, her poor vision worsened by the gray curtain of rain.

A coach and four had come to a rocking halt in the road. Gilt outlined the elaborate crest on the door, a crest Prudence did not recognize. She sucked in a breath as she realized why the coach had halted so abruptly.

It was surrounded by the murky shapes of six men on horseback. Their shaggy mounts pawed the ground as one man, who was evidently their leader, barked a command at the coachman. Even in the feeble light, the coachman's face was ghastly pale. Thunder rumbled once more, farther away this time.

Prudence's nails dug into the exposed roots of a hickory tree as one of the bandits wrenched the door of the coach from its hinges. A woman's rhythmic shrieking split the night. The leader slowly raised his arm. Lightning glinted off the sleek barrel of his pistol. But it was not the pistol that caught Prudence's attention. It was the tiny ball of gray and white fluff that catapulted from an overhanging branch to cling to the roof of the coach.

"Sebastian!" she screamed.

All caution forgotten, Prudence flung herself down the hill, half careening, half sliding through the mud-slicked leaves.

The scream was Sebastian Kerr's undoing. He twisted on his mount, searching the hillside for the source of that unearthly cry—his Christian name in a place where he had no name. In a moment of madness, he half believed it was his mother's voice, hoarse with fear and longing.

The night exploded in a blur of sound and movement. Sebastian's horse pivoted with him, fighting against the sting of the bit. With hardly a blink to betray the motion, the coachman swung his heavy stave, catching Sebastian full in the abdomen. A weapon discharged with a flash of light, fouling the air with the acrid stench of fire and gunpowder, as Sebastian sailed off his horse. He landed hard on the road, his ankle folding beneath him with an ominous crack. The inane screaming of the woman within the coach went on and on. For a savage moment, Sebastian wished he had shot her.

The other horses reeled, churning the road into a sea of mud as they scattered into the night, their caped and masked riders bent low over sinewy necks. The coachman's gloved hand lifted. Sebastian froze, awaiting the killing blow from the knobby stave. Instead, the coachman brought his shiny whip down on his team, jolting the vehicle into motion. The coach thundered away, rocking wildly with the speed of its flight.

The night was still again, surrendered to the patter of the rain and the distant rumble of thunder as the storm tapered to a steady downfall.

Sebastian lay in a haze of mud and pain. Rain washed into his mouth. Had his mother called his name? He closed his eyes, hearing her melodic French, feeling the brush of her soothing hand against his brow. As the breath robbed by the stave returned, he became conscious of the pulsing throb of his ankle. What a fool he was! It must have been his father calling him. He squeezed his eyes shut as a wave of pain rolled up his leg. His father's thick Highland burr rode on its crest. *Sebastian! 'Tis a silly name for a silly lad.* He flinched, awaiting the thud of a mud-caked boot against his ankle.

All that pelted him, though, was rain. He opened his eyes. Reality returned, as cold and substantial as the muddy goop cradling his elbows. He quenched a flare of resentment at his companions for deserting him. He could hardly curse them when he had taught them everything they knew. *Never risk waiting on the wounded,* he'd instructed. *A fallen man is a noose for the next man.* They had learned their lessons well. Sebastian winced at the thought of D'Artan's lifted eyebrow when his men returned to Edinburgh empty-handed.

A wave of weariness battered him. The night had started badly. There had been the unexpected storm, then the first coach they'd accosted had refused to stop. The next coach had to be cursed with a stubborn coachman and a plump, squealing matron. And finally, the mysterious creature charging down the hill . . .

Sebastian braced himself on one elbow and peered through the rain. A girl sat in the mud a few feet away, seemingly oblivious to the steady wash of rain, the stained velvet of her skirts, the heavy ropes of hair tangled around her face. And oblivious to him. Her head was bent and she was crooning *his name* to a sickly ball of fur nestled beneath her chin. He felt an odd catch in his throat to hear his name spoken in such adoring tones. Even his handsome English mistress did not cry out his name with such feeling during their liaisons. For a brief moment, he felt ridiculously and insanely jealous of the kitten cradled to the girl's bosom.

"What a naughty beast you are, Sebastian," she chided tenderly, smoothing the bedraggled fur of the trembling creature. "I've been searching for you everywhere. I thought Boris had gone and dragged you off again."

The kitten gave an insulted mew at the mere thought of such an indignity. His yawning pink mouth made him look large enough to swallow himself. Sebastian rather wished he would.

He cleared his throat meaningfully, shifting his glare from the irritating feline to the girl. Their gazes met. Her eyes immediately narrowed to a puzzled squint.

Clutching the kitten in one hand, she scrambled over to him, crawling heavily across his ankle. "You're hurt, aren't you?"

Sebastian gripped his leg, his knuckles white. "I am now."

She sank back on her knees. "Shall I fetch the sheriff? He is an acquaintance of mine."

Sebastian groaned, wondering if this night would ever end. "Naturally. He would be."

The kitten squirmed free of her grasp and trotted up

Sebastian's leg, pausing to sheath needle-sharp claws into his kilt. Sebastian yelped.

The girl snatched at the beast, jerking Sebastian's kilt up to an alarming height. "There you go again, you wicked cat. How naughty you are. You must forgive him, sir. I fear he possesses an irrepressible spirit of mischief."

"I've been accused of the same failing myself," Sebastian murmured, distracted by a tantalizing glimpse of creamy skin as she leaned over him.

She finally succeeded in untangling kilt and cat. Her fingers smoothed the mud-splattered tartan, then she grew very still.

"I know who you are," she whispered. "You're the Dreadful Scot Bandit Kirkpatrick."

Her gaze shifted to the silk mask that covered the upper half of his face. She reached for it.

Sebastian caught her slender wrist. "Feel free to call me Dreadful."

She took the hint well. Her arm relaxed, and he released it. His reticence didn't stop her from leaning forward on hands and knees to peer into his face. To Sebastian's dismay, excitement, not fear, brightened her expression. He ought to send the silly lass away, he thought, but if he wasn't to perish in this cold, muddy road, he needed her help.

"I've read all about you." Her voice was touched with awe. "You are the scourge of the Northumberland border. The faceless terror of both Scotland and England. A blight on the justice system of all nations. A grim reminder of the savagery and greed that lurk in the heart of civilized man. No traveler is safe from you. No noble crest a protection against your wiles. You rob and kidnap and ravish—"

"—and cheat at whist," he interrupted, fearful her impassioned recital of his dastardly crimes would send her into a swoon of ecstasy. "While I cannot suppress a thrill of pride at your detailed and much exaggerated account of my debauchery, at this moment I am only an injured man lying in the rain with a throbbing head and a broken ankle. There is a crofter's hut nearby. Will you help me to it?"

She leaned even closer, eyes wide with hope. "Are you abducting me?"

"No."

Her face fell in disappointment.

"Very well then." He rescued his pistol from the muck and leveled the thick barrel at her chest. "Help me."

She helped him. She slipped the kitten into her pocket, where it set up a steady howling until she fished it out, murmuring something about hairpins. She tucked the creature in her other pocket before bracing her shoulder beneath Sebastian's and half-lifting him to his feet.

Her strength surprised him. She was a head shorter than he, but her slender frame was imbued with a steely grace that enabled her to keep her footing even when he stumbled. When his ankle struck a jagged stump, he would have crumpled in agony were it not for the bracing arms she slipped around his waist. As they forded a shallow stream, he halted abruptly, knowing he could not take another step. They clung to each other like lovers, her arms tight around his waist, his brow pressed to her cheek. Rain washed over them, melding them together.

"I can't go on," he breathed into her hair. His burr thickened as exhaustion and pain stripped away his cultured tones. "Leave me now and get back to your home, lass, before I kill the both of us."

"Nonsense." The sharp practicality in her voice roused him. "You said the hut was right over that hill and over that hill is where we shall go. What sort of Christian would I be to leave you here to die?"

"A bonny smart one."

The slope was a nightmare of slick leaves. More than once, the girl's hand closed over his, guiding it to a gnarled root he could use to claw himself upward. He had almost reached the crest of the hill when his bad ankle gave out and he slid halfway back down. He felt his mask tear away, but did not care. He lay with his cheek pressed to the black silt, welcoming the fog of stupor that reached for him.

The girl caught his sash, rousing him anew. Pain shifted to fury. He lifted his head and roared, "Damn it, girl, leave me be, or as God is my witness, I'll shoot you."

"That might present a problem as I have your pistol."

The fog cleared from Sebastian's eyes as he stared into the gaping muzzle of his own gun. The girl knelt in front of him, looking more like an impish wood nymph than an English lady. Her dress clung to her in tatters and mud streaked every exposed inch of flesh.

She stretched out a grimy arm. "Give me your hand."

His lips twisted in a wry smile. "Are you abducting me, lass?"

"Aye, laddie, that I am," she said, mocking his burr. "Haul yer bloody arse up this hill before I'm forced to shoot ye."

Sebastian's head fell. He did not know it could hurt so much to laugh. Without raising his head, he lifted his arm. Their muddy fingers linked. He gave her hand a brief squeeze before resuming his torturous crawl to the top of the hill.

The crofter's hut nestled at the end of a lonely hollow. A silvery burn gurgled beside it, overflowing its own twisting banks to lap at the rubbled walls. The hut looked as if it had been dropped from a windy sky, and the roof slapped on as an afterthought. The windows were crooked, the door askew. Prudence resisted the urge to tilt her head to see if the hut would straighten. Her heartbeat quickened at the thought of entering a bandit's lair.

A sheet of wind and rain buffeted them as she shoved at the door. It did not budge.

"Kick it," the Dreadful Scot Bandit Kirkpatrick commanded.

She looked at him doubtfully, then gave the door a dainty kick.

"Not like that. Put all your weight into it."

Prudence drew back her leg. Not only did she put all of her weight into it, she put all of his weight into it as well. The door burst open and they crashed inside and to the floor. Prudence's pocket squirmed in protest.

The bandit groaned. "You're killing me. I should have let you fetch the sheriff. He might have shot me and put an end to my misery."

She sniffed. "Don't be ungrateful. Sarcasm doesn't become you." She wiggled out from beneath his weight. "Rescuing robbers is a relatively new pursuit for me."

"They didn't teach it during your London season?"

"I never had a London season."

Kneeling, Prudence peered into the shadowy corners of the hut. A distant flicker of lightning showed her a rusty lantern and tinderbox hanging on a wooden peg. She crawled to it and waited for the next flash to strike a flint and touch a match to the tattered wick. A halo of golden light illuminated the dusty corner. She stood, waving the lantern in a sweeping arc.

The hut was dirty, abandoned long ago to skittering creatures and cobwebs. The only furniture was a rough-hewn table and chair set before a stone hearth. Heaps of ashes and chunks of half-burnt wood littered the grate. A pile of sticks huddled beside the hearth. There was no bed, but a stack of blankets made a rumpled pallet in the far corner. The two windows were covered not with glass, but with heavy black sacking, tattered and worn bare in spots. Prudence shivered. The air felt damp and cool against her wet skin. She hurried back across the hut and shoved the door closed, muffling the rain to a cozy drumbeat on the thatched roof.

The bandit still lay by the door. He had not spoken for several minutes, and she thought he might be unconscious. Her breath quickened as she knelt beside him, bringing the gentle glow of the lantern toward his face.

She gasped as the lantern was snatched out of her hand and thrust in her own face. Recoiling, she shielded her eyes from the blinding glare. From behind that awful light came a voice stripped of all humor by violence and desperation.

"Get back! If you see my face, your life will be worth naught. Neither to me or my men."

Prudence blinked, suddenly afraid. She spoke calmly, with great effort. "If you don't get out of those wet garments, *your* life will be worth naught. How am I to tend you if I cannot see you?"

There was a long silence. Then he said, his voice still edgy, but thin with pain, "Put the lantern in the corner. The light should suffice."

She obeyed. This time when she approached him, he did not protest. She could see little but the gleam of his eyes and the shadowy outline of his features.

"I'm not sure I can rise again," he said.

While she dragged the blankets nearer, the kitten climbed out of her pocket and jumped to the floor. He teetered around on unsteady paws, exploring the hut. Prudence caught the man under his arms and tugged. He shoved with his good leg until they'd worked him onto the pallet. She propped his ankle on a folded blanket, then knelt beside him again. Even in the dim light, she could sense him studying her face. She hid her discomfort by busying herself with the task of unwrapping his plaid and unhooking the drooping ruffles of his jabot.

"What do they call you?" he asked.

"Prudence."

He gave a short laugh. "Surely not. Faith, Hope, Charity, or even Rash Impetuosity, but not Prudence."

"I'm afraid I lose all rational thought when it comes to cats. I'm normally a very prudent girl." She reached across him to peel his wet linen shirt from his muscular shoulders.

His hand cupped her arm. His grip was disarmingly gentle. "A prudent girl wouldn't be alone in an isolated hut with the Dreadful Scot Bandit Kirkpatrick, would she?"

His knuckles brushed her arm, and her skin tingled at the brief contact. She could not decide if she had been threatened or warned.

With a brisk motion to hide her sudden trembling, she spread a blanket over his lap and held out her hand. "Your kilt, please?" She was thankful she could not see his expression.

To muffle his pained grunts as he unwound the garment, she asked, "Is it romantic being a bandit? Do you rob from the rich and give to the poor like Robin Hood?"

His voice hardened. "Aye, I give to the poor. Myself. I am the poor."

"That's an uncharitable attitude, don't you think?"

"Have you ever been poor?" He held out his arm, the kilt dangling from one finger.

She took the wet garment and shook it out. "Actually, I'm penniless."

"Penniless?" He snorted. "Only the rich say 'penniless.' I'd be willing to wager you've never gone hungry for it, have you?" Anger thickened his brogue. His r's began to roll like a storm-pitched sea. "There's a powerful difference between being poor in velvet and poor with no food in your belly. Have you ever stolen food from a dog for your dinner? Have you ever been beaten senseless because you hunted all day and couldn't catch more than a stringy squirrel?"

She laid a soothing hand against his bare chest. "Forgive me. I always manage to say the wrong thing." The skin beneath her palm was lightly furred. She had never touched a man's chest before, and its muscular warmth surprised her. "I have no right to judge you."

He grunted a response as if embarrassed by his impassioned outburst. Her hand slid downward to gently probe his abdomen.

He jerked in a breath. His flesh contracted violently.

Prudence snatched her hand back. "I didn't mean to hurt you. I saw the man hit you there. You're going to have a terrible bruise tomorrow."

"I'll worry about that tomorrow," he said brusquely.

He closed his eyes and turned his face away. She watched him for a few minutes, and when he didn't move, she thought he must be sleeping. She pulled a dusty blanket over him and tucked it tenderly around his shoulders.

Prudence was wrong. Sebastian wasn't sleeping. As soon as she slipped away from him, he opened his eyes, following her every move with avid curiosity. She stood before the fireplace, peering around the hut. He wished she would stop squinting. He had an absurd desire to see the color of her eyes.

Equally absurd was the way he'd felt when she'd touched him. Pain had not prompted his stomach to leap at her light caress, but the startling tenderness of her fingertips. He could not remember the last time a woman's touch had elicited such a wrenching response.

She knelt before the hearth and built a small fire with the sticks that had been left there. Her movements were economical, but graceful. He wondered at her age. She seemed nearer to being a woman than a girl. She had demonstrated no maidenly shrinking while helping him undress. Her hands had been soothing and practical. She had done what needed to be done without blushing or stammering. The girl was an enigma, and Sebastian intended to figure her out.

Prudence soon had a cheerful fire crackling on the hearth. She stood and stretched with the lazy grace of a woman who believes she is alone and unwatched. Sebastian's breath quickened as she lifted her arms and began struggling with the tiny row of buttons down the front of her bodice. Her garments were soaked. It was only natural that she would want to get out of them. What was not natural was the mischievous stirring of Sebastian's body as she eased the gown over her head. In other circumstances, he might have understood it, but not while lying beaten, broken, and half-dead on a chilly dirt floor.

He saw her shiver in her thin petticoat and chemise. As she bent to pry off her muddy shoes, the wet fabric clung to her body in all the wrong places. The firelight shining behind her illuminated the supple curves of her long legs and the soft swell of her breasts. Sebastian groaned.

She whirled to look at him, her hands flying up to cover her breasts. He slammed his eyes shut and thrashed a bit as if in pain. He was in pain, but not as she thought.

As soon as he judged it safe, he snuck one eye open. The girl was sitting on the edge of the hearth, combing the tangles from her hair with her fingers. Her hair was a deep velvety brown and hung almost to her waist.

Warmth from the fire billowed toward Sebastian's pallet. His eyelids grew heavy. He nestled deeper into the blankets, caught in the hypnotic allure of Prudence's fingers stroking through the rich cascade of her hair. He wished it were his own fingers.

As if by magic, he felt the feathery warmth of hair beneath his fingertips. Prudence's kitten butted its head against his palm, demanding attention. Sebastian stroked beneath its furry chin with one thumb, feeling the deep vibration of a purr that would have been more deserving of a lion. The kitten curled contentedly into the crook of his elbow.

"Sebastian," he whispered. "A silly name."

Like Prudence.

He was already drifting into sleep when he remembered the girl still had his pistol.

Prudence waited for as long as she could bear. Her petticoat and chemise were warm and dry, her hair only damp. She had chewed off three of her fingernails. As she hooked the lantern on her finger and crept toward the pallet, she remembered her aunt's chiding refrain. *Curiosity is most unbecoming in a lady.* Prudence's papa had not called it curiosity, though. He had called it a sharp mind for deduction. What Papa had failed to tell her was that a deductive mind was not an asset suitors desired. Prudence seriously doubted if a desperate criminal would be any more appreciative of it.

She knelt beside the pallet, her petticoat cushioning her knees as she held the lantern aloft.

The highwayman had shrugged aside most of the covers. Only a single blanket rode dangerously low on his hips. One serious sigh might dislodge it. Downy hair the color of honey covered his chest. Prudence's wide-eyed gaze traced it to where it tapered to a thin line, then disappeared beneath the blanket. Moving the lantern, she shifted her gaze back up his body. He was of average height, but the wide breadth of his shoulders made him look bigger than he was.

A smile touched her lips when she saw the ball of gray fluff tucked into his elbow. The sleepy kitten lifted his head and gave her a disgruntled look. Prudence touched her finger to her lips in a plea for silence. With a faint squeak, the kitten stretched and rested his chin on his paws.

Prudence's mouth went as dry as cotton as the lantern flame shed a halo of light over the highwayman's face. His tawny hair was badly in need of a trim. She reached to brush it back from his brow before she realized what she was doing. Snatching her hand back, she inadvertently touched the hot tin of the lantern. She stifled a gasp of pain, telling herself one burn was better than another.

Lifting the lantern higher, she hungrily studied his features. The sun had burnished his skin to a warm, sandy color that nearly matched his hair. His low-set brows were a shade darker. A thick fringe of charcoal lashes rested on his cheeks. Aunt Tricia would do murder for such lashes, Prudence thought. Not even copious amounts of lamp black could duplicate them. His nose was slightly crooked, as if it had been broken once, but its menace was softened by the faintest smattering of freckles across its bridge. A pale crescent of a scar marred the underside of his chin. Shallow lines bracketed his mouth and creased his forehead. Prudence suspected they had been cut not by time, but by wind and weather. She judged his age to be near thirty.

The lamplight played over his mouth like a lover, and Prudence felt her chest tighten. It was a wonderful mouth, firm and well formed, the bottom lip fuller than the top. Even in sleep, the slant of his jaw tightened it to a sulky pout that would have challenged any woman. Prudence wanted to touch it, to make it curve in laughter or soften in tenderness.

She leaned forward as if hypnotized.

"Amethyst."

The word came from nowhere. Her gaze leaped guiltily from the bandit's lips to his wide-open eyes.

Two

Prudence was caught in a trap of her own making, paralyzed not by the accusing circle of light, but by the stranger's eyes, which were the misty gray color of summer rain. She felt like a dowdy moth beating its wings against a star.

"Amethyst?" she repeated weakly. Perhaps the bandit was dreaming of gems he had stolen.

"Your eyes," he said. "They're amethyst."

She blinked. Prudence had no difficulty seeing things close to her, so there was no need to squint now. If she closed her eyes, she suspected she would still see his face, etched indelibly on the slate of her mind. He did not touch her, but she could not move. Poised there in the light, she waited for him to reproach her or yell at her or shoot her. She bit her bottom lip, then loosed it quickly, remembering how her aunt said the childish habit emphasized her buckteeth.

Sebastian studied her frankly, his earlier suspicions confirmed. The girl was utterly lovely. The delicate alabaster of her skin gave her even features a surprising fragility. A nearly imperceptible cleft crowned the tip of her slender nose, and the primness of that nose was belied by a faint overbite that hinted at an alluring pout. Stubby dark lashes framed her violet eyes. The lamplight sought out burgundy highlights in the velvety tumble of her hair.

Sebastian caught a coil of that hair between his fingertips.

It was as soft and heavy as it looked. He had forgotten the pleasure of touching a woman's hair without getting powder on his hands. The steady throb of his ankle waned as a new throb shoved blood though his veins in a primal beat.

His eyes narrowed in a lazy sensuality Prudence mistook for drowsiness. "Put out the lamp," he said.

She obeyed, relieved that she had escaped being scolded or shot. Darkness drew in around them. The firelight cast flickering shadows on the far wall.

"Lie down beside me."

Her relief dissolved at the husky warmth of his voice. The darkness shrouded his features, reminding her he was a stranger, with all the dangerous edges of any unknown man met in the seductive solitude of night.

She twisted her petticoat between both hands. "I'm not very tired, thank you."

"You're not a very good liar either." His hand circled her slender wrist. "If I offend you, you may kick me in the ankle. I'm relatively harmless right now."

Prudence doubted he'd be harmless with both legs broken. No man with a mouth like that was harmless.

"I won't hurt you," he said. "Please."

It was the "please" that did it. How could she resist such good manners in a highwayman? After a moment of hesitation, she stretched out beside him, her arms and legs as rigid as boards. He slipped an arm beneath her shoulders in a casual embrace, and her head settled in the crook of his shoulder more easily than she would have hoped. Rain pattered a soothing beat on the thatched roof.

"Have you no family to worry over you?" he asked. "Won't they be frantic when you haven't returned?"

"I'm supposed to say yes, aren't I? So you'll hesitate to throttle me lest they should burst in."

He chuckled. "Perhaps you're not such a bad liar after all. Have you heard rumors of me throttling women?"

She thought for a moment. "No. But a friend of my aunt's, a Miss Devony Blake, claims you ravished her last summer. It was the talk of every picnic and ball for months. She swooned quite prettily each time she told the horrid tale."

"Which I'm sure she did," he said curtly, "in frequent and exacting detail. What do you think of this Miss Blake?"

Prudence buried her face against his collarbone. "She hasn't a brain in her silly blonde head. It was more likely that she ravished you."

"So only a girl without a brain would ravish me?" His fingertips traced a teasing pattern on her arm. "Tell me—will this aunt of yours be wondering where you are?"

"She had gone to a midnight buffet when I went out. Perhaps she'll think I snuck out for an illicit tryst." Prudence smiled at the improbability of the thought.

Sebastian did not find the idea amusing. His arm tightened around her shoulders. "Did you?"

"Aye, that I did." Again, she mocked his burr with uncanny accuracy. "To meet the bonniest fellow betwixt London and Edinburgh."

Sebastian's ankle started to throb again. "Your lover?" he asked quietly.

"No, silly—my Sebastian."

Hearing his name spoken in his mistress's adoring tones, the kitten lifted his head with a drowsy purr. Sebastian took advantage of the distraction to slide his hip next to Prudence's, feeling unaccountably elated at her words. The kitten deserted the crook of his elbow and climbed onto Prudence's chest by way of her stomach.

"Fickle beast," he muttered.

He reached over to pet the animal, and his hand found the kitten's silky fur at the same moment as Prudence's. Their fingertips brushed, and she laughed breathlessly.

"It seemed such an ordinary morning when I awoke," Prudence said. "I had my bath. I put up my hair. I ate my prunes and cream." Her voice sounded odd to her, more like Devony Blake's than her own. "If anyone had told me I would be having such an extraordinary adventure by nightfall—I mean, lying in a highwayman's arms—I would have thought them insane."

He pulled his arm from beneath her and propped himself up on his elbow. "And if anyone had told you a highwayman would be kissing you?"

She swallowed. "I would have judged them a madman, lunatic, bedlamite . . . "

Her voice trailed off as his fingers entwined with her own. His head bent over her, blocking out the meager firelight, and he touched his wonderful mouth to hers. She shivered at the unfamiliar heat. He tenderly brushed his lips across hers, and with each tantalizing pass deepened the pressure, melding his lips to hers as if they had always been meant to be there. His mouth was every bit as smooth and firm as she had fancied.

"Delicious," he murmured as he pressed tiny kisses along her full bottom lip and each corner of her mouth.

No one had ever called her "delicious" before. Prudence thought she might swoon, but then he might continue to kiss her. Or worse yet, he might stop. She quenched a sharp flare of disappointment as he did just that.

His lips brushed her eyelids. "Close your eyes." His hand cupped her chin; his thumb slid sleekly across her bottom lip. "And open your mouth."

"I—I don't know," she said, her words coming in nervous spurts, "if anyone has suggested this to you before, but you have an inclination toward bossiness. It is a character flaw that might be remedied if—"

Before she could close her mouth, he swooped down and gently caught her lower lip between his teeth. Her gasp was smothered by the sly invasion of his tongue. His hand tightened on her jaw, holding her mouth open until she hadn't the will or the inclination to close it. Then his fingers slipped around to the nape of her neck in a velvety caress. His tongue swept across her teeth and delved deeper. Prudence thought she might die when she felt the shock of its warmth against her own. She should have been repulsed. Decent women did not kiss this way. But somehow having her mouth taken and stroked by this man was not repulsive, but captivating. Her own tongue responded with a tentative flick.

The highwayman groaned as if in agony, his strong fingers twisting in her hair.

She pulled back, suddenly remembering his wounded ankle. "Am I hurting you?"

"Aye, lass. You're killing me. And I love it."

Sebastian's own delight deepened as he realized she had never been kissed before. He found her innocence entrancing, her awkward response a sensual charm all its own. His mind raced ahead to other experiences he would love to introduce her to.

He kissed her until their mouths melded in a hot blend of honey. Prudence could not have said when one kiss ended and another began. He was a robber born and bred, stealing her breath and will with each tantalizing swirl of his tongue. He needed no pistol or steel, but only the rapier-sharp edge of his erotic charm. As pleasure spread its guilty wings in the pit of her stomach, Prudence accepted his dark and unspoken invitation to explore his own mouth with her tongue, shyly at first, then with a growing hunger.

She did not realize what her surrender did to Sebastian, that the touch of her trusting tongue against his own drove him on to the point of madness. All she knew was that she felt as weak and helpless as a kitten in his embrace.

Prudence's own kitten perversely chose that moment to wander away. Their entwined fingers were no longer stroking the cat, and the bandit seized the opportunity, sliding his hand across her chest until it cupped the supple swell of her breast with infinite tenderness. His fingers were both subtle and deft, and for a hazy moment Prudence was unaware of the source of this new and drunken pleasure. Her chemise had dried stiffly, but his searching fingertips easily found the taut peak of her breast beneath the crisp linen. He teased the aching bud between two fingers, sending tingling waves of sensation to every inch of her body. The shock was as great as if he had touched her bare skin.

Shame flooded her cheeks with a fresh heat. What was she doing? He would think her as brazen a hussy as Devony Blake. Guilt and panic smothered her pleasure.

She turned her mouth away from his and shoved against his chest. "Please, stop. I beg you."

He lifted his head. His fingers froze in their tantalizing motion, but his hand still lightly held her breast. She listened to his ragged breathing for a long moment before she found the courage to face him. Even in the poor light, she could sense the tightness of his jaw, the steeliness of his assessing gaze. If he decided she was teasing him, they both knew she was lost.

"You said you wouldn't hurt me," she whispered.

His lips brushed her throat, touched her ear lobe. "Does this hurt?" His thumb grazed the peak of her breast. "Or this?"

She arched her neck, helpless to disguise her shiver of pleasure. "No. Yes. I don't know. I just want you to stop."

He blew gently into her ear. "Why did you come here with me?"

"Not for this."

"Are you so sure?"

Prudence's mind was so addled she wasn't sure of her own name. "I came because you needed help." It sounded unconvincing even to her.

He shook his head with maddening certainty. "You came because you were bored. Because it had been too long since anything exciting happened in your life. I saw your face in the rain. I saw the hunger in your eyes."

The highwayman had lied, she thought. He was hurting her. The bald truth of her life cut her like a blade.

She tried to turn away, but he caught her chin in his hand. "It doesn't take long," he said, "for a woman like you to tire of fops in velvet and lace, with their soft hands and powdered wigs. They write poetry in your name, but they're too timid to kiss you as you want to be kissed."

Prudence felt like crying with relief. She had been wrong. He knew nothing of her life.

Sebastian drew back as he felt her shudder. At first he feared he had made her cry.

A soft hiccup of laughter escaped her lips instead. She sighed and stretched out a regal arm. "'But soft! What light through yonder window breaks? It is the east, and Prudence is the sun.'" She collapsed in giggles.

The girl was babbling, Sebastian thought, and he wasn't a man tolerant of babbling. But he would have gladly listened to her babble as he eased her petticoat down her slim hips and pulled her chemise over her head. He buried his face in the soft, shiny mass of her hair at the tempting vision. Her hair smelled sweet and clean, like lilacs in the rain.

"You don't need poetry, Prudence. You are poetry."

She lay very still beneath him. Her hands lightly clasped his shoulders, neither drawing him nearer nor pushing him away. Sebastian knew he had a decision to make. A broken ankle would not stop him from taking this charming girl if he so chose. At this point, he wasn't sure a broken neck would. Still, the urgency of his need for her warred with the lethargic stirrings of his jaded conscience.

He had promised not to hurt her. And he was wise enough to know that for some women seduction could hold as much pain as rape. If he sent her home to her aunt filled with the shame of wanton surrender to a stranger, the price of her fling with the stormy night might be too great. Then there was always the risk of a child. A bastard. Like himself. Sebastian knew of ways to lessen that risk, but his hunger for this girl was so strong, he did not trust himself to use them.

He lifted his head. "I don't suppose," he said earnestly, "you'd let me take off all your garments and touch you if I promise not to do anything else."

"I'd rather you didn't. But thank you, sir, for asking."

He flung himself off her with a despairing groan. His ankle rolled to an awkward position, and he winced. Every ache, throb, and weary muscle of his body tingled to life, magnified by the misery of his thwarted desire.

She touched his arm. "I really am grateful. You're very kind not to—"

He jerked his arm away and pillowed his head on it. "Keep your gratitude to yourself, unless you'd care to have no need of it."

She fell silent. Sebastian's flare of guilt only annoyed him further. "Oh, go ahead and talk, won't you? Talk about something. Anything. Preferably something damned unpleasant to take my mind off my . . . ankle. Talk about hairy monks. Dead frogs. Quote some more bloody Shakespeare."

"Why do you rob?" she asked musingly.

"Why does anyone rob? For money."

"Money for what?"

He opened his mouth to make a flippant answer and was as surprised as she when the truth came out. "Money to win back my father's land and castle from the black-hearted MacKay who stole it."

She lifted herself up onto her elbow. He could barely make out the shape of her in the dark, but her interest and curiosity were a palpable thing. He realized he had just told her more than he'd told most of the men he'd been riding with for the last seven years.

"How did you lose your land?" she asked.

"Luck doesn't run in our family. My grandfather threw in his lot with Bonnie Prince Charlie in '46. When he was defeated, the English Crown stripped us of our titles. MacKay took the land. When my father died, he took the castle as well."

"Will money buy it back?"

"No. But money will buy influence and enough respectability to fight Killian MacKay."

"Have you ever considered honorable employment?"

"Once. When I was younger and stupider than I am now. But when you come out of the Highlands, the Lowlanders spit on you. I couldn't afford the Grand Tour to complete my education. What could I do? I could steal, fight, and scare the hell out of people. So I put my talents to good use."

"Have you enough money to buy another castle?"

"I want this castle. Dunkirk was my father's only pride. I'll do anything to win it back."

A note of wistfulness touched her voice. "You must have loved your papa a great deal."

Sebastian closed his eyes. "I hated the bloody bastard. I wished him dead with my every breath." He yawned. "Good night, Miss Prudence."

Prudence was silent for a long moment. "Good night, Mr. . . . Dreadful." She smoothed the blankets over them both. "You must take better care. Robbing is a dangerous vocation. Hazardous for your soul as well as your neck."

He opened one eye. "Would you weep if they should hang me?"

"I believe I should."

"Then I shall take greater care than ever before." He caught her hand and laid it gently over his heart, as if it belonged there.

Prudence stared at the ceiling until she could no longer distinguish between the pulse of the rain and the steady beat of the highwayman's heart beneath her palm.

Sebastian awoke to find himself adrift in a pool of sunshine. For an instant, he believed himself to be in the bedchamber of his mistress's London townhouse. But where were the fluted posts of the tester, the luxuriant softness of the feather bolsters, the smooth, cold marble walls? His mistress could not tolerate sunlight and kept the heavy drapes drawn until well after noon.

He rubbed his groggy eyes and looked around, then smiled with bemusement.

Prudence had propped the door open with a rusty poker and torn the thick sacking from the two windows. A gentle breeze stirred the heady scent of honeysuckle outside, and sunlight streamed into the hut, carrying with it the fragrant warmth of the newly washed earth. The morning sun even poked its way down the chimney to dapple the immaculate hearth. The tiny hut had been swept clean. Sebastian had little doubt that he was now the dustiest thing in it.

Prudence's tattered broom looked more suited for riding than sweeping. Her kitten divided his bouncing energies between chasing the broom and knocking dust motes into the sunbeams. As Prudence lifted the broom to swipe the thick cobwebs from the beamed ceiling, Sebastian folded his arms behind his head, basking in the pleasure of watching her.

She caught her tongue between her teeth in a gesture of childish concentration, and hummed beneath her breath. Every few seconds, a piping note escaped. Dirt smudged her cheek. Sunlight laced the heavy fall of her hair with burgundy. She still wore nothing but the chemise and petticoat. As she passed the doorway, the sun threw the curves of her long legs and slender rump into silhouette. A pang of regret tightened Sebastian's groin, and he cursed under his breath. Whatever had possessed him to be so damned charitable last night? But as his gaze followed her, even his lust was tempered by a strange contentment.

She made him wonder what it would have been like to be born a crofter's child instead of the bastard son of a brutal Highland laird. How would it feel to awaken each morning to such a cozy scene? A clean-swept cottage. A humming wife. It wasn't difficult to imagine three or four wee ones tottering after Prudence's petticoat.

His face darkened as he banished the image. Any woman he might marry would be too rich to know one end of the broom from the other. Nor would she care to ruin her tiny waistline bearing his brats, even if she was young enough. That dream was over and best forgotten. Only Dunkirk mattered now.

He spoke, and his voice came out with an edge he had not intended. "If I'd have slept any longer, you'd probably be hanging curtains and hooking doilies."

She jerked around, dropping the broom with a clunk. A wispy cobweb drifted down and settled over her hair like a wedding bonnet. The sight did not improve his temper.

It unnerved Prudence to have him glowering at her from beneath his low brows. She shrugged apologetically. "Cleaning is a habit with me. My mother died young. I used to look after my father when we lived in London." She inched toward the chair where her gown hung. "How is your ankle?"

"Still broken. My man Tiny will probably have to break it again before he sets it."

She winced.

He struggled to a sitting position, grimacing as his stomach muscles stiffened in protest. "I was hoping you'd be gone when I awoke."

She gestured lamely toward the floor. "There was so much dust. I thought I'd straighten things a bit."

"I'm sure Tiny will appreciate it when he's taking his afternoon tea. But you'd best go now. He's a bit unpredictable. He might decide to break your leg instead of mine."

She wavered between a smile and a frown. The vision of being tormented by someone named Tiny lacked real menace. She wished he would stop glaring at her. There must be something she could do to make him look at her as he had the night before. Her face brightened as she spotted the bowl on the table.

She scooped it up and carried it to him as if it were the Holy Grail. "I washed your pistol. It was all muddy."

Sebastian made a small noise at the back of his throat as he peered into the bowl at the submerged weapon. He plucked it out with two fingers. Water streamed from the polished wooden barrel. She was right about one thing. The pistol wasn't muddy anymore.

She looked so pleased with herself that his impending roar faded to a choked, "Thank you."

Smiling lazily, he brushed the cobweb from her hair. His eyes softened to sleepy gray, and Prudence's heart beat faster. Her aunt must be right, she thought. Men fancied brainless women. It hadn't even occurred to him that she had washed the gun to keep him from shooting her.

As he leaned forward, shooting her was the last thing on Sebastian's mind. She had learned her lessons of the night well. Her dark lashes swept down to shutter her eyes. Her lips parted as she tilted her face to his. He groaned and buried his hand in her hair and his tongue in the warm, wet recesses of her mouth. He wrapped his arm around her back, and the pistol dangled forgotten from his fingertips.

An angry roar from the doorway drove Prudence into his lap. "What's it to be, Kirkpatrick? Are ye goin' to tup the puir lass or shoot 'er?"

Sebastian lay a warning finger against Prudence's trembling lips. "Chin up, love," he whispered. You're about to make the acquaintance of my merry men."

Three

Prudence slowly turned to face the men. Kirkpatrick kept his arm anchored firmly around her waist.

The two men did not look merry at all, she thought. Even the sunlight quailed before the blond giant standing in the doorway. As he ducked under the lintel, the floor shuddered beneath the booted hams of his feet. He could only be Tiny.

He threw back his head with a laugh that shook the timbers. "I frighted ye, didn't I? Ye taught me well, lad. Stealth before wealth."

His long, ratty beard and halo of blond hair made him look more like a misplaced Viking than a Scottish border raider. Prudence half expected him to throw her over his shoulder and carry her off to his longship. She pressed her back to Kirkpatrick's chest, and his hand flattened against her stomach with a soothing stroke.

She recoiled farther as the puckish creature perched on the windowsill gave a nasal coo of horror. "Fer shame, Kirkpatrick, where's yer mask? Ye musn't think much of the wee lovey, do ye? Shall I take her fer a walk now or later?"

Prudence thought he was the ugliest child she had ever seen. Then she realized he was not a child at all, but a young man, his features pinched to foxlike sharpness. His thin arms were strung with muscles like pianoforte wires. His lips smacked as he sucked the nectar from a honeysuckle blossom and leered at Prudence.

"That won't be necessary, Jamie," Kirkpatrick said. "The lass is blind."

"Blind?" echoed the giant.

"Blind?" repeated Prudence.

Kirkpatrick pinched her sharply. She squinted obligingly.

"You heard me," he said. "She's blind. She can see nothing but a wee bit of light and a few shapes. That's how she came to tumble down that hill last night."

Jamie crumbled the blossom in his freckled fist. "And what was she doin' on that hill? Pickin' daisies?"

Before Kirkpatrick could answer, Prudence said, "I was having a picnic."

Tiny's brow folded in a thunderous frown. He crossed arms as big as birch trunks across his chest. "Bloody wet fer a picnic, weren't it?"

Kirkpatrick gave her hair a warning tug. She ignored him. "Not earlier in the day. You see, I'd been lost for hours until your laird was kind enough to rescue me and bring me here . . . to his castle." She blinked at the air a full foot down and three feet over from the source of the rumbling voice.

"Our laird?" hooted Jamie.

"His castle?" echoed Tiny.

Prudence felt around the floor, wincing as a splinter buried itself in her thumb. "I'd best get my things. Laird Kirkpatrick said one of you footmen would be kind enough to escort me to the road where I might await conveyance to my home."

"Did he now?" Tiny frowned. "Our laird is the purest soul of generosity."

Sebastian smirked. "So they tell me."

Prudence rose. Jamie vaulted off the windowsill and into the hut. Sebastian's jaw tightened, but he refused to let so much as a twitch of an eyebrow betray him. He knew they weren't convinced of her harmlessness yet. He hoped to God she realized it as well. He folded his arms across his chest to hide his clenched fists.

Prudence took a tentative step forward, arms outstretched

to grope the air. Careful not to make a sound, Tiny nudged a stool into her path. Sebastian flinched as her shin slammed into it.

"Excuse me, sir," she said.

She felt her way around the table with a crescendo of convincing thumps. Just as her hand reached the back of the chair, Jamie snatched away her gown and held it gleefully aloft. Silver hairpins tinkled to the floor. He picked one up, bit the pearl, then tucked it between his lips.

Prudence felt each rung of the chair back, frowning with great perplexity. "I'm sure this is where I left my gown to dry."

Jamie tossed the velvet into her face. "Here ye go. Must have slipped off."

"Thank you," she said, her voice muffled.

She pulled the gown over her head. All three men watched avidly as she buttoned the bodice and tugged on her damp shoes.

Straightening, she clasped her hands together. Sebastian's spirits sank as he realized what she was waiting for. If only the cantankerous cat would wander over and brush against her ankles. Tiny spotted the kitten at the same moment Sebastian did. It crouched behind one of the table legs, a cottony puff of a tail quivering in anticipation of pouncing on Tiny's boot.

Tiny bent double and shoveled the creature into his palm. He held it up to eye level, peering at its disgruntled whiskers.

Prudence squeezed her eyes shut, fighting back tears. She did not dare protest or reveal she knew he held Sebastian. He could easily snap the animal's neck between two fingers.

A low rumble filled the hut. Her eyes flew open. At first, she thought the massive man was growling at her cat, then she glimpsed the grin on Kirkpatrick's face. Tiny was purring.

He rubbed the kitten's belly against his bristled face, his eyes narrowed to blissful slits. "I love cats. Me mum always kept one at the hearth."

"I love 'em too," Jamie said. "When there ain't nothin' bigger to eat."

Prudence shuddered.

"Do the wee beastie have a name, lass?" Tiny asked her.

"Sebastian."

Jamie snorted. "That's a silly name."

Sebastian winced. "Give the lady her cat, Tiny. Jamie, take her to the road. Take her *directly* to the road. Then come straight back. Do you understand?"

Jamie doffed his shapeless cap with a mocking bow. "I ain't daft, me laird."

Tiny tucked the kitten in Prudence's arms.

"Thank you ever so much, Mr. Tiny."

Prudence had to take one last chance. She felt her way along the wall until her toe touched Sebastian's pallet. She knelt beside him, painfully conscious of the two pairs of eyes boring into her back. Her vacant gaze gave her the perfect chance to study him. She did not need to study him. His face was committed perfectly to her memory. She would see it each morning when she awoke and each night when she closed her eyes. Sunlight revealed tiny crow's feet, but robbed nothing from his devastating good looks. She touched his cheek, committing its texture to her memory as well.

"Thank you for your kindness, sir. It will not be forgotten."

He gave her hand a quick, hard squeeze. "That it won't."

She turned away before the tears could well in her eyes. Jamie offered her his arm. She stood there stupidly, ignoring it until he linked it in hers.

"Did ye ever hear the joke about the blind whore and the armless sailor?" he asked as he led her to the door.

Sebastian watched her go with a sense of triumph. Then the doorway was empty. The sun lost its sparkle, settling into the dull cast of mid-morning. He grimaced, deepening the brooding lines around his mouth.

Tiny propped his hip on the table. The wood groaned under his weight. "I feared for ye, lad, when I checked the old oak fer a note, but found none. I thought the law had got ye."

Sebastian refused to meet the other man's measuring gaze. Tiny knew him better than anyone did. They had run the moors together when they were boys. Tiny was the only one who had ever had the courage to place himself between Sebastian and his father's fists. It had cost him two teeth and earned him Sebastian's unswerving loyalty.

"Ye know D'Artan won't like this one wee bit," Tiny went on. "If the lass talks, it could be yer neck and his as well."

Sebastian felt a cold mask fall over his face; the mask of his father's face, the jovial ferocity he had always longed to smash. "No, Tiny. If she talks, it'll be her neck."

Tiny shook his head wearily and crossed the hut to squat down beside him. Sunlight struck silver as he tossed the hairpins in Sebastian's lap. "Ye'd best treasure them. They're all ye've got to show fer last night's work."

Sebastian waited until Tiny had gone to cut a splint before gathering the hairpins. He handled them reverently, as if they were tipped with something far more precious than pearls.

Jamie was the most unpleasant creature Prudence had ever encountered. She ached to be alone with her thoughts, but he chattered on blithely with jokes more suited for a brothel than a lady's company. She edged away from him when he paused to scratch his crotch and spit. By the time they reached the road, he had dragged her into one wet bramble bush, two rabbit holes, and a tree trunk. Her shins, she knew, would be black and blue by the morrow, and her delicate skin itched already with what threatened to be poison sumac.

Jamie looked both ways down the deserted road, scratching his head. Prudence took a step backward, fearful something might leap out of the ragged mop.

"I hate to leave ye here all by yer lonesome," he said. "Ye could be set upon by robbers. Ye know how robbers are. They love blind girls." He leered at her. "Blind girls can't kiss and tell."

"I'll be fine. If you could just sit me down at the side of the road, I'm sure someone will come along soon."

She resisted the urge to kick him as he led her to the middle of the road and pushed her to a seated position. "There ye go, luv. Sit right here in this patch of wildflowers. Ain't they pleasant?" His gamin nose wrinkled. "Smell them now."

Prudence could smell nothing. The muddy road sucked at

her skirt. He must think she was blind *and* stupid, she thought. She smiled brightly at the nearest tree. "Thank you. You are a true gentleman."

He circled her until he stood behind her. "I'll be on me way now. Good day." He ran in place for a moment, then stood utterly still, holding his breath.

Prudence began to hum softly, as would any genteel lady who had been left on a flowery bank to await the next coach. After three stanzas of "My Shepherd Is The Living Lord," Jamie sighed in defeat and melted into the woods. Prudence did not stir. The morning sun lengthened toward noon.

Finally, she dared to peek behind her. Sunlight glinted off glossy foliage. The chirp of a lark broke the waiting silence of the forest. Seeing and hearing nothing else, she gathered her muddy skirts and fled toward the meadow.

A tousled head shot out from behind an oak. Hazel eyes narrowed, and Jamie muttered to himself as Prudence scaled a fence, her bedraggled dress a splash of purple against a field dotted with yellow buttercups.

He tugged his ears and chortled. "Damned agile for a blind lass, wouldn't ye say, Kirkpatrick, me lad?"

He sprinted toward the hut, leaping rocks and dodging trees like the mad Highlander he was.

Prudence rolled through the window at the end of the upstairs corridor, blessing the iron trellis and weighted window sashes her aunt had chosen during her perpetual remodeling. Prudence's own window had been latched. She pulled off her shoes and tiptoed across the parquet floor. Clipped footsteps echoed on the polished wood. She looked around frantically. Not a doorway or alcove in sight. She pressed herself to the wall as if she might somehow disappear into the elaborate scrollwork. Old Fish, the aged butler, rounded the corner, sucking loudly on his sunken cheeks.

He passed her by without a second glance. "Good morning, Miss Prudence. Your aunt sent word that she was off to London for a fortnight. She trusts you to amuse yourself."

Prudence stared after his rigid back, her eyes huge, then looked down. Her skirt hung in tatters around muddy, scratched ankles, and the buttons of her dress popped like springs from loose threads. A tangled wad of hair hung over one eye.

Her shoulders slumped. She had just had the most extraordinary adventure of her life and not one soul had even missed her.

She slipped into her small room, no longer bothering to muffle her footsteps. The terrible silence of the house closed in around her. She had freed her kitten to cavort in the walled herb garden, but now wished she had brought him up for company. Hoping a soothing bath would lift her spirits, she rang for a maid. The cozy confines of her tent-bed looked tempting, too. It would be simple enough to plead a headache and spend the rest of the afternoon there. Heaven knew her aunt did it often enough. But her aunt was not always alone when she did it.

At that thought, pain burst through Prudence, so intense it was almost physical. She turned too quickly, sweeping a porcelain figure of the goddess Diana from her dressing table. The figure shattered on the floor, leaving only the jagged circle of a mouth to chide her for her uncharacteristic flare of temper.

Two maids dragged in the tin tub. They swept up Diana and took the clothes Prudence commanded they burn without betraying so much as a flicker of curiosity.

After her bath, Prudence donned a linen wrapper and sat at her dressing table. She dragged her hair away from her face in a severe chignon. Not a single damp tendril was allowed to escape. She anchored it at the nape of her neck, methodically shoving in the hairpins. Heavy hair, she thought. Impossible hair. It took powder poorly. It would not curl without scorching. How many times had her aunt suggested she chop it off and purchase a fashionable wig? If she refused, it was best that she wear it flat and close to her scalp so no one else would notice how impossible it was.

You don't need poetry, Prudence. You are poetry.

The husky burr haunted her. She dug her fingers into her forehead as if she could somehow stop its echo. The highwayman had buried his face in her impossible hair. His warm, sweet breath had stirred the heavy coils. He had looked deep into her eyes and asked if he could touch her. She jabbed another pin into her hair, relishing the distraction of the pain.

She opened a cherrywood box and drew out a pair of heavy spectacles, then perched them on her slender nose. Her father had taken time out from his inventing to fashion the pair for her.

Lifting her head, Prudence faced her reflection. The impetuous girl who had spent the night in a highwayman's arms was gone. In her place was a plain woman whose features were too even to be given even the distinction of ugliness. Prudence Walker. Plain Prudence, dutiful daughter, sensible niece. Thick shells of glass hid her eyes. Even at eleven, she hadn't the heart to explain to her papa that the blurred edges of life were sometimes kinder than clarity.

The mirror swam before her and her reflection turned as misty as gray eyes the color of sunlight on steel.

Four

The leaded glass window distorted the world into sparkling diamonds of green. Sebastian heard the door behind him open and close. Before turning, he shifted his weight to disguise how heavily he leaned upon his cane.

The Persian carpet muffled D'Artan's steps. He seated himself behind the walnut desk as Sebastian faced him. The older man leaned back in his chair and steepled his bony fingers beneath his chin. A cryptic smile touched his thin lips. He did not offer Sebastian a seat. The study was devoid of all but the desk and D'Artan's thronelike chair. Sebastian knew what D'Artan was doing. He would maintain his enigmatic silence until Sebastian started to babble. Sebastian was determined not to give him that satisfaction. He clenched the gold-claw handle of his cane.

D'Artan, however, knew Sebastian as well, if not better, than Sebastian knew him. The faint twitch of Sebastian's fingers only deepened his smile.

His mellifluous French poured over Sebastian as smoothly as his silvery cap of hair poured over his scalp. "Your wound? Does it trouble you?"

"No. It's nearly healed."

Sebastian was lying. Before a hard rain, the throbbing of his ankle could bring tears to his eyes. He still awoke trembling and sweat-drenched from nightmares of the sunny morning when Tiny had rebroken the bone. The opium Tiny had forced him to smoke had dulled the pain, but not the memory. Nor had it dimmed the memory of a girl's voice, as soft and alluring as velvet crushed against the nap. Sebastian did not care to speak of that night. He did not want D'Artan's sneer to sully it.

He tapped his cane on the carpet. "Quite an elegant retreat you have here."

D'Artan crooked an eyebrow. "Lord Campbell was kind enough to grant me use of his country estate while he is residing in the city."

"Still the darling of Edinburgh, are you? Playing upon Lord Campbell's sympathies for the tragic French émigré fleeing the terrors of the revolution?"

"The British are notorious for their lack of imagination except when it comes to their own thick skins. They see in me their fate should the revolution cross the Channel." D'Artan uncorked a decanter and poured two brimming hookers of Scotch. He handed one to Sebastian. "That's one of the reasons I summoned you here. Lord Campbell's admiration has finally culminated in something more substantial. I leave for London tomorrow for an appointment with the King. I'm to be elected to the British House of Commons and gifted with a tidy annual pension of five thousand pounds."

Sebastian choked. The whisky seared his throat as he threw back his head and laughed. "Old George must be going daft again. How would the King and Lord Campbell react if they knew they were harboring not an émigré but a revolutionist, and that your tidy pension will be sent to Paris to buy gunpowder and guns?"

D'Artan shrugged. "No gunpowder. No revolution."

"No revolution. No war with England. I doubt the King will be so hospitable when he finds his own country looking down the barrels of those guns."

"The spread of the new order is inevitable." D'Artan lifted his glass. "All for the glory of France."

Sebastian hiked his own glass. "All for the glory of D'Artan. Just how high are your aspirations? Chief Citizen of Great Britain perhaps?" He wiped his mouth with the back of his hand in an uncouth gesture he knew D'Artan would despise. D'Artan drummed his long, tapered nails on the desk, eyeing Sebastian's cane with distaste. "It was very unfortunate, this accident of yours. But not as unfortunate as the indiscretion that followed, eh? Your man spoke to me of a certain young mademoiselle."

Damn Tiny anyway, Sebastian thought. He was as protective as a wolf bitch guarding her pups. He braced himself for the blow he sensed coming.

"Far be it for me to begrudge you your liaisons," D'Artan continued, "but don't you think it unwise to reveal your face to some gibbering little light-'o-love?" Reproach dusted his voice, but did not alter his expression. Sebastian had always thought D'Artan's face was eerily unlined for a man his age. "Was it not you who told me the mask added the attraction of danger and immediacy to your . . . romantic interludes?"

Sebastian wondered if he had ever really said anything so callous. He must have been feeling smug after the Devony Blake encounter. "I did not choose to reveal myself. My mask fell away. As for the girl, she neither gibbered, nor was she my light-'o-love."

D'Artan cleared his throat. "That's even more unfortunate. You should have pressed your suit to make her so. A threat of scandal might have silenced her effectively."

"I don't recall rape being one of my duties."

D'Artan shrugged as only the French could. "Why consider it a duty? Consider it a privilege of the position."

Sebastian turned back to the window, needing a moment away from those steely eyes to steady his breathing. The dark oak paneling of the chamber absorbed both sunlight and air. He unlatched the window and shoved it open. A gentle breeze wafted in, bringing with it the scent of honeysuckle and the teasing warmth of a perfect summer day. An unexpected edge of longing closed Sebastian's throat.

He laid his fist on the windowsill. "If you are so well informed, then you must also know that the girl you speak of was blind."

D'Artan gave a genteel snort. "A bit off the path from the usual pencil peddler, wasn't she?"

Sebastian swung around. "The incident is over. I shall never see her again. What does she matter?"

"She doesn't matter." D'Artan pounded the desk, allowing Sebastian's anger to fuel his own. "But you do. You matter to France and you matter to me. As Sebastian Kerr, you can gauge support for the new French government in the best circles of London and Edinburgh society."

"I've been meaning to talk to you about that. I don't suppose the tidbit I brought you about the Marquess of Dover's speech *against* the National Assembly had anything to do with his unfortunate phaeton accident in the park."

D'Artan shook his head sadly. "Such a pity about his legs. They say he may walk again someday. But I didn't summon you here to discuss the Marquess's heavy hand with his horses." He rose and paced behind the desk, his hands locked at the small of his back. "I've indulged your little penchant for highway robbery thus far, but I won't put my new position and the influence it will bring at risk. You've become far too cocky. You're turning into a legend along the border! They're composing ballads about the adventures of the dashing Highlander. Those mealymouthed English magistrates are beginning to envy you. Who do you think their wives dream of when—"

"Enough!" Sebastian roared.

D'Artan acknowledged Sebastian's shift from French to English with a pained spasm of a smile.

"You'd take care to remember that my 'little penchant for robbery' filled your coffers with gold long before Lord Campbell would even grant you an audience. Who do you think has been paying for all those precious cannons and pistols you've been smuggling to France?" Sebastian's burr deepened. "Forget the girl. She was dressed in fashions at least two years old. She's probably some impoverished squire's sister. I doubt she travels in the same circles of society as I do."

"You could be right," D'Artan said with maddening calm. "However, there's too much at risk now. If you are caught, it would take very little effort to trace your name to mine. Then all of my work would be for naught." He sank back into his chair and shuffled the papers on his desk as if they had become of primary importance. "Before I return from London in August, I would like her dispatched. Something simple. A fall from a horse. A hunting accident. You know how to arrange such things."

Sebastian turned and groped for the edge of the windowsill like a blind man. The trim green of the manicured lawn mocked him. Why were the gentry so determined to create a miniature England wherever they went, he wondered, to prune and smooth away all traces of the wilderness and majesty that was Scotland? He hungered for the snowy peaks of Ben Nevis, the wild heathered moors of Strathnaver.

A new resolve tautened his jaw. D'Artan didn't know it, but by the time he returned from London, Sebastian would be trapped forever in a prison of such neatly bordered hedges and marble fountains. It would be a trap of his own choosing, though, and he would be free of men like D'Artan for the rest of his life.

Prudence's words rang through his head in the dulcet tones of a chiding angel. *Robbery is a dangerous vocation. Hazardous for your soul as well as your neck.* Perhaps it was not too late to escape with a scrap of his soul, before he became the kind of man who would kill the light in amethyst eyes for the sake of greed and politics.

D'Artan rose and crossed to him. "If you decline to protect yourself, I shall be forced to send one of my other men to track her down. I don't believe they have your high, but painless, rate of accuracy. I should hate for there to be a mess."

Sebastian did not bother to hide the contempt in his voice. "That won't be necessary. If my path should again cross the girl's, which I don't believe it will, I shall take care of the situation myself."

D'Artan fondly slapped his shoulder. "Well done, lad. You are a credit to your French blood. Your mother would be proud of you."

"I think not, Grandfather. I believe it is my father who would be proud of me."

Sebastian shrugged the old man's hand away and strode from the chamber, twirling the cane as if it were only an affectation. D'Artan watched through the window as his grandson crossed the rolling lawn, his gaze dark and thoughtful.

An enraged shriek shattered the quiet. Prudence's spine went rigid. Her book slid from her lap.

"Prudence!" The high-pitched screech was followed by a bellow. "Prudence! Come get this damned beast out of my wig!"

Prudence's eyes widened behind her spectacles. "Sebastian," she breathed.

She leaped out of the chair and pelted down the corridor toward her Aunt Tricia's bedchamber, skirts held high. Before she could reach the door, the kitten barreled around the corner, wig caught between his teeth. As his paws hit the waxed parquet, he slid. His claws shot out in a vain attempt to slow his skid, gouging a web of scratches across the precious inlay. He slammed into the opposite wall in an explosion of powder, then sat there, shaking head and wig until it was impossible to distinguish between them. Prudence dove on him, separating wig from kitten just as her aunt flung herself from her chamber in an avenging cloud of disheveled silk.

Tricia pointed a shaking hand at Sebastian. "That beast . . . that monster . . . that vicious creature . . ." As Sebastian licked the powder from his paws with wounded dignity, she sputtered into incoherence. Tricia refused to call the cat by name, or even acknowledge that he had a name.

Seeing that her aunt's hysteria was rapidly approaching a swoon, Prudence offered her the matted wig.

She snatched it from Prudence's hand, squealing anew with dismay. Her eyes narrowed. "I should have had Old Fish feed that beast to Boris while I was in London."

Prudence thrust the cat behind her back, blinking guilelessly. "Auntie Tricia, don't frown so. It emphasizes those tiny lines in your brow."

Tricia's face smoothed instantly, as if a porcelain mask had dropped over it. She touched the delicate skin beneath her eye with a long, crimson fingernail before breathing a sigh of relief. The careless frown had not crumpled it.

Cat forgotten, she fluttered back toward her chamber. "Come, Prudence. You may watch me dress."

"My heart's desire," Prudence said softly. She kissed the naughty kitten on the nose before freeing it, and followed her aunt.

The bedchamber reeked of powder and lilac water. Gowns littered the room like the helpless victims of a gruesome explosion. Prudence shuddered at the thought. She swept a lace petticoat from a brocaded stool and sat at her aunt's feet, resting her chin on her palm.

As she watched, Tricia smoothed lamp black over her auburn brows, darkening them to graceful wings. The trick gave her an expression of continual surprise, as ingenuous and natural as her use of cosmetics was artful. "My face is a canvas," she delighted in telling Prudence. "It is my responsibility to make it an unforgettable work of art." Prudence agreed that it was a work of art, although Tricia used more paint than Michelangelo, yet it was done in such a subtle way, she never appeared garish or overly made-up in the fashionably pale circle of society.

"You know, my dear Prudence," she said, dotting her puckered lips with carmine rouge, "this is the most important day of my life."

"I thought the most important day of your life was the day you married the viscount."

Her aunt sighed heavily. "Ah, yes, my poor Gustav."

"Gustav was the German prince," Prudence reminded her. "Bernard was the viscount."

Tricia looked momentarily perplexed as she hooked a lace collarette around her alabaster neck. Prudence imagined her counting her former husbands on mental fingers.

Tricia threw up her hands with a girlish flutter. "Gustav. Bernard. What does it matter? The past, however sweet, is past. Today we welcome my new fiancé to Lindentree." She cupped Prudence's chin in her soft, white hand. "He is eager to meet you. I've assured him you won't be a burden to us after we're wed. I told him how my poor Gustav adored you."

"That would have been poor Rutger. Gustav was already dead when I came to live with you. And Rutger didn't adore me. He simply tolerated me because I kept the household accounts. Bernard adored me."

Tricia leaned over. Her cheek missed Prudence's by several inches. The brief squeeze of her hands on Prudence's shoulders assured her she would have liked to kiss her if it wouldn't have mussed her powder. "*I* adore you. You are as dear and reliable as my Boris."

Prudence frowned. Being compared to a slobbering and fitfully stupid Great Dane was a dubious compliment at best.

Tricia clucked her tongue against her teeth. "Do stop grimacing, dear. You're not getting any younger." The crunch of carriage wheels on the cobblestones sent her into a frenzy of activity more befitting the second coming of Christ. "Oh, dear God, it's him!" She threw a cashmere stole around her shoulders. "Why don't you go powder that mop of yours? And straighten those dreadful spectacles. Do you want him to see you squinting like a Chinaman?" Without waiting for Prudence's reply, she tucked a perfumed rosette into her bodice and sailed from the room, hiking her rustling skirts to show off the tiny bows on the back of her slippers.

Prudence remained seated for a moment, a row of faceless wig stands surveying her. At last she stood, sighing. She could not seem to shake the cloud of depression that had beset her since the night she had dared to cross the Scottish border. It was as if some other border in her life had been crossed. Now the road before her loomed straight and gray and unbearably long. Her gaze wandered to the window, drawn by the trilling song of a thrush and the haunting scent of the honeysuckle twining up the trellis.

Beside the window, four gilt angels clutched a pier-glass in their chubby paws. As Prudence surveyed her reflection, their petulant smirks mocked her. She smoothed streaks of powder from the unadorned poplin of her skirt, bracing herself to meet yet another of her aunt's suitors.

In the seven years that she had lived at Lindentree, Prudence had grown accustomed to the steady parade of doddering dukes and deposed princes. They all shared three characteristics. They were foreign, wealthy, and preferably infirm. Tricia did have her standards too; she had never married two men from the same country. She had amassed quite a fortune in this fashion, as well as the titles of countess, baroness, and princess of a tiny Austrian country Prudence had never been able to locate on any map.

If her aunt chose to believe she was marrying for love, who was Prudence to enlighten her? The old gentlemen carried to their graves the memory of happy days spent in the embrace of a doting, beautiful, and relatively young bride. Most of them were too nearsighted to notice Tricia's steady stream of lovers. Prudence just hoped this one could walk and did not drool.

She tucked a stray piece of hair back into its tight knot and adjusted her steel spectacles with a defiant jerk.

"Come, Prudence." She curtsied to her reflection. "Shall we go meet your future uncle? I have no doubt he will simply adore you."

The afternoon sun slanted across the rolling lawn. As Prudence stepped out onto the porch, a coach rattled past, heading for the yawning door of the stable. Boris danced around its wheels, barking hoarsely. A wiry coachman tipped his wide-brimmed hat at her. Prudence lifted a hand to shade her eyes from the sun's glare, and looked around for her aunt.

At the bend of the long, sweeping drive, Tricia and a man stood in the shaded embrace of a willow. Shadows dappled his broad shoulders. This one must be better preserved than most, Prudence mused as she caught her skirts in her hands and started across the lawn. His back was neither swayed nor humped. He wasn't excessively tall, but the width of his shoulders dwarfed Tricia's dainty grace. Although he stood with legs planted firmly apart and held a slender cane in one hand, he gave no impression of being bandy-legged. As Prudence drew nearer, she could see he wore no wig. His hair was powdered a sandy gray and caught in a neat queue at the nape of his neck.

Tricia's laughter tinkled like a bell. No man, Prudence thought, not even a man aged to insensibility, could fail to appreciate the charm of that laugh. Tricia's skirts swayed in the teasing breeze as she laid a hand on the sleeve of the man's frock coat. She tilted her face to him, listening to his low, murmuring voice with obvious avidity. As the man bent to touch his lips to hers, Prudence ducked behind the nearest tree, embarrassed to be intruding on such a tender scene.

Old Fish emerged from the house at that moment, bearing a silver tray of glasses.

Tricia's voice rang out. "Here comes the wine. And there's my niece behind that tree."

Prudence silently cursed the slenderness of the birch.

"Come, my darling," Tricia continued, "and join in our celebration. I hope it will be the first of many for the three of us." She added sotto voce to the man, "My niece is rather shy. You shall have to overlook her."

Why not? Prudence thought, having heard her aunt perfectly clearly. Everyone else did. She doubted if her aunt's fiancé would be overjoyed at the prospect of adding the burden of a spinster niece to his household. She edged out from behind the tree and followed the curve of the cobbled drive, resisting the urge to drag her feet and kick at rocks like a stubborn child.

Old Fish reached the willow when she did. The stranger plucked a wineglass from the tray and turned to greet her.

Gray eyes laced with the mists of the Highlands sparkled down at her.

Prudence stood hypnotized as he made a courtly bow and brought her hand to his lips. The most terrible thing was not that he was the Dreadful Scot Bandit Kirkpatrick. The most terrible thing was not that he was going to marry her aunt. The most terrible thing was that he did not remember her.

His polite expression was as blindly indifferent as a mole's. The vacant sweetness of his smile was more painful than if he had pulled out a pistol and shot her dead right there.

Tricia linked one arm in Prudence's and one in his. Prudence's arm hung limply as Tricia beamed up at her fiancé. "There. I knew the two of you would be fond of each other."

He murmured a noncommittal agreement and sipped his claret.

"After all," Tricia prattled on, "it would have been tragic if the two people I adore most in the world did not come to love each other."

"Simply dreadful," Prudence murmured. Her voice brought his head upright. Wine dribbled down his white stockings into his buckled shoes. Tricia squeezed both of their arms. "I knew you'd get along famously. My dear Sebastian and my dear, dear Prudence." He met her gaze over the top of Tricia's wig. As his eyes widened, a shiver raked Prudence's spine. How could she have remembered the exotic attraction of his eyes without remembering the paralyzing danger that lurked in their smoky depths?

Five

Sebastian could not take his eyes off Prudence.

"Sebastian. Sebastian, dear, would you please pass the butter?"

Tricia's voice was no more than the nagging whine of a persistent mosquito. Sebastian handed her the gravy tureen. A table full of inquisitive eyes blinked at him. He jerked his attention back to Tricia and swapped gravy tureen for butter dish, chuckling feebly.

"Forgive me, darling. The long journey has addled my wits."

He would have to take more care, he thought. It would not do for anyone to notice his intense preoccupation with the prim creature dining on the other side of the table. He silently cursed Tricia's wretched sense of hospitality. She had invited not only the neighboring Squire Blake and his simpering daughter Devony, but the county sheriff, Sir Arlo Tugbert, to celebrate his arrival at Lindentree. If Tricia's niece dared to speak, the sheriff would have more to celebrate than an engagement before this interminable supper was done. Sebastian picked at his smoked herring and satisfied himself with studying Prudence beneath the sweeping veil of lashes he had always detested.

From Tricia's description of her unmarried niece, he had fully expected to meet a bucktoothed hag. A perplexed frown crinkled his brow. He could not look at her without having the enchanting vision of a lass soaked with rain and breathless with laughter superimposing itself over her now flawless composure. It was like watching a misty watercolor run over the harsh but simple lines of a pencil drawing. The effect was jarring. Sebastian gripped the crystal stem of his wineglass without realizing it.

Her every gesture captivated him as he searched for some hint of that other girl, the girl who had haunted his dreams since that rainy night.

She ate with head bent, seemingly oblivious to the bright titter of conversation and tinkle of silver on crystal. She cut her herring into tiny bits before tucking each neat square between her delicate lips. She ate so slowly, Sebastian began to count each chew under his breath.

She paused between bites to push the heavy spectacles back up her slender nose. Her thick hair was caught in a tight chignon at the nape of her neck, and Sebastian felt unaccountably angry. What right did she have to go around looking like someone's maiden governess? He hungered to loosen her hair, to drive his hands through it and see if its softness was as compelling as its memory.

"Tell us about yourself, Lord Kerr," said the squire, jerking Sebastian's attention back to Tricia's guests. "To hear our Tricia tell of you, it seems you are angel and saint rolled into one."

Out of the corner of his eye, Sebastian saw Prudence stop chewing. He forced himself to hold Squire Blake's gaze and not glance at her. The squire was a heavy-jowled man who looked as if he had been stuffed into his starched cravat and exploded. A cauliflower wig sat slightly askew on his head. Rice powder clung to the deep creases around his eyes.

"Like most men," Sebastian said, managing to smile, "I fear I am more sinner than saint. You musn't let Tricia's admiration sway you."

Tricia patted his hand. "Don't be modest, you silly boy." She leaned forward, including the entire table in the charmed circle of her confidence. "Sebastian is a Highland laird. He has a sumptuous castle in the mountains which has been in the Kerr clan for centuries. It is simply the height of romance—soaring turrets, a moat, a drawbridge."

"And a dungeon, I hope," Sir Arlo said. "No home would be complete without one." His prominent Adam's apple bobbed as he laughed at his own joke.

Sebastian's smile waned. He possessed no fondness for sheriffs, nor for landed English gentry. He could not help but notice the proprietary way the tall young man had pulled out Prudence's chair for her, and the possessive glances he had been casting at the top of her head throughout dinner. Sebastian felt like stabbing him with his two-pronged fork.

Tricia pursed her lips in a pout. "I've been trying to talk Sebastian into honeymooning at the castle. Won't you all help me convince him?"

Sebastian covered her hand with his own. Had she always chattered so incessantly? He hadn't noticed it in the bright babble of London society. "Now, Tricia, I told you Dunkirk would be much too primitive for your delicate tastes. I've been abroad for years, and there are a slew of renovations needed at the castle. Perhaps later in our marriage."

She gazed at him in obvious adoration. "I shouldn't care as long as I was with you."

Prudence pushed her plate away as if she had suddenly lost her appetite. Here it comes, Sebastian thought. She was going to denounce him. He was a madman to have stayed once he saw her. He should have leaped back into his carriage and fled.

She lifted her head. The thick glass of her spectacles hid the lethal beauty of her eyes. "Sebastian?" she said coolly. "Is that not an unusual name for a Scotsman?"

Sebastian felt his jaw tighten of its own volition. "My mother was French. She had a fondness for Bach."

Prudence toyed with her glass. "It's fortunate Mozart was not her favored composer. You might have been christened Wolfgang."

A muscle in Sebastian's jaw twitched. A nervous bubble of laughter escaped from Sir Arlo.

Prudence pressed on. "And your father?"

"A Highland laird. Like myself."

A corner of her mouth curved upward. "Ah, a great man. You must have been very fond of him."

Damn the lass, Sebastian thought. He wanted to reach across the table and shake her until her icy demeanor shattered. "I was," he said softly.

"I couldn't help but notice your limp," she went on. "Were you injured recently?"

Sebastian had seen bulldogs with less tenacity.

Tricia rescued him with a sympathetic cluck. "I fear my Sebastian suffers from an old war injury."

Prudence's gaze did not waver from his face. "What war might that be?"

He could feel his smile stiffening to a grimace. "You wouldn't have heard of it. It was a Highland clan war."

She blinked innocently. "I thought they'd been outlawed since the Scottish rebellion of '46."

She'd pushed him far enough. Sebastian leaned forward, his smile wicked, his burr deepening. "'Tis no surprise you did not read of it in your newspapers. 'Twas a gruesome affair that all began when a careless lass could not learn to still her flapping tongue." His eyes sparkled. "After she was found strangled with her own hair ribbons on the moor—"

With a violent gasp, Devony Blake shoved herself away from the table. She collapsed in the brocaded chair in a quivering heap of ruffles and lace.

Tricia jumped up and trotted around the table. "Oh, dear. How very, very thoughtless of us. You know how Devony swoons at the merest mention of Scotland, and here we are going on and on about it."

Prudence went back to her meal, dismissing Sebastian's glare with infuriating calm.

Devony's father shoveled another forkful of herring into his mouth. "She'll be fine in a minute. Loosen that fichu, won't you, so she doesn't suffocate."

While Tricia loosened the offensive fichu, Sir Arlo knelt beside Devony's chair and fanned her with his napkin.

Squire Blake gestured with his fork, sending bits of herring flying. "You must forgive my daughter, Lord Kerr. She had an unfortunate encounter with one of your countrymen. Abducted and used by a shameless Scots highwayman, I fear. Never be the same."

Devony's long lashes fluttered.

Sir Arlo patted her wrist. "It was that cursed Kirkpatrick. I suppose his infamy has spread even up to the Highlands."

Sebastian lifted his glass to hide his mouth. "I've heard of him."

Sir Arlo gave an angry snort. "Damned impudent monster thinks he can go about robbing decent people and ravishing innocent young girls."

Sebastian would have hated to disillusion the righteous sheriff, but Devony Blake had been neither innocent nor ravished the night they had spent together. He was beginning to see where Prudence had formed her opinions about him. The thought did not give him comfort.

Determination strengthened Sir Arlo's weak chin. He looked almost handsome for an elusive moment. "I swear I'll have my noose around the bastard's neck before this summer is done."

Sebastian resisted the urge to loosen his cravat. If Prudence chose, the sheriff would have his noose around the bastard's neck before supper was done.

Sighing breathily, Devony sat up. Sebastian tried to remember why he had ever been attracted to her. Thank God he hadn't taken off his mask for that one.

"I am so mortified," she said. "But every time I think of Scotland, I remember that horrible night." She swayed, showing signs of swooning afresh. Her vacant blue eyes went misty. "That man. I shall never forget him. His brawny arms, his relentless hands, the heat of his mouth on mine—"

With a neat jerk of one elbow, Prudence overturned her wineglass. Claret cascaded across the pristine linen tablecloth and into Devony's lap.

Devony leaped up with a shriek, swoon forgotten. She snatched the napkin from Arlo and swabbed at the red stain spreading across her delicate pink organdy skirt. "Oh, no, my new gown! Must you always be such a clumsy cow, Prudence?"

Prudence murmured an apology and neatly speared another bite of herring. While everyone else attended to Devony's fitful hysterics, Sebastian lifted his glass to Prudence in a mocking toast.

Her spectacles reflected the light of the chandelier with

twin candle flames, rendering her expression as inscrutable as if she were now the one masked. He did not like the effect.

He dared to address her directly. "Tell me, Miss Walker, how did you come to live with your aunt?"

As Prudence opened her mouth, Tricia looked up from dabbing at Devony's skirt and said, "Prudence came to live with me after my brother died. Livingston was an inventor. Much older than me, of course."

"Of course," Squire Blake seconded gallantly. "Tricia has always been the baby of this county." He cast a hopeful glance at his empty plate.

Tricia rose dutifully and rang for dessert, leaving Devony in the sheriff's capable hands.

Sebastian's long fingers tapped his glass. "An inventor. How interesting. What did your father dabble in?"

Prudence didn't even get her mouth open this time before Tricia trilled, "Silly things. Nothing of any importance. Muskets. Pistols. Gunpowder."

Sebastian ceased his tapping. The echo of fingernails against crystal rang in the silence.

"Before Papa died," Prudence said hastily, "he was working on a powerful fulminic acid to replace gunpowder."

"An interesting concept," Sir Arlo said. "It might have saved me a few hundred misfires from slow-burning powder."

She nodded. "Papa could have saved the King's Army a fortune in gunpowder as well if he had succeeded, but George wasn't interested. Had it been wig powder instead of gunpowder, I've no doubt the King would have financed any experiment Papa cared to undertake."

A slow, dangerous smile curved Sebastian's lips. "I prefer the claymore myself, but I've always been curious about a certain point. Tell me, Miss Walker, what did your father think of the effect of water on gunpowder?"

A tiny dimple appeared at one corner of Prudence's mouth. "He found it to have a dampening effect, my lord."

Sebastian leaned back in his chair and crossed his arms over his chest. "Yes. I supposed he would."

"Prudence was her father's assistant," Sir Arlo said, almost proudly.

"Scandalous task for a young girl." Tricia dabbed her nose with a perfumed handkerchief at the memory. "Whenever I'd visit, there the poor little creature would be—her clothes reeking of sulfur, her face streaked with charcoal."

"Graphite," Prudence corrected her aunt gently.

"Oh, pooh!" Tricia said. "Enough talk of such silliness over supper. Livingston's ridiculous experiments got him nowhere but blown to kingdom come in front of the Royal Society and half of London. I've never been so mortified."

Squire Blake waved his fork. "He shouldn't have poured that hooker of brandy into the mercury. Such a waste of fine brandy!"

Tricia nodded. "All his hopes of obtaining an honorary peerage from the King came to naught. Why, all we could find to bury of him were his shoe buckles and wig! Knowing how addlepated he was, he probably wasn't even wearing them. It was sheer good fortune that he sent Prudence back to their lodgings for his spectacles or we'd have found nothing of her but her hairpins."

A sick feeling blossomed in the pit of Sebastian's stomach. "Fortunate indeed," he murmured.

He studied Prudence to see what effect Tricia's callous speech might have on her. The hue of her skin was so delicate, he would have judged further paling impossible. He was wrong.

She pushed herself back from the table. Even against the stark white of the tablecloth, her knuckles looked pinched and pale. "I seem to be taking a headache. If you'll be kind enough to excuse me from dessert, I shall retire to my room."

She didn't wait to hear Tricia's objections. She fled the dining room, nearly colliding with a plump maid bearing a silver tray of cherries doused in flaming brandy.

The maid steadied the tray, rolling her eyes as Prudence disappeared. "Good Lord, Lady Tricia, that girl'll be the death of us all one day."

Sebastian waited for Tricia to defend her niece and upbraid the servant for her familiarity.

Instead, Tricia's lips curved in a feline smile. "Come, Squire Blake, put out that fire, won't you? Cherries are your favorites. I only hope Sebastian likes them half so well."

Tricia's hand stroked his thigh beneath the shield of the tablecloth. Sebastian hardly noticed as his gaze drifted back to the half-eaten herring and empty dessert plate on the other side of the table.

He stood abruptly, spilling his napkin to the floor. "If you'll excuse me, dear, I must tend to my coachman's . . ." The rest of his excuse was lost in a mumble as he strode from the dining room, bumping into the plump maid hard enough to send her teetering.

The corridor was empty. Sebastian lengthened his strides, his cane never touching the floor. The sleek marble tiles of the entranceway seemed to stretch forever. At last he saw her, a slight figure, head bent, hand poised on the banister as she started up the stairs. The grace of a thief served Sebastian well. His hand closed over her wrist before she ever heard his footfalls.

She spun around on the step above him, her eyes dark and stricken behind the fragile glass. His hard grip softened. His thumb rubbed lightly over the tripping pulse in her wrist.

There was so much he longed to tell her, so much he needed to say. But at the same moment, they both became aware of Old Fish behind them, puttering around the potted orange tree with a watering can.

The brittle eloquence Sebastian had perfected in London failed him, leaving him as awkward and graceless as a schoolboy. "Your father, Miss Walker . . . I'm terribly sorry."

"It was a long time ago." Her hand clenched into a fist, but she did not pull away.

Sebastian wondered how much anger she hid beneath her cool veneer. He should warn her of the cost. He had bit back his own anger for years, rolling dutifully beneath every blow until he could feel nothing at all. He longed to pull her head down to his shoulder and let the bitterness dimming her eyes spill into the healing balm of tears.

Old Fish stooped over the plant, his back to them. Sebastian couldn't stop himself. He reached up and stroked her cheek with the backs of his fingers. Her skin was satin cream, just as he remembered. "Some wounds take longer to heal than others."

She flinched as if he had struck her. Her gaze flicked downward to his cane. "Like your old war wound?"

His hand fell, and she turned away in a crisp swish of poplin. "You'd best get back to your guests, my lord. Your fiancée is waiting for you."

As she climbed the steps, her back and shoulders perfectly straight, Sebastian blew out a slow breath of frustration. He swung away from the stairs and met Old Fish's cold gaze. The butler's thin nostrils flared at the merest scent of scandal.

Before he could protest, Sebastian took the tin pot out of his hand and flipped it upside down. Nothing came out. He shook it before handing it back. "The tree might grow quicker, my good man, if you'd take the trouble of putting water in the pot."

Smiling angelically, Sebastian tucked his cane under his arm and marched back to the dining room.

Prudence slammed the door to her bedchamber shut, twisted her key with trembling fingers, and braced her back against the door. Her chest heaved as if she had climbed a steep mountain instead of a staircase. She took several long, shuddering breaths, fighting the feeling that she was being pursued. The silence that surrounded her was broken by a bright burst of Tricia's laughter floating up the stairs. It was not her aunt's flippant description of her papa's death that had ignited Prudence's hunger for escape. It was the frank sympathy in Sebastian Kerr's eyes.

Since Sebastian's arrival, Prudence had somehow tolerated the walk from the drive to the house with Tricia clinging to his arm like a limpet. She had suffered through the awkwardness of tea, although the buttercrumb tarts crumbled to sawdust in her mouth each time he looked at her. She had endured supper and the maddening swing of his expression from perplexed curiosity to something bordering on hostility.

But when he'd looked at her as if he ached to reach out and enfold her hand in his, her pretense of dignity had snapped. She pressed a hand to her burning cheek. She had never dreamed he would be so bold and foolish as to follow her, to say he was sorry about her papa, to touch her face . . .

Violently, she stripped off her gown, then tore at the stays of her corset, bending them beyond repair. She was in no mood to summon a maid to undress her as if she were an invisible doll.

Indignation flooded her. Sebastian Kerr had a surfeit of arrogance to attend one of her aunt's dinner parties in such a bizarre manner of dress! He had worn no wig. The powder that had burnished his tawny hair was light enough to be more of an insult than if he wore none at all.

She threw her gown in the armoire and jerked out a cotton night rail. She pulled it over her head backward, lost the armholes, and spent the next few seconds trying to extricate her head, muttering all the while. Then her head popped out and her hair came tumbling down, scattering hairpins across the faded rug.

Sebastian's unfashionable tan had made Sir Arlo, with his powdered visage, look like a day-old corpse. His charcoal knee-breeches had matched exactly the color of his thick lashes, and had clung to his thighs in a most unseemly manner. His cutaway frock coat had been devoid of all lace but for a narrow band around the cuffs. And most shocking of all had been his unstarched cravat. Its soft, loose folds had framed beautifully the piquant play of emotions across his face.

Prudence plucked the rest of the pins from her hair and dragged a gilt brush through the heavy mass. The brush caught in a tangle. She tugged, taking a perverse satisfaction in the pain. She started to braid her hair, then stopped. What difference did it make? There was no one to see her in the privacy of her simple chamber. She slammed a nightcap on her head with enough force to cover her eyes.

A hairpin jabbed her heel as she padded blindly to the bed. She crawled beneath the counterpane, pillowed her head on folded arms, and glared up at the tent-bed's canopy. Tricia had a massive mahogany bedstead with fluted posts and embroidered tester. Prudence's small bed was crafted of light iron and shrouded with white muslin. Polished brass finials topped the bedposts.

As she rolled to her side and pounded her bolster into submission, she had the discomfiting sensation that she was eleven years old again and struggling to understand why Papa must send every extra tuppence to his "poor orphaned little sister."

"Be patient, my Prudence," he would say. "All it will take is one word from the king and your future will be secure. Our day will soon arrive." Prudence was still waiting.

While she and her papa had lived in rustic comfort in a two-room apartment in London, Tricia had luxuriated in the Northumberland countryside, collecting and discarding Hepplewhite pier-tables and fawning beaux with equal panache. Prudence had tried not to resent her lovely aunt.

To Prudence, Tricia's infrequent calls to their cluttered lodgings had been like the earthly visitations of a satin-swathed fairy. Tricia would pat her cheek, her fingers cool beneath their net gloving. An irresistible sympathy would warm her amber eyes as she pressed a perfumed kerchief to her dainty nose. For a brief moment, basking in the glow of Tricia's attention, Prudence would find it not so terrible to be smart and skinny and plain.

The sympathy in Sebastian's touch told her otherwise. Prudence flung herself onto her stomach. Sympathy was too kind a word. Perhaps someday she would learn to separate it from pity.

Coach wheels rattled on the cobblestones of the drive. Tricia's lilting farewell drifted up through Prudence's open window. Devony Blake, she thought, was now free to go home and dream of her mystery bandit with the relentless hands and heated lips, while Tricia was left to do more than dream with a man who was a greater mystery than she knew.

Prudence sighed, wishing her kitten was snuggled beside her. He was probably in the herb garden, chasing moonbeams and dreaming of bewhiskered fairies. Why should he be at her side when she needed him? What could she expect of a beast with a treacherous name like Sebastian? Especially a male beast.

A board creaked on the stairs. She pulled the counterpane over her head. A hushed whisper was followed by a throaty giggle, then the giggle was muffled abruptly in a manner

Prudence did not choose to explore. A door closed. The house fell silent.

Prudence lay still until her legs grew stiff and she wearied of breathing the air beneath the stifling confines of the covers. How dare the scoundrel pity her? she thought, throwing back the counterpane.

She rose to pace the room. Moonlight slanted like prison bars across the rug. A brisk night breeze stirred the ruffled curtains. Her restlessness grew until it bordered on wildness. She picked up a book and tossed it down, then strode to the ceramic water pitcher.

It was empty.

It was just like the maids to forget to fill it, she thought. No doubt Tricia's pitcher was brimming over with cold water. Old Fish had probably shaved the ice himself for her ladyship's pleasure.

Prudence's throat suddenly felt as parched as if she'd trekked across the Sahara without benefit of a camel. She tightened her jaw, telling herself she would not remain a prisoner in her bedroom for the rest of her life, simply because her aunt had the insensitivity to marry a highwayman.

She donned a wrapper and stuck her head out the door to peer both ways. The long corridor was empty. A single candle in a glass sconce cast a gentle glow on the polished cedar floor. Old Fish always kept a candle burning for his mistress. Tricia hated the dark.

Prudence crept into the hall, her bravado dissipating along with her savage temper. The days when she would have gone to her aunt's chamber for a drink were done. Heaven knows what sordid sight might greet her there.

She sank down at the top of the stairs and peered through a lyre-shaped baluster. Her hands curled around the cool wrought-iron. Moonlight and shadows dappled the entranceway below. A candle left guttering in the drawing room cast a shallow pool of light across the marble tile. Prudence listened, but heard only the odd creaks and groans of any house abandoned to the stillness of night.

She glided down the stairs. The mahogany banister felt clammy beneath her palm.

As she stepped off the last stair and turned toward the mundane comfort of the kitchens, a band of relentless muscle shot around her waist and jerked her against an unyielding male chest. A firm hand clamped over her mouth, stifling her would-be scream to silence.

Six

Prudence waited for the steely arm wrapped around her waist to lift and tighten across her throat. She could well imagine the conversation between Tricia and her fiancé over breakfast the following morn.

Sebastian's sulky mouth would look appropriately penitent. "I'm dreadfully sorry, pudding. I mistook her for a robber and accidentally strangled her to death."

Tricia would tap Sebastian's arm playfully with her fan. "You silly boy. How unfortunate! You didn't leave a mess, did you? I had that marble floor installed only last February."

Prudence slowly realized he was holding her only firmly enough to still her fevered struggles to a helpless wiggle. It was a measure of the strength of the man that he could restrain her without hurting her. She felt a gentleness in his touch, an unspoken wish to exert no more force than was necessary to hold her. He dragged her into the shadows beneath the stairs, pressing his back to the wall for leverage. Her weight fell helplessly against him; her hips were pinned to the muscular contours of his thighs. He splayed his legs to keep his balance.

His breath, laced with tobacco and brandy, stirred her nightcap. "Quiet, lass. I won't hurt you. If you'll quit squeaking and squirming, I'll let you go. I swear it."

She ceased her struggles. His muscles relaxed, but his

forearm remained snug beneath her breasts, and his warm palm still cupped her mouth. The heat of his body trapped her in a silken web perilously near to an embrace. As he buried his face in her unbound hair, she realized the danger she believed herself to be in might be of a different sort altogether. Perhaps he had made his promise not to hurt her in haste. The pain he was capable of inflicting was both sweet and deadly.

He eased his hand from her mouth. His fingers lingered for a tantalizing moment against her lips.

She took a shuddering breath and summoned some shred of dignity. "Would you please unhand me, sir?"

She might have imagined the briefest brush of his lips against her bared shoulder before he freed her. "As the lady wishes."

She stepped away from him, but her knees betrayed her. He reached out to steady her. She jerked her nightcap straight before turning to face him.

He leaned against the curving wall with arms crossed. Shadows hid his face. Prudence felt exposed in the bright ribbon of moonlight streaming through the fanlight over the door. She sensed rather than saw his gaze slide downward over the thin cotton of her wrapper. She shivered, though the night was not cold.

"I thought you'd never come," he said.

"I fear to disappoint you, Lord Kerr, but I did not come downstairs for a rendezvous with you."

"Are you so sure? Or are you lying to yourself again? As I recall, you weren't too clear on your reasons for accompanying me to the crofter's hut either."

"I might suggest that you were the one unclear about my motives, not I."

He stepped into the light. If Prudence had found his dress to be immodest at supper, she was doubly alarmed now at his casual disarray. He had discarded his frock coat. His white shirt was half unbuttoned, and moonlight gilded the fur of his chest to gold. His hair was freed of its queue and tumbled loose around his face in a way more becoming than Prudence would have ever admitted. She took an involuntary step backward.

He circled her like a tawny panther. "You're a cool one, aren't you? I admire that in a man."

She chose to ignore the implied insult, studying the marble tiles as if she'd never seen them before.

"You'd make a fine faro player," he went on. "I dare say you've never tried your hand at it, though."

"Of course not." She lifted her head to face him. "Although I'm sure you'd number it among your many skills, along with highway robbery and lurking under stairways."

"Don't forget cheating at whist. What did you come down for, Miss Walker? Dessert?" His crooked smile was infuriating.

"I thought you might need help finding the silver," she snapped.

"Ah, the mouse roars. Is that why you believe I came to Lindentree? To rob your aunt?"

Prudence wished that was what she did believe. "No." Her voice lost its stinging note. "I believe you came to Lindentree to marry her."

He stared down into her eyes, seeming mesmerized for a moment. He lifted his hand to touch her cheek, then let it fall. "You should have worn your bloody spectacles. You could fall down in the dark and hurt yourself." He walked over to the pier-table, his limp more pronounced than before. Picking up a china shepherdess, he laughed shakily. "You have only yourself to blame. It was you who told me you would cry if I were to hang. You who suggested I might pursue my lust for gain in a more honorable fashion."

"Such as marrying a rich woman?"

"Aye." His long, elegant fingers caressed the delicate china. Prudence wondered if he was assessing its value. "It's a timeworn but socially acceptable method of amassing a fortune."

"You and Tricia have more in common than I realized." Prudence paced into the glow from the drawing room and back, frowning distractedly. The wrapper foamed around her calves. "Tricia always marries men with money. I have been over and over it in my mind and I can't figure out why she would marry you."

She turned back to face him. He stood silhouetted in the

moonlight like a rumpled pagan god, and her cheeks flamed as she realized what a stupid question it had been. The reason for Tricia's choice was all too clear—as clear as the silvery light bathing the slanted planes of his face. Tricia had finally found a man more beautiful than she.

He shrugged his broad shoulders. "I lied. I told her Dunkirk was still mine. And soon it will be. With an English countess as my wife and her purse strings to back me, even MacKay won't be able to stop me from claiming it. A few more robberies and I'll have enough in my account to maintain the illusion of riches—at least until we're wed."

Prudence kept her tone deliberately light. "Why marry? Why not just purchase your own title? Our prime minister hands them out like tissue paper. All you must do is prove an annual income of ten thousand pounds."

"What should I list as my vocation? Robber? Notorious criminal?"

She inclined her head, hiding a reluctant smile. "It will be quite a coup for Tricia to add a Scottish laird to her collection of French counts and Austrian barons."

"And if she knew I was a deposed Scottish laird?"

"As long as you escaped with the family treasury, she wouldn't care. The more deposed the better. Tricia loves a lost cause."

Prudence was unprepared for the touch of his fingers as he tilted her chin up. Her skin tingled at the warm shock of the contact.

"Is that what you think I am?" he asked. "A lost cause?" His gaze searched her face, lingering on her lips.

Her smile faded. "What you are, my lord, is of no concern to me."

With that cool dismissal, she turned away and caught the skirt of her wrapper in her trembling hands.

As she started up the stairs, he caught her arm, and she felt something akin to desperation in his grasp. "I never expected to find you in a household like Lindentree."

She could not look at him. "Are you sorry?"

"Sorry is only the half of it, lass. I never wanted to lay eyes on you again."

He did not protest when she gently disengaged herself

from his grip. Prudence was barricaded safely behind her bedroom door before she realized her face was wet with tears.

Sebastian rose at dawn to prowl the sleeping house. The hollow silence and the vacant blue gaze of the china shepherdess in the entranceway drove him out into the manicured gardens. In a few short weeks, they would be his gardens. Beads of dew sparkled on mint green blades of grass. He reclined on a marble bench and watched the sky melt from gray to pink to powder blue. A slim Ionic column sprouted from the polished flagstones. It was a column that went nowhere and supported nothing, and to Sebastian it expressed perfectly the elusive flaw of Lindentree's gardens. They were beautiful, but purposeless. Much like their mistress.

When they had met in London a few months ago, Tricia had seemed the perfect companion to his grandfather's education—amusing, enthusiastic in bed, widowed, wealthy, and possessing more titles than any woman or man he knew. He had studied her with painstaking care, using his natural talent as a mimic to learn her speech patterns and manners. Any gentleman, he knew, would be well complemented by having such a woman as his mistress.

But Sebastian was no gentleman. He knew it was only a matter of time before he turned around at some London party and came face to face with Killian MacKay. Then all of society would know him for what he was—a common thieving bastard. To escape D'Artan and build any sort of future in a society that should rightfully despise him, he needed not a mistress, but a wife.

Sebastian stood. The serenity of the gardens only mocked the hard edge of his restlessness. At every corner, at every bend of the path, stood iron trellises draped with velvety blossoms of honeysuckle. He plucked a bloom as he passed and pinched away the tender tip. His tongue darted out to catch the golden bead of nectar that welled on the delicate stamen.

He closed his eyes, haunted by the fragrant memory of

Prudence's unbound hair. Had his besotted senses imagined it or had her hair been scented with the elusive breath of honeysuckle? It took little imagination for him to conjure up the way she had felt when she had gone soft and pliant in his arms the night before. Her modest wrapper had done little to disguise her gentle curves. He could have held her all night.

Sebastian opened his eyes. He had not lied to her. He had hoped never to lay eyes on her again. Prudence Walker was dangerous. Far more dangerous than his grandfather knew. There was more at risk than just a shipment of gunpowder or the old man's election to the House of Commons. Sebastian's entire future hung on her discretion. His fingers curled into a fist.

I would like her dispatched.

The memory of D'Artan's icy commission darkened his eyes. He had never deliberately disobeyed his grandfather. He had learned long ago to laugh in his father's face, knowing he would get no more than a busted rib or a bloody nose for his insolence. But with D'Artan, one was never sure what one would get.

Sebastian opened his palm. The crushed bits of the honeysuckle blossom scattered in the wind.

The dining-room door swung open. Sebastian glanced up for the twelfth time, only to be rewarded by the shriveled countenance of Old Fish. He returned his attention to his poached eggs, resisting the urge to growl.

His earlier request for breakfast had been met with a cool stare.

"The countess never takes breakfast before noon," Old Fish had said.

"That's all very well," Sebastian had replied. "But I'd like something to eat now. Noon is five hours away."

The butler had sniffed, and dared a glance at the clock on the mantel. "Perhaps I could serve chocolate in your chamber."

Sebastian was not accustomed to ordering servants. He would have barked a command and boxed Jamie's ears for such impudence, but he'd been momentarily perplexed at how to handle the butler. The vision of what Old Fish's expression might be if he boxed *his* ears had given Sebastian the impetus he needed for a gracious smile.

"A very kind offer indeed, but I believe I'll take my breakfast in the dining room." Sebastian had paused. "Every morning."

With a flare of his aristocratic nostrils, Old Fish had bowed his surrender.

Sebastian had seated himself at the end of the long table, fully prepared to be served day-old gruel. But Old Fish had been determined to get the last word, whether it was spoken or not, and Sebastian had watched helplessly as course after course of steaming food was wheeled in and placed on the cherry sideboard. Hot scones slavered with honey followed fresh kippers and chilled rosettes of butter. Thick slabs of bacon glistened next to mounds of strawberries and clotted cream. Even Tiny would have been hard-pressed to do justice to such a feast. Too late, Sebastian had realized he wasn't hungry.

So he'd picked at his eggs and absently calculated the value of the silver warming dishes perched over the tiny candles. His gaze swung to the door each time it opened, as if by the sheer force of his will he could conjure up the person he wanted to see.

Old Fish hovered at his elbow. "Will there be anything else, sir?"

Sebastian laid down his knife, realizing with chagrin that he had been eating with the blade. His untouched fork gleamed amidst the snowy folds of his napkin. "I believe that will be all." He cleared his throat. "Tell me, Fish, does Miss Walker ever take breakfast in the dining room?"

The butler's thin lips compressed to a line of disdain. "She does not. I see no point in disturbing the servants for Miss Walker's breakfast. She prefers to pick up a scone in the kitchens and carry it to the library." He sniffed. "Very considerate of her, I might add."

What sort of bizarre household was this where the servants were not to be disturbed for their masters' comforts? Sebastian wondered. He would like to disturb personally anyone who intimated that Prudence wasn't worth cooking for. How many times had she gone without breakfast or a warm fire to be "considerate"? When he was master of Lindentree, she would lack for nothing. He would see to it.

"Has Miss Walker already been to the kitchens this morning?" he asked.

"Nearly an hour ago."

Sebastian jumped up. His knife clattered to the floor. "Very well. That will be all. Thank you." He raced for the door. "The kippers were tasty," he said over his shoulder to the gaping butler. "Nice butter too. Is there a trick to getting those little pats to look like roses?"

He was gone before Old Fish could reply.

Sebastian followed an arched corridor to the library he had discovered earlier that morning. The carved doors were shut. As a humming maid rounded the corner with an armful of linen, he pressed himself into a curtained alcove. He stepped out after she passed and gave his frock coat a nervous tug. When he was master of Lindentree, he would have to stop skulking like a second-rate French spy. *But that's what you are*, he reminded himself. Only Tricia's wealth held the power to set him free.

He pushed open the library doors and, seeing her, bit off a curse that would have made Tiny blush.

Prudence jerked her head up, her eyes widening in alarm.

"Pardon me," he said. "I stubbed my toe."

He had not stubbed his toe. He'd cursed because the alluring creature of last night had vanished once again. The fragile vision that had haunted him all morning might have only been a dream—her hair tumbled, her nightcap askew, the delicate bones of her face framed by lace—all gone as if they had never been. The twist of Sebastian's heart was more grief than irritation. Perhaps, he mused, he was dealing with a set of twins possessed by a diabolical sense of humor.

Prudence's unbound hair had been replaced by a chignon so tight it made his head ache to contemplate it. Her spectacles perched on the tip of her nose, and her mouth had a pinched look about it. She untucked her legs from the wing-backed chair and brushed a stray crumb from the dun muslin of her skirt.

He closed the door. "I need to speak with you. Can we be undisturbed here?"

She laid aside her book with obvious reluctance. "I suppose. I don't believe Tricia knows where the library is."

He frowned. "How long has she lived here?"

Prudence blinked owlishly over the rims of her spectacles. "Ten years."

Sebastian pulled up a brocaded stool and sat at her feet. The library was a cozy room, scented with the must and leather of well-worn books. Two long casement windows overlooked a meadow drenched in buttercups. It was refreshing to look out a window and see something more natural than clipped, rolling lawn and leering stone Apollos.

Now that he had finally found her, words deserted Sebastian. As he glanced at the book she had been reading, he smiled wryly. "Sur la combustion en general?"

She covered the book with a protective hand. "Monsieur Lavoisier shared many of Papa's theories regarding fulminating powders."

"I wasn't aware you were continuing your father's research."

"I'm not." She picked up a pile of letters stacked beside her chair. "But these men are. Their pleas come in the post every week. They want my father's notes, his formulas. But I can't help any of them when I don't know what went wrong in his calculations." She laughed weakly. "Some of them even want money."

Sebastian frowned at the pile. "Pesky lot, aren't they?"

"It's dwindled. It was much worse right after he died. They used to appear on Tricia's doorstep, accost me at church . . ." She sighed. "I can't help but wonder where they all were when Papa was begging for money to fund his own experiments."

Sebastian wanted to touch her hand, but satisfied himself with caressing the worn spine of the book. Silent minutes stretched between them. They both started talking at once, then lapsed again into awkward silence.

"Go ahead," he said.

She clasped her hands around her knees. "No, you."

He flexed his long legs. "Why haven't you betrayed me to your aunt?"

She sniffed with dignity. "If Aunt Tricia is silly enough to marry a highwayman, who am I to stop her?"

"Who are you indeed? I've been asking myself that question since I met you."

"I fear you would be disappointed by the answer."

She took off her spectacles and folded them into her pocket. Sebastian had placed himself near her in the hope that she would. He saw that shadows smudged the delicate skin beneath her eyes, as if she, too, had slept poorly. But the soft amethyst of her eyes was untarnished. He could not help staring at her, riveted by the pure curve of her cheek the view from the stool afforded him.

"It's just as well you sought me out, Lord Kerr. I had planned on seeking an audience with you later in the day. I did not think you would be up so early." She evaded his gaze. "My aunt seldom rises before noon. It never occurred to me that she might be awake at this hour . . . or that you might be awake or—"

He took pity on her flustered state. "I have no idea if Tricia is awake or not. Per my own request, my bedchamber is in the west wing."

She met his eyes then, and there was reluctant admiration in her gaze. Sebastian felt like a knave. His bedchamber *was* in the west wing at his request. But he had held Tricia at bay on the pretense that he didn't want the implication of their intimacy to corrupt her young niece. Both Tricia and Prudence would pale if they knew how desperately he really longed to corrupt her.

Prudence cleared her throat in a purposeful manner, and he got the distinct impression he was preparing to interview a governess.

"I wanted to meet with you, my lord—"

"Sebastian," he interjected.

"—to assure you that I will do everything in my power not to be a burden to you and my aunt once the two of you are wed. I don't know if my aunt has made you aware, but I am quite capable of keeping detailed household accounts. I can tend to the more tiresome details of running a manor house such as Lindentree, freeing you and Tricia to attend balls or hunts or whatever social activities you choose for your amusement." She bowed her head, and his gaze locked on the sleek cap of her hair. "I'm somewhat ashamed to admit that I lack a certain authority over the servants, but fortunately they adore Tricia, and even the lazy ones will do whatever she asks."

He continued staring at her in stunned silence.

"I am also quite proficient in needlework. I can do simple mending, which should save you the trouble of hiring a seamstress for the more menial tasks."

Sebastian wanted to stop her before she applied for the post of chambermaid, but her dignified recitation had rendered him speechless. He wondered what she would say if he offered her the post of his mistress. But no, that would be too cruel. And too easy.

At his silence, her voice faltered. "I can even turn my hand to light cleaning if you desire."

"Of what? My pistols?"

The words shot out before he could stop them. She lifted her head, her eyes wide in mild reproach as if she did not find his jest amusing. Her fingers knotted in her skirts. "Lindentree is the only home I know. My aunt was kind enough to take me in after my father"—she hesitated for the briefest moment—"exploded."

Her discomfiture pained him. He leaned back on the stool, his eyes searching her face. "What of suitors, Prudence? Don't you wish to marry one day?"

She met his gaze coolly. Her quiet words held not a trace of self-pity. "I am twenty years old. I have received two separate marriage proposals in my life. Within five minutes, I'd talked both men out of believing they loved me. If they had loved me, I would not have been able to talk them out of it."

Her blatant honesty disarmed him and tightened an aching knot in the pit of his stomach. "Does that suit you? Is this the life you choose? No husband. No home of your own. No children."

She shyly inclined her head. "I must confess to a fondness for children. I had once hoped to have some of my own."

Sebastian rose and strode over to the window before she

met his gaze and saw how badly he would like to put his child in her. He balled his fist against the casement, staring blindly at the summer morning.

When he spoke again, his voice was gruffer than he intended. "You need not worry, Miss Walker. Lindentree will be your home for as long as you desire to make it so."

He heard the swish of her skirts, the click of her spectacles unfolding, but did not trust himself to face her.

"Thank you, sir. I trust you will not be sorry."

Behind him, the library doors opened and closed. He pressed his forehead to the warm glass, baffled by what had transpired. He had come to the library to cajole, to swear, or to threaten her into secrecy concerning his identity, and she had ended up begging him—a lying, thieving, no-good scoundrel—for a small corner in her own home.

What manner of woman was she? And why was he so powerless to stop thinking of her? His eyes narrowed with determination. With luck and a bit of charm, he intended to find out. He reached into his coat pocket and pulled out one of the pearl-tipped hairpins he had carried since the night they had met. He rolled it between his fingers, hearing once again the sweet beat of the summer rain.

Seven

Prudence backed through the library door, trying to juggle a tart and flip the page of her book at the same time. Safely inside the library, she shoved the door shut with her foot. A light snore rattled the silence, and she froze. Her heart thudded a warning. As she turned, the tart slipped from her fingers and landed on the polished wood floor with a splat.

Sebastian sprawled in the wing-backed chair, his white stockinged feet propped on the stool. His head was thrown back, his mouth slightly ajar. A book lay across his lap, rumpling the neat creases of his tan breeches.

She knew she ought to scrape up her tart and silently creep away. Sebastian Kerr would soon be master of this house. If he chose to deny her the haven of the library in the first peace of the day, that was his right. But the slanting rays of the morning sun poured over him, seeming to drag her forward. Just one look, she promised herself. Just to satisfy her perverse curiosity about the reading habits of a notorious highwayman.

Clutching her own book, she glided toward him, bedazzled by more than the sunshine. The fragile light spun a white-gold web around Sebastian. He looked like a medieval prince awaiting a kiss to break his enchantment. Before she realized it, Prudence was leaning forward, her lips parted.

Sebastian's thigh shifted, and she gave herself a harsh mental shake.

She could hardly afford to indulge in such girlish fantasies about her aunt's fiancé. He was just a man like any other man. She forced herself to focus on his faults—the little hiccup at the crest of each snore, the pale scar under his chin. She bent over him. Why, his teeth weren't even perfect! One of his front teeth had a corner chipped out of it.

He stirred again, and she almost giggled at the thought of him awakening to find her peering into his mouth like a horse trader.

She eased the book from his lap, but she didn't have to turn it over to recognize it. It was Lavoisier's famed tome on gunpowder, the very book he had discovered her reading the day before. He had made it to the second page before falling asleep.

Her bewilderment shifted to unreasoning ire. The book slid from her rigid fingers, hitting the Persian carpet with a soft thud. How long had he been lying in wait for her? The man should be with his fiancée. What right did he have to ruin her morning? To insinuate himself into her library, her chair, her book? Was there nothing in her life he would leave alone, unchanged by the casual mockery of his touch? She glared down at him, unwillingly noticing how his dark lashes fanned across his cheeks. Sleeping people looked so terribly vulnerable.

She took three deliberate steps backward, off the carpet, held her arms straight out in front of her, and dropped her book. It slammed into the floor with the force of a gunshot.

Sebastian flew out of the chair, groping at his waist. Prudence didn't know whether to laugh or be ashamed when she realized he was searching for his pistols. His wild-eyed gaze lit on her.

She blinked, all innocence. "I'm dreadfully sorry. I didn't know you were in here."

He sank back into the chair and dragged a hand through his tousled hair. "Good Lord, girl. You took ten years off my life."

She noted that he wasn't too senile to nudge the treatise on gunpowder under his chair with his heel.

She knelt to retrieve her own book. "I didn't mean to disturb you. I'll be going now."

"No!"

She stared at him, frozen in place on her knees.

He gave his frock coat a sheepish tug, as if realizing how much desperation had tempered his command. "Stay, please. There's ample room for both of us here."

Prudence didn't know if the Colosseum of Rome held ample room for both of them. Before she could protest, though, he was kneeling beside her. His knee brushed hers as he picked up her book.

He gave a mock stagger at its weight and read the title aloud, his tongue stumbling over the unfamiliar Latin. "*Philosophiae Naturalis Principia Mathematica* by Isaac Newton." He handed it to her. "I'm glad to see you've taken up some lighter reading, Prudence. I was beginning to wonder if you ever had any fun."

His teasing grin revealed the chip in his tooth. It only made him look dashing. Prudence knew she should have escaped before he recovered his smile.

She hugged the book to her breasts like a shield, babbling as she always did when nervous. "Newton is quite fascinating, you know. The *Principia* explores his hypothesis that the force of attraction between two bodies varies directly . . ."

Her voice trailed off as she became mesmerized by the clean scent of his hair, the lazy little flick of his tongue across his upper lip.

He lifted an eyebrow, challenging her to continue.

She stood abruptly. "You wouldn't be interested."

He straightened too. "You're wrong, Prudence. I would be very interested."

"No, you wouldn't." She took a step backward. "I—I'm boring. Everyone says so."

"Nonsense. I find Norton's theories quite intriguing."

"Newton," she corrected, taking another step away from him, acutely aware of the closed door at her back.

He reached for her book, as if by touching it he could somehow hold her there. Her fingers dug into the leather spine. Oddly enough, it wasn't the considerable charm of his physical presence that tempted her to stay. It was the tender earnestness in his eyes. It would be too easy to believe he actually wanted to sit with her among all these books, and laugh and talk about the things that interested them, as she and Papa used to do. When she looked up, though, Sebastian's gaze was lingering not on her book, but on her lips.

A strange heat flooded her cheeks. She fumbled behind her for the door handle. "Perhaps another time."

As if sensing he had pushed too hard, too fast, he stepped back. "Come tomorrow morning, won't you? We could talk . . ."

A peculiar expression stole over his face, and she followed his gaze downward. His foot was planted firmly in the middle of her tart. Raspberries bled into his immaculate white stocking.

Prudence clapped a hand over her mouth before a throaty giggle could escape. Tricia said her laugh was vulgar, as low and common as a London hussy's. Beneath his lowered lashes, Sebastian's eyes sparkled dangerously. Prudence opened the door, deciding it was wisest to pretend she hadn't noticed his foot was mired in her breakfast.

"Perhaps tomorrow." She bobbed a harried curtsy. "Good day, my lord."

His elegant bow could have graced any London drawing room. "Good day, Prudence."

She backed into the hall, turned and ran, skittering around the corner and out the door to the garden. She collapsed against the wall, smothering her merry peals of laughter with her skirt.

Sebastian trailed his hand through the rippling cool water of the fish pond. A goldfish nipped his thumb. He straightened with a sigh and leaned on the balustrade. The sun toasted his cambric shirt against his shoulders. He longed to tear away his queue and let the warm wind rush through his hair.

From the bowling green below the terrace, Squire Blake waved a turkey leg at him. Sebastian wondered if that would be him in twenty years. Corpulent and crude, satisfied to spend his days playing games with other overgrown children and his nights learning clever new ways to fold his cravat. He shuddered.

"Have you taken a chill, darling? Shall I have Fish fetch your coat?"

Sebastian suppressed another shudder as Tricia's trilling voice raked down his spine. What sort of inane question was that, he wondered. Probably just another excuse to stuff him into a frock coat. He swung around to face his fiancée. She sat a few feet away, going through her correspondence with Old Fish. Just recently risen from her bed, she wore only her elegant *robe de chambre*—and, of course, a wig and full complement of makeup. Her damp fichu clung to her bosom. A trickle of sweat eased down her flushed cheek, melting the powder in its wake. Beneath the flattering candlelight of London ballrooms and her bedchamber, he had never noticed the folds of skin loosening at her throat. He felt a pang of sympathy mixed with irritation. It must be stifling under that wig.

"No, thank you, dear," he said, dredging up a pleasant smile. "I haven't taken a chill."

She tittered. "Perhaps a goose walked over your grave."

A Great Dane, more likely, he thought as Boris galloped across the lawn below, scattering the peacocks.

Tricia blew him a kiss and went back to dictating her correspondence. Catching the butler's eye, Sebastian decided he might need that coat after all. Old Fish's glare was as shivering as a glacier.

His hands clenched the balustrade. He wouldn't have to worry about a grave for quite some time. The only thing likely to kill him at Lindentree was boredom. Rising at five each morning to haunt the library wasn't improving his temper either, especially since Prudence had failed to appear after their last meeting. He was a slow reader, and had struggled to page fifty of the gunpowder book without gaining any insight into her character.

Squire Blake tromped up the glassy slope, sucking the last drops of grease from the turkey bone. The afternoon stretched interminably before Sebastian. Tea. A round of bowling on the lawn. Dinner. Sipping brandy while listening to Tricia pound on her new pianoforte. A late supper. No wonder Squire Blake was so obsessed with his digestion. In the past week their whole lives had consisted of an endless parade of meals broken only by an occasional hunt or ball. Sebastian smothered a yawn with the back of his hand.

A boom shattered the silence, rattling the glass in the casement windows.

Sebastian spun around. "What the hell . . . ?"

Tricia slapped a sheaf of letters on the stone table. "Damn that girl! I warned her."

Her robe rippled around her feet as she stalked into the house and down the long corridor to the east wing. Old Fish trotted behind her. Sebastian followed at a safe distance, fascinated by the abrupt change in Tricia's demeanor.

Black smoke rolled out of the kitchens. Tricia slammed a handkerchief over her nose and charged into the smoky fray, batting at the air. Old Fish hung back, clutching the door frame. The smoke slowly cleared, revealing a scene of such charming chaos that Sebastian felt himself grinning like a fool.

White gobbets of dough spattered every visible surface. They clung to the cracked glass of the windows, dotted the brick hearth, and dangled from the herb rack like yeasty pearls. The iron door of the oven hung askew on its hinges. Inside, a tongue of flame licked at a charred ball. Wooden bowls, spoons, and platters littered the floor and table. Two maidservants huddled in the corner, coughing into their aprons. Sebastian-cat perched on the table, lapping cream from a shattered pitcher.

In the midst of it all stood Prudence, enveloped in a charcoal-smudged apron, her hair piled on her head in an untidy mass. Flour dusted her spectacles. Sebastian threw back his head to laugh, but as Prudence faced her aunt, something in her stance stopped him.

She laced her fingers together. Her slender throat convulsed as if she were swallowing a knot of dread. Still, she managed to summon a weak smile. "Good afternoon, Auntie."

She hadn't seen him. Sebastian slipped into the narrow alcove between pantry and cupboard, wanting to spare her the embarrassment of his presence.

"It weren't my fault, mistress." A stringy cook charged forward, brandishing a rolling pin. "The girl slipped in while I was takin' my afternoon nap."

Tricia's wig quivered with rage. Sebastian suddenly realized how much shorter than Prudence she'd be without it. "How many times have I forbidden you to use the kitchens for your horrid experiments?"

"I'm very sorry. I didn't think—"

"Of course you didn't think. You didn't think about how many pounds it cost to have these windows shipped from London, did you? Or about who might be able to repair the range before my supper party tonight? This is the fifth oven you've destroyed, you careless girl."

As Prudence knotted her apron in her hands, Sebastian's hands clenched into fists. Old Fish retreated a discreet distance, but not too discreet to hear everything that was said.

Hands on her hips, Tricia surveyed the wrecked kitchen. The ribbons on her bodice heaved wildly. Sebastian-cat chose that unfortunate moment to lift his head from his feast. His whiskers dripped cream. He shook his head, spattering yellow droplets across the satin skirt of Tricia's robe.

She gave an unintelligible shriek. "How dare you let that furry monster into my kitchens!"

Her hand flew back. Prudence snatched up the cat and cradled him against her chest. Tricia's hand hung poised in the air, her crimson-tipped fingers curled like claws.

Sebastian held his breath, paralyzed, as the image fractured into jagged shards of memory. How often had he stood crippled with fear and frustration at such a scene? Then his vision cleared. His eyes narrowed. He wasn't a child anymore. It might cost him his engagement, his fortune, and his future, but if Tricia dared lay her hand against Prudence's smooth cheek, he would show her why his enemies called him Dreadful.

Prudence was paler than cream, but the hands locked around her cat were steady. She met her aunt's gaze without blinking, her chin tilted in calm defiance.

"It was an accident," she said.

Tricia slowly lowered her hand. "You and your father are prone to them, aren't you?"

Only Sebastian saw Prudence's barely perceptible flinch, for Tricia had already turned, her skirt swishing. Sebastian ducked deeper into the shadows.

"You can't expect me to clean up this ungodly mess," the cook protested.

"I certainly don't," Tricia tossed over her shoulder. "My niece made the mess. She can clean it up."

The cook tapped the rolling pin in her palm with waspish satisfaction. The maids giggled into their aprons. Tricia swept from the room, her entourage of supporters in tow. Old Fish reappeared to slam the door, jarring a glob of dough from the herb rack. It plopped into Prudence's hair. Sighing, she set the squirming kitten on a stool.

As she surveyed the kitchen, she swiped at her hair, leaving a smudge of flour where the dough had been. The small gesture betrayed her dejection more than tears or curses. Sebastian emerged from his corner, no longer able to ignore the ache in his own heart.

When she saw him, Prudence hid her shock behind a stern frown. "And where did you come from?"

He smiled. "You forget—lurking is one of my best talents."

"Remind me to remember that."

He began to open the windows. The lingering tendrils of smoke drifted away on the wind. "It seems my bride has a bit of a temper." He threw open the last window with more force than he intended. The warped pane shattered and crashed to the floor. "Damn. I'm so clumsy." His sulky grin was less than repentant.

Prudence gathered up pieces of the broken pitcher in her apron. "Tricia's not so bad. You can't really blame her, can you? It *was* the fifth oven."

"What were you working on?" He wracked his brain, hoping to impress her with something he'd learned from her book. Studying the floured table, the thick bowl of goo resting next to her elbow, he asked, "Was it corning powder? Some sort of detonator?"

A brilliant pink tinged her cheeks, and she sighed. "Tea cakes. I was working on tea cakes."

"Tea cakes?" If she hadn't looked so crestfallen, Sebastian would have laughed.

She scraped at the dough on the table with renewed vigor. "Cooking seems to be the only form of chemistry that eludes me. I've never been any good at it. But I was so encouraged. The icing turned out quite well."

She dipped her finger in the bowl, then tucked it between her lips with a soft moan of satisfaction. The innocent gesture wreaked havoc on Sebastian's heartbeat. A tiny bit of icing clung to the corner of her mouth. He wanted to lean over and lick it away, knowing full well the hunger he felt had little to do with tea cakes. If she only knew the dangers of tempting a starving man.

Unable to resist, he traced the inner curve of her lips with the tip of his little finger. As her eyes widened, he slid his finger into his mouth.

A smile of genuine pleasure curved his lips. "Delicious. Perhaps you're not such a bad cook after all."

The sweetness lingering on his tongue was ashes compared to her answering smile. "We should both remember that lying is also among your special gifts."

He reached down and drew off her spectacles. Her eyes revealed only a faint wariness. Would she be as compliant if he worked the pins from her hair, buried his fingers in the silky mass, traced the delicate curve of her jaw with his lips?

With a brisk motion, he polished her spectacles on his sleeve, leaving the cambric streaked with flour. He set them back gently on her nose, pretending not to see the shaky breath she drew.

Reaching around her, he plucked an apron from a wooden peg. "We'd best get to work if we plan to have this kitchen in order before Tricia's supper party."

"You don't have to help me."

"You didn't have to help me either. But if you hadn't, I'd probably be dead or crippled right now. Toss me that broom, won't you?"

She obeyed, not quite able to hide her grin. "You cut quite a dashing figure in an apron. It's a pity Tiny can't see you now."

"I shudder to think of it. Why don't you stick a spoon in that icing? It would be a shame to let something so sweet go to waste."

She gazed into the bowl, smiling a sad little smile. "Yes, I do believe it would."

Old Fish paused outside the kitchen door, his bony fingers splayed on the knob. Frowning, he leaned forward, pressing his ear to the fine oak. Voices murmured in soft accord. A soft clink was followed by masculine laughter. What was the insolent chit up to now?

He drew in a deep breath and threw open the door. A flash of white disappeared into the pantry. Prudence stood in the middle of the kitchen, broom in hand.

She blinked at him. "May I help you, Fish?"

Her voice was cool, almost subservient, but Fish knew she was mocking him.

His sharp gaze traveled the immaculate kitchen. A wooden bucket of wash water sat at her feet. The table, floor, and walls had been scrubbed clean. Even the oven door hung straight. The only sign of the earlier destruction was a gaping square where the window glass should have been. A breeze wafted in, sifting the pungent aroma of the mint drying on the herb rack.

He reached for the pantry door. Before he could touch the knob, the door slipped open a crack. Sebastian-cat strolled out as if he owned the kitchen.

Old Fish backed away, sniffing. "I believe your aunt requested that you remove this animal from the premises."

"Why, thank you for reminding me, Fish. Would you be so kind as to take him out to the herb garden for me?"

Before he could protest, Prudence draped the beast over his shoulder like an infant and blithely departed, humming under her breath. The kitten snagged his claws in Fish's coat and glared at him cross-eyed. Fish scowled at the cat, then gazed thoughtfully at the bucket of water. But, no. He might have a hard time explaining that one.

With a beleaguered sigh, he unhooked the cat and started for the garden, holding the squirming creature at arm's length. He vowed to himself that he would keep a stricter eye on prim Miss Prudence. Her weekly excursions to church did not fool him. No proper young lady would dabble in such unnatural sciences as chemistry. Unchecked, the little heathen might resort to dabbling in things more sordid. He would not have his mistress's reputation tarnished by Miss Prudence's folly.

With a furtive glance behind him, Fish opened the nearest window and gave the cat a toss.

Prudence snuggled into the velvet cushions of the window seat. Sebastian-cat rolled over on her lap, baring an irresistibly furry hump of a belly that demanded stroking. She absently obliged, her thoughts elsewhere.

A warm breeze wafted through the open window. June was waning, melting into the sultry heat of July. The humid air curled the tendrils of hair escaping from her braid and freed the intoxicating scent of the jasmine twining up the trellis. Light spilled from the wing that housed the servants' quarters, breaking the darkness into cozy squares.

A snatch of laughter drifted into the night, followed by a chorus of tipsy song. Prudence smiled ruefully as she recognized the most recent ditty immortalizing the amorous adventures of the Dreadful Scot Bandit Kirkpatrick. If they only knew the half of it! She wished she could go down to the servants' hall and somehow join their merriment undetected. All the windows between her chamber and their quarters were solid rectangles of darkness.

Sebastian and Tricia had set off that morning in a rattle of coach wheels and merry peals of Tricia's goodbyes for a ball in Durham County. They would not return before dawn, if then. For the mistress of Lindentree, the last three weeks had passed in a veritable cyclone of social activity, as Tricia presented her betrothed to every squire, duke, and earl in the county of Northumberland. That accomplished, she set out to conquer the neighboring counties. Much to her satisfaction, all the gossip was of Sebastian—his elegant but casual dress, his refusal to wear a wig or pomade his hair, his sun-bronzed visage.

At his first ball, he had scandalized half the county by listening earnestly as a foppish young marquess explained the intricate powdering of his hedgehog wig. Sebastian had then taken the fellow by the elbow and suggested that a live hedgehog would require less care and be considerably more attractive. When Tricia had repeated that story, Prudence had choked on her tea and been forced to excuse herself from the table.

By the end of the second week, baring pates was becoming outrageously fashionable. Even the doddering Duke of Poitmontou dared to arrive at an afternoon picnic with his bald scalp glistening like a baby's rump. His duchess had fainted, knocking her wig askew and revealing that her own head had been rubbed bare by the weight of the wigs she had worn for half a century.

Some of the younger men had taken to exposing their faces to the sun. On his last visit, Sir Arlo had shyly exhibited his own sallow tan for Prudence's approval.

She sighed at the memory. Sir Arlo hadn't had time for many visits to Lindentree lately. There had been a fresh rash of robberies along the Scottish border.

The Dread Kirkpatrick's boldness increased daily. Some whispered he would soon desert the highways to prey on the manors themselves. At the mere mention of his name at tea the day before, a serving girl had dropped a tray of china and burst into tears, earning herself a scolding from Fish and a slap from Tricia. No one, fortunately, associated the bandit's raids with Lord Kerr's frequent trips to Edinburgh to review his Highland holdings.

To Prudence, Sebastian was unfailingly polite. He went out of his way to draw her into a game of whist or coax her to attend a ball at a neighboring estate. She now carried two pastries to the library each morning, knowing she would find him poring over a book or sorting through her correspondence, sifting the pleas for money from those truly interested in her father's work.

He might seem an elegant ruffian to the gentry, but with her he practiced perfect decorum, even gentleness. She rewarded his kindness by sliding his fork nearer his place at supper, and clearing her throat in warning when he absently picked up the brandy decanter and brought it to his lips.

The previous night, she, Sebastian, and Tricia had gathered in the parlor like a proper family while Tricia pounded out a melody on the pianoforte and lifted her fuzzy soprano in song. Prudence had glanced up from her embroidery to find Sebastian watching her over the rim of his brandy glass. His eyes were narrowed as if he were searching for something he had misplaced. It reminded her of her father's lost expression when he could not remember where he had left his wig. His quizzical frown tugged at her heart, and her aching hunger to help him find what he had lost unnerved her. She had excused herself, her temples pounding with another of her interminable headaches.

Prudence was jerked back to the warm summer night by the ringing crash of an iron spoon against a kettle. Someone had decided the addition of a makeshift cymbal would greatly enhance the bawdy chorus. She leaned forward, straining to hear more clearly the quavering rasp that sounded suspiciously like Old Fish.

A hobgoblin face popped out of the darkness.

Prudence screamed. The hobgoblin gave a nasal shriek of terror. Sebastian-cat's fur stood on end as he dug his claws into Prudence's night rail, then fled, dragging long scratches down her thigh. Prudence scrambled backward out of the window seat and the hobgoblin vanished, as if an unseen hand had abruptly jerked off its wings.

A curious bumping and scraping was followed by a string of curses in a burr so thick, it was nearly unintelligible.

Prudence snatched a hairpin from her dressing table and crept back to the window. She peered down into the rustling ivy, wielding the hairpin like a tiny dagger.

Glossy leaves flew as the mysterious gremlin popped back up with a triumphant crow.

"I knew it was ye! By God, he told me to stay away from the house, but I seen ye from the stables, and I swore it was ye."

She recoiled anew from the malnourished, freckled visage. "Jamie," she whispered in dread.

Eight

"Aye, lass. 'Tis Jamie Graham. In the flesh." His hazel eyes narrowed dangerously. "Ye're seein' better than ye used to, ain't ye?"

Prudence took another step backward. "I went to London. I had an operation." She was a terrible liar and they both knew it.

To her shock, he flung a wiry leg over the windowsill and climbed into her room. No man other than her papa had ever set foot in her bedchamber. She hugged her night rail tight around her.

"Maybe it was a miracle," he said. "You one of them Catholics?" He wiggled his bony fingers at her. "Did a priest sprinkle holy water in yer eyes? I don't want no one sayin' Jamie Graham don't understand miracles. Me own da's a minister of the kirk."

In her surprise, she forgot her fear. "Your father is a minister?"

"Aye, that he is." He leered at her. "Don't it show?"

"Of course," she said faintly. "I suspected it from the first moment we met."

He brushed dirt and leaves from the seat of his pants onto her pristine rug. "Damned ivy."

Prudence drew herself up. "I wish it had been rose bushes.

It would have served you right for daring to spy on a young lady."

Her indignation did not trouble Jamie. His gamin face crinkled in a smile. "Nice place ye got here." In horror, she watched as he flung himself on the bed, crossing his ankles and resting his head on folded hands as if he planned to stay. "Very nice indeed."

He gave the down mattress an experimental bounce before jumping up. His boots left dirty smudges on the counter-pane. She jerked up her bolster, brushed it off, then clutched it in front of her. Her eyes widened as Jamie careened around the chamber like an elf run amok.

He scooped up her gilt hand mirror and surveyed his foxlike face from all angles, then puckered up and blew his reflection a kiss before lifting her hairbrush to his matted mop. At her helpless sound of dismay, he turned the brush over in his hands and studied it with a sly smile.

"Worth a pretty shilling, if ye ask me."

"I didn't ask you," she said, desperate to rid her chamber of the horrid creature.

He tried on her spectacles and splashed a dab of rose water behind each ear. "The ladies love a good scent on a man, don't they? That's what Sebastian told me." He spun around on the stool. "Look what it's done for him. Two lovely lasses under one roof. Which room does he come to first every night? Yers or hers?"

Prudence's trembling ceased. She felt dangerously close to using the hairpin in her hand. Jamie had good reason to be thankful it wasn't a loaded pistol. "I don't think rose water was what Sebastian had in mind. Would you please leave my room?"

Jamie's mischievous grin faded. He rose, shrugging his thin shoulders. "Never say Jamie Graham don't aim to please the ladies. I thought ye might be lonely while Sebastian was out gallivantin' with the other one."

He started for the window, casting her a wounded glance from beneath his sparse auburn lashes.

"Wait." Prudence startled herself as curiosity overcame both anger and fear. She might never have a better opportunity to learn about her aunt's enigmatic fiancé. "Is Sebastian Kerr his real name?"

Jamie shrugged again. "It is now. Used to be Kirkpatrick. Sometimes we just call him Kirk." Sighing, he sank down on the window seat. "Why is it every time I'm in a lass's bedroom, I end up answerin' questions about him?" His voice shifted to a whining falsetto. "What color does he like? What's his favorite food? What pleases him in bed?" He snorted. "If I knew that, they wouldn't need to worry about it, would they?"

"He wouldn't be very pleased to know you'd been here, would he?" She dared a sweet smile.

He acknowledged her threat with a mocking smirk.

"Have you ever been to his home in the Highlands— Dunkirk?"

"Aye. Tiny snuck me up there one night when we was hidin' out."

"What is it like?"

Jamie shook his head at the memory. "A crumblin' hole of a castle perched at the edge of heaven itself."

Prudence sat down cross-legged on the carpet, still clutching the bolster. "If it's such a hole, why does he risk everything to gain it back?" Her real question remained unspoken. *Why will he even marry Tricia for it?*

"'Cause he don't want a stinkin' MacKay to have it. The MacKays and the Kerrs have been sworn enemies since the massacre at Culloden. Sebastian's ma came all the way from France to be MacKay's bride. Sebastian's da kidnapped her and kept her for his own. MacKay swore revenge. When Sebastian's da dropped dead in his boots, MacKay took Dunkirk. Sebastian was little older than a lad. There was nothin' he could do to stop him."

"Did you know Sebastian's father?"

"No." Jamie shuddered. "But Tiny told me about him. He was the meanest son-of-a-bitch whose boots ever shook the heather. Did ye see the scar under Sebastian's chin?"

She nodded slowly, hesitant to remind Jamie of her nearness to Sebastian in the crofter's hut.

"That's where his da's ring caught him when he dared to

shed a tear at his own ma's burial. 'Men don't cry,' he told him. And the lad little more than a babe himself!'"

Prudence twisted the bolster in her hands, caught off guard by the dangerous welling of emotion in her throat.

"Lass?" Jamie's voice was surprisingly kind.

She lifted her head, blinking back unshed tears.

He cocked his head to the side, studying her. "Back at the hut, Tiny didn't understand what Sebastian saw in ye. Ye ain't really his sort, if ye know what I mean. But I can kind of see it now. Ye ain't so bad. When ye came out of the house that first day, I thought it might be ye he set out to marry. It would have made good sense to keep ye quiet that way."

She pursed her lips thoughtfully.

Jamie shifted his weight from window seat to windowsill. "Look, lass, just watch yer back when he's around."

She stood, letting the bolster drop to the floor. She barely felt the brush of the kitten against her ankle. "Why?"

"Ye know what they say about curiosity and cats." He drew his forefinger across his throat.

She glanced down at her cat. When she looked up again, the window was empty and Jamie was running fleet-footed and silent across the lawn. Prudence stood for a long time, staring at nothing and shivering in the warm night breeze.

Nine

A ghostly tapping came on the window. Prudence stiffened in her bed, holding her breath. Tap. Tap. Tap. Her fingers curled around the counterpane as she weighed the wisdom of pulling it over her head. Not Jamie again, please, she prayed silently. Not two visits in the same week. The tapping ceased. She rolled to her side, hoping she was dreaming.

A shower of pebbles struck the window, shattering a glazed pane with a tinkling crash. A slurred curse followed. She leaped out of bed and tiptoed to the window, picking her way among the shards of glass.

She peeped out the window.

A figure stood on the lawn below, bathed in a puddle of moonlight. "'But soft! What light through yonder window breaks? It is the east and Prudence is the sun.'"

She ducked behind the curtains. She *must* be dreaming, she thought. Why else would a Highland bandit be standing beneath her window misquoting Shakespeare?

"'Arise, fair sun, and kill the envious—'"

She jerked up what was left of the window. Sebastian's idea of a stage whisper was enough to awaken Tricia's dead husbands sleeping in the family crypt. "Ssssh! Have you lost your senses, Sebastian? One more word and I shall rouse my aunt."

The reproachful look he gave her would have shamed an

infidel. Prudence's breath caught in her throat. She had forgotten what a dashing figure he cut in full Scottish garb. A belted kilt matched the black and green tartan of his stockings. A silver brooch secured the pleated plaid draped over one shoulder. His knees were bared to the warm night air.

She frowned as the import of his dress sank in. "Whatever are you doing? You're supposed to be in Edinburgh."

He bowed mockingly and almost stumbled. "I stopped off in London to pay my respects to King Georgie."

She leaned out the window. "This is no time for jests. What will Tricia do if she finds you on the lawn dressed like that? What will Sir Arlo do?"

"He'll probably shoot me again."

Prudence's hands froze before she could slam the window back down.

Her mouth went dry. It could be a trap. She was the only one at Lindentree who knew his true identity. Jamie's warning spun through her mind. She would be a fool to step into the deserted night with him. She poked her head back out the window, prepared to send him away with a scathing denouncement.

He gave her the lopsided smile of a rumpled Highland angel. "I need you, Prudence."

A piece of glass stabbed her toe as she threw on her wrapper and ran for the door.

Prudence pounded across the dew-slick lawn, her wrapper billowing wildly behind her. She tripped over a short box hedge and silently berated herself for forgetting her spectacles. Her nightcap bobbed over her eyes. As she rounded the corner of the house, her heart shuddered to a stop. The lawn below her window was deserted. Moonlight shone on empty grass.

She must be dreaming, she thought. When she looked down at herself, she'd probably be naked.

She dared a glance downward. The comforting folds of her modest wrapper still enveloped her.

A muffled grunt drew her forward. Sebastian leaned

against the iron trellis. His arms were crossed, his stance casual. Freed of its queue, his hair tumbled around his face. The soft light of the new moon dusted the tawny strands to silver.

As he stepped away from the trellis, his legs gave way and he crashed back into the unyielding iron. His long lashes fluttered down over his eyes. Even in the thin light, his pallor was apparent. Before the plaid sank back into its folds, Prudence saw the dark stain spreading across his white shirt.

She snatched off her nightcap and pressed it beneath the plaid. Fear made her gruff. "You fool. Were you going to stand out here all night and bleed to death?"

"The thought did occur to me. Would you have felt any remorse when Boris dragged my mangled corpse up the front steps in the morning?"

"None at all. Though it might have spoiled my breakfast."

She dabbed at his shirt, praying he would not feel the violent trembling of her hands. The nightcap seemed to be soaking up an alarming amount of blood.

He gave a drunken hiccup. "Sad waste of a perfectly good nightcap. It looked enchanting on you."

He shuddered at her touch, and she realized it was not liquor that slurred his words and gave him that stupid grin, but the pain he was struggling to hide.

Tears stung her eyes. She lowered her head before he could see them.

He brought the tip of her heavy braid to his lips. "The pain's not so bad. The ball only grazed me. The powder burn hurts worse than the wound."

She dared not meet his eyes. "A few more inches and it would have been your heart."

"No danger of that. I left my heart here." His voice faded as he buried his face in the curve of her throat, resting some of his weight on her shoulder.

"We must find a safe place for you."

She hooked his arm over her shoulders, supporting his weight when he would have staggered. Together they slipped through the long casement-windows in the parlor.

Sebastian shook his head, then faltered, the motion making him dizzy. "Not my chamber. It's not safe. Tricia's been known to make nocturnal visits." His hands fluttered. "Like a bat."

Prudence struggled between laughter and wanting to drop him. She could think of only one room in the house that no one bothered to visit. She was so unfailingly tidy, even the maids stayed away from her bedroom unless summoned.

As she pushed open her door, a ball of down twined around her legs with a questioning mew. She shushed the kitten and eased Sebastian down on her rumpled bedclothes. He fell face first into her counterpane, sighing with contentment. She gently righted him, then moved away to light the candle.

When she turned back, Sebastian was fumbling with his buckled shoes.

She caught him, bracing him with her shoulder as he began a precarious slide toward the floor. "Whatever are you doing?"

"My shoes. I mustn't get mud on your pretty sheets."

She righted him. "Don't be silly. I don't care one whit about the sheets."

He wagged a chiding finger at her. "You would if you'd never had any."

She laid him back on the bed with tender exasperation and knelt between his knees to pull off his shoes.

"When you're master of Lindentree," she said, deliberately keeping her voice light, "you can buy me all the sheets I need."

"It would be my pleasure. Satin sheets. Silk sheets. Have you ever slept on Chinese silk? It's like nesting on a cloud."

Heat freshened Prudence's cheeks as she dropped his second shoe on the floor. She feared to meet Sebastian's eyes across the supine length of his body, afraid she might find mirrored within them the foreign images his words summoned—bodies entwined, sliding and rolling in clouds of blue silk. Then ice water doused her fevered vision, as she remembered Tricia airily describing her new addition to her London town house—an Oriental bedstead, replete with drapes of Chinese silk.

She dumped his legs on the bed, ignoring his wince of pain. "Don't go anywhere. I'll be right back."

She darted through the sleeping house to the kitchens. After finding what she needed there, she raced into the dining room. Pawing frantically through the mahogany hutch, she discovered a stack of linen napkins. Tricia would not miss them. Their crest dated at least two husbands back. She started to leave, then hesitated. Tricia kept laudanum in her bedchamber and had been known to dole it out for Prudence's headaches, but Prudence was reluctant to disturb her. She satisfied herself with snatching the decanter of Scotch whisky from the sideboard.

Back upstairs she closed the door to her chamber behind her, carefully turning the key in its lock. Sebastian had propped himself against her bolster. The alien breadth of his shoulders dwarfed her narrow bed. His eyes were alert, but misted with pain. He absently stroked the kitten nestled between his knees.

Prudence knelt beside him, setting aside her burdens, and managed a shy smile. "Let's take a look at that shoulder, shall we?"

Before she could blink, a tiny dagger leaped from Sebastian's stocking to his hand. "You can cut the shirt, but not the plaid, please. It's the Kerr plaid. The only one I have." He flipped the dagger in his hand, offering her the hilt.

She swallowed hard and took it. Many were the unwitting enemies a Highlander had dispatched with the *skean dhu* tucked into his stocking. The hilt was warm where it had rested against Sebastian's bare calf.

She unfastened the brooch at Sebastian's shoulder, taking care not to snag the tartan with the heavy pin. As she unwrapped the plaid with tender hands, she was ever mindful of his gaze fixed on her face. On closer examination, she realized how worn and frayed the garment was. Only the sturdy weave and Sebastian's loving care held it together. It was no matter, she supposed. Once he and Tricia were wed, Tricia would buy him all the tartan he desired.

Prudence slashed the shirt with more enthusiasm than she intended. Sebastian's flinch reminded her of the whisky.

"Here. Drink some of this before I go on." She held the decanter to his lips.

He drank. The amber liquid trickled down his chin, and she wiped it away, her fingers lingering on his lips.

"Perhaps you should drink some of it," he said. "It might steady your hands."

She lifted guilty eyes to meet his mocking gaze. He knew as well as she that it was not his wound that made her tremble.

She peeled the blood-soaked fabric from his shoulder. The wound itself was little more than a deep scrape, puckered at the edges. A soft sound of sympathy escaped her at the sight of the ugly powder burn that blackened his chest and shoulder. The curling hair at its edges was singed.

She held up an earthenware crock. "Butter and egg yolks. Ambroise Paré claimed it to be an excellent lotion for powder burns. Papa agreed."

"Your papa was a wise man."

She dabbed at his wound with a moistened napkin. "Wiser than most people realized." His skin contracted as she lightly smoothed on the cool butter. "Lean forward," she commanded.

He obeyed. Her arms circled him, securing the bandage of knotted napkins around him. Her braid fell against his thigh and her breasts brushed his chest before she sank back to her knees, lowering her eyes.

Beneath the downy hair on his chest, she could see other nicks and scars, some pale and faded with time. Had he gotten them the same way he had gotten the scar beneath his chin? she wondered.

She busied herself with folding the remaining napkins. "How will you hide this from my aunt?"

"It won't be hard. Tricia hasn't seen me without my shirt for quite some time."

Prudence gave him a skeptical look. "She will after you're wed."

He shifted restlessly and peered up at the canopy. "This room is just as I imagined it. White and starched, everything neatly in its place, devoid of affectation, elegant yet simple."

"Like me?"

He slanted a half-smile at her. "No one would dare call you simple."

The kitten stirred, butting his head against Sebastian's thigh. Prudence stroked him. "Sebastian-cat is very fond of you. Perhaps I should change his name. To avert confusion."

"Perhaps you should," he said, an odd note in his voice. "Sebastian is a silly name anyway."

She lifted her head to protest, but his eyes were closed. She knew he wasn't asleep yet. The grooves around his mouth had deepened with weariness and pain. He had crossed his arms over his chest in an age-old gesture of self-protection.

Prudence gently tucked the counterpane around his shoulders. There would be no harm in letting him sleep for an hour or two. It was early yet. She'd have ample time to smuggle him away before running the risk of Tricia discovering him. She sat quietly until his breathing lapsed into the uneven rhythm of troubled sleep.

Tiptoeing across the room so as not to disturb him, she snuffed the candle and drew open her curtains to the fragile moonlight. She returned to sit on the side of the bed, basking guiltily in the sheer pleasure of studying Sebastian. His lush lashes fanned out on his cheeks. His air of vulnerability in sleep erased the wary edge he bore in wakefulness. He moaned faintly, and she pressed her palm to his brow, feeling for fever, then brushed back his tangled hair.

Quickly she withdrew her hand. She had no right to touch him. He was Tricia's. He only belonged to her in the stolen moments of the night.

She sighed as weariness touched her. With the briefest hesitation, she lay down on top of the counterpane beside him and curled into the warmth of his side.

Her father's hand gently stroked her hair. She must have fallen asleep on the hearth rug again while waiting for him to finish his experiments. She snuggled deeper in the cocoon of warmth, relishing the hypnotic flow of his fingers across her scalp.

Prudence opened her eyes, realizing with perfect clarity

that it was not her papa, but Sebastian who cupped her head in his palm. In her sleep she had slid down until her head rested in his lap. The soft, worn folds of his plaid enveloped her.

She kept her breathing steady and deep with effort, unwilling to reveal she was awake. She could not remember the last time she had been touched with affection. Tricia might pinch her cheeks to stir the color in them, or kiss the air with her rouged lips, but there was always the fear of mussing her wig or smearing her powder. Tricia's love was a mere ghost of fondness, all style and no substance. Prudence would never dare throw her arms around her aunt for fear she might crumble away, leaving nothing but a heap of powder to scatter in the wind.

Sebastian's touch was beguiling in its simplicity. It made no demands and asked no questions. She might have been a child or a kitten nestled trustingly against his thigh. His touch was rife with a tenderness hard-won, for she knew he had known little of it in his life. She lay still for as long as she dared, aware that it was wrong, but wanting to remember what it felt like to be cherished. As the gray light of dawn softened the sky, she shifted in his lap, knowing she must warn him.

His eyes were open, somber and muted like the dawn.

She opened her mouth to speak, but he lay two fingers across her lips and smiled tenderly. "I've always wanted someone to take care of."

He leaned forward, and his lips touched hers. His kiss was achingly tender, laced with the bittersweet tang of the whisky on his tongue. Her fingers nestled in the soft hair of his chest.

A rooster gave a rusty crow.

Prudence pulled away with a panicked glance at the brightening sky. "You must go."

His mouth took on the sulky tilt that would have seemed petulant on any other man, but only made him look more dangerous. "Oh, I don't know. Wouldn't it be amusing to see Tricia's expression when she found us this way?"

Struggling to hide how badly his illicit kiss had shaken her, Prudence unwrapped the plaid with brisk motions. "It would not be amusing to see the hangman's expression when he came to take you to the gibbet."

Sebastian's face closed as if his mask had fallen over it. "Very well. Jamie's loft then. It's where we hide booty. The surly imp's threatened to cut off the toes of any groom who ventures there."

Prudence readjusted her wrapper around herself, and draped the remains of his shirt across his shoulders. Then they slipped through the silent house. For once, she was thankful for Tricia's indolent habits. Most of the servants did not bother to leave their beds until well after sunrise. As they stepped through the terrace doors, she felt Sebastian's arm tighten around her shoulders.

"What is it?" she whispered.

"Could you get me the whisky? If I'm going to be holed up with only Jamie for company, I might have need of it."

She propped him in the garden against a statue of Zeus and raced back for the whisky. Sebastian's tiny dagger lay forgotten on her nightstand. She dropped it in the pocket of her wrapper before flying back down the steps, driven by the first clink of activity from the kitchens.

Prudence and Sebastian ducked into the shadowy stables. A horse nickered in sleepy curiosity. Sebastian leaned against a feed bin while Prudence climbed the splintered ladder to Jamie's lair.

Jamie awoke with a snarl, jerked a loaded pistol out from under his head, and leveled it at Prudence's chest.

She backed away, hands in the air. "Sebastian needs your help. He's been shot."

Jamie jumped up with a curse that pinkened Prudence's ears. Too late, she realized he was naked. To her bleary eyes, he appeared to be one large, annoyed freckle. She swung around, clapping her hands over her eyes in mortification.

"I warned the silly fool not to go alone," Jamie muttered.

She peeped between her fingers. He had pulled on a pair of worn knee-breeches.

"It's yer own bloody fault, ye know," he added.

"My fault?" she squeaked. "I didn't shoot him."

"Ye might as well have." He grabbed her hand in his bony paw and jerked her down the ladder. "Tiny was right. He ain't had any wits about him since he met ye. If he'd have taken me with him, I'd have nailed the bastard that shot him."

Sebastian's velvety burr came out of the musty darkness. "Then Tricia wouldn't have had an even number for her supper parties."

Jamie spat in the hay. "I should have known. It was Tugbert, weren't it? Cursed sheriffs. I hate the bloody lot of them."

Prudence once more wrapped Sebastian's arm around her shoulders. Jamie took his other side. Bearing his weight between them, they soon had him up the ladder and settled in the narrow heap of straw that served as Jamie's bed.

Jamie loomed over them like a jealous bulldog, his thin lips pursed in a childish pout as Prudence tucked the plaid around Sebastian's shoulders. "Keep him warm, won't you?" she said.

"Have ye given him any opium?"

"Of course I have," she retorted. "I keep some under the bed next to my hookah pipe."

Jamie muttered something unintelligible.

Feeling a sharp poking against her thigh, she fished the *skean dhu* from her pocket. "I almost forgot to give you your dagger."

Jamie snorted. "Why don't ye cut out his heart while ye've got it so handy?"

Sebastian's icy glare was enough to make Prudence glad he was incapacitated at the moment. She did not care to mop up after two wounded men. Jamie stomped down the ladder in disgust. Prudence stood, knowing she should go, but reluctant to abandon Sebastian to the churlish gremlin's care.

Sleep and whisky had dulled Sebastian's pain and restored the sparkle to his eyes. The snowy white bandages deepened the golden hue of his skin. Grinning, he lifted the decanter to her.

She laughed. "You look quite the rogue."

"If you could have pilfered a cigar, I'd be a happy man."

A new mist claimed his smoky eyes. She sensed that it

would take more than a cigar to make him a happy man. Within the frame of the open hayloft behind him, the sky took on a buttery cast.

A soft breeze ruffled Sebastian's hair. "You haven't even asked about your devoted beau."

"Beau?" she echoed stupidly. Her hand flew to her mouth. "Good Lord, did you kill Sir Arlo?"

He sighed. "No. Though I'll probably live to regret it. I could have killed him."

She peered into his face, fascinated by his matter-of-fact tone. "Why didn't you?"

He toyed with the pleats of his kilt. "I was afraid you'd think poorly of me."

"Why, that's a silly reason for not killing someone!"

He arched an eyebrow.

She hastened to explain. "I'm not suggesting you should have killed him. You should have *not* killed him for a better reason. Because he was a nice man. Or because his mother would have grieved. Or simply because you're not the sort of man who goes about killing people."

"Or robbing them? Or marrying them for their wealth? Or lusting after their virgin nieces?" He stared into the whisky decanter. The cut glass splintered the first rays of the sun into amber crystals. His low tones mesmerized Prudence. "The sort of man I am wishes he had taken you that night in the crofter's hut. He wishes he had put his child in you so all of our choices would have been made for us." He swirled the whisky, took a large swig, then wiped his mouth on the back of his hand. "That's the kind of man I am."

A piping voice floated up through the hayloft. "Fish, you've gone quite insane. I do believe you drank the whisky yourself."

Prudence met Sebastian's eyes, horror-struck. "Good Lord, it's Auntie Tricia."

Ten

Old Fish's whine was borne on the morning wind. "You insult me, Countess. I never indulge in spirits. You should have seen the girl. It was scandalous. Creeping about in her nightclothes. Why, she wasn't even wearing a nightcap!" Indignation trembled in his voice. He might as well have pronounced Prudence naked. "She snatched the whisky and went skipping across the lawn like some sort of wanton—" The rest of his speech was mercifully muffled.

"I never dreamed the old lech had such a vivid imagination," Sebastian whispered.

They stared at each other, paralyzed by the approaching voices.

Jamie popped up the ladder like a wild-eyed jack-in-the-box. He captured Prudence's arm and started back down, jerking to a halt when he realized the rest of her wasn't following.

"Get down there, ye silly chit. Do ye want them to come up here?"

"No, of course not. But what shall I tell her?"

Jamie didn't give Prudence time to ponder. He shoved her across the loft and stuffed her down the ladder. She missed the last three rungs, scraping her shins and landing in the hay as Tricia and Old Fish entered the musty stable.

Prudence stumbled around to face them, disheveled and

wide-eyed with guilt. Untidy wisps of hair escaped her braid. She opened her mouth, but nothing came out. Sebastian's cool confession was still thundering through her brain. *The sort of man I am wishes he had taken you that night in the crofter's hut. He wishes he had put his child in you . . .* Her hand flew to her abdomen. Why couldn't she be the sort of girl who fainted?

She would have thought it impossible, but as she stared at her aunt and Old Fish, the butler's eyes bugged out farther. Another half inch and they would surely pop out and roll across the hay. Prudence realized too late the reason for his shock.

Jamie swung off the ladder, landing on the balls of his feet like a cat. "Where'd ye go, luv? The fun was just beginnin'."

He laid his wiry arm across her shoulders. Old Fish cleared his throat. Jamie looked up as if seeing them for the first time.

"Shame on ye, pet. Ye didn't tell me we had guests."

His copper hair was ruffled, as if he had run his fingers through it. His chest was bare, and the first three buttons of his breeches were unfastened. A mortified heat swept up Prudence's throat, and she seriously reconsidered swooning.

Jamie swaggered forward, sloshing whisky over the rim of the decanter. His gaze traveled boldly over Tricia's jade green negligee. She closed it at the throat with a demure hand, blushing prettily. Prudence gaped, so amazed at Jamie's transformation that she forgot her own embarrassment. Ugly or not, he exuded a smug sexuality that was almost palpable.

Tricia's eyes were all for Jamie. Prudence felt invisible. She wondered if anyone would notice if she dropped to her stomach and buried herself in the hay.

"You realize," Tricia said, fluttering her lashes, "I shall have to speak to your master about this little . . . indiscretion."

To Prudence's amazement, Jamie dropped to one knee at Tricia's feet and brought her hand to his lips. "I'm a poor lad, me lady. I ain't got no other post. Would ye have my lord send me away penniless"—Prudence would have sworn his tongue flicked out to touch Tricia's hand—"and hungry? I am humbly sorry." He looked about as remorseful as a freckled Lucifer.

Tricia gave a breathless cluck. The bows on her towering satin mob-cap trembled becomingly. Prudence had always suspected she slept in her wig. "We shall have to give it some thought, won't we? Perhaps I can persuade Lord Kerr to be merciful when he decides your fate."

A muffled snort from the loft reminded Prudence that Lord Kerr was already deciding Jamie's fate. She blushed anew.

Tricia swept across the stable like a regal queen and stopped in front of Prudence. Prudence stared at the flounces of lace on her aunt's bosom, unable to meet her eyes. Shame flooded her as she realized for the first time that she was guilty of a crime far worse than dallying with Jamie. She was in love with her aunt's fiancé. In another month, even God would have a name for a woman like her—adulteress.

She waited for Tricia to scream at her or box her ears or send her packing. She was acutely aware of Jamie leaning against a splintered post, arms crossed over his bare chest, a smirk on his thin lips. He was enjoying her discomfiture almost as much as Old Fish. The loft above held its waiting silence.

Tricia gently cupped Prudence's chin, tilting her face upward. Her soft, tinkling laugh filled the stable. "Why, you cunning little creature! Who would have thought it? My Prudence and the coachman!"

Tricia's eyes danced with warmth and delight. She pulled Prudence into her arms. Prudence hung limply in her aunt's embrace, her eyes wide circles of shock. Jamie lifted his hands in a baffled shrug. Old Fish opened and closed his mouth like a beached herring.

There was no mistaking the bemused pride in Tricia's voice as she led Prudence toward the door. "Come, you naughty child, we have much to discuss. You should have come to your aunt sooner. I thought all you were interested in were those dusty old books of yours." As they ambled into the awakening morning, Tricia cast Jamie a coquettish look over her shoulder. "Men can teach you what pleases men, but it takes a woman to teach you what will please you."

Prudence dared a glance back. Sebastian was leaning out of the hayloft, listening with interest.

"Don't think I'm judging you, darling," Tricia went on. "Most of the women I know cut their proverbial teeth on groomsmen and houseboys. But you should learn to protect yourself from mishaps. It would be exceedingly awkward to explain away—"

As Prudence's cheeks flamed bright red, Tricia mercifully became aware of Old Fish following behind them, ears perked to their conversation.

She gave the butler an airy wave. "Bring a tray of chocolate to my chamber, Fish." Prudence cringed as Tricia gave her a motherly squeeze. "It's just as well my Sebastian is in Edinburgh. I shall have time to prepare him for this. He's quite protective of you, you know. I believe he thinks of you as far more than a niece."

A cold shiver raked Prudence's spine. Tricia knew, she thought. Oh, dear sweet Lord, she knew.

A frown furrowed her aunt's brow. "I do believe he thinks of you as a daughter."

Behind them a pained yelp was muffled to a strangled cough. Tricia spun around as the door of the hayloft swung shut with a bang.

Prudence was reading in her room two nights later when a knock came on her door. It was followed by an aristocratic sniff. "Lord Kerr wishes your presence in the study."

"Very well, Fish."

Prudence smoothed the skirt of her pale green watered silk gown and slipped on her spectacles. She studied her reflection in the mirror, then dropped the spectacles back in her pocket. Tugging two strands of hair free from her tight chignon, she fluffed them around her face, then sighed. Her nose was still too pointy, her eyes too big.

"'Vanity of vanities; all is vanity,'" she murmured to her reflection.

She waited at the door for Old Fish's doddering steps to recede before slipping into the hall. As she approached the study, the door opened and her aunt emerged. Tricia hastily shut the door behind her.

She captured Prudence's hands and brought them to her rouged lips. "Courage, my child," she whispered. "I begged him to go gently with you."

Then Tricia was gone in a cloud of musky gardenia and Prudence was left to face the heavy door alone. Sebastian's gentleness was the last thing she needed. She pushed open the door.

Nothing was visible of Sebastian but a thatch of sandy hair, a cloud of smoke, and a pair of polished top boots resting on the windowsill. She cleared her throat.

He scraped the chair around and jerked the thin cheroot out of his mouth. "Good evening, Miss Walker."

She bobbed a curtsy. "Good evening, Uncle Sebastian."

His lips twitched. He took a long drag off the cigar, and a thin wisp of blue smoke wafted out the window. He indicated the leather chair in front of the desk. Prudence sat.

Sebastian thumbed through a sheaf of papers, his heavy brows drawn together in a stern line. "Miss Walker, your aunt has asked me to speak to you about a certain breach of propriety that occurred at Lindentree during my recent absence."

"What might that be, sir?"

He kept his gaze on the papers. "I am referring to a pilfered decanter of Scotch whisky. In the future, if you care to supply either yourself or your male companions with spirits, you are to come to me and I will dole it out to you." He looked up at her then, and his eyes were sparkling. He seemed to have difficulty catching his breath. "Your aunt is deeply concerned about a moral decline which has led you to become a thief in your own home."

Sebastian's attempt at sternness failed as he blew a cloud of cigar smoke up his nose and collapsed in a wheezing, sputtering heap. His muscular shoulders heaved. He threw back his head, mopping tears of laughter from his eyes as Prudence flew out of her chair in an indignant fury.

"Isn't that just like her! She chastises me for stealing the whisky, but not for dallying with the coachman!"

She paced the study in long, swishing strides. "That's the

first time Tricia has ever looked at me with anything resembling pride." Sebastian hiccuped. Prudence turned on him, planting both hands on the desk. "Go ahead and laugh. It's not your reputation in shreds. You don't have Old Fish looking down his nose at you as if you were Jezebel and the whore of Babylon rolled into one."

Sebastian clapped a hand over his mouth in mock dismay. "Miss Walker, your language. You shock me!"

"After a morning of Tricia's tutelage, I could shock you even more."

He sat up with interest. "Was it bad?"

"Horrid. Not even Papa's *Icones Anatomicae* prepared me for *that*." She lowered her voice to a husky whisper. "She taught me things that would make your toes curl."

He fanned himself with the papers. "You don't say? Do go on. You know, you should get angry more often. It's enchanting. Your eyes snap, your cheeks pinken. Quite an amazing transformation from my meek little niece."

Prudence dared to sit on the edge of the desk. "Niece? You wound me. Tricia swore you thought of me—"

They shouted in unison, "—more as a daughter!"

Prudence snatched the papers from Sebastian and beat him about the head as her own fury dissolved in mirth.

"Careful, careful," he said. "Take pity on a wounded man, won't you?" He raised a hand, too weak with laughter to defend himself.

She dropped the papers. "I forgot. How is your shoulder?"

"Much better. The butter and eggs did the trick. I'd be fine if Boris didn't think me a scone. He keeps sniffing me and licking his chops. Of course, after three days of Jamie's company, even Boris has his charms."

One of the papers had slid off the desk. Prudence stooped to pick it up.

Her smile faded as she glanced at it. "A masked ball prior to your wedding." She handed him the invitation. "How quaint."

He smoothed the creamy vellum. "And original. How did Tricia ever think of it? Perhaps the ten masked balls we attended last month inspired her."

Prudence drew her spectacles from her pocket and put

them on. "You should enjoy it, my lord," she said, her voice as cool as the steel frames against her skin. "You have such an affinity for masks."

She turned to go.

"As do you, Miss Walker."

Prudence paused, but did not turn around. She knew he was no longer smiling. She managed to keep her back straight and her hands steady until she had left the study and pulled the door shut behind her.

She leaned against the door, welcoming the dig of the oak paneling into her spine. There was no sound from within the study. Tears scalded her eyes, and she realized with a shock that they were not tears of guilt, but tears of anger. The rage felt good, cleansing her of the melancholy that threatened to buffet her. She jerked off her spectacles. Damn Tricia anyway!

Tricia. It had always been Tricia. Bright, tinkling, gay Tricia. Prudence would simply have to understand that Tricia needed the money more than they. Tricia was an orphan. Tricia had no one. Prudence and Papa must be content with their books and each other. Prudence would understand. Prudence was such a good girl.

She dashed the tears from her eyes with a clenched fist. She was tired of understanding. She was tired of being a good girl. Being a good girl meant giving up Sebastian and his lovely mouth forever.

A bust of Plato sneered down at her from a velvet draped pedestal. Prudence shoved her spectacles on his marble nose and started for her room, jerking out hairpins as she walked.

&

Prudence sought out Jamie the next day. As she neared the holding pen, his amorphous form solidified into angular sinew and muscle. Sunlight sharpened his hair to carrot orange, and she shielded her eyes from its brilliance. He was straining against a blob of russet—the mare Tricia had presented Sebastian as an early wedding gift. Early and premature, Prudence dared to hope.

She folded her arms on the fence. The air was laden with moisture, and the sultry heat sent sweat rolling down her sides, pinning her heavy damask dress to her stays like a second skin.

Jamie tugged the lead, guiding the wild-eyed yearling in a trotting circle. "Hullo, luv," he said. His voice was dry. "How could ye stay away so long? Are ye tryin' to break me proud heart?"

She gave him a reproachful look. "It didn't look so proud when you were drooling at my aunt's feet the other morning."

"Jealous, sweeting?"

He clucked, and the spindly horse trotted within his reach, shivering and prancing. He soothed her with an expert touch on her haunches. She stopped shivering and slipped easily within the circle of his arms. He drew a halter over her head.

"You're very good at that," Prudence said.

"Never let it be said Jamie Graham don't know how to gentle a lady. What did ye expect? Ridin' crops? Whips?"

She shrugged. "Some men take 'breaking a horse' literally."

"Some men are fools." He turned his back on her to run a brush down the mare's flank. Though he hummed softly under his breath, his jaw was taut.

Prudence climbed up to sit on the fence. Her stockings snagged on the rough wood. "You don't like me very much, do you, Mr. Graham?"

His even strokes did not falter.

She took a deep breath. "I need your help. I want Sebastian."

"Ye don't need me for that. Go find him. He's never minded obligin' a lady in need."

She flushed and looked down, toying with the dusty folds of her skirt. "Not like that." She struggled to find the words, any words, that might leave her a few shreds of dignity. "I want him to care for me."

"Oh, bloody hell!"

Jamie threw the brush. It struck the fence with a bang. Prudence flinched and the mare loped away, seizing her sudden and unexpected freedom.

Jamie turned on her, his eyes blazing almost as bright as

his hair. "Has it ever occurred to ye, Lady Walker, or whatever it is ye fine folk call yerselves, that with me ain't the safest place to be?"

A hot wind barely stirred the air as Prudence glanced around. The meadow was isolated. Even the brick chimneys of the house were hidden from view by a slight rise in the land.

The muscles in Jamie's arm knotted. "I may not be big, but I'm strong. I could pop yer wee neck 'tween me thumb and forefinger." He snapped his fingers to demonstrate the ease of it. "If Sebastian is too besotted to kill ye, I am the next most likely choice."

"Kill me?" Even to herself her voice sounded as if it were coming from very far away. "Why would Sebastian want to kill me?"

" 'Cause with one dainty sigh, ye could send us all to the gallows. Word's out there's a steep price on yer head and Sebastian's got his orders to follow like any other man."

The sun paled before Prudence's eyes. "I don't believe you. You shouldn't tease so. It's cruel."

"Cruel?" He puffed out a sigh. "I've been watchin' ye the last few weeks. Ye don't ask fer much, lass. The least I can give ye is the truth." He buried his fists in his pockets. "Don't worry. Sebastian's a good man. He'll make it quick and painless if he's able."

It might be quick, she thought, but it was far too late to make it painless.

She clambered down from the fence, praying her legs would support her. "Such lies are very unbecoming, Mr. Graham. If you didn't want to help me, a simple 'no' would have sufficed."

"Believe what ye will, lass. But take care."

Jamie clucked softly and the mare trotted to him. As Prudence walked back toward the house, he watched her go, his cheek pressed to the horse's silky mane.

The sun scorched the back of Prudence's neck. Her sturdy shoes rustled the dry grass. She couldn't remember the last time it had rained. Or could she? She squeezed her eyes shut and almost stumbled. When she opened them, they burned as hot as the air.

Jamie was lying, she thought. She said the words aloud and it made her feel slightly better. The petty little wretch, she added to herself, was only jealous of the attentions Sebastian had paid her.

Are you so sure? whispered a small voice inside her head. She knew that voice. It was the voice that reminded her she was too old to waste time woolgathering about a husband and children. It was the voice that soothed her back to sleep when she awoke tangled in the bedclothes, her body aching with some nameless longing, her cheeks wet with tears. It was the voice that kept her sane and safe by quenching all of her dreams and yearnings.

She stomped up the hill. Of course she was sure Jamie was lying. After all, Sebastian had come to her when he was wounded. To her—not to Jamie or Tricia.

And why wouldn't he? the voice asked. *Especially if you won't be around long enough to betray him.*

But he said he wanted her.

He spoke of need, not caring. The bulls in the field have the same needs. Why not want you? Why not slake his lust on you rather than some loose-tongued housemaid? You won't be around later to cause any embarrassing scenes.

Prudence gave herself a harsh shake, fighting to silence the rational demon within her. "Sebastian has shown me only kindness," she said aloud, ignoring the curious stare of a gardener watering the hedges.

What better way for Sebastian to keep an eye on you than to be always underfoot? What better way to seek out your weaknesses, await the opportune moment to silence you forever?

She stumbled to a halt as all the voices of her reason blended into one devastating truth.

If the kitchen blew up again, who would be suspicious if she happened to be standing beside the oven? And no one would be shocked if a bite of her own cooking killed her. Sebastian would cut such a dashing figure in mourning! The grim black would set off the sandy highlights in his hair to perfection. Her nails dug into her palms as she strode across the lawn.

Sebastian's own words condemned him. *If you see my face, your life will be worth naught. Neither to me or my men.* A stark chill cut through the heat, making her shiver.

Sebastian. Beautiful, considerate Sebastian. A thousand small kindnesses crumbled to bitter ash in the wind. Sebastian handing her a book she was too short to reach. Sebastian trimming her kitten's claws with his own tiny dagger, his hands deft and gentle. Sebastian wrestling the icing bowl away from her, demanding the last lick with that slow, sweet grin of his.

Not sweet, she corrected herself coldly. Cunning. She dashed away a tear before it could fall. He might murder her, but he would not make her cry. Sebastian Kerr wasn't worthy of her tears.

She marched up to the front door and flung it open. Before she could take three steps inside the house, Sebastian emerged from the parlor.

He looked up from the book in his hands and grinned. "There you are. I've been waiting for you. I think I've found something in this book about the properties of mercury." He pulled out a creamy envelope tucked between the pages. "And this came in the post today. You'd best open it first. It looks important."

She stared at him. She wasn't prepared for this, for his devastating good cheer, his rumpled shirt. He had abandoned his boots again and his hair tumbled loose around his face. He looked good enough to eat—luscious and forbidden, like the ice cream Tricia had once brought from London for one of her parties. Prudence had eaten it until her stomach ached, then been sent to bed without supper for her gluttony.

Pain knifed through her heart. What a fine actor he was! She couldn't bear it. She wanted to hurt him as much as he'd hurt her. Her furious passion disappeared behind an icy veil.

She looked him up and down, her lips twisted in a smile of cool disdain. "Perhaps you should fetch your boots, my lord. If you keep going about garbed in such a manner, everyone at Lindentree is going to know you're nothing but a common peasant."

His smile faded. His hands dropped to his sides. Her heart spasmed in regret as a raw, bewildered pain touched his features. It was gone so quickly, she might have imagined it, and was replaced by something dark and wary. She gathered her skirts, but he did not move.

She was forced to brush past him to reach the stairs. As her breast grazed his unyielding chest, he caught her wrist in a bruising grip, pulling her against him. His eyes searched her face.

She returned his gaze with insolence, terrified he would hear the wild thudding of her heart, the mad rush of blood through her veins. The tension in his body strummed so tight, she expected him to shove her against the wall and throttle her right there in the entranceway.

They both heard the telltale scrape of a chair behind them. She called toward the dining room in a parody of calm, "I'll be taking dinner in my room, Fish. I have a terrible headache."

Sebastian released her abruptly. As she climbed the stairs beneath the probing heat of his gaze, she discovered she wasn't lying. Her head was pounding nearly as hard as her heart.

Eleven

"Sebastian, old boy, it's your play."

Sebastian jerked his gaze away from the window. A bleary-eyed cycops was peering at him. He suppressed a faint shudder as Squire Blake lowered the quizzing glass he wore on a gold chain around his neck.

"Attentiveness, my boy, is the key to success when playing such lovely and intelligent creatures as these."

Devony giggled and Tricia clucked her tongue against her teeth in the chiding manner Sebastian was beginning to loathe. He briefly entertained the notion of choking her with the curtain cord the next time she did it..

His smile tightened to a grimace as he threw his card down, winning the trick. "Your pardon, Squire. My concentration is somewhat lacking this afternoon. I can assure you it is not the charm of my companions which distracts me." As far as Sebastian could tell, his companions had no discernible charms.

Devony struggled to hold on to her cards with fingers that sported long carmine daggers for nails.

Tricia tapped the back of Sebastian's hand with her fan. "We were hoping it wasn't us." She winked at Devony. "If we thought it was, it would make us terribly 'whistful.'"

Her dreadful pun sent them both into tinkling peals of laughter. Devony dropped her entire hand of cards on the table. Squire Blake's chortling led to a fit of coughing so intense, Sebastian feared it might end up in apoplexy, and he half hoped it would.

The light tap of footsteps outside the door jerked his head up. It was only one of the maids dusting a brass spittoon. He hid his disappointment behind a black glower that sent her scurrying back down the corridor. When would he stop expecting every footstep, every murmur, to be Prudence?

She had contrived to spend not one minute alone in his company in the past week. When she did emerge from her room long enough to dine, he would glance up to find her eyes fixed on him with a look of such dark betrayal that it made him ache. Her stack of letters on the pier-table lay untouched. He paced the library each day at dawn, listening to the hollow echo of his own footsteps. That morning, he had finally crawled back into bed and lolled until noon, only to awaken more sluggish and irritable than before.

Beneath the table, Devony's beribboned slipper crept up his calf for the third time. Tricia twined her ankle around his other leg. He felt as if he were in the grip of some serpentine vine that would suck him under the table to meet a hideous fate.

The ormolu clock on the mantel ticked away endless minutes as Devony rearranged her cards and took the customary century to decide which one to play. Sebastian tugged at his cravat without realizing it.

He felt as if he had been trapped in the oppressively delicate parlor for a lifetime. Tricia's hand at decorating was everywhere—in the fragile china Muses along the gilt mantel, the tiny roses embroidered on the brocade cushions, the ethereal lines of the Sheraton tea table. It all made him feel like an awkward giant set down in a dollhouse. The others seemed to recede, to shrink before him—prattling puppets in a mock tea party.

Panic threatened to overwhelm him. Each day brought him nearer to his wedding day, when he would be master of Lindentree and live forever in this miniature world. His gaze shot again to the door as he fought the barbaric impulse to climb the stairs and drag Prudence out of her room by her tight little chignon. If she wanted to see a how a common peasant behaved, by God, he'd be more than happy to show her!

Empty teacups littered the table. Sebastian glared at his cup. He hated tea. He longed for an icy keg of ale, chilled in the fast running waters of a spring-fed burn. His gaze wandered hungrily to the window. Sunlight flooded the sunken garden, its brilliance intensified by the dark bursts of clouds shifting across the sky. A teasing breeze wafted through the open windows.

His throat tightened as a ball of gray fluff detached itself from a yew hedge and hurtled past the window. Boris followed, a sleek gray shadow, running low and hard. Sebastian half rose out of his chair as Prudence careened out of the hedges behind the dog, her unbound hair streaming behind her. The severe lines of her black gown were marred by wild disarray. She stumbled over the trailing hem of her petticoat and nearly fell.

Devony drummed her fingernails on the table. The squire snapped open a silver case and sucked a pinch of snuff up his bulbous nose.

Sebastian gazed around wildly, wondering if he had imagined the entire scene.

"Didn't you see that?" he demanded.

Tricia fanned herself with her cards as Prudence darted between the hedges at the foot of the garden. "It's only Prudence out for her afternoon stroll."

Devony tapped one of her cards thoughtfully. "Lovely day for a walk, isn't it?"

"Nothing like a daily bit of exercise to aid in the digestion," Squire Blake said, and sneezed into his handkerchief.

Sebastian slowly sank back in his chair. It was no wonder Prudence insisted on fading into the scrollwork. They all treated her as if she were invisible.

As she passed out of sight among the grove of lime trees bordering the lawn, he glanced down to discover he had mangled the cards in his hand.

"More tea, sir?" Old Fish's white-gloved hand proferred a tray.

"No!" Sebastian barked. His answer came out louder than he intended.

Old Fish sniffed in obvious derision of any gentleman with the audacity to refuse tea. "Very well, sir. Perhaps later."

Sebastian caught his arm. The tray wavered. "Not now. And not later. Not this evening. Not tomorrow morning. Not ever. *No more tea.*"

The butler's pasty complexion went a shade paler. Sebastian realized the others were staring at him. He fought the urge to check his palms for tufts of hair or feel his brow for the beginning knobs of horns.

He stood, dropping his destroyed cards. "Do excuse me. My leg is throbbing. I believe I'll take a nap."

He forced himself to press a kiss to the powdered mask of Tricia's cheek. Leaning heavily on his cane, he left the parlor, shuddering at the sympathetic clucking that followed him.

As soon as he was out of sight of the parlor, Sebastian dropped his cane in the potted orange tree in the entrance hall. He strode out the front door and across the lawn, taking care to skirt the parlor window.

The gardens and lawns yielded no sign of Prudence. He passed through the grove of lime trees and into the blessed wildness of a rolling meadow. The tall grasses swept to life around him, tossed and flattened by the warm wind. Patches of cornflowers and buttercups waved through the soft green. If he could only walk fast enough and far enough, surely the earth itself would swallow Lindentree and its mistress without a trace.

The darkening clouds sifted the sunlight, throwing the meadow into shadow.

"Prudence?" His cry sounded faint and dismal in a silence broken only by the distant whisper of wind.

The sun chose that moment to defy the clouds and flood the meadow. He shielded his eyes. A dense forest of pine hung in a blue haze at the edge of the fields. He strode toward it, lured by the promise of a cool respite to quench his burning restlessness. As he entered the forest, the crisp tang of pine penetrated his fuzzy senses, along with the steady chirp of a cricket. The long, fragrant boughs swayed in hypnotic rhythm, lulled by the wind murmuring through them.

Sebastian's borrowed serenity was shattered as a woman's piteous cry shamed the voices of the forest to silence.

He ducked beneath a shaggy branch. Prudence knelt on a smooth rock that jutted over a still pool, her face buried in her hands.

He knelt beside her, his heart pounding in his ears, and gently touched her heaving shoulder. "What is it, lass? What is the matter?"

She threw back her head, baring the delicate line of her throat to the caress of the sun. Tears spiked her short dark lashes. "I was too late." She pointed down the hill behind her in horror. "Oh, Sebastian!"

He almost lost his balance as she flung herself at his chest. He had no way of knowing if her passionate declaration was meant for him or her cat. He was too busy pondering the charms of having his coat kneaded by her slender fingers.

She snuffled into his cravat, and he cradled her head in his palm, staring beyond her at the object she had indicated. Tufts of coarse gray fur protruded from the mossy hollow. A baffled frown creased his brow.

"Prudence, where are your spectacles?"

His matter-of-fact tone startled her into silence. "On my dressing table, I suppose. I forgot them. I had been dressing for tea before I rushed out."

He could not help but notice that she had also forgotten her corset and stays. The scandalous softness of her breasts against his chest made him feel giddy and slightly breathless.

She wiped her eyes with his cravat. "The garden gate was only open for a few minutes. I had no way of knowing Boris was loose. My poor, dear Sebastian," she murmured. "How terrible . . . "

"Terrible indeed for the unfortunate squirrel," Sebastian said dryly.

She gazed up at him, wide-eyed. His lips twitched. Slowly she turned to gaze down the hill; her eyes narrowed to brilliant slits of violet. Sebastian-cat chose that moment to dart out from the trees, back arched. With a halfhearted bark, Boris padded after him. The kitten skittered sideways, spitting like a tiny demon. A swipe of one furry paw raked a trail of crimson down Boris's shiny nose. With a wounded yelp, the hound slunk back into the woods, his tail tucked between his massive hindquarters.

The kitten rolled onto his side and began to groom himself with his rough pink tongue. Sebastian threw back his head with a burst of deep-throated laughter.

"But I thought Boris had eaten—" Prudence clapped a hand over her mouth, but not before a merry peal of joy escaped. Tears of relief streamed down her cheeks.

Sebastian wiped them away with his fingers. "Squire Blake is more likely to eat your kitten than that cowardly mutt. I saw the old chap eyeing the peacocks only yesterday at tea."

That sent Prudence into a new fit of laughter. Helpless with mirth, she clung to his shoulders. He anchored a lean arm around her waist and hugged her against him. His lips brushed her cheek. Too late, they both realized his embrace was not that of an uncle.

The eternity of the past week melted as Sebastian's mouth drifted to the curve of her cheekbone and he tasted the softness of her unpowdered skin. Her eyes were pressed shut as if she could somehow deny the lingering descent of his mouth, even as her hands closed in helpless fists against his shoulders. He pressed a kiss to her feathery lashes; the salt of her tears burned him. He soothed the sting by dipping his tongue between her parted lips; only to ignite a slow, steady burn in his loins. His arm curved around the small of her back, dragging her hips against the aching cradle of his thighs. It was no longer enough to be inside of her lovely mouth. He wanted to be inside of her everywhere.

Dear God, he thought. He was falling hopelessly in love with this beautiful, clumsy, bespectacled spinster.

He buried his face in the sheltering hollow of her throat. "Oh, lass, I've missed you so."

A long, still moment passed.

Prudence shoved at his chest and sprang to her feet as if the rock had sprouted flames. Her heavy mane of hair tumbled around her shoulders.

Sebastian climbed to his feet, still shaking with desire. "One glimpse of your hair in London and they would know why powder and wigs are beginning to pall."

She tilted her nose in the air, but not before he saw dread darken her eyes. "You followed me," she said. A note of accusation tinged her voice.

He took a congenial step forward. She took a wary step backward.

He locked his hands at the small of his back, striving to look every inch the country gentleman. "When I saw you go rushing off, I was naturally concerned. It is ironic that I should be the one to remind you, but there are robbers about the countryside. You shouldn't be out unchaperoned."

"And it is ironic that I should be the one to remind you, Lord Kerr, but there are also robbers in my aunt's parlor. One place should be as safe as the other. It would be as simple for you to drop Plato's bust on my head as drown me, although considerably less tidy."

Sebastian was still too addled to understand what she was babbling about. His gaze traveled over the skin exposed by the unbuttoned throat of her gown, then glided over her body, down to her bare toes peeping out from her torn stockings. "I should hate to think what men like my own might do if they found you in such a vulnerable state."

She sniffed. "You don't hate to think of it at all. Quite the opposite, I'm sure—*Uncle* Sebastian," she added for pure spite.

His brows drew together. "What manner of scoundrel do you think me?"

It infuriated Prudence that even though she knew he was a lowly assassin, she could still be entranced by the teasing touch of his lips, the fluid play of emotions across the imperfect beauty of his features.

Her jaw tightened, and she turned her back on him before he had her mumbling an apology for forcing him to kill her. "I think you the lowest sort of scoundrel. If you desire to play loving uncle to my doting niece, you should search for another actress. Some silly chit you can teach to cheat at whist and dandle on your knee before you slide your filthy dirk between her shoulder blades."

She shivered as his hand slipped beneath her hair to cup her neck. She would have preferred a pinch or a slap to this lethal tenderness.

"I'd love to dandle you on my knee," he murmured. "Or anywhere else for that matter." His thumb slid around her throat, and she knew he could feel the havoc he was wreaking with her pulse.

She tugged free of him. "Do stop it! I hate it when you're kind."

Sebastian's hand closed on her forearm. Her words were finally beginning to penetrate the warm haze of his emotions.

Prudence could feel the heat of his touch through her thin cotton sleeve as he pulled her around to face him. "Would it be more in character if I strangled you with your stockings?"

She could no longer hide the fear that flared her nostrils and set her lower lip to trembling.

Sebastian's hands fell to his sides. His eyes darkened to the color of the storm-threatening clouds rushing across the sky. "My God, lass, I was only joking. What have I done to make you fear me so?"

Impotent rage surged through her. "Nothing yet. But I know what you intend to do. You must have found my little speech very touching when I promised not to be a burden to you. You knew quite well that I wasn't going to be around long enough to be a burden to anyone." As she spoke she walked backward, unwittingly nearing the sharpened crag of rock and the deep pool sleeping beneath. "It galls me most that you weren't honest enough to take responsibility for your own decision. You let your men think another wanted me dead when all the time it was you." Her heel touched the edge of the rock.

Sebastian lunged for her. Fear twisted through her, and she wheeled around to flee.

Too late, she realized she was on the edge of the rock. Her foot met only air and she tumbled off the warm rock into the chill water.

The pool dragged her into its depths. The shock of falling opened her mouth and water rushed into her throat. She pushed her way upward, skinning her knuckles on rock. Her skirts clung to her legs. A slimy strand of weed tangled around one knee. She clawed at it, feeling a jagged flare of pain as a fingernail tore away. The panic that had closed her throat before she could take a breath erupted now in a frantic dance that twisted the ropy weed tighter around her leg.

With a shudder of relief, her body went limp. As she floated in the weed's embrace, her head fell back. She watched the muted play of sunlight drifting on the water until the world went as gray as Sebastian's eyes.

Twelve

A cloud covered the sun, severing its warmth like an unseen hand. Lightning streaked the sky as Sebastian stared at the pool.

Prudence's fall into the water had set off bubbling ripples across the dark mirror of its surface. His grandfather's words echoed through his mind like the distant rumble of thunder: *I would like her dispatched. Something simple. A fall from a horse. A hunting accident. You know how to arrange such things.* As Sebastian watched, the ripples settled, leaving the pool an unmarked sheet of indigo.

"Prudence?" A tentative echo carried his whisper back to him. On the other side of the pool, a tree frog lisped into song.

Sebastian pulled off his shoes. A hoarse note of panic touched his voice as he called her name again. The forest let out a wistful, sighing breath. The swaying trees creaked a reply. From the depths of the pool, though, came nothing but silence. How simple it would be to turn around, walk back to the house, and pretend he'd never passed this way.

He tore off his coat with a curse. His dive broke the water with the barest hint of a splash. His hands groped in the murky water at what felt like hair. It came away in his grip and he was left holding a fragile clump of grass and dirt. He strained his eyes to see, still blinded by the light above. A glimpse of pale white started his heart thundering in his ears.

His powerful body shot toward the absence of darkness. His hands closed in a convulsive movement around the fleshy coolness of Prudence's arm. Her skirts billowed at her waist. Her hair floated around her face in a silky web. Her eyes were closed, her lashes pressed like ferns against her cheeks.

Sebastian jerked. Nothing happened. Around him the watery world faded to gray as the last bit of air in his lungs fed his hungry brain. He raked his hand down Prudence's thigh and felt the weed cutting into her skin. He tugged with his dying strength. The weed snapped. He half pushed, half dragged her to the surface, shoving her head above the water before his own.

The first raindrops splattered on the surface of the pool as Sebastian drew in a shuddering breath. Nausea tightened his stomach, and for one dizzying moment he feared he would faint, sending them both spinning into the pool's darkness without a trace. The rock jutted over them, a black shadow against the graying sky.

He gathered his limbs for a lunge toward the far bank. His arm locked around Prudence's throat, holding her head out of the water even when his own slipped beneath. Water trickled between his lips. His toes stabbed a spongy cushion of mud. He crawled through the crackling reeds, dragging Prudence with him until their feet cleared the water. Her body rolled like a dead weight onto the grassy bank.

Sebastian did not recognize his voice as his own while he untangled the wet strings of hair from her face and begged her not to die. Praying to a God he had long ago forsaken, he chafed her icy cheeks with his palms and tore open the bodice of her gown. Her chest did not stir. Curses and entreaties choked his raw throat as he gathered her in his arms and shook her violently. Her head fell back in limp surrender, and he leaned forward, pressing his forehead to her throat with a despairing sob.

A whisper of breath stirred his hair. He slowly lifted his head, staring with wonder at the convulsive rise of her chest. She hiccuped softly, then snatched in a breath that drove out racking coughs from deep in her lungs.

He steadied her over his arm until her struggles with the water ceased. She collapsed against him, and he cradled her across his lap, murmuring her name in a litany of thankfulness. He kissed her nose and cheeks and ears, as if to ensure she had lost no precious features in the murky world of near death. He smoothed her hair with shaking hands. She lay like a child in his arms, her eyes still closed. But her lips parted lightly with each breath and a flush of rose bloomed in her cheeks.

"Poor sweet lass, I almost killed you," he whispered.

His gaze raked over her, and he cherished each gentle rise and fall of her chest. When he finally noticed how her sodden chemise clung to the soft swell of her breasts, he was unprepared for the sensation that swept him. Feeling like the thief he was, he cupped her sweetly rounded breast in his palm.

Bending down, he lay his lips against hers, wanting nothing more than to mingle his breath with her own in an affirmation of her life. Her lips were cold. He warmed them with his own until they parted beneath the pressure of his silky heat. With a will of its own, his tongue dipped inward, finding a surprising warmth to match his own. His breath quickened as her tongue stirred to meet his, drawing him into her with an innocent allure that made him shudder.

His trembling fingers caressed her breast through the thin cotton. Her nipple hardened, and the knowledge of her arousal dug deeper into his heart than a dagger.

It was more instinct than the faint shift of her breathing that made him open his eyes and meet her gaze. Her own eyes were dark and luminous, wide with a startled curiosity that trapped his hand in its guilty motion. A flush shot from his throat to his face, and he hated himself for it. He could not decide which offense Prudence would deem worse—nearly letting her drown or fondling her like a common whore while she lay helpless in his embrace.

He waited for her to shove him away, for the silent

reproach to fill her eyes. The rain fell harder now. It slicked his hair to his head and streamed over his face. She blurred before his eyes as she reached up and gently wiped the rain from his lashes.

The tender gesture was Sebastian's downfall. He pulled her against him, holding her so tightly his arms ached. Her own arms went around his neck. Her small hands curled into fists against his nape as he scooped her up and carried her beneath the sheltering boughs of a willow. The green leaves enveloped them in a glossy canopy that slowed the rain to a steady drip. Still he held her, his face buried against her throat, reluctant to loose her for fear she would flee.

"Sebastian?"

His name was a velvety purr against his lips.

"Mmmm?"

"A tree is hardly the place to be. We could be struck by lightning."

He swung her around, laughing exultantly as he lowered her to her feet. "My ever practical Prudence." He cupped her face in his hands and stared deep into her eyes. "It's far too late for me. I've been struck by something fiercer than lightning."

Prudence shivered as he lowered his lips to hers, and it had nothing to do with a chill.

"You don't know how badly I've wanted to hold you," he said. Each of his words were accentuated by a soft kiss that left a tingling trail along the curve of her mouth. "To make you drop that prim and proper mask you hide behind."

Her fingers curled in his damp hair as her lips brushed his cheek, tasting the light stubble that had risen since he had shaved that morning. He was such a tantalizing combination of roughness and smoothness. She longed to explore his varying textures with a hunger that terrified her.

She made a soft sound of despair. "You should have left me to drown. It would have been kinder."

He tilted her chin up and gazed into her eyes. "Jamie warned you, didn't he? I should have expected it. The lad's grown quite fond of you."

She gave a weak hiccup of a laugh. "He threatened to snap

my neck at our last meeting. I'd hate for him to take an active dislike to me."

"That's just Jamie's way. The more he likes you, the surlier he grows. I thought he was going to shoot me one Christmas when he was overcome with the joy of the season." He nudged her gown aside and nuzzled her collarbone, licking the rain from her skin with a greedy tongue. "I could never hurt you. You were mad to think I could."

She pushed against his shoulders. He stiffened.

She backed away from him. "But you *are* hurting me. This *is* madness. You are going to marry my aunt in less than a week. Remember?"

He stalked her around the tree trunk, spurred on by desperation. "Why should we let a little thing like that come between us?"

Her eyes widened. He took advantage of her shock, wrapping his arms around her and crushing her mouth in a kiss as darkly different from the one beside the pool as death was to a faint. His lips were hard and unrelenting, demanding an answer from her that no book had prepared her for. She opened her mouth to him, feeling her body go molten and liquid against the rough edges of his own as he bore her back against the willow trunk. Velvety petals of ivy cradled her.

Sebastian's hands rubbed her back, then slid lower, cupping her hips and bringing them against his own with fierce strength. The soaked fabric of knee-breeches and gown was only a fragile skin between them. A foreign sweetness rocked through Prudence's veins, paralyzing her with fear and pleasure. She felt herself sliding down the tree, down some dark, erotic abyss of Sebastian's making into delicious surrender. She knew if they reached the ground together, she would never fight her way back from beneath his will.

She balled her fists between them and shoved with all of her strength. His chest felt like a rock. It did not budge. He gazed at her from beneath his lashes, and she knew he was one breath of sanity away from taking her to the ground, with or without her consent. For a long moment, the only sounds were the rain beating against the leaves and the rasp of his breath as he struggled to regain even tenuous control over his desire.

Tears slipped silently down her cheeks, and his grip softened.

"Do you know what you're doing to me?" he asked.

"Inconveniencing you?" She averted her eyes. "Causing you some momentary physical discomfort?"

His palms slammed into the tree trunk on either side of her. "What you're doing to me," he said, his burr thickening perceptibly, "they don't teach in anatomy books. You're breaking my bloody heart. And I didn't even know I had one."

She ducked beneath his arm. "Please, Sebastian. I was wrong. *This* is wrong. I can't do this to Tricia. She's been kind to me. Given me a home."

He braced his weight against the tree. "And love, Prudence? Has she given you love?"

She had no answer for that and slipped quietly from the willow's canopy. Sebastian followed, flinging the curtain of leaves aside. They faced each other in the pouring rain.

"I am sorry to disappoint you," she said, "but I am not part and parcel of my aunt's estate. I know you're accustomed to taking what you want, but you can't have everything." She was shivering again, and Sebastian ached to put his arms around her. "Please stay away from me. I will be civil to you for my aunt's sake, but if you approach me again in any way that can be deemed improper, I will be forced to tell her the truth about you."

He knew Prudence meant what she said. Her determination was written in her whitened knuckles, in the painful rigidity of her spine. She twisted her hair into a nervous knot before realizing she had nothing to hold it with.

He reached into his pocket and withdrew a small tartan packet. He held it out to her without a word, and she unfolded it with trembling fingers. Nestled in the precious scrap of wool were five silver hairpins tipped with pearls.

"You've misjudged me, Miss Walker," he said, his voice bitter. "I know I can't have everything. I learned that long ago. But for once in my life, can't I have what I really want?"

A small sob broke from her, and she reeled away. She scooped up her bedraggled kitten and fled across the meadow, a slender figure, bare-footed and loose-haired, running as if something were pursuing her. Sebastian's fists slowly unclenched. The rain washed over him, running into his eyes. He watched as Prudence was swallowed by the curtain of rain and he was left alone with the mocking rumble of thunder.

Old Fish plucked the cane out of the potted orange, snorting with disgust. He held it with two fingers as if it were a serpent. If he had his way, he would use it for kindling.

He leaned the cane against the pier-table and sifted through the stack of envelopes there. The front door opened, and he winced as a cool gust of rain struck him in the face.

Prudence ran in and shoved the door shut with her shoulder. A dripping, squalling beast clung to her arm.

Old Fish gazed down his nose at her, noting every aspect of her shocking state of dishabille. "Will you be taking tea with your aunt, Miss Prudence?" His voice oozed polite contempt.

She pelted past him without a word, trailing mud across his polished tiles and up the stairs.

He waved a creamy envelope after her. "Wait, Miss Prudence. You have another letter . . ." His voice trailed off at the slam of her bedchamber door.

Ungrateful wench, he thought. The girl was a disgrace. No manners at all. He eyed the cane thoughtfully. If she were his niece, he'd use it to give her a good beating. He studied the envelope in his hand. Crimson wax sealed the heavy folds, giving it an aura of importance.

Old Fish held the envelope up to the light, but could see nothing. He brought it to his nose and sniffed it, then lowered it, shrugging his bony shoulders.

Miss Prudence never received correspondence of any import. It was more likely a plea from one of those blasphemous scientific societies her father had supported, begging a donation. Miss Prudence had no funds of her own. He would not have Lady Tricia plagued by such infidels.

He gathered up the entire stack of letters and strode into the parlor. Ignoring the curious maid who was attempting to start a fire on the hearth, he tossed the letters on top of the sputtering kindling. The fire flared. He brushed off his hands, smiling with smug satisfaction as the dancing tongues of fire licked at the wax seal, staining the flames to the color of blood.

Thirteen

The coaches rocked up the long drive, their lanterns casting bells of light through the darkness. Liveried footmen flung open the gilt doors, and masked figures darted toward the house, their capes splashes of white around their feet. There was something bewitching about their flight, as if a magical being had breathed life into the garden statues, sending them tripping and laughing across the lawn. The discordant hum of violin and harp being tuned drifted up through the floorboards with the melodious ring of a sonnet.

Prudence watched from her window, separated from the gaiety below by more than a fragile pane of glass. It could have been another world, another galaxy. If any of Tricia's guests had glanced up, they might have seen her there, half hidden by the drapes. None of them did.

She finished her braid and dropped her hairbrush in her lap, then pulled a shawl around her night rail, although the night was warm. The sky unfurled above like a dark banner sprinkled with stars. Tricia could not have arranged better weather for her masquerade ball. God would no doubt favor her with sunshine and blue skies for her wedding two days hence, and perhaps even a rainbow to span the garden folly where she and Sebastian would exchange their vows.

Prudence hugged her shawl tighter. She had been lonely

for most of her life. But this loneliness cut deeper—bone deep—deep enough to last a lifetime.

Behind her, the door to her chamber opened and shut with a soft click. She didn't turn around. "If you've come to finish me off, Jamie, there's a letter opener on the dressing stand."

Jamie blew out a huge sigh. "What sort of welcome is that? I had the very devil of a time sneakin' past Old Pruneface."

"Old Fishface," she corrected him, then swung around in the window seat.

Jamie was a bright splash of tan and russet against the muted cream of her walls. "Sebastian ain't goin' to kill ye, is he?"

"Yes, he is. Very slowly. It may take years."

Jamie raked his fingers through his hair. "I ain't no happier about this weddin' than ye are. Do ye think I want to spend the rest of me days as a stableboy to some uppity countess?"

"There are worse fates."

"Aye, it could be me marryin' the wench." He walked over to the window seat. Together they watched the torches along the terraces wink to life. "It ain't about money. It ain't even about that godforsaken castle of his." He stabbed his finger at the window as another opulent coach spilled out its guests. "It's about *them*. He's always wanted to be one of them. Like his mum. Like the Kerrs shoulda been if the MacKays hadn't taken it all."

"Then he's about to get everything he wants, isn't he?"

"Everything he thinks he wants," Jamie muttered. "But what do ye want, lass?"

She brushed his hand from her shoulder. "I want to be left alone."

"And I think ye've been left alone far too much in yer life." With surprising gentleness, he dropped to his knees and clasped her icy hand between his freckled paws. "Ye've got to help me, lass. Ye're the only one who can."

She tried to withdraw her hand, but he held it fast. Fighting to keep her voice cool, to swallow the tears brimming beneath her calm, she said, "Sebastian has made his choice painfully clear."

"Ye don't understand. Sebastian ain't had a lot in his life, but he's always had his freedom. He'll wither up and die here as sure as he would in prison."

Her hands curled into fists. "I have no control over Sebastian's future."

With a hoarse oath, Jamie jumped to his feet and began to pace the chamber. "Aye, and a bright one it is at that! All stuffed into a frock coat fer the rest of his life. Drinkin' hard to dull his hunger fer the wide-open moors, the silvery shimmer of rain on a loch. It won't be dull, though, will it? He and the countess, they'll have their wee tussles between the sheets—lovers whose names they won't remember when the morn comes." He picked up the letter opener and jabbed it toward her. "What of yer own future, Prudence? What do ye have to look forward to when Sebastian grows into a fat sot? A peep under yer skirts as ye climb the stairs? A drunken fumble in the garden? I wager that'll be enough fer an old spinster like—"

"Damn you!"

He ducked as Prudence's hairbrush came sailing at his head.

Straightening, he glanced behind him and whistled. The force of the blow had torn a jagged chunk of plaster from the wall. Prudence was on her feet. Her eyes snapped violet fire. "You insolent"—she groped for a word vile enough to describe him—"Scot!"

A slow grin spread over Jamie's face. "Bonny good shot, lass." He waved the letter opener in front of her. "Would ye like to try this next?"

"I'd like to bury it in your gullet, you evil little wretch."

She lunged for it. Jamie danced just out of her reach. "Have ye ever really fought fer anything ye wanted, Pru? Really scrapped for it, tooth and claw?"

"You want claws? I'll give you claws." Her fingernails swiped the air, but Jamie was gone.

He cleared the bed in one bound, swinging around the bedpost like a demented monkey. "I bet ye've spent yer whole life sayin' 'Aye, sir. No, ma'am. Never mind me, sir. I ain't of any import.'"

His simpering attempt at a curtsy was Jamie's mistake. Prudence gave the stool under her dressing table a vicious kick. It flew across the room and slammed into his shins. He dropped like a stone.

She leaped on top of him, and he threw up his hands to protect his face. She grappled for the letter opener clenched in his fist, but her struggles slowly stilled as she realized that Jamie was howling not with pain, but with laughter. Her rage abated as reality sank in. She, Prudence Walker, virtual paragon of temperance and restraint, was lying on top of Sebastian's man in her night rail, gasping, sweating, and fully prepared to do murder. What in God's name was happening to her?

She sat up, brushing a stray tendril from her eyes with a shaky hand. Jamie curled on his side, snorting and snuffling. When she started to rise, his hand shot out and circled her wrist.

"If you won't help yerself, Pru," he said, his eyes strangely earnest, "help Sebastian."

She hesitated for only a heartbeat. "What do you want me to do?"

He sat up cross-legged behind her. "I want ye to listen very carefully. The first thing ye're goin' to have to do is learn how to fight dirty. Sebastian ain't never known no other way . . ."

As he spoke, his deft fingers were already unbraiding her hair.

In the ballroom below, three men garbed in long velvet surcoats lifted their trumpets and blew a discordant blast. Boris threw back his massive head and howled in accompaniment.

Old Fish appeared at the top of the four shallow marble steps leading down into the sunken ballroom. He sucked in a deep breath and intoned, "The demigod Pan and his companion, the goddess Diana."

"God pity the goats," Sebastian muttered as a beaming Squire Blake and a simpering Devony materialized on the stairs.

The mock heralds wandered off like a deck of mismatched playing cards. The Great Dane padded after them, drooling into his Elizabethan ruff. Old Fish gathered his scythe and went in search of new victims. Sebastian wondered if it had been Tricia's idea to dress the butler as Charon, the grim spirit who ferried the dead across the river Styx to Hades. It *was* rather appropriate. As Tricia linked her arms in the Blakes' and led them through the dazzling array toward Sebastian, his suspicion that he was in hell deepened to certainty. He tossed back a glass of champagne in one gulp.

Tricia had defied her own edict, abandoning a Greek costume for that of a medieval maiden. The satin of her kirtle gleamed like a ruby among the pale creams and ivories of togas and robes. A towering cone perched on top of her elaborate wig. Sebastian watched with renewed interest each time her flowing veil fluttered near one of the candle sconces.

Squire Blake clumped toward him on plaster hooves. "Sebastian! Always a delight, old chap." The horns perched on top of his wig bounced with enthusiasm.

"Always," Sebastian murmured, bringing Devony's hand to his lips.

Her lashes fluttered as her gaze swept over him, taking in the elegant cut of his knee-breeches, the falls of lace at his wrists and throat, the scandalous absence of a mask. "Why, Lord Kerr, whatever are you masquerading as?"

His lips tightened in a thin smile. "An Englishman."

Devony clapped her hands. "How clever!"

Tricia shot him a pout. Their first real quarrel had been over his costume, or lack of it.

"Deucedly clever," the squire echoed. "An Englishman, you say. I'd never have thought of it." He captured Tricia's hand as the orchestra struck up a new tune. "Shall we dance, my lady? Your days of freedom will soon be over." He grinned at Sebastian. "After Saturday, I shall have a jealous husband to contend with."

Sebastian's cheek twitched with the effort it took to keep his smile from turning into a grimace. Squire Blake swept Tricia into the humming merry-go-round of a minuet, trailing laurel leaves. The folds of his linen toga slid lower over his hairy belly with each clumping step.

Devony faced Sebastian expectantly.

He caught her by the shoulders and turned her around. "Look over there, Devony. Isn't that Sir Arlo with the pitchfork and green wig? Won't you serve as hostess in Tricia's absence and dance with him? He looks rather forlorn." He shoved her in the sheriff's direction, ignoring her sputtered protests.

Alone again, he sank against the marble pilaster with a sigh of relief. Shoving his fists into his pockets, he prayed he could keep from striking the next person who congratulated him on his impending wedding. The irony of the night was not wasted on him. All of his life he had dreamed of being in such a room, surrounded by a whirl of motion and light. His head had been tilted to hear such magnificent music since he had first heard his mother sing, but now the melody of the violins was no more than a grating whine. He had learned too late that gilt was not true gold, and that the masks had more substance than the souls they hid.

Where was Prudence? he wondered. Probably in her bedroom with her nose buried in some damn book. He had started from the ballroom three times to seek her out, but Tricia kept appearing to drag him into the dance. Her attentions had been both needier and greedier since he'd shut her out of his bedchamber. After their wedding, there would be no more locked doors between them.

Dewdrops of crystal draped the chandeliers. Thousands of candles cast sparkling diamonds of light across the dancers. Sebastian's gaze drifted upward. A vaulted ceiling capped the ballroom like the sky of heaven. His eyes traced the delicate pattern of honeysuckle carved into each molding. What a difference there was between the cold wood and the real blossom with petals as soft and velvety as Prudence's skin!

He wished for the eloquence to make her understand. If he had a choice, he would carry her away from Lindentree tonight, find a ramshackle cottage, and fill it with their babes. They would need neither wealth nor titles; they would need nothing but each other. But he wasn't marrying Tricia only for wealth. He was marrying Tricia to escape D'Artan before his zealot grandfather turned him into the kind of man who would murder a girl like Prudence simply for seeing his face. His time was running out. D'Artan's election to the House of Commons had been announced in the London *Observer* only last Friday. He would return from London in less than a week.

When Sebastian next met with his grandfather as Tricia's husband, he would have within his grasp enough wealth and power to laugh in the old man's face. He remembered another time, laughing in his father's face and biting back tears of pain as the blows fell, knowing he was daring his father to kill him, but not caring.

The heavy perfume of the pomaded heads curled through the air like tentacles. Sebastian started for the terrace doors. He had to escape, to find a place where he could breathe again.

Tricia appeared like magic at his side. "Miss me, love? Our Pan nearly hooved me to death. My toes are quite sore. Would you rub them later?"

Before he could answer they were surrounded by a cloying circle of well-wishers, the Blakes and Sir Arlo among them.

"Splendid ball, Countess!"

"Outstanding champagne!"

"The prologue to a fine life together."

Their words bounced off Sebastian like a foreign language. He watched Tricia greet them, trying to remember a time when he had found her pleasant company. It really wasn't her fault. If he had never met Prudence, perhaps he would still find Tricia's smile charming instead of vacuous, her breathless patter witty, not shallow.

Old Fish appeared on the stairs, obviously relishing his role as a portender of doom. "The . . ." He paused, at an uncharacteristic loss for words, and glanced at the figure next to him. "The creature—Cupid."

Sebastian cringed as a nasal voice rang out. "The creature? What kind of intro is that? Every other bloody bugger gets to be gods and semi-gods. How come I have to be a creature?"

Fish took a step backward, dodging the dangerous swing of the arrow in Cupid's hand. Painting it gold had done little to disguise the fact that it was a real arrow, its tip sharpened to a lethal point.

Tricia freed Sebastian's arm. "Why, it's that naughty coachman of yours! He's crashed my ball." Her eyes sparkled with delight. "I shall have to take him to task."

She gathered her skirts and flounced across the floor. The curious eyes of her guests followed her as she greeted the half-naked savage with a wag of her finger and a peck on the cheek. Jamie hiked up his loincloth and swaggered after her, his bony chest puffed out like a robin's and his unpowdered hair blazing like a sunset. Apprehension tightened its fingers around Sebastian's throat.

"Hullo, master," Jamie said as he reached Sebastian.

Under the pretense of ruffling his hair, Sebastian caught his ear and gave it a vicious twist. "And who do you think you are?"

"Ye heard the old man. I'm Cupid, the messenger of love." He leered at Devony. She giggled into her hand.

"You know very well what I mean. I can't think what you're doing—"

They both froze as Sir Arlo's voice rang out. "I know I hit him, Sir Marstan. There hasn't been a robbery for weeks. The vicious bastard—forgive me, ladies—probably crawled in some hole to die. I believe we honorable folk have seen the last of the Dreadful Scot Bandit Kirkpatrick."

Jamie took advantage of Sebastian's inattention to wiggle away. With a mocking wink, he dragged Devony into a rollicking jig that had little to do with the waltz playing. Old Fish started down the stairs, obviously determined to keep an eye on the mischievous imp.

There was no one to announce the lone figure who appeared at the top of the stairs. But no one needed to. A maid screamed and dropped her tray. Devony Blake crumpled to the floor in a pretty faint. The musicians crashed to a halt. The dancers stumbled into one another as all eyes turned to the stairs.

Sebastian sucked in a breath. His eyes narrowed to slits as he met the amethyst gaze of the Dreadful Scot Bandit Kirkpatrick herself.

Fourteen

Dead silence hung over the ballroom. The apparition on the steps might have sauntered straight out of one of the handbills nailed on trees all over Northumberland. From buckled shoes to belted plaid, the Highland costume was complete. Sebastian's tartan socks clung to slender calves. The wood-grained butt of a pistol protruded from the scarlet sash.

A low murmur rippled through the crowd, then Squire Blake's voice boomed out as he picked his daughter up off the floor. "What a splendid costume! I wish I'd thought of it myself."

The murmur deepened. Jamie began to clap. Squire Blake joined in, bouncing Devony's wig askew. Like lemmings, the other guests followed suit until the room rumbled with the thunder of applause. As Sebastian's gaze found him, Jamie ducked behind a nude statue of his cherubic namesake.

Sebastian shot through the crowd, neatly and with one purpose. He stopped on the step below Prudence and caught her wrist in a bruising grip.

"Are you asking me to dance, sir?" Her voice brushed him like velvety wings, yet her soothing tone had the opposite effect on Sebastian. He glanced over his shoulder, noting the curious gazes fixed on them. He did not dare speak, so he contented himself with jerking her into his arms.

Her feet left the floor as he swept her from the steps in a

dizzying circle. The orchestra limped through a handful of false notes before soaring on the joyous chords of a waltz.

Candlelight deepened Prudence's hair to burgundy wine. The sausage curls Jamie had wrung from her stubborn locks flowed down her back with a life of their own. Sebastian's own black silk mask caressed cheeks as fine as alabaster. An excited whisper arose from those nearest them and sped around the ballroom as the crowd realized Lord Kerr's partner was not only undeniably female, but very attractive.

More than one pair of eyes slid to Tricia. Her thoughtful frown quickly shifted to a dazzling smile. Sir Arlo fingered his chin, his own eyes narrowed with puzzlement as he watched the graceful pair circle around the room.

Even through the folds of tartan, Prudence could feel the biting warmth of Sebastian's fingers splayed against the small of her back. He held her dangerously close, pressing against her, and the cold pistol in her waistband dug into her belly.

His breath was hot and angry against her ear. "Didn't Tricia teach you proper etiquette? You should never tuck a loaded pistol into your drawers."

She smiled sweetly. "They're not my drawers."

They were only three turns from the terrace doors when a tug on Prudence's plaid brought them up short. Sir Arlo stood behind them. His genial smile sent prickles of warning down Prudence's spine.

As Sebastian murmured an excuse, his steely gaze promised her retribution. Then he was gone without a backward glance, moving deftly through the crowd, smiling charmingly as he plucked a glass from a maid's tray.

Sir Arlo fingered the tartan. "Amazing reproduction. So very authentic."

Prudence gathered the plaid tighter around her. "I've always had a hand with a needle. A tuck here, a tuck there."

Arlo pulled an incongruous quizzing-glass from the folds of his toga and studied the brooch at her shoulder. "Utterly fascinating. Such a delicate filigree. It's French, you know. I would have sworn there was only one like it in all of England."

Flirtation did not come naturally to Prudence, but she felt

compelled to try. She disengaged the tartan from his fingers, smiling brightly. "Imagination, Sir Arlo. You simply have to use your imagination."

His keen gaze did not ease her fears. "Oh, I am, Prudence. I am."

The shrill coo of Devony's laughter broke the awkward silence between them. Prudence glanced over to see Sebastian's head tilted near to Devony's, his graceful fingers draped over her bare shoulder. Tricia swept toward him with yet another guest in tow.

Prudence could no longer bear Arlo's inquisitive scrutiny of her face. She should never have let Jamie talk her into this madness. The entire charade had been a fool's game. And she was the fool.

She touched her fingertips to her temple. "My head is pounding. I must beg you to excuse me."

She slipped through a cluster of chattering, linen-draped Muses, praying she could make it across the ballroom and out the doors before she was stopped. Still, she could no more keep her eyes from seeking a last glimpse of Sebastian's elegant form than she could have halted her breathing. The sight of him jerked her to a waiting stillness.

His stance was rigid, his brows lowered in a forbidding line. But the sulky cast of his mouth warned her that his anger with her was a mere shadow of what touched him now. It amazed her that no one around him was aware of his turmoil. A trill of laughter rose and fell. The harpist plucked a melody comforting in its funereal blandness. Tricia clung to Sebastian's arm. And Prudence knew enough about gunpowder to sense that if someone struck a flint near him, he would implode, leaving only a pile of smoldering ash on the marble tiles.

She inched nearer.

". . . and Viscount," Tricia was saying, "this is my soon-to-be husband, Sebastian Kerr. Perhaps you can return for the wedding Saturday."

An urbane, French-accented voice prickled the tiny hairs at the nape of Prudence's neck. "I had no inkling you were engaged, my dear. What a delightful surprise."

"The night seems to be rife with them," Sebastian said.

Prudence peered over Sebastian's shoulder and realized she had been wrong. Someone else *was* aware of Sebastian's seething emotions. Either she was a poor judge of character, or the viscount's murky eyes fairly glistened with suppressed glee.

The old man's thin lips pursed in a bemused smirk as he gestured to the ballroom with a flutter of his elegant fingers. "I was traveling in the neighborhood upon my return from London. I should never have intruded had I known the countess was entertaining." He indicated his impeccable breeches and frock coat. "I fear I am not suitably attired for such a fete."

"A pity," Sebastian said. "You would have made an admirable Cerberus."

Tricia tapped her ruby lips. "Was he one of Zeus's sons?"

Prudence spoke up without thinking. "Cerberus was the three-headed dog who guarded the gates of Hades. Whenever anyone entered Hades, he would fawn upon them, but if anyone tried to leave, he would devour them . . ." Her voice trailed off as she was suddenly aware of everyone's eyes upon her. Sebastian's angry gaze was tinged with reluctant pride.

Tricia dismissed her with a chiding cluck. "Oh, pooh! Who wants to be costumed as a dog? We have Boris for that. Did you know, Sebastian, that I met Viscount D'Artan during my stay in Paris? That was before those horridly rude peasants confiscated his estate. I was still wed to Pierre at the time."

"Raynaud," Prudence corrected her aunt absently. Only Tricia, she mused, would equate the volatile revolution in France to bad manners.

The viscount's eyes were still fixed on her, and their tarnished gray depths disquieted Prudence. He found her hand among the folds of tartan and lifted it. His lips were surprisingly warm, but she suppressed a shiver.

"My niece, Miss Prudence Walker," Tricia said as an afterthought.

The viscount stared at her as if mesmerized. "Charmed. I had the pleasure of attending one of your father's exhibitions in London once. The man was a genius."

"I thought so." Prudence withdrew her hand, fighting the urge to wipe it on her kilt.

"I was intrigued by his work with fulminics," the viscount went on. "Having once had a laboratory in Varennes, I fancy myself as something of a chemist."

Tricia looped an arm through his. "That dreadful rabble forced the poor viscount to flee his own country. They burned all of his holdings."

"How unfortunate," Prudence murmured.

He shrugged. "*C'est la vie.* Your countrymen have been more than kind to me. I have just returned from London after accepting a post in the House of Commons. I should love to call on you next week to discuss your father's work."

"If you've been traveling," Sebastian said coldly, "we shouldn't wish to detain you."

The viscount gave Prudence an elegant bow before meeting Sebastian's eyes. "I trust we shall meet again. Very soon."

"Tell me, Viscount," Tricia said, jealously capturing his attention again, "is it true they serve no tea in those dreadful prisons of yours? I shudder to think of what Marie and Louis must be suffering. They are such a delightful pair. Pierre took me to visit them once." She began to draw him away. "Or was it Raoul?"

The viscount's reply was a silken murmur as they melted into the crowd. Prudence turned to Sebastian. Her question died on her lips as his icy gaze raked her from brooch to stockings.

"I believe you owe me a dance, Miss Walker. And an explanation."

Before she could protest, he swept her into his arms once more.

Prudence could feel every shift of his muscles as he spun her in an ever widening circle. His gray eyes had gone from smoldering ash to molten steel. She had never dreamed a man could look so attractive and so given to murder at the same time. She threw back her head, fighting to catch her breath as the gowned figures blurred to milky fog. She could no longer tell which gods were real and which were marble. They all had the same sly expression, like gloating Heras waiting for an omnipotent Zeus to cast her from Mt. Olympus.

Prudence's toes only grazed the floor as Sebastian danced her out the doors and onto the flagstoned terrace.

She stumbled when he abruptly released her, then his roar shattered the night. "Och, lass, ha'e ye no' a wee brain in yer puir, daft head?"

She blinked up at him. "Pardon me?"

"I said 'Och, lass, ha'e ye no' a wee—'" He turned his back on her, flexing his hands on the stone balustrade in an obvious struggle to regain some control of his temper and restore his command of the English language.

After the blazing light of the ballroom, the terrace enveloped them in cool darkness. The music and laughter seemed only a brittle echo. The fountain at the bottom of the stairs tinkled a melody of its own.

After a minute Prudence spoke, her voice musing. "It has suddenly occurred to me, Sebastian, that I've never seen you truly angry."

He swung around. "They don't call me Dreadful," he said, backing her up with each word, "because I'm a clever whist partner."

Her back hit the opposite balustrade. She swallowed hard. "Perhaps it's your skill at faro—"

She gasped as he jerked the pistol out of her waistband, then threw up her arms, forgetting it wasn't loaded.

He checked the weapon with brisk competence. "Contrary to what the good sheriff may have told you, I'm not given to murdering unarmed women." He shot her a look from beneath his lashes. "However strong the temptation."

She lowered her arms, feeling like an idiot. He handed the pistol back. "It completes your ensemble quite nicely."

She turned around and laid the gun on the balustrade, desperate to escape his accusing gaze. She had miscalculated. Sebastian was not angry. He was furious.

"I'd like to know one thing, Miss Walker." He grasped the balustrade on either side of her, effectively barring any attempt at escape. He did not touch her. "Are you threatening me?"

She forced a light shrug, remembering Jamie's advice. Duplicity and half-truths did not come naturally to her. "That would be unwise, would it not?"

"Not if you thought you were safe with me."

She gathered her courage and turned to face him. "Am I safe with you, Sebastian?"

Warmth emanated from his lean body. She could sense the fury that tensed his muscles abating into something softer and far more dangerous. The night breeze stirred her hair, untwining the scent of jasmine from the loose strands.

Sebastian's nostrils flared. He drew one finger down the lacy jabot at her throat. "You fill out my plaid quite nicely."

His silky tone mesmerized her, and his compliment took on a new bite as he lowered his head. The heat of their breath mingled before his mouth touched hers. His tongue traced the outline of her lips, then dipped inward with a tantalizing stroke. Her fingers clutched his coat as the steady, lingering pressure of his mouth on hers paralyzed her.

His lips traveled across her cheek to her ear, each kiss a separate entity, as rough and tender as his gruff whisper. "In the Highlands, when a woman wears a man's plaid, it means only one thing. She belongs to him."

His mouth closed over hers with a fresh heat. His teeth scraped her lips as his tongue sought out the honeyed mysteries of her mouth. Wrapping an arm low around her back, he pulled her against him, rubbing his chest to hers. He groaned at the feel of her soft, unfettered breasts. Too late, Prudence remembered he knew all the secrets of her attire.

When his hand slipped beneath the plaid and between the buttons of his own shirt, there were no corset or stays to separate his seeking fingers from the buoyant curve of her breast. He caught the aching bud of her nipple between his thumb and forefinger, teasing it with a skill that drew a whimper from deep in her throat.

Her legs threatened to fold, but with a dangerous dip, Sebastian was there, his palm a searing heat against the scandalously bare skin behind her knee. His hand began a maddening ascent up her thigh, pushing the kilt ahead of it, then sliding beneath. Her pulse thundered a warning as she recognized for the first time the wisdom of stockings and garters, chemises and petticoats. Sebastian's fingers stroked the sensitive, trembling flesh of her inner thigh, moving inexorably toward the worn trews tucked between her legs.

With a frightening shock, Prudence realized she wanted him to touch her there. What sort of wanton had she become? But her shame melted in the bracing warmth of his kiss. Her hands cupped his strong neck, feeling his convulsive swallow as his fingers continued their hungry quest.

His palm cupped her, rubbing blindly against the softness beneath the trews. She threw back her head, stifling a gasp as his thumb brushed her in a deliberate caress, setting off a quaking explosion. She could feel her body opening like a flower, slickening with the dew of an aching emptiness she'd never dared acknowledge. She entwined her body to his, looping her arms around his neck, pressing her lips to the delectable throb of the pulse in his throat.

Suddenly, his hand stilled against her. Sebastian caught her hair and forced her to look at him. Her vision gone misty with need, she smiled tremulously at him.

A black fury darkened his eyes. Her smile vanished. What had she done to anger him so? Icy needles of shame pricked her. Her wanton behavior must have disgusted him. How could she have been such a fool? She lowered her eyes, thankful for his mask as the heat of a blush stained her cheeks.

Growling, he sank his teeth into her swollen lower lip. She shuddered against him, expecting pain but finding only pleasure. Something in his grip had changed; it was now as implacable and relentless as the dark passion that rose between them. His arm slid lower down her back, his hand curving around her rump, as his mouth plundered hers with punishing heat. His knees slipped between hers, parting her legs and lifting her to the balustrade in one smooth, balletic move. He dragged her against him, wrapping his arms around her as his palm was replaced by a greedier hardness rubbing against the soft folds of tartan between her legs.

She strained away from him as a fear deeper than that of discovery and stronger than the fragile strands of new desire beat frantically in her belly. She turned her face away. "Sebastian, please, don't . . . I can't . . ."

He caught her chin between two biting fingers and tilted

her head back. The scattered light cast harsh planes across his features. His lashes swept down, but not before she caught a glimpse of the hungry Highland beast sleeping beneath his thin veneer of manners. An unreasoning terror swept her.

She shoved against his chest, near to swooning in the fear that he might shove the trews aside and ravish her right there on the terrace. How dare she condemn him for taking what she had unwittingly offered? Self-contempt for her own shameful surrender only enflamed her panic.

"Let me go!"

He caught her flailing wrists in one of his broad hands. The look in his eyes stunned her. It was pain, pain that haunted the hollows of his cheeks and deepened the grooves around his beautiful mouth. Pain of such a quiet intensity that a matching ache opened deep in her own heart. Her hands crumpled into loose fists and were still.

"What have you decided?" he asked. His voice was surprisingly cool and detached. "Are you safe with me?" She inclined her head. The mask absorbed the first of her tears. His warm breath touched her ear. "Don't start the music, Prudence, unless you're willing to dance."

The light spilling from the terrace door dimmed. "Sebastian? Are you out there?" Tricia called hesitantly.

He freed Prudence and moved to stand a few feet away. The imprint of his fingers clung to her wrists like icy bracelets. She slid off the stone railing and smoothed the kilt with trembling fingers. They had been in shadow, but she had no way of knowing how long Tricia had been standing there.

Sebastian stared down into the sunken garden with eyes gone as dark as the night. "I'm here, love. What is it?"

Tricia's skirt swept the flagstones as she pranced to him. Her hand curled around his forearm. "Can you come in, dear? The guests are growing bored."

"Of course." His lips brushed her temple, but his gaze passed beyond her to Prudence. "Anything for you."

They walked back to the door, then paused there, bathed in a golden pool of light. Sebastian leaned forward with deliberate grace and planted a tender kiss on Tricia's lips. Prudence's hands tightened on the balustrade. As they started into the ballroom, Tricia looked back, acknowledging her niece's presence on the terrace for the first time. Prudence wondered if it was triumph or suspicion sparkling in her aunt's eyes.

She tucked the pistol in her sash and trailed after them, knowing she could ill afford to burst into sobs as she longed to do. She caught her lower lip between her teeth. Her mouth felt bruised and swollen. She prayed the signs of Sebastian's passionate lovemaking were not as obvious to others as they felt to her.

She slipped through the crowd and out of the ballroom, her head pounding in earnest. The carved gilt doors closed behind her, dulling the music to a low pulse.

The steady throb in her skull sharpened to piercing pain as Jamie popped out from a curtained alcove, wielding his arrow like a demonic cherub. "Congratulations, girl. Well done indeed. I'd say ye got his attention."

She kept walking. "I certainly did. He despises me."

Jamie's face fell, then he brightened. "Don't take it to heart, lass. Me mum and da hated each other fer years. And look how dandy I turned out." She continued on toward the stairs, and he called after her, "There's a man outside in a fancy coach askin' after the daughter of Livingston Walker. Might that be ye?"

Prudence stopped. Her shoulders slumped. Not now, she thought. Not tonight. Her pride was in tatters. She couldn't bear to discuss silver compounds and saltpeter with some rabid inventor. At the moment, she didn't care if they all blew themselves up, the mysterious French viscount along with them.

She turned back to Jamie and straightened her shoulders. "Tell him I'm not here. Tell him I emigrated to Pomerania. Tell him I died."

Jamie scratched his head with the arrow. "Ye want me to make him go away?"

"Yes, Jamie," she said with weary patience. "As far away as possible."

She missed his gleeful grin as he notched the arrow in his bow and bounded out the door.

Prudence pulled off the mask as she climbed the stairs.

She rubbed the scrap of silk against her cheek, hearing again Sebastian's husky whisper of warning.

Don't start the music, Prudence, unless you're willing to dance.

The music from the ballroom floated up the steps, the haunting melody of a song begun too late. As Prudence crumpled the silk in her fist, her delicate features hardened into a mask of their own.

Sebastian stood in the darkness at the library window, listening to the muted spray of gravel as the last of the revelers' coaches departed Lindentree. His nostrils twitched as he drank in the rich, fallow aroma of the meadow beyond the window. Like an animal scenting freedom, he longed to step through the open window, to escape the man he had been, the man he would become. But there was no escaping the man he was; Brendan Kerr's blood coursed through his veins like poison. He closed his eyes against the mocking wink of the fireflies, feeling again the frantic tattoo of Prudence's fists against his chest.

He had only meant to teach her a lesson, to show her he was no affable Arlo Tugbert to dally with. What would be the harm of a stolen kiss? What cost a few lazy caresses? But the cost had been higher than he had anticipated.

His eyes flew open. He dug his fingers into the window casement, remembering the warmth of her silly, wistful smile, the loving caress of her hands against his throat. The painful honesty of her love had unleashed a wild tide of desire in him, a spiraling agony of want that bordered on madness.

He had frightened her. When he had looked at her and found her pupils dilated with fear, her hands shoving him away, he had felt himself receding, curling into that quiet, still place where he had once gone to escape his father's shattering bellow, and the repeated thud of fists against his mother's flesh.

Let me go, Prudence had pleaded. Sebastian shook his head to rid it of the haunting echo.

His father had not let his mother go. He had not let her go

when she shoved him away, not when she begged, and not when she screamed. It was only when she stepped up to the window of Dunkirk's tower, her body thick with their second child, that Brendan Kerr had been forced to let her go. He had tried to hold on, had hurled himself across the tower, grabbing frantically for her skirts. But the child in her belly had given her courage. She'd spread her arms and stepped into the sun, disappearing forever into the heathered abyss below Dunkirk.

Sebastian could still see the peace on her face in that moment, as the sun slanted across her golden hair. He had hugged his knees in the corner of the tower, tears coursing down his cheeks, and hated his mother for flying to freedom and leaving him behind.

Sebastian groaned and ruffled his hair. He could ill afford to probe old wounds. He had more pressing concerns, such as why D'Artan had returned early from London.

He couldn't believe the crafty old man had dared come to Lindentree. Now that he had learned of Sebastian's plan to marry, they both knew their next rendezvous would be their last. D'Artan might sulk for a while, but Sebastian prayed his appointment to the House would absorb most of the blow. D'Artan would have his own pension, his own entrance into London society. He wouldn't need his grandson anymore—not for money and not for secrets. He could work on liberating France and blowing up England all by himself.

Sebastian hoped their parting could be an amicable one. He suspected D'Artan was fond of him in his own stilted way.

Sebastian's only concern now was Prudence. His jaw tightened as he remembered the predatory look on his grandfather's face when he had seen her. The old man knew she was the girl in the crofter's hut. Sebastian reminded himself that, in two days' time, he would be powerful enough to protect her. As the penniless niece of a scatterbrained countess, she was vulnerable to D'Artan's machinations. But when he was master of Lindentree, he would ensure a disappearance or untimely accident involving *his* niece would not go unnoticed by the King.

Sighing, Sebastian latched the window. The knowledge that he would be able to protect Prudence did not give him the peace he sought. He climbed the stairs with a heavy tread. Since he had come to Lindentree his sleep had been mercifully free of nightmares, but he feared tonight might be different. Pausing outside Prudence's chamber, he touched the burnished oak door, as if he might somehow reach through the cool wood to the gentle warmth of her embrace.

Would he ever trust himself not to push open her door, lay his mouth across hers to muffle her protests, and bury himself in her tender, young body? His hand clenched into a fist and he hastened down the darkened corridor.

As he rounded the corner into the blessed privacy of the west wing, he saw that his door was cracked open. The soft glow from a single candle fluttered in the corridor. He cursed under his breath, in no mood to fend off Tricia's cloying advances.

He pushed open the door, and his jaw dropped at the sight before him. It was not Tricia, but Prudence who sat in his chair.

She hefted the crystal decanter braced between her legs. "Good evening, Mr. Dreadful. Would you care for a spot of brandy?"

Fifteen

Sebastian could not have looked any more shocked had she blown a cloud of cigar smoke in his face, Prudence mused. Under other circumstances, she might have found it comical. As he continued to stare at her, she gripped the decanter. The crystal cut against the tender pads of her fingers. Sebastian started to close the door, then propped it open, then pushed it shut. He circled her as if she were a wild beast, deserving of his utmost caution.

Prudence bowed her head. She had brushed the sausage curls out of her hair, and it lay like a heavy cloak across her shoulders.

He pointed at the half-empty decanter. "Did you drink all of that?"

She gave an apologetic shrug. "I accidentally kicked it when I heard you coming. I'm afraid Old Fish will be displeased."

He glanced at the darkening circle beside her chair with obvious relief. She lifted the decanter to her lips to take a nervous sip, but he plucked it from her hands.

"Must you be fortified with brandy to converse with me?"

"I didn't come here to converse with you."

He made an odd noise, as if his throat had suddenly gone dry.

She pointed to the garments folded neatly on his satin-wood bureau. "I came to return your plaid."

Sebastian turned his back on her, gulping a swig of brandy before setting the decanter on the mantel.

He addressed the andirons. "Did it ever occur to you what might happen should Tricia find you here?"

"She won't."

He swung around, gazing suspiciously at her. "How can you be sure?"

She blinked at him over the rim of her spectacles. "Tricia is in the habit of lacing her nightly toddy with laudanum. I took the liberty of adding a few extra drops."

He threw back his head with a pained shout of laughter. "You'd make a fine lady bandit."

"Better than you. I wouldn't go getting shot and falling off my horse all the time. You should give serious consideration to another livelihood."

"I have. The husband of a wealthy countess."

She looked down and smoothed her night rail over her knees.

He sighed. "You sit there like the most innocent of angels and tell me you've poisoned your aunt. I'm afraid I can't help you hide the body. Murder isn't my forte."

She gave him a wounded look. "Nor is it mine. You know I'd never hurt Tricia." She glanced away, unable to meet his gaze. "Not deliberately anyway."

He knelt in front of her, covering her hands with his. She clamped her knees together to keep them from trembling.

"Prudence, I want you to listen very carefully. I am not a nice man. I am a reprehensible criminal and a duplicitous scoundrel. I would sell my proverbial grandmother for a chance at a woman with a title. My uncharacteristic bursts of morality and self-control where you are concerned are liable to lapse at any moment with grave and lurid consequences." He chucked her chin upward, favoring her with one of his most beautiful smiles. "Are you listening?"

She managed a weak nod and an answering smile.

"Very well." He rose and flung open the door. It crashed into the opposite wall. *"Then get the bloody hell out of my bedchamber!"*

Prudence jumped a foot in the air. She stood, painfully aware of his gaze raking over her as she glided toward the door. She wore no wrapper. The soft flax of her night rail brushed like fairy wings against her skin. The modest garment shielded her from throat to wrist to ankle, but was helpless to stem the teasing invasion of candlelight and shadow.

She reached around Sebastian and closed the door. The top of her head brushed his chin. She heard his quick, indrawn breath.

He strode away from her, loosening his cravat. His laughter was strained. "For a smart girl, you make some very odd choices. You come to an isolated corner of the house. You drug the only person within screaming distance. Did it ever occur to you that even if you choose to go, I might keep you here?"

"I'm not afraid of you."

He spun on his heel, jerking off his coat. "Then you're a fool. I wouldn't be the first lecherous male relation to take advantage of a female dependent, not even among your high-handed gentry."

She bent to pick up his cravat, and tenderly folded it. "Are you trying to convince me or yourself?"

"I'm not sure. But you'd best leave before I succeed."

With a show of nonchalance, she resumed her position in the chair. Sebastian tore open the ties of his shirt. Like a lover's seeking caress, the flickering candlelight found the gold scattered over the smooth muscles of his chest. Her mouth went dry, and she pushed her spectacles up on her nose.

He stared helplessly at her, as if he hoped she might have vanished. Dragging a hand through his hair, he freed the leonine mass from the satin queue. His expression was so wild, she half expected him to lapse into an unintelligible burr or leap upon her with a Highland battle cry. The latter might be a relief. At least she would know where she stood with him.

"All I'm trying to say, lass," he said, his soft tone raising gooseflesh on her arms, "is that you don't really know me."

She met his gaze evenly. When she spoke, her voice was so

dispassionate she might have been cataloguing a chemical formula rather than a life. "You fled the Highlands at the age of thirteen before Killian MacKay could boot you out of your father's castle. The first thing you stole was a wheel of cheese because you were hungry."

He sank down on the edge of the bed.

She continued. "You weren't a much better bandit at that time than you are now. You were caught and thrown into jail to await your hanging. A relation of your mother's found you, had you released, and took you to France. He picked off the lice and gave you your first real bath and a brief, but thorough, education." She paused. "How am I doing?"

"Marvelous," he said flatly. "Do go on."

"You returned to Scotland a few years later, both older and wiser, and began your remarkable stint as the Dreadful Scot Bandit Kirkpatrick, spreading terror and mayhem along the Scottish border, plotting and dreaming of the day when you could return to the Highlands and avenge yourself on the dastardly MacKay."

"Careful. You're lapsing into melodrama."

"Sorry. It's a weakness of mine."

"I've noticed. Along with charging rashly into situations you're unprepared for."

Prudence felt her composure slipping. "After the ball tonight, I felt I had nothing to lose."

He slipped off the bed with catlike grace. She resisted the urge to turn as he circled her chair.

His elegant fingers cupped her chin from behind, and he tilted her head back. "You, my dear, have everything to lose." His lips brushed hers in a brief, dry caress.

She shivered as he released her. Her scalp tingled and she realized with wonder that he was brushing her hair. He drew the bristles upward, lifting and separating the silky strands into a crackling cloud.

She inclined her head shyly, daring to luxuriate in the delicious sensation as he swept the brush along her hair. A decadent joy coursed through her at the innocent pleasure of being tended to. When she was a child, her papa had spent hours patiently working the tangles from her unruly hair. The same feeling of security touched her now, but it was

tempered with the dangerous knowledge that between herself and this man, security was only a fragile illusion.
Sebastian caught her hair at its crown and drew the brush
back in a long, lingering stroke. A tiny moan of satisfaction
escaped her throat, and she closed her eyes.

His silken burr caressed her, tempting her to drop all
defenses. "So you know who I am. Shall I tell you who you
are?"

She laughed nervously without opening her eyes. "No
mystery there. I've no bandits or mysterious French relations
lurking in the wings. I'm only Prudence Walker, spinster
niece and poor relation of Tricia de Peyrelongue."

He lifted the brush, exposing her delicate ear to the
soothing heat of his breath. "You came to live with Tricia
after your father died. She clucked sadly over what a plain,
little thing you were and said you had too many brains to
ever make a decent match."

Prudence flinched. She would have pulled away, but his
hand replaced the brush. She was caught by his possession
of her hair.

His voice poured over her, soft but merciless. "In the years
that followed, she paraded past you a steady stream of
leering younger sons, pompous parsons, and elderly squires.
With each dreaded foray into the parlor to meet your *suitors*,
you became smarter"—he twisted his hand in her hair,
binding it tightly away from her face—"and plainer."

Tears pricked her eyes. How could he be so cruel? He freed
her hair, and it fell around her face and shoulders. She was
thankful for its sheltering weight as burning humiliation
tinted her cheeks.

But Sebastian was ruthless. He walked around the chair
and squatted in front of her. "What did Tricia tell you? Did
she tell you your nose was too thin, your teeth too prominent?"

Prudence bit her lower lip and turned her face away from
his avid scrutiny.

He cupped her cheeks in his palms and forced her head
back. His thumbs curved around to trace the dark wings of
her brows. "Did she murmur her sympathy over your heavy
brows, your pale skin?"

"Stop it!" She could not bear for him to see her cry, and lifted her hands to break his grip.

He captured both of her wrists in one of his hands and took off her spectacles. She cringed away from him, blinking back tears.

"Aren't you weary of hiding, Prudence? Behind these spectacles? Behind books? Behind Tricia? Hasn't it been lonely all these years?"

She struggled to pull out of his grasp, helpless to stop the tears from trickling down her cheeks. "I wasn't lonely. I had a happy life before you came along."

"A happy life? Buried behind books. Living other people's lives because you had no life of your own. A happy life? Without one breath of excitement to stir it?"

"Is that why you think I came here tonight? For excitement?" She finally broke his grip and bolted from the chair. She stood with her back to him, clinging to the bedpost for support.

He slowly straightened. "Why did you come here, Prudence?"

"Because I thought you cared for me." She added softly, almost as an afterthought, "I would have left you alone. You didn't have to remind me I was ugly."

His laughter rang out, harsh and mocking.

She fled for the door. With one long stride, he reached it before she did and she collided with his unyielding chest. When she would have recoiled, his arms enfolded her, holding her hard against him until her struggles subsided. She buried her mouth in the fur of his chest, refusing to begrudge herself the last taste she would know of his arms.

He rubbed his cheek across her hair. "Tell me, Miss Walker, if you're so damnably smart, how could you believe the twisted musings of an envious woman far past the bloom of her own youth?"

His heart thundered against her lips. For a long moment, she did not comprehend his words.

"Can't you see what Tricia's jealousy has done to you?" He again caught her face in his hands, smoothing her hair away. "You are the most uncommon and utterly beautiful woman I have ever laid eyes on. I've wanted you from the first

moment you trod upon my broken ankle." Her eyes widened
in misty wonder, and he laughed. "And, oh, when you look at
me like that, all I want to do is lay you beneath me and taste
every inch of your lovely fair skin."

Prudence's breath came out in a squeak. "You can't be
serious."

"Let's get this off, shall we, and I'll show you how very
serious I am." He bunched the soft flax of her night rail in his
hands and began to draw it upward.

She clung to his shoulders. "But you haven't even kissed
me."

His tongue traced the outer rim of her ear. "I will," he
whispered. "Everywhere."

His hands rode up over her hips, drawing the night rail
with them. "The candle," she said frantically.

"I know. One candle is not enough. I'd like to carry you
down to the ballroom and make love to you beneath the
chandelier." His knuckles brushed her belly. "I wonder what
Old Fish would think about that."

She squirmed in his arms. "Sebastian! You say the wick-
edest things! I meant for you to put the candle out."

He drew back, smiling a tender, lopsided smile. "No more
hiding, love. No more masks." He pressed his mouth to her
ear. "Please, my darling, be naked for me."

Prudence had never imagined herself the recipient of such
an odd request. But Sebastian's loving smile was irresistible,
and she lifted her arms in surrender. He gently pulled the
night rail over her head. A heated blush crawled up her skin,
and she squeezed her eyes shut, believing like a child that if
she could not see him, he might not be able to see her. His
soft groan proved her wrong.

Her hands flew up instinctively to cover herself, desperate
to hide the flaws of legs too long, breasts too heavy for her
slender frame. He caught her hands, lacing his fingers
around hers and bearing them back against the door on
each side of her head. Even with her eyes closed, she could
feel the heat of his gaze on her.

Sebastian drank in her beauty. Her hair absorbed the
candlelight, deepening to rich and magical hues. The sight
of it spilling like wine over her alabaster breasts both

inflamed his tender lust and tempered it with a curious desire to protect. It was as he suspected. Prudence's stiff-necked pride hid a blossom as precious and fragile as petals of honeysuckle.

She hid her face in her hair. "Please. I'm so embarrassed."

"Of what? Perfection?"

She dared to open her eyes.

He brought their linked hands down to brush the creamy skin between her breasts. All traces of humor had vanished from him. "Everything I've ever possessed that was worth having, I've stolen. You're the only gift anyone has ever given me."

He lifted her palm to his lips. Prudence took a step away from the door and melted into his embrace, knowing she would never forget the wanton sensuality of her nude body pressed against the crisp folds of his clothes. His mouth closed on hers in a flood of aching tenderness.

Sebastian hardly dared to believe the miracle of holding her pliant body against him. He had dreamed it too often to accept that it was real. A thread of guilt wound its way through his anticipation, but he hastily shoved it away. Prudence had come to him, on his terms, not her own. She suckled his tongue in an innocent attempt to draw him more deeply into her. Her nipples stiffened against his chest, and he felt a dizzying surge of response in his groin. He could feel himself straining against his breeches, hungering to be freed, hungering, too, to allow his hands and mouth to wander over this beautiful, generous creature. But he could not yet trust himself enough for that.

Her hand twined through his hair as he bent his knees and gently took her breast into his mouth. His tongue swirled around the dusky peak, and he felt her deep shiver.

"Sebastian, please. I can't even think!"

He slipped to his knees, filling the delicate cleft of her navel with his tongue. "For once in your life, Prudence, stop thinking."

Prudence had no choice but to obey as his reverent hands parted the silky pelt between her legs. He muttered an oath that sounded more like a prayer as his fingers slipped beneath to explore the honeyed folds and hollows of her body with tender expertise. She shoved aside his shirt and gripped his shoulders in a desperate attempt to find some substance in a reality melting to shuddering pleasure. The cool wood of the door pressed to her back and hips seemed to be part of another, saner world. Her instinct to shrink away from him was consumed in the flames of a more primitive instinct to arch against him, to open herself to the stroking persuasion of his eloquent touch.

She panted softly as his thumb discovered her heated nectar and teased it forward until he found the taut, aching bud hidden by her velvety folds. Her knees buckled at the pleasure, and he slipped an arm around her, cupping her hips as he buried his mouth against the dark fur at the V of her thighs in the tenderest of kisses.

Her shy gasp was lost in a new sensation as he sheathed his finger inside her, pressing forward with gentle determination until he felt her wince of pain. Her body quivered in disappointment as he withdrew.

"Oh, God, Prudence, you're so tight."

"I'm sorry, Sebastian." Her voice was very small. "I don't mean to be."

His groan was one of exultation as he curved his arm around the backs of her thighs and lifted her straight into the air. He pressed his cheek to the delicate skin of her belly. She clung to his shoulders as he spun around and dropped her neatly on the bed.

As he peeled off his shirt, she reached for a corner of the satin counterpane to cover her nakedness.

"My sweet Prudence," he said, trapping the counterpane under his knee as he joined her on the bed, "I was not rebuking you. The . . . um . . ." He searched for words, curbing with effort his characteristic frankness. ". . . deliciously untried condition of your body only serves to demonstrate what a fine and precious privilege you are bequeathing to me." He propped himself up on one elbow and ran a finger down the flat plane of her stomach.

Her brow crinkled in a frown. "How would the Dreadful Scot Bandit Kirkpatrick say that?"

Sebastian's slow, sensual grin sent the blood coursing through Prudence's body in a primal throb. He pressed his mouth to her ear. "Something scandalous like, 'Och, lass, ye ne'er had a mon inside ye the way I'm goin' to be inside ye.'" His finger dipped into her, smearing the honeyed dew to ease his passage. His burr thickened with desire. "Ye want me, angel. Ye're hot and wet and needin' a mon like me to fill ye."

Prudence had always loved words, but she had never before known their full power. "Scoundrel," she breathed, melting into his tender touch.

Sebastian dared to slip another finger into her, knowing only preparation could ease the pain to come. She turned her face to his, groping blindly for a sustenance to soothe the aching hunger flowering within her. He smoothed a thread of hair from her moist lips and laid his mouth over hers. The world narrowed to the wet heat of their fused mouths and bodies. Her legs fell apart, giving his hand dominion over her. His fingers began to move of their own volition, matching each thrust of his tongue. When he felt her arch and rock against him, he forgot patience, forgot gentleness, forgot everything but the promise of ecstasy tightening around his fingers as he buried them roughly in her. An involuntary whimper escaped her throat.

He half lifted his weight as if he might pull away. "I can't bear to hurt you, lass."

"I know that." She ran her fingertip along the pale, rigid scar under his chin. "You won't hurt me. You're not your father, Sebastian."

He stared down at her, his eyes as unfathomable as smoky diamonds. "Is there anything Jamie didn't tell you?"

She averted her gaze as she ran her hands over his arms, delighting in their muscular resilience. "Tricia always said I was a nosy miss." She cupped his throat and pressed her lips to his scar.

Sebastian's skin tingled from her cool touch. Nothing in his life had prepared him for her. Not the perfunctory stabs at pleasure he had made before he met Tricia, and not their expert couplings which had left him breathless, spent, and completely hollow. For Sebastian Kerr, there had been little of love in the making of it. He had suspected long ago that he was as crippled as his father.

Now here was this innocent woman-child daring to tell him he was wrong. And offering herself to prove it.

He enfolded her in his arms, encompassing her as if he could somehow draw the warmth and rich texture of her skin into his own. She buried her mouth against his shoulder with a wordless murmur.

He kissed her hair. "Let me pleasure you, angel," he murmured, and slid down her body, through the pools of candlelight dappling her creamy skin. Her delicate scent was maddening, all honeysuckle and jasmine and musk. Prudence's urge to clamp her knees together went unheeded as a deeper urge rocked her. Sebastian parted her thighs with gentle hands. His mouth touched her, seeking to give solace where before he had given pain.

If she had been standing, she would have fallen. Her hands entwined in his hair; the tawny strands slipped like silk between her fingers. She lay back, hypnotized by a languid desire to close her eyes and surrender to the delicious sensations. His beautiful mouth pleasured her, doing things she had never, not even in her most heated dreams of him, imagined. The novelty of it was dark and mysterious and unbearably sweet. A moan tore from her and she arched her slender back, holding nothing from him. Without disturbing the maddening rhythm of his mouth, Sebastian thrust his fingers deep within her. She cried out his name in a voice she did not recognize as a blinding wave of pleasure broke over her, cresting again and again until she lay breathless and shivering among his pillows.

When her eyes fluttered open, he was leaning over her, his grin softened by concern. "I thought you might have swooned."

Her own lips curved in a shy smile. "I'm not the sort of girl who swoons."

He touched his lips to hers. "I'll have to see what I can do about that."

His hand lowered to unfasten the hooks of his knee-breeches. Prudence nibbled her lower lip to keep it from trembling. Not wanting him to see her fear, she reached across the bed and smothered the candle as he slipped out of his breeches.

The darkness enfolded them like a black velvet curtain. Her hand fluttered out to find him. She nuzzled her cheek against his chest, content to be held while her eyes adjusted to the light of moonbeams scattering through the chintz drapes. The cost of Sebastian's patience was betrayed by the thundering of his heart.

She tilted her face up for his kiss and their naked bodies entwined in languorous communion, his muscled thigh entrapping both of her legs, his belly pressed to hers. Her skin contracted violently at the sleek heat of his engorged manhood. He eased himself over her, bracing his weight on his elbows, and she slipped her arms around his neck.

Sebastian stared down into her eyes, seeing in their violet depths what he least wanted to be reminded of at this moment. It would be so easy to bury his guilt and doubt in her trusting body, but somehow he could not take her in dishonesty. She had come to him, but he had to ensure that she understood the cost of it.

He met her gaze unflinchingly. "You know this changes nothing. I still must marry Tricia."

Some selfish demon within him howled its anguish as Prudence disappeared. It was that simple. One second she was there. The next, she was gone. She stared at him without blinking. All that had been melting warmth between them cooled to unnatural stillness.

The blood drained from her face as if his words had somehow pierced her heart. "Let me up."

His demanding hardness brushed the silky curls between her legs. His muscles contracted with the temptation to drive himself into her honeyed sheath, to shatter her icy composure with a vivid reminder of his heat. To make her cry out his name once again with passionate abandon.

A trickle of sweat eased down his brow. "You can't ask me to stop now. It's not fair."

Prudence was too wise to struggle. "What do you know of fairness?"

Desperation gave his voice a hard edge. "You came to me. I thought you understood the way of it."

"Let me up." She enunciated each word with crystal clarity.

He flung himself off her as if she had shot him. Prudence

had never known such an aching emptiness. Without the
warmth of Sebastian's skin covering her, she felt vulnerable
and ashamed of her nakedness.

She sat up on her knees, clutching the counterpane to her
breasts. "You said you cared for me. How can you marry
her?"

He glared up at the mahogany tester, his head resting on
one folded arm. "I have no choice. She can give me what I
need."

"What do you need, Sebastian? Money? Access to a title? A
town house in London?"

His voice was low and flat. "Respectability."

She threw back her head as laughter burst wildly from her.
"Respectability? I've had respectability all my life, and I can
promise you it's nothing extraordinary." She pressed the
heels of her palms to her stinging eyes. "Tell me one thing. If
I were an heiress, would you marry me?"

His narrowed gaze shifted to her. "In a heartbeat."

She dove for the edge of the bed, dragging the counterpane
with her. With the reflexes of a born thief, he lunged for her.
His arms encircled her waist, pulling her back against him.
Her hair spilled over his face. He caught her flailing wrists in
his hands, subduing her with all the gentleness he could
muster.

"Listen to me, Prudence. We have a chance at happiness
that few people in this world ever have. I can be with you and
cherish you for our whole lives. Let me take care of you."

She crumpled against him. "What are you offering me? A
few hours before dawn after Tricia has drugged herself
insensible? A stolen kiss in the pantry? A new gown on my
birthday?"

He touched his lips to her hair. "I am offering you a lifetime
of tenderness. Tricia will never suspect us."

Prudence twisted in his arms until she faced him. "And if
you get me with child? What then? Will you pass it off as the
stable boy's? The butler's?"

An unexpected heat brushed his cheekbones. "I can protect you from that. There are ways." He hoped he was
sincere. The vision of her slender body swelling with his
babe inspired a poignant longing that shook him.

He made no attempt to stop her as she pulled out of his arms, sliding off the bed. The unmistakable bitterness in her eyes quenched his last spark of hope—yet he could not stop trying.

"You know your aunt better than anyone does. Do you think Tricia will take no lovers after we're wed? It's the way of things in her world."

Prudence crossed to the door and knelt to gather her night rail, her shoulders bent beneath the weight of the counterpane. "But not in mine."

Sebastian Kerr, who had bit back his pleas his entire life, said softly, "Please, Prudence. Don't leave me."

Her hands paused in their motion. She looked back to find him naked in more than his unabated need for her. His haunted gaze caught and held hers.

She dropped the night rail over her head, letting the counterpane fall in the same motion. Sebastian caught a glimpse of her skin.

Her hand touched the doorknob.

He leaped from the bed and crossed the room in two strides. His own hand covered hers. "You mustn't tell Tricia who I am. Both of our lives may depend on it."

She stared at the door.

His fingers tightened around hers. "Swear you won't."

She lifted her gaze to him, and he stepped back, recoiling from the contempt in her eyes.

"I swear it." She opened the door. "It would have never worked between us anyway. Because I don't have the money. And you, Sebastian Kerr, don't have the guts."

The soft click of the door shutting in his face echoed louder than a pistol shot.

Sebastian wandered over to the chair like a blind man. His toe touched something hard, and he stopped his foot just short of crushing the cool steel and delicate glass of Prudence's spectacles. He set them carefully beside his hairbrush. Among the bristles, a long dark hair entwined around his shorter blond ones.

Sighing wearily, he stared at his plaid, which lay folded in a neat square on the bureau. He picked it up and buried his face in the soft, scratchy wool, breathing deeply of Prudence's fragrance before it became no more than a memory.

Prudence's hands trembled as she twisted the key in the lock. She pressed her forehead to the bedchamber door, gathering her courage to turn and face the painful sterility of her tent-bed. There it was, bolster tidily fluffed, edges of the counterpane tucked neatly around the mattress. It would never know the weight of a man, the shameless sprawling of blankets, the fragrant aroma of cheroot smoke and brandy. The bed was as neat and prim as a coffin.

Her knees, still weak from Sebastian's loving, faltered. She swung around and gripped the edge of her dressing table, coming face to face with her own reflection. Loose tendrils of hair spilled over her face, eerily dark against the white of her skin.

Tonight was the end. The end of everything.

The hollow tick of the clock on the mantel mocked her as a liar. Tonight was only the beginning. The interminable moments of Tricia's marriage stretched before her in a prison of minutes and years.

She might be able to bear it if Sebastian grew bored with her cool reticence. It would just confirm her worst suspicions—that she was only a diversion to him, a mild flirtation easily forgotten in another woman's willing arms. Would he seek out Devony or some other Northumberland County belle? He was a well-traveled man. Even now he might have a mistress lodged in London or Edinburgh.

But deep in her heart, she knew Sebastian would not relent. He would continue to batter her feeble defenses with his love. How many tender glances across the supper table would it take? How many teasing games of whist? How many harmless strolls around the garden? How many of his lazy, beautiful smiles before she surrendered and became his mistress, condemning their love to tawdry dust? He had already broken her heart. If they became what society deemed they must be, he would break her very soul.

She looked down to discover her fingernails had gouged an ugly scratch in the walnut dressing table. She gazed at her wild-eyed reflection, believing either herself or the mirror would shatter beneath the weight of her intolerable future. She could still scent Sebastian on her skin. She had been brought to the brink of something wondrous, only to be cheated of it by his ambition and her pride. She hugged herself, rocking back and forth. The pain was all jagged edges twisting in her gut. There wasn't enough laudanum in all the world to dull it.

Sebastian's pistol gleamed against the wood of her dressing table. She had forgotten to return it. The sleek barrel had been polished to a high sheen with utmost tenderness. No instrument of death should be so compelling, she thought, so flawlessly beautiful.

With a strange calm, she lifted the lid of her cherrywood box. The satin lining still held the recent indentation of her spectacles. She ran her fingers along the seam and the false bottom lifted easily. The leather pouch and slim rod lay nestled in the folds of velvet as they had on the day her papa had given them to her. Insurance for the future, he had called them.

As her fingers followed the familiar routine with method ical precision, she felt as if she were watching herself from a great distance. She tipped the pouch, filling the barrel of the pistol without spilling a speck of gunpowder. She tamped down the ball with the slender gold ramrod. It wasn't until the gun lay heavy across her palm, fully primed, that she began to shake. Unable to bear another tick of the clock in the stifling silence, she dragged on her wrapper, then unlocked and flung open the door.

Her fevered strides carried her down the stairs and through the ballroom. The chandelier was dark, and the long room was drenched in moonlight and shadow. A broken champagne glass lay overturned in a puddle of amber. With every step, a dark anger grew in her. She wished she could be there in the morning when Tricia's glib fiancé tried to explain why her dead niece was floating like Ophelia in the goldfish pool.

She stopped, dashing away a furious tear. Why should she shoot herself? She ought to shoot Sebastian. She wheeled around to pace the length of the ballroom. The tall pier-glass between two windows threw back the image of a harried Medea, startling among the pale, impassive marble gods.

God gave you a brain, child. Use it.

Papa. It had been Papa who had first sensed the reckless passions that lurked beneath her calm, Papa who had urged control, assuring her she could think her way out of any dilemma. But her brain was no match for this bitter agony, this unbearable longing for something she would never have. She stared down at the gun in her hand, knowing she could not use it.

She could not remain at Lindentree either, though. She refused to stand beneath that floral bower and watch while Sebastian burned their lives to ashes. She would go up-stairs, pack her trunk, and quietly take her leave on the next coach to London.

Her resolve was no comfort. She still wanted to smash something. She tore open the terrace doors. A gaudy scarlet mask skittered across the tiles, caught by the fingers of the wind.

The voice came out of the shadows, its clipped tones softened by empathy. "Where's your charming costume, Prudence? Did you feel compelled to return it to its rightful owner?"

She turned slowly, staring at nothing as the man reached over and gently pried Sebastian's pistol from her limp fin-gers.

The masquerade was done.

Sixteen

Jamie shimmied up the trellis. A mist of rain slickened the iron, and as he reached for the window sash, his foot slipped. He slid down, barking his knee on a crossbar. Grunting an oath, he started up again.

A muscled forearm clamped around his throat.

Jamie choked. His feet flailed at empty air. The night went gray before a veil of translucent black descended over his eyes. Heat filled his ears, roaring like the sea beating against distant cliffs. His hand fumbled at his stockings, fingers straining toward the hilt of his *skean dhu*. The forearm cut into his windpipe and the precious air fueling his hand was cut off abruptly.

The wet grass slammed up to meet him. Through the roar in his ears, he kept hearing the words, "He got to you, didn't he? Damn his black soul! He got to you. Answer me, damn you!"

Powerful hands gripped his shoulders. As his head bounced on the turf, Jamie was thankful the lawn had been softened by the day's dismal rain. He caught a bleary glimpse of handsome features contorted in rage, eyes darkened to murky accusation.

Fearing Sebastian might kill him before he could choke out an explanation, Jamie used the only weapon he had. He opened his mouth and emitted a keening shriek. Even in his rage, Sebastian winced. He was forced to stop shaking Jamie and clap a hand over his mouth before the entire household of Lindentree descended on their heads.

He lay on top of Jamie, stilling his squirming. "How much did the bastard offer you?"

Jamie mumbled a garbled answer. Sebastian lifted his hand so he could repeat it. "A thousand pounds."

Horrified wonder touched Sebastian's eyes. "Oh, my God. I know men who would kill their own mothers for fifty."

Jamie frantically clutched Sebastian's forearms. "Listen to me. I didn't come to kill the lass. I came to warn her. I tried to see her today, but all that fish-faced butler would tell me was that she was locked in her room with an achin' head."

Sebastian's eyes narrowed thoughtfully. That part of Jamie's story was true. His own repeated attempts to return Prudence's spectacles had met with icy silence from behind a locked door. At mid-morning, he had given them to a sneering Old Fish, concocting some story about finding them in the library.

Jamie stirred restlessly. "Ye're goin' to have some fancy explainin' to do when that fine lady of yers catches ye rollin' on the lawn with yer own coachman."

Sebastian freed him, and they both sat up, breathing hard.

Sebastian rubbed at a grass stain on his kilt, absently smearing it into the tartan. "He won't stop, will he?" he said. His voice was strangely distant. "Not even if I become king of all England. His precious appointment means more to him than her life. He means to see her dead."

Jamie shifted uneasily. "What are ye goin' to do?"

Sebastian pulled a pistol from his sash and checked the charge with cold efficiency. "Whatever I have to."

The wet grass felt suddenly cooler, and Jamie shivered.

Sebastian looked at him, really seeing him for the first time. He caught his elbow in a hard grip. "Be packed and ready to leave by the time I return." His eyes softened as he lifted his gaze to the shiny blank panes of Prudence's window. "Go to her. Tell her to pack light and be ready to ride."

Jamie's homely face split in a grin.

Sebastian stood, tucking the pistol back into his sash. "If I'm not back by midnight, take her and go without me. She won't be safe here. Trust no one but Tiny." He paused. "And tell her I love her."

"Aye, that I will. Let no one say ye can't count on Jamie Graham."

Sebastian gave his bony shoulder a brief touch, then he was gone, running low toward the stables. Jamie watched until he vanished into the mist, then turned to scale the wily trellis. His sense of purpose sharpened his reflexes, and he made it without mishap. Balancing on the top rung, he tapped at the window with his grimy nails. The room within was dark. When an even sharper knock earned no response, he shoved at the sash. The window was not latched. It slid up without a sound.

He flung his leg over the sill and climbed into the room. "Pru?" he whispered.

Silence greeted him. His eyes adjusted with the rapidity of someone who has spent much of his life working in the dark. A chill touched him. The room was empty.

Prudence's brush and mirror lay in symmetrical precision on the dressing table. The small tent-bed was neat and unrumpled. The room looked as if it had been unoccupied for a long time. Jamie nearly screamed when something hairy rubbed against his ankle.

He scooped up the little cat, bringing him to eye level. "I eats wee fellows like ye fer breakfast, ye know. I don't like 'em."

Sebastian-cat was not intimidated. He pawed his way onto Jamie's shoulder and nestled his nose in Jamie's matted hair.

Jamie surveyed the empty room, shaking his head. "I don't like this either. Not one wee bit."

Mist rose in ribbons from the cooling earth. Sebastian slapped the reins on the bay's neck, driving it through the dense forest with as much haste as he dared. A sheaf of wet leaves smacked his face, and cold water trickled down his neck into his shirt. He hugged the damp plaid tighter at his throat. The pistol in his sash lay heavily against his hip. He lowered his mask. Tonight the Dreadful Scot Bandit Kirkpatrick would make his last ride.

He dodged a glossy branch, his mind racing in time with the horse's hoofbeats. The time had come to end it with D'Artan. This was not as he would have chosen it, but the crafty old man had left him no choice. Without warning, Sebastian remembered his first glimpse of his grandfather.

Sunlight had poured through the iron-barred window of the filthy Jedburgh cell, shimmering off the gold brocade of D'Artan's frock coat. He had bent over Sebastian with a murmur of ruffles and lace. He smells like a woman, Sebastian had thought. D'Artan gripped his chin with two fingers, as if he did not care to dirty his hands. He tilted Sebastian's face to his with ease, for beneath the fragile, white skin of his fingers was steel. Sebastian's mouth tightened in a mutinous line to hide his fear. They were going to hang him. He had heard the guards laughing about the infamous Jedburgh law—execute the criminal first, try him afterward.

A deeper fear touched him when he met the old man's gaze. "My Michelline's eyes. My daughter gave you her eyes."

His mother's name spoken in his mother's language.

Sebastian had heard no French since she had died. The melodic notes poured over him like honey. It wasn't until much later that he discovered the honey was tainted, like everything else about his grandfather.

D'Artan had introduced him to all that was civilization—a heady, bittersweet seduction. The memories rushed back over Sebastian. Sinking up to his chin in his first hot bath. Smoking his first cigar. The dark, bitter taste of cognac on his tongue. His first woman. Lisette had been so clean and had smelled so sweet, he had believed she must be a princess. Only after he'd killed a man on the dueling field defending her honor did he discover she was a whore, a mere travesty of what she pretended to be—an empty mask, like everything else D'Artan had given him.

After the first woman came the polished elegance of his first set of pistols and their return to Scotland. His task was simple enough. Rob the English. Fill his grandfather's coffers with enough gold to ship gunpowder and weapons to the revolutionists in France. Sebastian was but one tiny fly buzzing along the Scottish border, drawing England's attention away from France and the impending revolution. D'Artan found his career of highway robbery to be a colossal joke on the English. The old man lived for the imminent day of war with Great Britain.

After the revolution, D'Artan's web of intrigue slipped like a rope around Sebastian's neck. Always in front of him, like a carrot on a stick, dangled the hope of returning to the Highlands, of winning Dunkirk back from MacKay. But the harder he strained, the more the rope tightened.

Sebastian guided the horse through a ravine, where the rain had swollen a trickle to a shallow, rushing burn. He emerged on a narrow path and dared to kick the horse into a canter. Chunks of mud flew from the bay's hooves. The moon peeped through the rushing clouds, slanting its beams across the thinning trees.

The wash of light tipped the wet leaves with silver. Once Sebastian would have cursed the rain. Now he inhaled deeply, savoring a fragrance as clean and fresh as Prudence. His pulse quickened at the thought of holding her again. He would bring her to a place like this. He would lay her down on some misty hillside and let the forgiving rain wash over their skin. Then they would go and he would build her a house. Not a drafty old castle perched on the edge of nowhere, but handsome cottage nestled beside the sky-blue waters of a loch. On sunny days they would sit outside and watch their children tumbling in the grass.

To hell with Dunkirk and MacKay.

A shadow blurred the moonlight. He caught the faint hint of movement from the corner of his eye. It could have been a bat flitting through the trees or a leaf twirling to an early death, but Sebastian's instincts were honed to razor precision. He dug his heels into the bay's flanks as the underbrush exploded in a flurry of silvery droplets and heaving horseflesh. Three dark shapes hurtled after him.

Sebastian bent low over his horse's neck. Her coarse mane whipped tears into his eyes as he careened down the narrow path.

D'Artan.

Rage blurred his vision. Once again, the old man had beat him to the ambush. Was he so damned predictable? He jerked a pistol out of his sash, cocked the hammer, and twisted around to fire.

The rope strung across the road caught him neatly across the chest. His weapon exploded with a shattering roar, imprinting an arc of light on his pupils. He sailed from the horse, his flight ending with the dull thud of a rock striking the back of his head.

Mud cradled him. A twig poked his thigh. He must not be dead, he thought. But his limbs were sprawled in an uncooperative puddle. His bad ankle throbbed. He lay there, helpless to stop the mist swirling around him from creeping into his head. A comfortable languor claimed him. Clouds rushed across the pallid moon as he waited for one of D'Artan's men to blow off his head.

A horse nickered as a pair of boots hit the ground. The moon swooped down toward him. Sebastian blinked, bringing into focus a pleasant face crinkled in a mask of concern.

"Terribly sorry, old chap." Long aristocratic fingers probed the back of his head, then reappeared smeared with blood. "I'm afraid you're going to have the very devil of a headache in the morning."

"Tugbert," Sebastian whispered.

His lashes fluttered down, ushering in the merciful oblivion carried by the cool fingers of mist.

Seventeen

Sebastian's ankle ached as he was led from the damp cell. The rope binding his hands behind his back chafed the raw skin. His jaw itched. He longed to claw at the first prick of stubble, and thought with dull amusement how civilized he had become that it should bother him. His mouth tasted like he'd been chewing rusty nails and his throbbing head felt stuffed with cotton batting.

As they reached the slat of light at the end of the slim corridor, Tugbert gave him an unmistakable shove. Sebastian stumbled and whirled around, his dubious patience at an end. His fierce glare was enough to make Tugbert step backward, rope or no rope.

Then the sheriff's eyes lit with smirking amusement on something behind him.

Sebastian turned slowly. Its emptiness made the small, dusty room seem larger than it was. A watery dawn seeped through the window. For a long moment, the only sound was the hiss and sputter of a tallow candle drowning in its own fat.

Sebastian sucked in an audible breath as the niggling suspicion he had shoved to the back of his aching head hardened to icy certainty.

Prudence sat in a rustic, cane-backed chair, as prim and proper as if she perched on a Hepplewhite chair in some

Edinburgh tea room. Her posture was perfect, her gloved hands folded demurely in her lap. A lavender dress of watered silk set off her fair skin to perfection. Her hair was caught in a chignon and molded to the delicate bones of her head in a shiny cap. Not one wisp was out of place.

She lifted her head. Light reflected off the glass of her spectacles, erasing her eyes. He started to shake.

His harsh laughter grated in the silence. "I was a fool to trust you, wasn't I?"

"You left me no choice." Her voice was calm, resolute.

"You swore."

"I did not break my oath. I told Tricia nothing."

He smiled nastily. "Of course you didn't break your oath. You're a respectable woman."

Without warning, he lunged for her, not sure himself what he might do if he reached her.

Tugbert wrapped both arms around him and jerked him back.

Prudence lifted a white-gloved hand. Despite her steady voice, that hand trembled. "Arlo, please. It's all right. You may let him go."

"I hardly think that would be the wisest—"

Sebastian twisted away from him. "You heard Miss Walker, *Arlo*. I can hardly strangle the lady with my hands bound."

The sheriff stepped back to lean against the wall by the door, his arms crossed, his eyes wary. Sebastian paced the room, stretching his legs.

"Why, Prudence?"

She took a deep breath. "It would have been wrong for you to marry Tricia. You don't love her."

He kicked a stool. It bounced off the wall and splintered. Then he turned on her, his fury erupting. "Are you so desperate for a man that you'll even take one at the end of a rope?"

Tugbert tensed. Prudence bowed her head. A barely perceptible blush crept up the luscious curve of her neck.

"I couldn't let you marry her," she said. "Don't you see? It would have destroyed us all in the end."

"So you'd rather see me dead?"

She shook her head. "You're not to be hanged. You're not even to be brought to trial."

Sarcasm thickened his burr. "How did you manage that? Offer your bookkeeping services to the King?"

She glanced at Tugbert. Sebastian's gaze traveled between the two of them, then his mouth quirked, his smile a weapon of unmistakable contempt.

"So the two of you have everything worked out. How cozy! Perhaps you can name your first brat after me."

Tugbert stepped forward. "If you only knew to what depths your chicanery has driven this good young woman—"

"Arlo! You promised." A note of panic touched Prudence's voice. Sebastian caught a glimpse of something beneath her cool expression—something fearful and passionate.

"If I weren't a gentleman . . ." Tugbert let the words hang in the air. His ashen hair was caught in a neat queue at the nape of his neck. Without his wig, he didn't look nearly so foppish. "You are to leave Northumberland, Kerr, and return to the Highlands. If I catch you anywhere near the English border again, I *will* hang you." He paused. "With pleasure."

Sebastian walked over to the window to stare blindly at the rust that had flaked off the iron bars and fallen to the windowsill.

After a moment he spoke to Tugbert, but he slanted a dangerous look at Prudence. "Give me a moment alone with her."

"I'd say not, sir. If you think I'm mad enough to—"

"Do as he says." Prudence's voice held a quiet note of command. "Please."

Tugbert sputtered indignantly. "Very well, then. I'll be outside the door. *Right* outside the door."

Sebastian watched him go, darkly amused. "You've got him dancing like a marionette. Tricia would be proud of you."

He came to stand directly in front of her. She fidgeted with her soft kid gloves.

"Look at me."

She reluctantly lifted her head.

"I said look at me," he repeated, the terse request more effective than a roar.

She paused for a moment, then drew off her spectacles and

slipped them into her pocket. She tilted her head back and studied him through the thick fringe of lashes.

His jaw tightened. "Do you think you'll forget, Prudence? When you're lying alone these cold winter nights to come, do you think you'll forget the way I kissed you, the way I touched you?"

When she would have lowered her eyes, he squatted in front of her. She turned her face away.

"You won't forget me. I swear it. I'll haunt you for the rest of your lonely, miserable life. Even if you marry Tugbert and he comes to your bed blushing in his long nightshirt, who do you think you'll see when you close your eyes? It won't be him. It will be me."

"Stop it! You don't understand."

His mouth curved in a shadow of his tender smile. "I understand one thing. I was a fool to let you out of my bed. You night have thought twice about betraying the father of your babe." He leaned toward her, putting his mouth next to her ear. "Stay out of my way, Prudence Walker. I won't make the same mistake again. I promise you that."

He stalked to the wall, refusing to look at her. She rose, her spine poker-straight. Her legs did not falter until she reached the door. He turned around and for a maddening instant, he thought she would crumple. He could not have caught her if she had. She recovered, though, swaying briefly. The haunting fragrance of honeysuckle tickled his nostrils as she brushed past him.

Sebastian pressed his eyes shut, determined that Tugbert would not see him cry.

Prudence walked past Arlo without seeing him. Something in her face kept him from stopping her. She gathered her skirts in her gloved hands and started down the muddy road toward Lindentree.

The warm wind burned her dry eyes. On the eastern horizon, streaks of peach shot through the muted gray. It promised to be a beautiful day—a fine day for a wedding. Her toe caught in a rut. She did not look back at the jail to check if anyone had seen her stumble, but hastened her steps instead. She must get back to Lindentree. She was needed there, for she would have to deal with her aunt's vapors when Tricia discovered her bridegroom had fled. Tricia relied on her. She must be strong. She could not afford to succumb to her own hysterics.

A needle of pain jabbed her head. Her fingers flew to her temples.

Do stop grimacing, dear. You're not getting any younger. Tricia's echoing clucks drowned out the nearby shriek of a jay.

Prudence dropped her skirts and broke into a run.

The first thing ye're goin' to have to do is learn how to fight dirty. Sebastian ain't never known no other way.

Jamie would be long gone by now. Sebastian would not return from his midnight ride, and Jamie was too bright not to realize something was drastically wrong. Mud spattered her skirts as she dragged her hem heedlessly through a puddle.

You won't forget me. Sebastian's voice thundered unbidden through her skull. *I swear it. I'll haunt you for the rest of your lonely, miserable life.*

She clawed at her hair, tearing out the hairpins in a vain attempt to stop the pain. Her hair streamed across her face, and the only reality became the thud of one foot in front of the other and the harsh rasp of her breathing.

She skirted the gatehouse and fled across the lawn, ignoring the curious stares of the sleepy peacocks. She crushed her skull between her palms, desperate to silence the accusing cabal of voices screeching through her mind. Her feet slipped on the slick grass and she fell to her stomach. Her thigh crunched against the spectacles in her pocket.

She lay for a long time, eyes squeezed shut, fingers tearing up tufts of damp earth. If she had stayed in the jail for one more minute, she would have been on her knees at Sebastian's feet, begging him to understand, pleading with him to take her away with him.

"Oh, Sebastian, why did you make me do it?" she whispered. "I hate you."

But as she baptized the grass with her bitter tears, she

would have given her dying breath to have his arms around her one last time.

Prudence dragged her fingers through the water of the fountain, parting the dead fronds, then watching them float together again. Leaves drifted from the trees in languid blobs of russet and yellow. To her, the garden was a pleasant blur. Her wrecked spectacles lay on her dressing table. Her new pair had not yet arrived from London. She did not care. The world looked better without them.

A cool rush of October wind caught the leaves in a spinning dervish before scattering them across the terrace. She pulled her shawl tighter and strolled past a leering Apollo. His scant drapes fell across the exaggerated masculinity of his marbled form. A fat, hairy spider strung a web between his knees.

Prudence shivered, unable to banish the spooky vision of her and Tricia growing old alone there, strolling arm in arm through the garden until cobwebs festooned their graying hair.

Tricia appeared like a ghost in the doorway. "There's a man here to see you," she said in a thick voice.

To Prudence's genuine dismay, her aunt had taken the disappearance of her handsome fiancé harder than the timely deaths of her seven previous husbands. Tricia's eyes were rimmed with red, her nose shiny, and her wig crooked and ratty-looking. Was it Prudence's own guilty imagination or did wounded accusation burn in her aunt's eyes?

"If it's the viscount again," she said, "tell him he may call tomorrow. If it's Sir Arlo, tell him I'm still ill."

She had no desire to discuss chemistry with the persistent Frenchman. And Sir Arlo, through no fault of his own, only reminded her of the grim path she had almost taken in the darkest moment of her life.

"It is the viscount," Tricia said, "but he's brought a man who says he has business with you."

Prudence frowned. "With me? Who would have business with me?"

"How should I know? I told him I was mistress of Lindentree, but he insists on seeing you." She sniffed. "He's a bit pompous, if I do say so myself."

Prudence followed Tricia reluctantly. After the fresh autumn wind, the house felt stale and closed. For weeks now, Prudence could hardly bear to be indoors. The house was an empty shell. She could not turn a corner without expecting to hear a warm, masculine burst of laughter or the jaunty click of a cane on the parquet floor. As Tricia followed the corridor to the parlor, Prudence breathed a sigh of thanks that her aunt had not put the guests in the library. Prudence had been there only once in the last two months. The lingering fragrance of cheroot smoke had driven her out into the garden, biting back tears.

D'Artan and his companion rose as they entered the parlor. The stranger would have looked comfortable in a drawing room a century ago. Lace erupted from the sleeves and collar of his frock coat, and powder flew from his elaborate wig as he bent over Prudence's hand with a courtly bow.

"Miss Walker, I presume?"

Prudence pinched back a sneeze before he could straighten. "I am."

The viscount gave Tricia a pointed look. A hint of her old pout touched her lips as she trotted obediently from the parlor. The tip-tap of her slippers paused right outside the door.

D'Artan lifted Prudence's hand to his lips. "Lovely as always."

As his companion plopped back down in a Sheraton chair, the delicate legs teetered dangerously. D'Artan introduced him, but Prudence was too interested in seeing if the dainty chair would hold his ample frame to give her full attention to his name. She wasn't sure if it was Lord Pettiwiggle or Periwinkle. D'Artan sank onto the settee, beaming like a satisfied cat.

The other man snapped open a silver snuffbox and tucked a wad up his nose. D'Artan took a pinch, and Prudence thought for moment the man might offer her some, but he checked the gesture. The box disappeared into the voluminous folds of his coat.

The chair creaked as he settled back. "I am here on behalf of George III, King of England." His voice boomed as if he had spent his entire life saying important things.

"The King?" she repeated. "What business could the King possibly have with me?"

"A petition your father filed has recently come to the King's attention."

Before she could stop it, an unladylike snort escaped her. "It's a bit late, wouldn't you think? My father has been dead for almost eight years."

D'Artan leaned forward, crossing his satin-clad legs. "As I'm sure you know, my dear, the King was indisposed for quite some time."

Mad as a March hare, she thought uncharitably.

"We attempted to locate your father as soon as the King reviewed his petition." Lord Pettiwiggle-Periwinkle shook his head sadly. "A regrettable and tragic circumstance. We tracked you to your London lodgings only to discover you'd gone. The missives we sent to Lindentree received no response."

"But I never—"

He continued in his chiding tones as if she hadn't spoken. What he had to say was obviously more important than anything she might add. "One of our agents was dispatched here a few months ago, only to be informed by a rather churlish creature that you had emigrated to Pomerania where you later died. My agent was forced to flee the grounds of the estate when this *enfant terrible* began to fire arrows at his coach. When our inquiries in Pomerania yielded nothing—"

Jamie. Prudence stared into her lap, biting back a smile. A rush of nostalgia blurred her vision.

"—I decided to investigate the matter myself. The King is very dismayed by the length of time that has passed. He and the Prime Minister have taken extraordinary measures to rectify their part in the sad affair."

He patted his coat and pulled forth a creamy envelope. Prudence recognized the Royal Seal and sat back in her chair, bracing herself for a lengthy and boring formal condolence.

"The King has little doubt that your father did outstanding scientific work and would have been of great benefit to the crown had he lived."

She murmured an agreement.

His throat rumbled. "So it is with great pleasure and approval of the King that I wish to confer upon you, Miss Prudence Walker, the only direct descendant of Livingston Walker, this patent of nobility. You are henceforth to be known as the first created Duchess of Winton."

A shocked squeak from the other side of the door was quickly muffled.

The man continued. "Your aunt's dear friend, the viscount, recently managed to convince the King that the title was worth little more than paper without some monetary compensation."

D'Artan reached over and patted Prudence's hand. She was too dumbfounded to protest.

"As I'm sure he has told you," the man continued, "the viscount pursues interests similar to your own from his laboratory in Edinburgh. The King believes an exchange of information between the two of you regarding your father's fulminic research would benefit all of England. So for this service to the crown, he has decided to gift you with an annual pension of ten thousand pounds."

Prudence sat as if frozen. "Am I to understand," she asked in a very quiet voice, "that I am now a duchess?"

Before the man could reply, D'Artan said smoothly, "A duchess of moderate wealth, my dear." With great ceremony, he dropped to one knee and folded her fingers in his cool hand. "Your Grace."

Tricia couldn't resist poking her head around the door as she heard a sound she hadn't heard in over two months—the rich, velvety notes of Prudence's laughter. Prudence rocked back in her chair, clapping her hand over her mouth. Both D'Artan and Lord Pettiwiggle-Periwinkle were staring at her as if she'd gone as mad as old King George. But she could no more stop her wild peals of laughter than she could stop the tears streaming down her face.

Part Two

Wi' lightsome heart I pu'd a rose
Frae aff its thorny tree,
And my fause luver staw my rose,
But left the thorn wi' me.
                    Robert Burns
                    1791

Eighteen

Edinburgh, Scotland
1792

The Duchess of Winton stood at the mullioned window, watching the rain stream down the sparkling panes. Tendrils of steam curled from the tiny glass in her hand and warmth wafted out from the marble hearth, but still she shivered. The cold crept up from deep within her. She took a sip of the heated liqueur. It slid down her throat, as dark and bitter a comfort as the night outside the window.

Street lamps cast misty halos of light over the glistening cobblestones of Charlotte Square. The teeming streets of Old Edinburgh might have been a galaxy away from this elegant symmetry of park and avenues christened New Edinburgh. Wrought iron gates and snarling stone lions guarded the neat rows of brick town houses. Across the park, the lights from other mansions winked like distant stars. A shiny carriage clip-clopped past. A man in a woolen greatcoat bustled down the walk, his shoulders hunched against the icy rain. Prudence wondered if Sebastian was out there somewhere, cold and wet and alone.

She closed her eyes, battered by the memory of a stormy night when she and Sebastian had clung to each other in a haze of mud and rain and fear. She would trade all of her warm comforts for a chance to go back to that damp, dusty crofter's hut and begin again. It was too easy to imagine Sebastian safe in this cozy drawing room—leaning against the pianoforte with negligent grace; clinging to Tricia's arm with those long, elegant fingers, the paragon of a doting husband while he winked at Devony.

Prudence's eyes flew open. Her lips tightened. Sebastian had made his choices. And she had made hers. A stranger's eyes glittered back at her from the darkened pane.

Who was the elegantly coiffed woman in the window? she wondered. In a room humming and twirling with laughing people, Prudence felt utterly alone with the woman she had chosen to become. She had swathed herself in armor of lace and silk, as soft as velvet and as hard as steel, burying the awkward, wistful girl who had dared to offer her heart to Sebastian Kerr. Her skin was porcelain, her heart ice, and no one would know or care if her own brittle laugh shattered her into a thousand pieces.

A raindrop skittered down the window, wavering like an errant tear past her cheek. She touched her finger to the cool glass.

A breathy whisper interrupted her reverie. "Lovely creature, isn't she? Wherever did she come from?"

"Tricia had her tucked away in the country," another female voice answered. "Lady Galt swears she's a Hapsburg princess. Her aunt was once married to one of their princes, you know."

"Tricia de Peyrelongue has been married to nearly everyone," a third woman said. "This one's in no haste to follow her lead. She's received three proposals since Christmas and turned down every one. Much to her aunt's chagrin, I might add. Tricia threw quite a tantrum after the last one. Perhaps the girl's holding out for a prince herself."

"A bit thin for my tastes. I've never seen her eat. You'd think she'd wear a bustle."

Prudence stiffened. After three months in Edinburgh society, she should have grown accustomed to the murmurs and stares, but they still unnerved her.

The brittle tinkle of champagne glasses was followed by a new whisper, this one low and masculine. "After she dared to debate him on the morality of his poetry, even Burns is besotted with her. And they say old Romney offered to paint her. For nothing."

"For nothing? Or with nothing on? She might be his next Emma Hart."

The ripples of laughter ceased as Prudence swung away from the window alcove. She lifted to her eyes her gold spectacles, which hung from a chain around her neck, and favored them with the glacial stare that had earned her the sobriquet "the Duchess of Winter." She noted with dull amusement that two of the women were wearing identical pairs of spectacles. Spectacles fitted with plain glass had become all the rage since "the mysterious young duchess" had made her Edinburgh debut. Their blind emulation both repelled and fascinated Prudence.

Beneath her challenging gaze, the women drifted away, leaving the musk of their perfumes lingering on the air. The plump hips of the girl who had pronounced her too thin swayed beneath her skirts. Prudence suspected she wasn't wearing a bustle either.

Their companion, a sheepish young man with long, unkempt hair, murmured a pardon and attempted to slip away. She crooked a slender finger at him.

He bobbed an awkward bow, raking a hand through his curls. "Your Grace?"

"Lord Desmond—Ned. It is Ned, isn't it?"

He looked absurdly pleased that she had remembered. Prudence squelched a flicker of shame.

"Ned it is, at your service, my lady. What can I do for you?"

She considered asking him to stand on his head and balance a wineglass with his toes, but the cruel impulse passed. She lay her fingers on his crisp linen sleeve. "I wish to discuss a certain wager I overheard last night between yourself and a young Mr. Cotton."

Lord Desmond colored prettily. "Cotton's a rapscallion and a commoner. Pay him no mind." He disowned his previous night's companions by glowering at the circle of gentlemen leaning lazily against the chimneypiece. They lifted their glasses with comical precision, pretending not to be watching.

Prudence led him away from the sheltered gloom of the window and into the fountain of light that poured from the candles of the chandelier, shimmering off the peach damask walls.

"You were discussing," she said, "which of you might first discover the source of my patent of nobility. Mr. Cotton suggested I could have performed some covert service for the King, such as shoving him out of the way of an assassin. You alleged that I might have performed a different sort of service for our liege."

"But I wouldn't . . . I never . . . I swear I didn't mean . . ."

Prudence would have sworn his arm grew warmer beneath his sleeve, and she pursed her lips in a studious frown. "You then went on to wager with Mr. Cotton the corpulent sum of one hundred pounds that you might be the first to elicit a smile from me tonight."

They had reached the hearth. The young men straightened, tugging at their cravats in preening abandon. The freckled Mr. Cotton fidgeted with an ivory snuffbox.

Prudence released her fawning captive. "I'm sorry, Lord Desmond, but you owe your friend a hundred pounds."

With those words, she dipped her slender shoulders in a curtsy and favored the gaping Mr. Cotton with a luminous smile. She knew—since she had been told—that her smile softened her features without dispelling the faint air of melancholy these child-men seemed to find so irresistible. As she turned to leave them, Ned groaned and Mr. Cotton whooped with triumph, slapping him on the back. Prudence lifted her skirts and slipped away, feeling the heat of their adoring gazes against her bared shoulders. A heady elation swept her at her power over them.

Sebastian had laid that power in her hands and left it there like a loaded pistol, primed for a touch that would never come.

Her smiled faded, her complicity in their silly games leaving a bitter taste in her mouth. The more practical part of her found their attentions ridiculous. But if they chose to mistake her sarcasm for wit and her melancholy for sophistication, who was she to enlighten them? At least she didn't have to pretend to be stupid. The neglected little girl within her basked in the fickle heat of their admiration.

She drifted through the dancers, her silk stockings whispering against her calves. The wistful notes of a Bach cantata spilled from the pianoforte. She plucked another liqueur from a maid's tray and downed it in one swallow, as if its warmth could thaw the icy claw tightening around her heart. It was nearing February, but it seemed as if the spring would never come.

She set her empty glass on a pier-table, longing for escape. But from across the crowded drawing room, Tricia's waving fan stopped her. Glancing at her aunt's elaborate gown, Prudence nearly smiled. Tricia's only concession to the simpler fashions inspired by the revolution in France was narrower panniers. She no longer had to turn sideways to enter a room.

She saw two men flanking Tricia, and sighed. Not another plump elderly count, she prayed. Since Prudence's unconventional inheritance, Tricia had renewed her old campaign to see her niece wed. Not only was Prudence stealing all of her attention, she had committed the unforgivable transgression of outranking Tricia in the nobility.

The Viscount D'Artan hovered near Tricia's elbow. It had been he who had arranged for their invitation to stay at the Campbells' town house. He had been their constant companion since their arrival, helping Tricia query solicitors about her missing fiancé and even tolerating Boris and the Blakes as Tricia's chosen traveling companions.

Prudence banished a shiver as she wove through the crowd. Both in the laboratory and out of it, the elderly viscount was as considerate of her feelings as a father. He had been painfully patient with her, even when she refused to reveal the exact formula that had killed her father until their research was more conclusive. But Prudence could not abolish the sense of desolation she felt each time she saw D'Artan. The viscount had come into her life and Sebastian had gone. That was her own doing, though, she reminded herself. Blaming it on the viscount would not change what she'd done. Nothing would ever change what she'd done. A garrote of pain squeezed her frozen heart.

D'Artan's attention was not on her now. His brows were knit into a silvery line as he glowered at the man next to Tricia.

Prudence caught her breath with an odd ache at the sight of him. A black and green belted plaid was draped over his broad shoulders. His beringed hand rested proudly on the hilt of his claymore. A leather sporran hung at his waist.

Tricia clung to the fall of ruffles at his wrist. "I must confess the Scottish sense of humor eludes me," she was saying as Prudence approached. "The horrid solicitor we approached yesterday did all but tell me my fiancé was but a figment of my demented imagination."

"Not an apparition, my lady, but perhaps only a scoundrel." The Scot's gruff voice was touched with a musical burr, not yet obliterated by the stilted English of Edinburgh society.

Prudence listened hungrily as he continued.

"As difficult as it may be to consider, there are men who would prey on a woman of your beauty."

And wealth, Prudence added silently. The man was as tactful as he was charming.

Tricia sniffled. A pair of handkerchiefs appeared. She took the lace-trimmed one the Scot wielded and dabbed at a sparkling tear. "I simply cannot accept that. My fiancé adored me. He must have been abducted. He would have never left me willingly."

Prudence slipped into their midst and gently touched Tricia's elbow. "We've received no ransom demands, Auntie. You promised to go on with your life if we did not find him here."

Tricia swatted her hand away. "That's easy enough for you to say. You didn't lose the man you loved."

Prudence inclined her head as heat rose to her cheeks. She remembered too vividly the night she had gone to Sebastian's room, the tender things he had said to her, the ways he had touched her. Shame and regret mingled, but always with it came the image of their bodies entwined on the satin counterpane.

Tricia's trembling lips curved in a brave smile. "Forgive me, won't you?" she said to the kilted stranger. "I had only hoped that, hailing from the Highlands, you would have some knowledge of the Laird of Dunkirk."

The man drained his glass of whisky in a single swig. "Aye, that I do, Lady Tricia. I am the Laird of Dunkirk and have been for nigh on fifteen years."

Prudence's dark musings were shattered as she lifted her gaze to meet the twinkling eyes of Killian MacKay.

A man slipped through the shadows of the garden wall, his gaze riveted to the glowing squares of light set deep in the mellow brick. Rain poured off the brim of his hat. He gave the signal, and five dark shapes vaulted over the wall. Somewhere in the back of the mansion, a door opened and the rich, brilliant notes of a viola poured into the garden.

"Ain't these fancy folk ever heard of bagpipes?" a voice muttered in his ear. "We're in Scotland for God's sake, not Paris."

"Quiet," Sebastian snapped. "We're going to be in the jail if you don't hold your tongue."

"It weren't my idea to come to Edinburgh."

"Would you rather we starve to death in the Highlands?" Sebastian adjusted the sack over Jamie's head with a jerk. "We've robbed every kirk there but your own father's."

Jamie sniffed, his annoyance muffled by a layer of burlap. "I was all fer it. Ye were the one who backed out."

"I'd rather rob my grandfather than your father. He's the one who's frozen all of my accounts at the Royal Bank. If I can get to my money, we can hole up in the Highlands until the spring."

"But if he spots ye first, ye won't be needin' the Highlands, will ye? Ye'll be in jail or hell, wherever he chooses to send ye."

Slush spattered as Tiny landed behind them. "If the two of ye are goin' to argue all night, we may as well trot around and tap on the front door. Maybe the butler'll let us in."

Jamie plucked a flask from Tiny's belt, shoved up his mask, and took a long swig. "Aaah! Nothing like stout Scotch whisky to thaw a man. All me best parts are frozen."

Tiny snorted. "No great loss fer the Edinburgh whores."

"That's yer opinion, not theirs," Jamie retorted.

At a snort of laughter from one of their cohorts, Sebastian swung around and hissed him into silence. With pistol drawn, he led them around the side of the house, pausing only to untangle his breeches from a dormant rosebush. The lit squares of the casement-windows gave him a shimmering glimpse of a world of satins and silks. It was a world that would never willingly give anything to the impoverished son of a Highland laird.

Sebastian had learned that lesson anew in the last few months. Bathing in icy streams. Shivering all night in ratty blankets. Eating dried meat so tough he had to chew it for hours just to taste it.

The dashing highwayman was gone, leaving only a silk mask and a tartan rag crumpled in his pocket as an epitaph. In his place was a common thief and a hungry man. What Sebastian Kerr wanted, Sebastian Kerr would have to take. Prudence Walker had taught him that much. He could afford to yield to his crueler impulses now, all because a woman had left him with nothing to lose but his freedom . . . and his life.

His numb fingers curled around the butt of his pistol. Beneath the burlap mask, he smiled coldly.

As Prudence stared up at Killian MacKay, the color drained from her cheeks as rapidly as it had come. Tricia's surprised protests faded to a sonorous buzz.

No villainous hunchback was this man, but a tall gentleman with a thick mane of white hair. Deep crannies scarred his leathery brow, but his shoulders were unbent and surprisingly broad for a man his age. She lowered her eyes before he could glimpse her shock. Her gaze was drawn to the white hairs scattered across his heavy plaid—not his own, but long, fluffy cat hairs. Could this truly be the heartless ogre who had cast Sebastian from his home?

"So you've never heard of a man who calls himself Sebastian Kerr?" D'Artan's voice brought Prudence abruptly back to the conversation. A faint sneer twisted the viscount's lips.

A silvery tension arced between the two men as MacKay hesitated for the briefest moment. "Never," he said.

Prudence pushed her spectacles up on the bridge of her nose. As Killian MacKay met her cool, challenging stare, they both knew he was lying. But they also knew that unless Prudence cared to explain why she colored each time her aunt's fiancé was mentioned, she would hold her silence.

Tricia gaped as Prudence slipped her hand in the crook of MacKay's arm and smiled up at him. "Perhaps we should give my aunt time to recover from such a shock. Have you visited the Campbells' library? It's quite extensive. Would you care for a tour?"

"I would love to." MacKay brought Tricia's limp hand to his lips, then bowed to D'Artan, his smile mocking. "Viscount, always a pleasure."

D'Artan's eyes narrowed to silvery slits as the warm crush of the drawing room parted before the striking pair.

The lamps in the library were unlit, though a crackling fire wafted the warm aroma of cedar into the air. Windows shiny with rain ringed dark walls of polished walnut.

Prudence's satin petticoat bustled about her as she sat on a narrow settee and arranged the skirts of her cranberry gown with meticulous care. MacKay sank into a wing-backed leather chair opposite her. For a long moment they studied each other in silence.

As a young man, MacKay had prided himself on a knowledge of feminine fashion. The girl did justice to the softer, more natural styles sweeping London and Edinburgh. It would have been as much of a crime to bury her flawless skin beneath a layer of ceruse as to hide her hair under a wig. The dark mass had been swept upward and arranged in heavy coils at her throat. A wide sash matched the pink satin of her petticoat and emphasized her slender waist. Her prim demeanor might have been comical on another woman, but her dignity rendered it oddly touching. MacKay wished he was past the age where being alone in such warm, dark intimacy with a lovely woman would stir him.

Prudence pushed up her spectacles in a gesture that she knew betrayed her tension, wondering what had possessed her to indulge this mad fancy. "Forgive me for being so blunt,

Laird MacKay, but I have been seeking a small bit of property in the north of Scotland. This castle you call Dunkirk— might it be for sale?"

MacKay sat up in his chair. The lass was betraying more than simple nervousness. No one in the drawing room had called him by name. "Dunkirk is little more than a crumbling ruin. 'Tis virtually worthless."

"Then it would not burden you to be rid of it."

He rose and walked over to the fireplace, as if seeking a warmth far removed from her cool stare. In his squared jaw, Prudence caught a glimpse of the stubborn patience that had let him wait sixteen years before taking revenge against the man who had stolen his bride. Her heart gave an odd thump at the sight of his broad shoulders silhouetted against the firelight.

"Dunkirk is not for sale," he said.

She couldn't help the note of pleading that touched her voice. "You are a wealthy man. I know you own most of Strathnaver. What value could an old ruin have for a man such as you?"

He gazed into the flames. "A sentimental value. A woman I cared for once lived there."

And died there? The words resounded clearly through Prudence's mind. For one terrible moment, she thought she had said them aloud.

When MacKay turned to face her, though, there was no fury or bitter rebuke in his eyes, only a gentle sadness. "I'm sorry I cannot oblige your wishes, my dear. But, you see, Dunkirk is not truly mine to sell. I am keeping it in trust for someone else."

The plaintive strains of an oboe drifted into the room. The music was both dark and unbearably sweet, an alien counterpart to the steady patter of the rain against the windows.

Prudence stood. "Forgive me, Laird MacKay. You're absolutely right. I cannot ask you to sell what never belonged to you."

With a mocking curtsy, she left him standing before the hearth. MacKay's hands trembled as he reached for the back of the chair. In the barren years since Michelline's death, Killian MacKay had prayed often for forgiveness. But it seemed that God had seen fit to send not a spirit of compassion, but an avenging angel with violet eyes and a whisky voice. His gnarled fingers bit into the sleek leather as he bent his head in silent prayer, asking not for mercy, but for courage.

Sebastian drew back his pistol and rammed the butt through the fragile glass.

With a practiced twist of his wrist, he unlocked the tall double windows. He was inside before the musicians could falter to a discordant halt.

A shrill scream threw the gathering into dead silence as six faceless, hulking blobs spilled into the room.

"Weapons on the floor, gentlemen," Sebastian called out, his voice disguised with a rasp made all the more convincing by his raw throat.

His command yielded only one pistol, a handful of canes, and an umbrella. A blue-haired lady crumpled in her husband's arms.

"We'd like a more substantial donation now," he said. "All jewelry, gold, and money into the sacks, please. . . . Very nicely done. Aye, that'll do very well, thank you," he added as the jingle of fob watches and gold chains filled the tense silence.

His men operated as he had taught them, moving with sacks open from one group to the next, never making eye contact and never breaking silence. It took Sebastian only a quick perusal to determine D'Artan was not there. Bitter disappointment welled in his throat.

The tantalizing aroma of warm pastries drifted to his nose. He carefully kept his gaze averted from a silver tea cart heaped with cakes. His belly felt as if it were touching his spine. His mouth watered. His stomach rumbled. If he ate one cake, he'd end up on his knees before them all, stuffing cakes into his mouth like the ravenous beast all these fine people undoubtedly thought him to be.

A young man with untidy hair hesitated to remove his heirloom ring. Sebastian jerked his pistol in an unmistakable gesture of threat. The freckled young man beside him nudged him into compliance, tossing into the sack himself an ivory snuffbox and a fat purse, which landed on the pile with a musical clink. Sebastian felt an unwelcome flash of empathy at the impotent fury reflected in the freckled man's brown eyes. He sincerely hoped he wouldn't be forced to shoot either of them before the night was done.

His gaze strayed again to the cakes. Six months ago he would have been a guest at such a gathering, sipping champagne and nibbling a sweet crumbling cake. A fist of memory buried itself in his gut—tracing Prudence's lips with the tip of his finger, the sweetness of her icing melting on his tongue. But that had been another world and another man. A man who had been foolish enough to let a pair of treacherous amethyst eyes besot him.

A shadow stirred on the landing above. Sebastian's gaze flicked upward. D'Artan stood at the curve of the stairs, smiling, his hand resting lightly on the balustrade.

Sebastian had taken three long strides toward the stairs when the bronze door at the end of the drawing room swung open and Prudence Walker walked unwittingly into the middle of his robbery.

Nineteen

"Sweet Almighty Jesus," Tiny breathed reverently, breaking his silence.

Jamie started to cross himself, then remembered he wasn't Catholic. His awe dampened to dread as he saw Sebastian swing away from the staircase to face the vision in the doorway.

Time stopped. Sebastian's finger convulsively squeezed the trigger of his pistol. Had it been cocked, he would have shot himself in the foot.

The gilded wood of the doorway framed Prudence perfectly, like a painting by one of his grandfather's favorite artists. Was it Gainsborough or Reynolds? A halo of candlelight stoked to life the shimmering highlights in hair swept softly from her face, then curled to frame the slender column of her throat. Light winked from the diamond brooch pinning her lace fichu at the lily-white cleft between her breasts.

Sebastian knew the softness of that skin, knew its frailty and its grace. But this was not the prim, proud woman he had last seen in a dirty jail in Northumberland. This was the elusive creature of his fantasies, utterly lovely and alight with yearning promise. His hothouse flower had not faded, but bloomed in his absence. The realization made him feel mean and hard in more ways than one.

Prudence peered around the room, biting her lip in consternation. She did not see Tricia. D'Artan must have escorted her upstairs after her pretty swoon. Hooded figures circled the frozen guests, sacks spread wide. What new game was this? She wasn't sure if she was supposed to freeze in place, attempt to evade the hooded figures, or go in search of a one-eyed dwarf possessing an original Hogarth engraving.

Devony was hovering behind a potted palm. Prudence leaned toward her and whispered, "What do we play? Statues? Blind man's bluff? Scavenger hunt?"

"Robbery," Devony said between clenched teeth. "We play robbery."

Prudence frowned, trying to remember the rules of that game. It was nearly impossible to keep track of all their childish entertainments. She studied the room, noting for the first time the pistols shoved into the waistbands of the men with sacks.

"Oh. Robbery." She glanced behind her, gauging the wisdom of slipping out and running for a constable.

It was too late. One of the robbers had spotted her and was coming her way. She tugged off Tricia's diamond ear bobs, prepared to surrender them without protest.

The man continued to approach, each step as measured as a waltz. A crude mask of burlap hid his face. The wide brim of his hat cast his eyes and mouth in shadow. His dingy linen shirt was stretched taut across broad shoulders. The other robbers froze, sacks spread, as his path melted the crowd between them. Prudence's heart tripped into an uneven beat.

He kept coming. For a breathless moment, she thought he would back her right up against the door. Finally he stopped, leaving mere inches between them. The heat of his body was a palpable thing, as masculine as the scent of tobacco clinging to his shirt. She glared at his chest, trying to control her breathing. She was afraid, but also angered by his impertinence. None of the other guests were being treated in such a callous manner.

He shoved his pistol in his breeches and opened his sack. "Your jewelry, my lady."

His graveled voice sent a frisson of fear coursing down her

spine. She dropped the ear bobs into the sack and drew her pearl necklace over her hair.

The faintest breath of jasmine buffeted Sebastian. His senses reeled. He could smell her and taste her as if the months without her had driven him to the point of madness.

"All of it. Your ring too," he snapped gruffly.

And your gown. And your petticoat. And your garters. And your stockings. And your chemise. His mind staggered at the fantasy of her disrobing before him, obediently casting each garment into his sack until he could ease her back against the door and finish what they had started that long-ago night at Lindentree.

Prudence slipped off a coral pinkie ring that couldn't have been worth more than a tuppence, then stood at a loss as he remained unmoving before her. His animosity both baffled and frightened her. His shoulders blocked out the rest of the drawing room. It was as if the whole world had narrowed to only her and this savage stranger.

She flinched and closed her eyes as he dropped the sack and buried his hands in her hair, ruthlessly stripping away the silver pins.

Sebastian did not want her hairpins. He simply couldn't resist the temptation to immerse his fingers in the silky cloud of her hair. He cast the pins in the sack, then let his gaze wander with arrogant boldness to where her breasts swelled against her lace and silk fichu.

Heat flooded Prudence's cheeks. She struggled with her brooch, trembling not in fear now, but anger. The pin snagged in the silk, then drew a thin crimson line across one breast. A small sound of pain escaped her. Then he was there, his warm hands displacing hers as he worked the pin from the delicate material with surprising patience. His hands lingered. His callused knuckles grazed the sensitive skin between her breasts with shivering delicacy. A curious knot tightened in her stomach. She studied the sandy hair scattered across the backs of his hands, too shaken to risk looking up.

A shudder passed through his rigid body. He gave the brooch a careless tug, shredding the precious silk.

As he turned away, dismissing her with humiliating swiftness, she cried, "Wait."

The crowd gasped as he pivoted on one heel, a faceless, wary figure.

She snatched off her spectacles and jerked the gold chain over her head. Her eyes blazed and contempt was written in her every word. "Don't you want these? They're real gold. They're not worthless like a bit of coral or a handful of hairpins. They should fetch you a fancy price."

She faced him proudly, hair tumbling around her face, her torn fichu fluttering in the wind that blew through the open windows. The thief's fingers brushed hers as they folded around the gold spectacles. He took them from her and gently slipped them over the bridge of her nose.

She blinked at him, mystified by the unexpected kindness.

He leaned forward and pressed his mouth to her ear. "Keep them, Miss Walker." The prick of his heathery burr lifted the hair at the nape of her neck. "The gold suits you far better than steel."

Then, with an imperceptible signal, he was gone and the others with him. A sheet of icy rain pelted the marble floor by the windows. As the drawing room exploded into movement, Prudence Walker slid to the floor in a puddle of cranberry satin.

A callused hand smoothed the hair away from her face. Prudence nuzzled her lips against it and murmured, "Sebastian."

The hand withdrew, and she became aware of an awkward silence. Slowly she opened her eyes. Killian MacKay gazed down at her, his kind eyes crinkled in careful assessment. Horror flooded her as she realized what she had done.

Her gaze darted around the bedchamber, finding Tricia mercifully occupied with Lady Campbell and Devony. A maid was draping her gown over the back of a chair. ". . . simply scandalous," Tricia was saying, her pale hands fluttering like birds. "Do you know she tossed my favorite ear bobs into his sack as if they were mere trinkets?"

With a worried glance at the bed, Lady Campbell wrung her own plump hands. "I do hope she recovers. Such a shock for a delicate young girl. I feel so responsible. Two houses across the square were robbed earlier this week, but I never dreamed they'd attempt us. Why, my Dempster is a member of the parliament!"

"She's awake, mum," the maid pronounced, sliding a hot brick wrapped in flannel beneath the counterpane at Prudence's feet.

They gathered around, peering down at her like curious moons in a canopied galaxy.

Tricia puckered up and kissed the pillow next to Prudence's cheek. "You gave us quite a scare, young lady. When Laird MacKay discovered you had collapsed, he was kind enough to carry you here to your chamber."

"Your body was blocking the door," Devony added, giving the impression that they might have left her there had it not inconvenienced the other guests. She shivered delicately. "I can't blame you for swooning. You should have seen that scoundrel tear the pins from your hair. We thought he was going to throw you over his shoulder and carry you off. Or ravish you right there against the door."

Prudence's color fled anew at the memory of Sebastian's rough mastery. Laird MacKay dampened her brow with a cloth and gave Devony an icy stare from beneath an oddly boyish fringe of snowy lashes. Lady Campbell's bottom lip quivered.

"I'm quite embarrassed," Prudence said. "I've never swooned before."

MacKay's lilting burr flowed over her. "No need for apologies, lass. You've suffered through a terrible experience."

Tricia rested her fingers on his broad shoulder. To Prudence's shaken vision, they looked like talons. "I think we'd all agree the best thing for my niece is rest. Would you care to join me for a warm toddy in my sitting room, my lord?"

MacKay settled back in the chair and stretched his long legs out before him. "I believe I'll sit for a while. The lass might sleep easier knowing there's a man to watch over her."

Tricia's eyes narrowed faintly as she gazed at her niece. That look meant trouble, Prudence knew. There would doubtless be a whole new parade of fawning suitors for her to review in the morning. For now, Tricia had no choice but to obey. Prudence swallowed her own protest. Laird MacKay looked as determined and immovable as a plaid mountain.

The women slipped out, leaving the maid napping just inside the open door. Prudence closed her eyes, pretending to fall asleep, but when she chanced to look, MacKay was studying her, his hooded eyes as bright and wary as a hawk's.

"Sebastian's an uncommon name for these parts, is it not?" he asked softly.

She propped herself up on the pillows, feeling equally as wary. "I have a cat named Sebastian."

She leaned over and peered hopefully under the bed. Where was the furry little monster when she needed him? Someday she would learn never to depend on a male of any species.

She straightened, her face flushed, and blew a stray wisp of hair out of her eyes. "He must be in the greenhouse terrorizing Lady Campbell's cockatoo again."

"If he's a bonny gray lad, he's more likely next door in the kitchen of my own town house, lapping cream from Cook's saucer and courting my Bella."

Prudence deduced Bella to be the owner of the incriminating cat hairs on his plaid. It was easy to imagine her—fluffy and white, a lolling pink tongue, brainless. Sort of a feline Devony Blake. "I fear my Sebastian has taken to pouncing after every set of pretty whiskers that comes along. Typical male," she added in a mutter.

"A bit jaded for one so young, are you not? Perhaps your aunt's misfortune with the rake who duped her has colored your opinions."

MacKay's words colored her cheeks. He smiled faintly, and she silently cursed her traitorous complexion. He looked as if he would like to say more, but at the moment the maid blew out a snore between pursed lips.

MacKay fluffed Prudence's pillow. " 'Tis late, lass. You've had quite an evening. We can talk tomorrow." His shuttered gaze warned her it was more than casual conversation he had in mind.

He awoke the maid and left. As the door shut behind them, Prudence began to tremble. She arched her foot to find the warm brick beneath the counterpane. Would Sebastian come to her? Did he dare?

She flung herself onto her side, gazing at the terrace doors. She must be truly mad. If Sebastian did come, he would probably shoot her first and exchange pleasantries later.

How could she have been so blind? The crude mask might have hidden the sheen of his hair and the smoky steel of his eyes, but her madly beating heart had tried to warn her. Even in his dingy garments, Sebastian had commanded the cream of Edinburgh society like a robber prince, a pirate king of the drawing room. In a few brief moments, he had stolen far more than costly baubles. He had robbed her of her precious sophistication, the cool aloofness she had fostered these many months to keep her from feeling anything at all—not grief, not regret, and not the overwhelming guilt that threatened her now. The rapacious heat of his hands had brought her every nerve tingling to life and rendered her as witless as Devony Blake.

How he must despise her! She had robbed him of all his fine plans, betrayed him to a man he held in the deepest contempt. But how to explain the fleeting moment that evening when his fingers had grazed her skin with aching tenderness? That instant when he had set her spectacles on her nose with the same gentleness he had once shown a flour-speckled girl in the ruins of Tricia's kitchen?

Prudence burrowed deeper into the sumptuous blankets, shivering in her thin chemise as the icy rain shifted silently to snow.

Sebastian's boots made wet prints across the terrace. The snow sank through the cracks in the leather, melting when it touched his woolen stockings. The heavy, wet flakes fell straight down, covering the bricks, clinging to the holly trees that bordered the terrace, and casting a net of fluffy white across Sebastian's hair.

He was oblivious to the cold. Pressing his fingertips to the icy glass of a French door, he stared into the room beyond.

The waning fire cast a cozy glow across the soft form humped beneath the bedclothes. He could almost feel the fire's warmth, even out on the chilly terrace. He felt like a child, his grubby fingers pressed against the window of a sweet shop, and he muttered an oath.

He had never meant to see Prudence again. Not in England, and certainly not in Edinburgh. He had never thought to again feel the heavy weight of her hair against his palms, or to brush her creamy skin with his knuckles. His hands clenched into fists as he fought the tenderness that threatened to overwhelm him. Damn her! Since the night she had come to him at Lindentree, his dreams had been fired by her lissome form, her honeyed kiss. He had let her walk away from him that night, but now he swore she would not walk away from him again.

He drew her pearls from his pocket, looping the shimmering strand between fingers cracked and stiff from the cold. They were so like her—bound by a fragile but enduring thread, cool upon first glance, but warming to his skin, coming alive to his touch with an opalescent fire.

He turned away from the door, then stopped, driving a hand through his hair. He had cursed his own tender heart a hundred times since that night at Lindentree. Had it brought him here only to betray him again? Surely one glimpse of her misty eyes couldn't erase the endless months of shivering in damp glens, unable to light a fire for fear of drawing the law. He had slept in a sullen knot, nursing his rage toward Prudence until it coursed through his battered body like molten flame, consuming all of his waking and dreaming thoughts with hot and inventive fantasies of revenge.

He knelt in the cold snow and slipped one of her hairpins into the lock of the French door. Before he could turn it, though, a numbing flame seared his throat. Would he find her alone? She had worn no betrothal ring or wedding band on her graceful fingers. But how else was he to explain her transformation? There must be a man—a wealthy man, to drape her in diamonds and satin, to weave gems around her slender throat. A man sharing both her life and her luscious body.

Sebastian's fingers tightened convulsively. The necklace snapped, sending pearls bouncing and flying to sink without a trace into the blanket of snow.

He straightened and threw his heaving shoulders against the wall, staring blindly at the broken thread dangling from his fingers.

"You haven't an ounce of grace in you, you clumsy, stupid boy."

Sebastian's features hardened. At first he thought it was his father's voice, thick with whisky, hoarse with contempt. But his father did not speak French. The falling snow frosted his lashes as he lifted his gaze to find not the spectre of his father, but his grandfather shivering beneath a lush beaver cloak.

D'Artan was arrogant, but not arrogant enough to come alone. Sebastian could sense the dark shapes crouched behind the box hedges.

"I knew I'd find you here," D'Artan said. "Your predictability is almost boring." His thin nostrils flared. "Scenting after her like a stag after a doe in heat. You can't help yourself, can you? You're just like your father. It's in your blood."

Sebastian refused to show D'Artan how deeply the words cut. "At least I have blood pumping through my veins. Not ice water." He took a step toward his grandfather. "I believe you and I have business to tend to."

"*Oui*, it seems we do."

D'Artan's amused gaze and a rush of warm air warned Sebastian. He spun around to find Prudence standing just outside the French doors. His oath was unutterably profane and as tender as an endearment. Christ, he thought, the little fool was barefoot.

"Sebastian? Is that you?"

Her voice was husky with sleep, and she was shivering in a thin silk wrapper. She looked as if she hardly knew where she was, much less whether she was awake. Snowflakes floated down to dust her dark hair. She was soft and disheveled in all the right places, a rumpled dream come to life. Even as Sebastian struggled to hate her, he moved toward her, forgetting he no longer had his plaid to wrap around her shoulders.

Her puffy eyes narrowed as she focused on the second dark shape. "Viscount?"

Sebastian's cold tone snapped her to immediate wakefulness. "Go back to your room, Prudence. Now."

The twitch of D'Artan's lips was more grimace than smile. "Oh, do stay, *ma chérie*. The party is just beginning. 'Tis only a pity it must be so brief."

Sebastian forced an amused sneer. "Won't you have trouble explaining our untidy corpses on the Campbells' pristine lawn?"

Prudence stared at the two men as if they had both gone mad.

D'Artan shrugged. "*Au contraire.* The wicked robber returns in the night to ravish the young lady he found so enchanting. But his attentions become a trifle . . ." He tapped his pursed lips, ". . . shall we say, rough, and his little death tragically becomes her big death. I burst in, too late to save my young charge, but not too late to wield justice against her cruel attacker."

Prudence had gone the color of the snow. With one fluid movement, Sebastian shoved her behind him. His hand eased toward the pistol in his breeches.

"Scream, Prudence," he ordered.

He held his breath, awaiting her scream, half hoping it would come. He was weary of running, weary of aching with cold and hunger.

"What should I scream?" she asked stupidly.

He swung on her. "Dammit, lass, just scream!"

His hissed command made Prudence jump. Her tongue darted out to moisten her lips. One scream from her would bring the house down on them all. Sebastian would hang. She didn't utter a sound. She just stood there, barefoot in the snow.

"Fascinating, isn't it?" D'Artan said. "To contemplate how far you could push her before she betrayed you with a scream . . ."

Sebastian's heart lurched. He averted his eyes, afraid Prudence might read within them a reflection of his own dark fantasies.

D'Artan burst into a silvery peal of laughter. "Such fools

you are! I could have killed you both a thousand times over by now."

Sebastian's hand remained poised over his pistol. "I know how you hate to dirty your own lily-white paws."

"Did you really think I would kill you?" D'Artan sank down on a stone bench, wheezing slightly. He wiped his moist lips with a dainty lace handkerchief. "Even if you are a besotted, bumbling fool, you are still my grandson."

Sebastian scowled, but he took his hand off his gun.

Prudence sat down abruptly on the low terrace wall. Snow melted into a wet circle on her wrapper, but she didn't seem to feel it. Shocked awareness dawned in her eyes. "One of you might have bothered to mention this to me," she said dazedly. "A simple introduction would have done nicely. 'Hello, Prudence, I'd like you to meet my grandfather,' for instance, or 'What a delight to meet you, Miss Walker. My grandson has spoken of you with great regard.'"

They both ignored her. D'Artan pulled a leather pouch out of his cloak and tossed it to Sebastian. It landed at his feet with a solid clink.

Sebastian cocked an eyebrow in disdain. "I don't want your blood money. I won't hurt her."

D'Artan slanted Prudence a look. "Oh, I think you would. After what she did to you, you can't tell me you haven't dreamed of fastening your fingers around her silken throat and squeezing—"

Prudence absently stroked her neck.

"Stop it, old man!" Sebastian turned away, hands on hips, seeing from Prudence's wary gaze that he had betrayed himself. His grandfather still knew him too well.

D'Artan's voice shifted to petulance. "But it's such a pretty throat. I've come to appreciate its beauty myself in the last few months. She is a charming companion. But you already knew that, didn't you?" He paused, certain he had Sebastian's full attention. "Your Prudence and I share many interests. Such as chemistry."

"Chemistry?" Sebastian echoed.

"*Oui.* It seems our dear girl is the only one who knows the formula to those fulminic detonators her father was working on when he died. But out of misguided nobility, she refuses to share it with me. The shortage of gunpowder is crippling our revolutionists. Such a substitute would be invaluable, especially when the new regime declares war on England."

Prudence stood, desperate to halt this sudden tumble of secrets long enough to let her think. "The revolutionists? I thought you were a royalist."

Sebastian's laugh was low and unpleasant. "My grandfather is many things, but a royalist is not one of them."

D'Artan strode to Sebastian, hissing him to silence. He picked up the pouch of gold and shoved it into Sebastian's hand. "Take it!"

Sebastian carelessly tossed the pouch into the air, catching it with the other hand. "Why? If she has more merit to you alive than dead, why do you want me to kill her?"

Prudence backed toward the French doors, her gaze fixed on Sebastian's face. It was as beautiful and merciless as Satan's.

D'Artan scowled at Sebastian. "I don't want you to kill her, you fool. I want you to marry her."

Twenty

The pouch fell flat against Sebastian's palm. A chill swept over him. His gaze met Prudence's and held. She looked as if he had thrust a knife through her heart.

D'Artan rushed on. "Think of it. We would have both her silence and her cooperation. I could smuggle the two of you to Paris tonight. By day, she could be your devoted little wife. But by night, oh, by night . . ." His eyes rolled in twisted ecstasy. "You could take your revenge, not once, but each and every time the urge struck you."

Although the cold should have made it impossible, Sebastian's groin tightened. A succession of images flashed in his brain, as cold and mercilessly erotic as a Caracci engraving. But drawn over them with the delicate brushstrokes of a master were other images: Prudence squatting in the mud with his pistol, grinning like an imp; Prudence brushing the rain from his lashes; Prudence thrusting the gold spectacles at him, her eyes amethyst fire in the candlelight.

What did he read in her eyes now? Regret? Longing? Fear? He reached for her. His hand dug into her forearm, callused fingers snagging on the sheer fabric of her wrapper. Despair brushed him with cold wings. Like a confection of silk and cream, she symbolized everything he could never have. The man he could never be. Was this how his father had felt when faced with the ethereal temptation of his mother's beauty?

Did he feel compelled to crush what he could never truly possess?

Without warning, tears spilled down Prudence's cheeks. He wanted to catch them on his tongue, to mingle them with the whisky-scented heat of his own mouth.

He groaned deep in his throat, shaking her roughly. "Damn you, lass. Save your tears for Tugbert or your other fancy beaux. They'll not work on me."

Yet even as he spoke, he pulled her into a fierce embrace, holding her face against his shoulder so she couldn't see his expression. He rocked her gently, pressing his mouth to the fragrant softness of her hair, remembering all the cold, lonely nights when he had hungered to hold her against him or hear the husky ripple of her laughter. This wasn't some brittle society belle or even the heartless bitch he wanted to believe she was. It was Prudence. She trembled, but she did not beg. Within him still lay the grudging admiration he had sheltered like a live coal in his heart. His stubborn, silly, brave Prudence.

Prudence couldn't remember the last time she had cried. But when she gazed into Sebastian's shadowed eyes, all the feelings she had fought to bury rose in a torrent, choking her with tears—her shame and sense of failure at her own betrayal, the need to make him understand how deeply he had hurt her by choosing Tricia's wealth over her love, the hollow emptiness of her life without him. But words abandoned her, and all she could do was snuffle like a child.

Sebastian tilted her tear-streaked face to his. Her eyes had gone misty, like fog-shrouded stars. Forgetting his grandfather, forgetting everything, he touched his lips to hers. Their mouths melded, their tongues entwining with an eloquence beyond words.

"Go on," D'Artan whispered, his voice demon-soft. "Take her back into the room. I can't blame you for wanting a taste before you buy. I'll stand guard. If she changes her mind about screaming, you can use this."

Sebastian slowly lifted his head to find D'Artan's handkerchief fluttering from the old man's fingers. Prudence stiffened in his embrace, but instead of stepping out of his arms, she pressed herself closer to him, her breasts warm and soft against the rigid muscles of his chest.

He searched her upturned face. A muscle twitched in his jaw. How dare she look at him with such trusting eyes? Didn't she know what kind of man he had become? What would she do if he dragged her toward the door? Would she scream? Struggle? And if she did neither, but let him work any dark wickedness he desired on her sweet young body, would he ever be able to live with himself again?

He pushed her away as if she'd scorched him, steeling himself with yet another image—Prudence walking away into a beautiful summer morning, leaving him in the stench and confinement of Tugbert's jail.

He turned on his grandfather, his expression as dangerous as a smoking pistol. D'Artan backed away without realizing it.

The old man had baited his trap with diabolical care, Sebastian mused. He weighed the pouch of gold in one hand, calculating how many hot scones it would buy. His stomach knotted at the thought.

He threw the pouch, refusing to look at Prudence. It struck D'Artan squarely in the chest. "If you're so bloody fond of her, why don't you take her to Paris? The two of you would make a charming pair."

Prudence sucked in a choked breath. As Sebastian strode away from them, her quiet words echoed down the narrow alley after him. "You've underplayed your hand, Viscount. Sebastian's affections don't come cheap."

Sebastian stopped, on the dangerous verge of striding back, pushing her into her room, and showing her until dawn just what his affections would cost her. D'Artan's henchmen rustled in the hedges. He started walking again, waiting for a pistol ball to smash between his shoulder blades. But from behind him came only the whisper of the falling snow.

As Sebastian disappeared into the snow-swept night, Prudence hugged herself. Her body was throbbing to miserable life. The wet wrapper clung to her thighs. She stared down at her numb feet as if they belonged to someone else.

D'Artan touched his finger to his lips. "Quiet, my dear. You

mustn't awaken your aunt. I shouldn't want her to discover
the extent of her fiancé's . . . shall we say . . . indiscretions. I should hate to see him hang for them."

Prudence fumbled behind her for the icy door handle. The
cold burned her throat. "As much as you'd hate to hang for
your own *indiscretions*, I'm sure."

"I'm delighted we understand each other." He bowed with
flawless grace. "Sleep well, Your Grace."

He ambled off into the night as if he'd simply chosen the
garden for a midnight stroll. Three dark shapes melted after
him. Prudence shivered against the door, her only warmth
the tingle of her skin where Sebastian had touched her.

Prudence stepped out of the bookshop and tucked her hands
deep into her muff. Her reticule dangled against her hip. The
cold wind whipped roses into her cheeks, but she was soon
warmed by brisk exertion as her kid boots crunched the
snow in long restless strides.

Free at last in the sprawling streets of Old Edinburgh! She
and Laird MacKay had snuck out like children while Tricia
napped, escaping both Tricia's herd of maids and D'Artan's
dour shadow. Another moment trapped in the sticky fibers
of the viscount's web, and Prudence believed she might have
run screaming from the Campbells' town house.

The past week had been sheer misery. When she had
pleaded a headache to avoid working in his laboratory,
D'Artan had haunted her like a solicitous ghost. He had
fetched her shawl when the parlor was chilly, dipped his
finger in her tea to check its warmth, gifted her with a rare
edition of Diderot's *Encyclopedia* and a foil-wrapped box of
chocolates. She had accepted his tender graces, her teeth
gritted behind her smile. Tricia and Lady Campbell had
exchanged amused glances, never noticing that Prudence
fed the chocolates to Boris and poured the tea into the
drooping bay tree behind the settee. She had just traded the
priceless *Encyclopedia* bound in Moroccan leather for a
lurid novella only Devony could enjoy.

She gave a little hop to avoid two small boys chasing a
careening ball from an alley. As she walked on to where she'd

agreed to meet MacKay, she fought to keep from searching every face she saw for a trace of Sebastian. She lost. The pain of his abandonment cut a raw swath through her. Each time she lifted her eyes, she saw him turning his back on her, walking into the night, leaving her to D'Artan's grim machinations. But who was she to blame him? Hadn't she turned her back on him as well? The tenderness of his kiss on the snowy terrace haunted her dreams until she awoke shivering and crying, her night rail tangled around her legs.

She passed a withered old woman who hawked her steaming chestnuts in singsong rhythm. Warm laughter burst from a coffee room. The scent of roasting chocolate beans drifted to her nose. By fading daylight, the shopkeepers lit candles in windows that sparkled like walls of glass. She wistfully remembered a winter eve in London when she and her papa had walked hand in hand down Fleet Street, admiring the shining displays of goods they could not afford and were content without. Life had been much simpler then.

A passing lamplighter wrapped in a woolen muffler gave her a brisk nod. She hastened on. Darkness was closing in. From behind her, she heard the crunch of stealthy footfalls. She glanced back and saw the lamplighter, a sooty shadow against the deepening darkness.

She rounded a corner, relieved to see the sturdy figure of Laird MacKay standing in the halo of a street lamp. A rush of affection brightened her spirits. The rugged Highlander had been her salvation in the past week. He had called at the Campbell mansion faithfully each day, displacing the glowering viscount from her side. Prudence knew now why both D'Artan and Sebastian despised him. He had lost D'Artan's precious daughter and Sebastian's mother to Brendan Kerr. But since the night of the robbery, the canny laird had made no further mention of a man named Sebastian, although Prudence often glanced up to find his gaze locked on her in smoky appraisal.

MacKay did not hear her approach. He was staring at a scrap of paper tacked on the lamppost. She slipped up beside him.

Her heart lurched as she saw what had captivated him. Someone had finally captured the Dreadful Scot Bandit

Kirkpatrick—an artist of consummate skill. The mask still veiled the upper portion of his face, but the slanted curve of his jaw, the teasing brackets around his mouth, and the broad planes of his throat were all Sebastian.

Prudence reached out as if hypnotized and touched a fingertip to the sulky line of his mouth. MacKay drew in a breath, and she knew she had betrayed herself.

She snatched the notice from the post and shoved it into her reticule. "Silly authorities. They shouldn't clutter up such a lovely city with this refuse."

MacKay caught her wrist in a grip that was anything but infirm. "Have you seen him? Do you know where he is?"

She jerked away, refusing to meet his eyes. "I haven't the faintest idea who you're talking about."

A ripple of cream on the next post caught her eye. She started for it. MacKay fumbled at his sporran, and the rustle of paper froze her in her tracks.

She turned. MacKay stood with arm outstretched, a handful of bills crumpled in his fist. The wind caught one and sent it fluttering down the street.

His eyes were beseeching. "You can destroy that one if you want. But they're putting them up faster than I can tear them down. Somebody's turned traitor on him, lass, and I'd be willing to bet it's that wretched grandfather of his."

Prudence looked up and down the long street, and realized with despair that every post sported one of the uncanny likenesses.

Her voice rose on a note of hysteria. "Why should *you* want to help him? I know who you are. You kicked him out of Dunkirk before his father's body was even cold."

MacKay crossed the distance between them in two strides. His nostrils flared. " 'Tis a lie. When I took Dunkirk, the boy had fled and Brendan Kerr's black soul was already roasting in hell." He passed a hand over his eyes as if he could somehow erase the pain etched on his features. "I used to see the wee lad, poaching my land, skulking in the brush like a wild creature. But I could never get close to him. Do you know what it was like to see his mother's eyes peering out of that dirty, bruised face?"

"Yet you took his precious Dunkirk away from him."

MacKay's shoulders slumped. "I wouldn't have run the lad off when Kerr died. I'd have let him stay on. I'd have taken care of him. Fed him, clothed him, sent him to school. But he never gave me a chance to tell him that. He wanted nothing from me. Why, I couldn't even catch him!"

He bowed his head. There was something about this man, some indefinable kindness Prudence had sensed from the first moment they had met. It was almost as if they'd known each other before.

She gently touched his sleeve. Hope sparkled in her eyes. "Don't despair, Laird MacKay. Perhaps if we both try very hard, we can catch him together."

His gaze softened as he brushed a tear from her cheek with wizened fingers. "If he can resist you, lass, the lad's a bigger fool than his father."

He opened his arms to her. Prudence was so weary of secrets, and MacKay's shoulders, like her papa's, seemed strong enough to bear even the worst of them. As she lay her cheek against the scratchy softness of his plaid, the lamplighter tore a handbill off a post and melted back into the darkness, his broad shoulders braced against the bitter cold.

Tricia reclined like a queen among her feather pillows. As Prudence approached the bed, her aunt clawed through a gold-foiled box and popped a chocolate in her mouth. Prudence wiped her palms on her skirt, wondering what occasion could have been so dire that her aunt would rise before noon.

Gauzy winter light sifted through the drapes, stoking to life the lush shades of a Gainsborough on the far wall. Pieces of correspondence were scattered across Tricia's satin counterpane.

"Good morning, dear. I trust you slept well." Tricia licked chocolate from her lips like a lazy cat.

Prudence hoped her spectacles hid her swollen eyes. "Like a babe," she lied.

"You retired rather late last night."

Prudence's wariness subsided. She was only to be scolded for her tardiness after all. "Laird MacKay took me to a coffeehouse. We began talking and lost track of the time."

Tricia arched an immaculately drawn eyebrow. "A bit scandalous for you to entertain a strange man in a public coffeehouse, don't you think?"

Prudence squelched an uncharitable thought about all the strange men Tricia had entertained in her bedchamber. "I'd say not. We are nearing the turn of the century, after all. Laird MacKay is both a pleasant companion and a gentleman."

"He must find you a pleasant companion as well." Smiling enigmatically, Tricia smoothed a creased scrap of paper on her knee. "I felt you should know, I have received two offers of marriage this morning."

Prudence's own smile was wan. "Two proposals before breakfast? Even for you, that's quite a coup."

"I have decided to accept one of them."

Prudence's smile faded. She had been waiting for this moment since Sebastian first disappeared. Tricia was ready to marry again and rid her household of her spinster niece. That was all right, Prudence assured herself. She would survive. She could afford a small house now, a few servants, books of her own. She would find contentment in living alone. And Laird MacKay had brought a daring and long-forgotten element back into her life—hope for the future. He was a wealthy man with an army of men at his disposal. With his help, perhaps she could find Sebastian and somehow make amends.

Tricia's words startled her back into the present. "I'd barely had time to peruse the first offer when your rugged laird came bursting in with such an ardent plea that I couldn't deny him an audience."

Prudence frowned. Laird MacKay had made no mention of such intentions the previous night. She hadn't even noticed him courting Tricia. "He seems a fine man," she said weakly. "It would be easy to grow quite fond of him."

"I'm relieved you feel that way. You see, Prudence, the proposals were not for my hand. They were for yours. And as your guardian, I feel it is long past time for you to wed. I will no longer tolerate your wavering. I insist you make a decision. Before the end of the week."

Prudence stared at her aunt, her mind stumbling over the

question she was afraid to ask. "If Laird MacKay made the second offer, who made the first?"

Tricia blinked in wide-eyed innocence. "Haven't you guessed?" When Prudence mutely shook her head, Tricia popped another chocolate in her mouth. "Why, darling, the Viscount D'Artan, of course!"

Twenty-one

Sebastian Kerr was a desperate man. As his horse plunged down the mountainside, he sawed on the reins, throwing his weight back to keep from tumbling forward and being crushed beneath the beast's shaggy hooves. His crude mask blinded him to the other riders, but the ground shook with the thunder of hoofbeats. He could smell their fear even through the smothering thickness of the burlap. The harsh rasp of his own breathing filled his ears. He longed to tear off the mask. It was little more than a sack cut with eyeholes— the sort of mask a scarecrow might wear, the sort of mask the hangman would slip tenderly over his head when he was caught.

Icy water splashed into the holes in his boots as his horse forded a swollen burn. The agitated shouts of their pursuers faded to the echoes of curses, as the Frenchmen chasing them drove their mounts to the edge of the cliff, only to discover their prey had vanished, borne on the sturdy wings of horses bred for the wild and rocky terrain.

Sebastian was the first to halt. He clawed at the strings of his mask and jerked it off, sucking in a deep breath of the cold, cleansing air.

A hairy hand curled around his bridle. "God's land, Kirk-patrick, what are the Frenchies doin' in the Highlands?"

Sebastian gave the furry paw a disparaging glance, keeping his voice deliberately cool. "How should I know? Why don't you ride up and ask them, Angus?"

He had to look up to meet the glowering eye of Big Gus McClain. A dingy patch covered the bandit's other eye.

Big Gus freed Sebastian's bridle and spat in the burn. "Ye mumblin' French in yer sleep and all, I though ye'd be the one to know."

The wind shifted; McClain's stench wafted toward Sebastian, making him itch for a bath. He longed to steal away with the precious ball of soap he had pilfered from a crofter's wife.

Tiny shoved his mount between the two men, grinning roguishly. "Everyone knows the French have a love of bonny music."

Jamie's nasal laugh rang out. The other men sniggered nervously. They had been tearing an organ out of a tiny kirk when the Frenchmen had approached.

"Or perhaps they're just regular churchgoers." Sebastian's smile was politely ferocious. It whetted Big Gus's suspicions that beneath his soft-spoken, clean-smelling exterior lay a man infinitely more dangerous than himself.

"Aye. Regular churchgoers," McClain echoed thoughtfully. "Maybe that they were."

The men dared to shoot Sebastian half-curious, half-admiring glances as their horses milled into motion, churning the water to icy froth.

Big Gus and his men were the scourge of the Highlands. Even by Sir Arlo Tugbert's exacting standards, they made the Dreadful Scot Bandit Kirkpatrick and his men look like fops at a tea party. Sebastian had been accepted into their ranks on the sheer menace of his reputation, but he had the sinking suspicion that if he didn't rape a virgin or shoot someone in cold blood very soon, his own corpse might be auctioned off to the Edinburgh Medical Society. He wondered if shooting himself would count.

The thunder of the other men's hoofbeats faded. Only Tiny remained. Sebastian's gaze strayed to the harsh line of the ridge. "Something's gone wrong, Tiny. Something's gone terribly wrong or he wouldn't have sent them after me. The bastard won't give up this time. What if he's changed his mind and decided he wants her dead?"

"Then she's one dead lass, ain't she?" Tiny's voice roughened at Sebastian's flinch. "Forget about her. She ain't been nothin' but a noose 'round yer neck from the moment ye laid eyes on her. Ye don't owe her anythin'."

Emotion sharpened Sebastian's eyes to steel. Tiny had seen that look before, late at night when the others were snoring in their bedrolls and Sebastian stared moodily into the dying flames of the campfire.

"Oh, I owe her something. And if I ever get my hands on her again, I'll give it to her."

He kicked his mount into a canter, crumpling the mask in his fist. He would live and die in such a mask. If D'Artan didn't get him, the hangman would. He had been a poor, deluded fool to let a lovely girl with husky laughter make him believe otherwise.

As Sebastian drew the mask over his head, the first snowflakes drifted out of the paling sky.

Prudence huddled against the coachman's shoulder as a gentle slope lurched into a steep uphill trail. She slipped a hand out of her muff and buried it in Sebastian-cat's silvery fur, flexing fingers stiff with cold. He rewarded her with an adoring purr, sheltered from the wind by her sturdy redingote.

Not even a blizzard would drive her back into the musty confines of the carriage. She had endured the first leg of the journey from Edinburgh with Devony's stays digging into her side, Squire Blake snoring in her ear, and Boris slobbering on her knee. At their last stop, ignoring Tricia's half-hearted protests, she had given her seat to Boris and chosen the company of MacKay's laconic Scottish coachman.

The coachman reached out a steadying arm as they jolted through another rut. Prudence's already battered hip struck an iron bolt, and she winced. They had been forced to stop twice earlier and push the lumbering vehicle out of the frozen ruts worn by the unexpected February rains. The last try had taken the combined efforts of the coachman, the two outriders, and all the occupants of the coach, including a snuffling Devony. Only Boris had been allowed to stay in the carriage. The Great Dane had poked his sleek head out the window like a visiting dignitary.

As they started up a slope gashed in the mountainside, the hooves of the outriders' horses tattooed a crunchy beat against the thin quilt of snow. Prudence sent a cloud of warm breath floating into the brisk air. A primitive excitement stirred in her breast at the beauty of this alien land. Jagged mountains split the bleak sky in misty peaks of blue and silver. On a slope across the glen, a herd of creamy sheep huddled, their inquisitive black faces turned to the sky. Far below, a loch twined through a narrow glen only to be swallowed by a swirling curtain of snow.

She shivered, thinking of Sebastian out there somewhere, lost in the wild majesty of the Highlands. But if he took the bait she and MacKay were so openly offering, he wouldn't be lost for long.

Prudence considered their plan worthy of any of Devony's sordid novellas. D'Artan's proposal had only forced their hand. She didn't know whether to giggle or cry as she imagined Sebastian's reaction when he discovered she was traveling to wed Killian MacKay, his most despised enemy, within the fortnight.

Once they reached Strathnaver and MacKay's castle, the plan was simple. She would have the coachman drive her around in MacKay's carriage, alone and unprotected, until Sebastian found her. Then all she had to do was calmly and rationally convince him that MacKay was not the wicked ogre he believed, but only a kind old man haunted by a lifetime of regrets. A man who had the riches and resources to help Sebastian build a new life free from both the shadow of his grandfather and his past. And free from her if he chose. Her cool plot always faltered at that point. She gave Sebastian-cat a hard squeeze. If their wild scheme didn't work, she feared she and MacKay would have only regrets to share.

She refused even to consider that Sebastian might have left Scotland altogether, spirited away by either D'Artan or the law. Or that he might strangle her before she had a chance to explain.

Her heart plummeted as the coach took a dive, then thumped to a halt with ominous finality.

Tricia slammed her parasol into the coach roof. "Onward, driver. Give the horses their heads."

"I'd like to give 'em yer head," the coachman muttered.

He climbed off his perch, tipping his hat to Prudence in apology. She clambered down after him with Sebastian-cat draped over one arm.

The coachman wrenched open the door. "Everybody out," he barked. "That slobberin' beast as well."

It was not Boris, but Squire Blake who first emerged, sheepishly rubbing his eyes.

"Well, I never—" Tricia huffed her way out with Devony trodding on her skirts.

The ribbons of Tricia's Leghorn hat streamed in the wind. The winter light was not kind to her complexion. Hectic patches of color stained her cheeks and nose. Powder gathered in the faint crevices around her eyes.

The coachman pointed into the coach. "Him too, or I ain't pushin'."

"But my big fellow might get his wittle paws all dirty," Tricia crooned.

Prudence's spirits sank. If they had to walk, Tricia would doubtless ask her to carry the dog.

Boris proved to be as stubborn as the coachman. Squire Blake hauled on his emerald-studded collar, but the dog would not budge. Only Tricia's coaxing finally moved him. Prudence watched in doleful silence as the last of the tea biscuits disappeared down his yawning maw. He padded out and sniffed at Sebastian-cat, then licked his rubbery chops. Prudence hoped they weren't to be without food for very long.

With the help of the outriders, they managed to jog the coach into a rocking motion. With a sickening creak, the wheels tilted, throwing the coach deeper into the rut.

Tricia swore at the coachman. He bellowed back at her. Boris caught the coachman's coattail between his yellowed teeth and tugged. Squire Blake tried to soothe them all while Devony burst into tears, wailing that wintering in Scotland was the most ridiculous idea anyone had ever had. If Prudence had chosen to wed that nice viscount instead of some Scottish savage, they could be jaunting through the south of France right now.

Prudence sank down on a rock. Icy daggers of wind dried the sweat on her brow. She pulled her shoulder-cape tight around her shoulders, chilled by the memory of D'Artan.

On the day her betrothal to Killian MacKay was announced, a pale mask had dropped over the viscount's face, his tension revealed only in the pinched creases around his lips. He had packed and vanished from the Campbells' that same afternoon.

An eerie cry echoed over the mountains. Prudence stiffened. The others fell into silence. A quivering ridge of hair stood erect on Boris's back.

"A wildcat?" Prudence asked hopefully.

The coachman refused to meet her eyes. He reached behind the leather seat for a battered musket as the outriders mounted and drew their own weapons. "Aye, lass. The wildest of 'em all. Into the coach, ladies."

Squire Blake dove after Tricia and Devony. The coachman caught the waistband of his breeches and hauled him back.

He thrust a squat knife into the squire's trembling hand. "Highlanders don't fancy Englishmen, but they do fancy Englishwomen, if ye take my meanin'. 'Tis no matter to me if those fancy bits of baggage get what they deserve, but I'd hate to see that nice little lass torn apart by a pack o' Highland rogues."

He turned to find Prudence standing behind him, her face drained of color, but her eyes sparkling with a fevered excitement. The coachman handed her into the carriage without a word.

The door slammed. Boris's eyes gleamed eerily out of the darkness. Prudence stuffed Sebastian-cat into the deep pocket of her redingote. It was a much tighter squeeze than it had once been. The Great Dane growled, fouling up the close air. After the icy purity of the mountain, Prudence felt as if she were smothering. Tricia stared blindly ahead, her face expressionless.

"I warned Papa we shouldn't have come to Scotland,"

Devony said. "I'll probably be ravished by that Dreadful Scot Bandit again."

"Not if I can help it," Prudence replied evenly. Her heart slammed against her rib cage in a wild song of hope.

"Why, I might even be ravished by an entire gang of bandits!" Devony added cheerfully.

The high-pitched wail came again to be answered by another, then another. The pounding of hooves roared nearer. A musket cracked.

"No," Prudence whispered.

She had envisioned a dramatic cry of, "Stand and deliver," followed by surrender. It had never occurred to her that Sebastian's men might shoot the nice coachman, or worse yet, that the nice coachman might shoot Sebastian.

"No!"

She flung open the coach door, eluding Tricia's wild grab for her skirts.

She spilled into the road in a tangle of petticoats. Her hands flew up to cover her face as hooves pawed the air above her head. She rolled to the side, cradling Sebastian-cat from her weight, then crawled frantically away, dodging the thrashing forelegs of one horse and the heaving belly of another. A filthy hand skittered across her hair. She ducked away. The man snarled a curse.

Her spectacles dangled from one ear. She grabbed them and bounded to her feet, jumping up and down to scan the melee for a glimpse of a blond giant, a carrot-headed elf, or a dashing highwayman in plaid and kilt.

Hulking goblins churned to and fro, hurling oaths and firing their pistols in the air. One of the outriders' horses, riderless now, plunged down the hillside. A motionless hump of lace lay beside one of the coach wheels. Prudence realized with horror that it was Squire Blake. The coachman went down under one blow of a blunt club. A squat creature leaped from his horse and ripped the carriage door off its hinges. He ducked into the carriage and reappeared with a shrieking Devony thrown over his shoulder. Her long blonde hair streamed down his back.

Prudence didn't realize she was screaming herself until a

brutal hand caught her hair. "Stop yer yappin', lassie, or Big Gus'll give ye somethin' to yap about."

The man forced her head back and thrust his face into hers. The stench of his breath choked her. Beneath the shapeless mask, Prudence saw no eyes, only a bulbous, milky film. A new scream tore from her throat. Sebastian-cat clawed his way out of her pocket and darted between the flailing legs of the horses. Ignoring the tearing pressure in her hair, she lunged after him.

As the butt of a pistol came down on the back of her head, Prudence realized too late that she had caught the wrong bandit.

Twenty-two

Lulled by the rocking jolt of the horse beneath her belly, Prudence slipped in and out of consciousness.

When the rocking stopped and the rough hand anchored at the small of her back vanished, she started awake. A rush of disorientation was replaced by creeping dread as she remembered what had happened. All of her fears flooded back, intensified by the blurry darkness, the cold, and the brusque cadences of strange masculine voices.

Her hand went instinctively to the chain around her neck. Mercifully, her spectacles were still there, tangled in her hair.

She slipped them on. A ragged Highlander squatted before a pile of brush. He glanced at the horse and caught her somber gaze. A leering grin twisted his mouth. The first crackle of flames sent light spilling over his face, illuminating a puckered slit where his nose should have been. The man gave a menacing rumble of laughter as Prudence flung herself off the horse.

She hit the ground running. The formidable dark shapes of Highlanders and trees blended as she fled from one cluster of men to the next, searching for Tricia or Devony. Mocking laughter followed her. Fires sprang up in the clearings between the trees, throwing an eerie web of shadow and light over the bandits' camp. She stumbled over a rolled blanket, biting back a shrill scream before realizing the hand that clutched her ankle was only a gnarled branch. She spun around and crashed into a broad chest.

A burly ogre caught her elbows and wet his lips with a hearty smack. A patch covered his right eye. "Miss me, darlin'? Big Gus was comin' right back. I wanted to get our blankets spread. A pretty wee thing like ye shouldn't have to sleep on the ground."

A man behind Big Gus guffawed. He jerked his thumb toward a gaping hole in the hillside covered by a tattered fur curtain. "*He* won't like it. Ye'd best tell him 'afore ye go spreadin' anythin'."

Prudence wouldn't have thought it possible, but Big Gus's expression turned even uglier. "Curse the bugger, Jordy. He was too damned drunk to go raidin' with us. Does he think he's goin' to just lay back and enjoy the spoils?"

"No," another man said. "He thinks the spoils are goin' to just lay back and enjoy him." He sniggered nervously.

Big Gus's good eye narrowed to a venomous slit. Prudence twisted around, following his sullen gaze to the cavern. The faint light of a lantern within gave it an unearthly glow.

Big Gus captured Prudence's hand in one of his scarred paws and tucked it under his arm. The butt of his pistol dug into her ribs. "To hell with the pretty lad. I caught this wee English lass and by God, I'm keepin' her."

Prudence's flight through the camp had gathered them quite an audience. At Big Gus's bold announcement, men who had been gaping quickly bent to unfold their blankets or spear a chunk of dried venison over the fire. But they could not stop their furtive glances toward the cavern.

Prudence did not care to meet the man within. Any man these savages considered more threatening than Big Gus must be Lucifer himself.

She took a deep breath. "Excuse me, sir." She tugged at Big Gus's fingers. "Sir, I must request a word with you."

He rumpled her hair, tossing a wink over his shoulder at the man behind him. "Ain't she sweet? I love an eager lassie."

She ducked from beneath his hand and drew herself up to her full height. "I am *not* an eager lassie. I am Prudence Walker, the Duchess of Winton, and the betrothed of Laird Killian MacKay of Strathnaver. If you will send a missive to him, I am certain he would be willing to post a substantial ransom for the safe return of myself and my party."

"Gus, I'm warnin' ye. He'll have yer throat for it," Jordy said.

Big Gus only grinned.

Prudence shook a finger under his bulbous nose. "I must warn you also, Mr. Big Gus. There will be severe repercussions should harm come to any of us."

"The lass is warnin' me. I think I'm in love." He chucked her under the chin. "Don't fret, me wee Prudie. The rest of yer party is bein' taken care of. Just like Big Gus's goin' to take care of ye. I won't even leave any bruises for yer fancy laird to find on his weddin' night."

The besotted bandit threw open his burly arms, enveloping Prudence in a greasy bear hug.

His jaw went slack. His arms dropped. But it wasn't until he inched backward that the other men could see why.

The barrel of his own pistol was rammed into the plump cushion of his belly.

Prudence's voice was as firm and unflinching as her grip on the pistol. "It would be very disagreeable for me to have to shoot you. I'd rather you tell me where I might find the rest of my party."

Big Gus tried to clear his throat and failed. "I was only funnin', little lassie. Big Gus wouldn't hurt ye."

She cocked the pistol. The click reverberated through the silent camp. "This is a new redingote. I should hate to get it all bloody."

Big Gus raised his hands in surrender and took a step away. Prudence caught a flicker of movement out of the corner of her eye and swung the pistol in a wide arc. "I wouldn't try it if I were you," she warned.

The men moved back as if hinged together, and exchanged uneasy glances. Prudence's grace in handling the weapon did not go unnoted. It rested in her net-gloved hand as comfortably as a satin reticule.

"That's right," she said. "I was born handling a pistol. My father was a—"

"Munitions expert?"

The soft voice sent a jolt of shock down her spine. She

jerked her head toward the cavern as a man emerged, pushing aside the fur curtain with lazy grace. Her heart lurched into a wild beat. His worn silk mask did nothing to hide the faintly amused quirk of his well-shaped lips. Long, thick lashes veiled his sparkling eyes.

Prudence's shoulders slumped in relief. Her arm dropped and the gun wavered. Then a shadow moved behind Sebastian. A sinuous arm twined around his waist, and a tousled blond head peered around his shoulder with feline curiosity. Prudence caught a glimpse of a small, fine-boned hand clutching a whisky bottle, blue eyes half closed in sensual languor, pink lips moist and swollen. She had found the first member of her poor, unfortunate party—Devony.

Her gaze shifted back to Sebastian. The glow of the firelight threw his figure into aching relief. His sandy hair was tousled. His shirt hung open. The first two buttons of his breeches were undone as if in invitation to the line of golden hair that spilled down the muscular plane of his abdomen.

He crossed his arms over his chest, rocked back on his heels, and gave Prudence his sweetest smile.

Her arm steadied and swung around with a life of its own, pointing the pistol straight at Sebastian's heart.

Twenty-three

Sebastian had faced death down the barrel of a pistol more than once in his life, but he'd never felt its breath blow quite so cold. Prudence wanted to shoot him. He could see it in her eyes, her stance, the heaving of her bosom beneath the torn redingote. She wanted to kill him.

She had never looked more beautiful.

He had finally succeeded in fanning the flames beneath her cool exterior to a roar. A lock of hair fell over her eyes. She tossed her head back, spilling the tangled mass around her shoulders in a rich cascade. The men stared at her with slackened jaws and glazed eyes as if God had dropped an angel in their midst—an avenging angel.

Without taking his eyes off Prudence, Sebastian caught Devony's elbow and jerked her forward. "You told me you and your father were alone."

Devony took a swig from the whisky bottle, then burped delicately. "We *were* alone. Prudence jumped out and ran away, leaving us at the mercy of those savages. Then the countess was carried off by that nice Viking gentleman."

Sebastian smoothed his mask as if he could somehow meld it to the bones of his face. "The countess?"

"*Her* aunt." Devony tucked a pensive finger between rosebud lips, weaving slightly. "Did I forget to mention the countess?"

"I doubt he gave you the chance," Prudence said icily.

Sebastian hated to admit it, but Prudence was right. He had struggled out of his whisky-soaked haze with barely enough time to jerk on his old mask before Devony had fallen on him, babbling about being ravished. He had not guessed it was himself she was intent on ravishing. But her arms had been warm and her mouth hot and wet. Before he could protest, she'd been fumbling with the buttons of his breeches and whispering the most interesting things in his ear—things she would like to do to him, things she would like him to do to her.

He had to be dreaming, he'd told himself. What would Devony Blake be doing in a cave in the Highlands? And wasn't it nicer than those dreams where he endlessly reached for Prudence just as she crumbled to ash in his hands?

But here was Prudence standing before him, not ash but seething flesh and blood, legs braced apart and the wood-grained butt of a pistol gripped in a hand itching to pull the trigger.

He thrust Devony aside and sauntered down the hill toward her. One of the men mumbled an oath under his breath. Big Gus mopped greasy beads of sweat from his brow.

As Sebastian drew nearer, the pistol began to waver. Prudence slammed the heel of her other palm against her wrist to steady it. He advanced until the cold muzzle of the gun touched the warm skin of his chest.

His lips curved in a mocking smile. He extended a genteel hand, ignoring the fact that both of her hands were occupied with the pistol. "Allow me to introduce myself, miss. You may call me Kirkpatrick."

Her delicate nostrils flared, warning him there were things she'd rather call him.

"Perhaps no one has explained our laws to you," he went on. "*We* are the bandits. *We* carry the weapons." He turned his hand palm-up. "The pistol, love."

At his casual endearment, a shudder swept through her. Sebastian hoped he hadn't miscalculated. If he had, he was a dead man.

"You heard my request, *Mr.* Kirkpatrick," she said. "I want to know the whereabouts of the rest of my party. My aunt. The coachman and outriders. Squire Blake." Her voice wavered. "And my cat."

Sebastian could see she was near to cracking, and braced himself against the tears welling in her eyes. "Very well. I shall see to their safety myself." He added softly, "You have my word on it."

She gave a less than genteel snort.

Jordy stepped forward. "Kirkpatrick, there's somethin' ye ought to know. The lass claims to belong to—"

Prudence swung the gun on him. Standing almost nose to nose with six feet of smirking male had dampened her eagerness to discover Sebastian's reaction to her engagement. Her dream of rational discourse with Sebastian now seemed not only highly unlikely, but dangerously naive.

Jordy backed into the crowd, trodding on the toes of the man behind him. "Never mind. It weren't important."

Sebastian reached around and gently plucked the gun from her hand. She glared at his chest.

Now that the danger was over, Big Gus roused himself. "Wait one bloody minute, Kirkpatrick. I finded her. I wants to keep her."

"She's not a puppy, Angus." Sebastian tossed the primed weapon at him.

Big Gus ducked. The man behind him caught the weapon between two fingers.

"I know she ain't no puppy. She's a lass. And a right comely one at that."

Sebastian peered into Prudence's face as if seeing her for the first time. His nose crinkled. "A bit plain for your tastes, isn't she?"

Prudence shot him a dark look.

Big Gus scratched his head. "I ain't noticed it."

She squirmed as Sebastian caught a handful of her hair and deftly knotted it on top of her head. He grasped her cheeks in his other hand and squeezed. "See what I mean. Plain as a sparrow."

Big Gus frowned as his temptress puckered into a herring. "The light weren't so good when I caught her."

With an impotent huff, Prudence jerked away and started down the slope. Sebastian caught her easily, spinning her into his arms. Her back slammed into his chest, as his hard forearm snaked around her waist.

She drove her heel into his shin. "Damn you, Sebas—"

He clapped a hand over her mouth. His furious whisper warmed her ear. "Don't call me that. These men are not ardent Bach admirers." His grip tightened. "I can't hold off Big Gus much longer. Perhaps it's time you decided if you'd rather share his bedroll or mine."

Her struggles subsided. As her delicious body went pliant in his arms, Sebastian's embrace changed subtly. He softened his grip until only the pads of his fingertips touched her lips.

She grew in a shaky breath and spoke against his fingers. "What's the cost of your protection? I'm well aware you do nothing without a price."

The arm around her waist relaxed. He pressed his palm against the curve of her abdomen and bent slightly so his hips burrowed into the elegant curve of her rump. "What are you willing to pay?"

"Bastard," she murmured, closing her eyes in defeat.

"That I am. Among other things." He tucked her hand under his elbow and backed toward the cavern. "I thought you were a man who fancied buxom blondes," he called to Big Gus.

"I like blondes," Big Gus said hopefully.

Sebastian laid a brotherly hand on Devony's shoulder and gave her a gentle shove down the hill.

"But, Kirk," she whined, "you promised we were going to—"

"You'll like Big Gus, Miss Blake. He came by his name honestly." Leaving them both sputtering, Sebastian flipped aside the fur and pulled Prudence into the cavern.

Before she could get her bearings, he shoved her down on a stool and squatted in front of her.

His fingers dug into her shoulders. "I'm going to check on the others. Unless you'd care to get better acquainted with Big Gus and his cronies, I'd suggest you stay put until I get back. Do you understand?"

Her new spectacles made her eyes look huge. She nodded mutely, and he freed her with reluctance.

As he turned away, her slender shoulders slumped. "I could have shot you, you know."

He brushed a stray lock of hair out of his eyes. "I know. For a moment there, I thought you were almost human."

Without another word, he ducked out of the cavern, leaving her alone.

Prudence shifted on the hard stool, still sore from the harrowing coach ride. Her bracing anger had fled as quickly as it had come, leaving only the sour weight of fear. Her weary thoughts ran in circles. Was Tricia safe? Had Sebastian-cat been trampled? What would she do if Sebastian found Squire Blake and the coachman dead?

Her gaze strayed of its own volition to the rumpled blankets spread beside the sputtering lantern. Had Sebastian touched Devony the way he had touched her? Had his beautiful mouth roamed Devony's body the way it had roamed hers? A sharp pain stabbed beneath her ribs at the vision of Devony's long limbs entwined with his. It wouldn't be the first time, would it? She stared at the ceiling of the cavern to keep from crying.

The cavern was little more than an animal's den gouged out of the cliffside and sheltered by a stone overhang. A bottle of whisky sat next to a glowing bed of coals.

She unfastened the pearl buttons of her shoulder cape and eased out of her redingote. Travel had rumpled the dove gray satin of her gown. A long tear in her skirt revealed a peek at her silk stockings and one lacy garter.

"Good·God, it is ye!"

She screamed as a figure swathed in rags crawled under the curtain.

He bounded across the cave and clapped a hand over her mouth. "Stop the bellerin', lass. They'll hear ye all the way to Glasgow." He unwound his scarf.

"Jamie!" she cried at the sight of his familiar, homely face and red hair. Not even a month's worth of dirt could dim the radiance of his tangled mop.

"No, it's Bonnie Prince Charlie come back to take Culloden." He snatched her hand in his. "Follow me. If what Jordy told me about MacKay is true, we ain't got much time."

"Time?" Prudence repeated, clinging stubbornly to the stool. "Sebastian told me to stay here. Did he send you to fetch me?"

"I've come to rescue ye."

"No need for that. Sebastian has already rescued me."

Jamie rolled his eyes heavenward. "Lord, give me strength. Where's Tiny when I need him? I came to rescue ye *from* Sebastian, ye daft chit."

Prudence frowned. The untidy knot Sebastian had fashioned of her hair flopped over her face. "You think he might do me some sort of physical harm?"

Sarcasm ripened Jamie's brogue. "Perish the thought! He'll probably order up a wee bit of tea to celebrate yer upcomin' weddin' to Killian MacKay. Shall we send fer Old Fish to serve them little pats of butter shaped like tulips?"

"Roses," she corrected him absently. Sighing, she flipped her hair back and rested her chin on her hand. "It's his own fault I was forced to accept MacKay's proposal. I've no intention of marrying the man. Once I explain that, I'm certain Sebastian will be reasonable about it."

Jamie knelt beside her. "What makes ye think he'll give ye the chance to explain?" She turned her face away from the unflinching honesty in his hazel eyes, but Jamie caught her chin and forced it back. "I've never seen him this way, lass. He might not mean to hurt ye, and he might even be sorry after, but by then it'd be too late fer both of ye. Don't ye understand?"

"She understands very well, if her honorable sheriff has completed her education on bandits, as I suspect he has."

Too late, the chill night wind ploughed across their skin. They looked up like guilty children to find Sebastian standing over them, his arms heaped with moth-eaten blankets and a small trunk Prudence recognized as her own. She wondered how long he had been standing there.

"Shall I catalogue my crimes as she once described them to me?" He tossed down the blankets and trunk. "I am the faceless terror of both Scotland and England. A grim reminder of the savagery that lurks in the heart of civilized man. I rob and kidnap"—he cast her a smoky glance— "and ravish."

Jamie straightened. "May I have a word with ye?"

"Out, Jamie."

Jamie grinned hopefully. "I thought I'd sit fer a spell while the two of ye get reacquainted."

Sebastian didn't even look at him. "Out. Now."

Jamie tossed Prudence a helpless glance, then ducked out of the cavern, leaving the fur swinging.

Sebastian turned his back on her and shook out the blankets.

"The others?" she asked softly.

"All safe. Tricia, Boris, and Sebastian-cat are under Tiny's ample wing. Devony has found Big Gus's charms more potent than his shortcomings, and your coachman and Squire Blake were alive when they were left at the carriage. I sent a man back to check on them."

"Thank you."

He grunted in reply.

She toyed with her skirt. "I must confess it was a bit unsettling to discover you'd returned to your life of crime."

He lifted his shoulders in a shrug more Gallic than Scottish. "I developed a certain fondness for eating in my stay at Lindentree. The workhouses were all full, and I'd been a Presbyterian and a rake a bit too long to commit myself to a monastery."

As he squatted to smooth the blankets, his homespun breeches clung to the arc of his narrow hips. Prudence wondered what had become of his brilliant kilt, but was afraid to ask. This man was a stranger. His icy demeanor held not even a hint of the gentle humor she remembered. The awkward silence between them deepened. She was desperate to show him her newfound sophistication, to prove she was no longer the clumsy, besotted fool he must remember.

"I received five proposals in Edinburgh," she blurted out.

He pivoted on his heel, lifting a polite eyebrow. "Any of them decent?"

"Only three," she confessed, wishing she had kept her mouth shut.

He turned back to his task. "I believe that brings your total to five decent and three lewd, my offer to make you my mistress included, of course."

Her composure faltered at hearing his tender declaration reduced to such crass terms. He unbuckled the leather straps of her trunk. As he held a scrap of paper up to the meager light, his soft laugh chilled her.

"An excellent likeness. Which of your lovers is the artist? Tugbert? The Scot I saw fondling you on the street? Or is this your own work? I don't remember sketching being among your interests, but you are a woman of many talents."

"You saw me? On the street?"

"Aye. I happened to be in the neighborhood."

His gruff tone did not fool her. She remembered the persistent shadow of the lamplighter on the evening she had met MacKay. Her heart skipped a beat. Sebastian hadn't left her at D'Artan's mercy. His ruse of apathy on the terrace had been just that. He had followed her. Watched over her. Perhaps even cared for her. But now his flinty gaze belied his affable grin. He looked less guardian angel than mocking Lucifer.

She wished he would take off the mask. The shadows it made of his eyes unnerved her. She watched his deft hands smooth the wanted notice, remembering all the times he had tried to make her afraid of him. They were strong hands, competent and swift enough to muffle a scream before it started. What would he say if she told him she slept with that handbill under her pillow each night? That it was creased and worn to softness by her touch? She opened her mouth, then closed it again, unable to bear the mockery of his laughter.

"Come now, don't be modest, dear," he said. "The phrase, 'Reward Provided Alive or Upon Staunch Evidence Of Death' simply rings with your flair for melodrama. 'Gray Eyed and Well Favored'? Such flattery! How did you know I was well favored? Did Tricia tell you? Or was it Devony?"

Prudence's lips tightened. When Sebastian saw she wasn't

going to deny or defend, his grin faded. He bent over the lantern, sneering. Her gaze locked on the unforgiving lines of his back as he turned the light higher.

Sophistication was a dismal failure. Perhaps she should attempt honesty.

She smoothed her skirts over her knees and took a deep breath. "I've missed you, Sebastian."

His fingers twitched, touching the hot chimney of the lantern. He bit off a curse and whirled around, jerking off the mask. Prudence gasped. There was little trace of Tricia's urbane fiancé in him now. Anyone who saw him would swear he was a Highlander, born and bred. His hair was long. The ends of the shaggy cascade curled against his shoulders, sandy bright against skin darkened by wind and weather.

He seemed broader, more muscular, and infinitely more dangerous. His savage demeanor led a devastating edge to his good looks—an edge honed to lethal sharpness by his expression of pure contempt. She had to struggle not to flinch beneath it. His anger in the jail was mere annoyance compared to this new bitterness.

Too late, Prudence realized she *had* stumbled into the lair of an animal—a predator, cunning and feral and hungry.

Twenty-four

"Why, I do believe you might ravish me!" Prudence said in both disbelief and wonder.

Sebastian's lips curved in a roguish smile. The wild tattoo of her heart shifted to a slower, more jolting beat.

"I wouldn't be much of a bandit if I didn't, would I?" he said. "I should hate to disappoint you. You'd have nothing to tell Sir Arlo over tea when you get home."

Her gaze dropped to the cozy nest he had fashioned of the blankets, then wandered to the entrance of the cavern. She knew their privacy was illusory. Big Gus's men lay just down the slope, their thieves' ears tuned to every stray crack of a branch.

"A scream would be a nice touch," Sebastian said in a conspiratory whisper. "It would enhance my reputation immeasurably."

She blinked up at him. Her natural curiosity won out over her trepidation. "Have you ever ravished anyone before?"

"No." He touched a finger to his lips. "But pray don't tell. I should hate for it to get out. I try to think of it as a timeworn tradition. Pirates, bandits, Americans, all sorts of ill-meaning scoundrels have succumbed to the temptation."

She pulled off her spectacles and squinted at him. "Have you been drinking?"

"Copiously. But staring down the barrel of that pistol gripped in your delicate little hand did much to sober me."

"Perhaps we should discuss this tomorrow when you're sober," she said, laying her spectacles on the folded redingote.

"Fine. I wasn't in the mood for discussion anyway."

He started toward her. She ducked beneath his arm and grabbed the warm bottle from beside the coals.

"Would you care for another drink?" she asked. With any luck, she thought, she might be able to coax him into drinking himself insensible.

He took a long swig from the bottle, and wiped his mouth on the back of his hand, sighing with satisfaction. "Whisky always make me feel powerfully lusty."

She snatched the bottle from him and tipped it to her own lips. There was no logical reason she should start being lucky now. Sebastian plucked the bottle away and tossed it over his shoulder, not caring that it was uncorked.

His warm fingers curled around her own. "Do you know how long it's been since I've had a woman?"

She glanced nervously at the blankets. "About fifteen minutes, if my calculations are correct."

He drew her against the unyielding length of his body. "Wrong again, Miss Isaac Newton."

Prudence shivered. Sebastian had touched her so many times in tenderness, holding the hard edge of his masculine strength in check. It was a shock to realize how much stronger than she he was. A dangerous thrill of anticipation shot through her.

Her fingers kneaded the nest of curly hairs spilling over his chest. She dared not look at his face, fearful her gaze might wander to his lips. "Villainy suits you poorly, Lord Kerr."

"Not as poorly as it did before I met you." He arched a devilish eyebrow. "I've been practicing." He twirled her in a neat circle and backed her toward the blankets.

She closed her eyes, dizzied by their primitive dance and the intoxicating warmth radiating from his bare chest. "I've never been ravished before," she said, her voice shaking. "I shan't be any good at it."

"There's really nothing to it. You just yell and thrash about. I'll do the rest."

He hooked his foot around the back of her ankle, tripping her and catching her in the same movement. He eased her to the blankets, following her down with inevitable grace.

Her hands seemed to belong to someone else. How had they gotten so enmeshed in the pale hairs of his chest? She slanted a look at him through her lashes. "Was Jamie right? Will you be sorry afterward?"

His jaw tightened. "Probably." He reached across her to kill the lantern. "But not during."

He was little more than a shadow above her, but the darkness only increased his substantial warmth and the husky reverberation of his voice. His fingers worked their way down the tiny pearl buttons of her bodice with ruthless skill.

As Sebastian shoved the gown from her shoulders, his deliberate roughness failed him. He had forgotten how delicate and pronounced her collarbones were, how fragile the hollows beneath. It would take little force from him to bruise her tender skin. His grip softened. His thumbs betrayed him, stroking the silky union of skin and bone, finding the velvety dip at the base of her throat where he longed to press his lips. Dear God, what was he doing? She was so fine, so lovely. He had no right to touch her with his rough scoundrel's hands. He leaned back, beguiled by the porcelain splendor of her skin against the dark wool blanket.

His harsh breathing filled the silence. Prudence held her own breath as his expression shifted like quicksilver between desire and bewilderment.

She had seen that look before. On the terrace at Lindentree when she had shoved him away. If she pushed him away now, he might walk out of that den and never come back. It stunned her to realize that she didn't want him to go. She wanted to search for some lingering hint of tenderness, some tantalizing whisper of *her* Sebastian behind his rough facade.

Mustering her courage, she touched his unshaven cheek as if he were a dangerous animal she hoped to tame. She slid her fingers around his neck, winding them in the shaggy curls at his nape. His lashes swept down. From the corner of her eye, she saw his other hand rising, fingers curling hopefully toward her breast.

"No!" She scooted back until her shoulders touched the wall, catching his wrist with two fingers as if she actually had the strength to hold him if he chose to press on. "Don't touch me," she commanded, her boldness surprising her. "I don't wish to be ravished. I wish to be seduced. You may kiss me if you like," she added primly.

His scowl melted to a wry grin. "As opinionated as ever, aren't you, Miss Walker?"

But his hand linked with hers, pressing palm to palm as he lowered his head. His warm, dry lips touched hers. When he would have thrust his tongue deep in her mouth, she closed her teeth against him. He gave a frustrated grunt, but as her own tongue explored the seam of his lips, it turned into a groan. After an endless moment of this exquisite torture, she let him into her, a tiny bit at a time, drawing back when he got too greedy.

Sebastian caught on to her game fast, easing his tongue into the hot, wet shelter of her mouth, then withdrawing to nibble and tease the sensitive inner skin of her lips. He caught on too fast. Prudence found herself clinging to his hand, not to keep it from roaming, but to find some substance in the shifting sands of pleasure and anticipation. She forgot to stop him when he leaned forward. He pressed against her until only their mouths, hands, and groins touched. With each deepening foray of his tongue, he rubbed the hard ridge of his arousal against the sleek satin of the gown trapped between them.

"Wait," Prudence said. She pulled away from him, fighting to control her trembling. "You must say something nice now."

His lips nuzzled her throat. "Take off your gown."

"No. Something truly nice."

Sighing, he pressed his lips to her ear. "Your hair smells like flowers."

"Mmmm. That *was* nice," she whispered.

He took advantage of her approval to plunge his tongue

into her ear. She gasped, unprepared for the answering flood of warmth between her thighs.

He traced her earlobe with his tongue. "You want to hear something else nice?"

She nodded, too dazed to notice that his hand had untangled from hers and was stealthily working its way up beneath her gown.

His voice was a husky whisper. "For every time you've pulled back on me, I'm going to do the same to you. I'm going to kiss you and tease you until you're begging me to love you."

She tilted her head to meet his intent gaze, her eyes glazed with desire and doubt. At the exact moment his lips met hers, his fingers breached her silken drawers, dipping into a honey as hot and sweet as her mouth under his.

Prudence quaked as his warm, rough fingers plundered her, soothing and maddening with equal grace.

She buried her face in his shoulder. "I'm afraid, Sebastian."

"So am I, angel. So am I."

But his fear didn't stop him from undressing her and laying her back on the coarse blankets, prepared to make good on his vow. Prudence fought back a shiver as the scratchy blanket met her bare skin. She closed her eyes, swimming in a sea of contrasts. Sebastian's unshaven jaw grazed her cheek. His chest hairs teased the aching tips of her breasts like a thousand gold filaments, sparking an electrical response that made her abdomen contract wildly.

The rosy glow from the coals bronzed his skin as he drew off his breeches. She stared at his mouth, his chin, the faint smattering of freckles across his nose, anywhere but his eyes or much lower. He seemed suddenly a stranger, alien but achingly male, and determined to ease the hollowness yearning inside of her despite her fear.

His hands cupped her breasts, teasing one nipple between his fingertips. She bit back a moan as his lips closed around the taut peak of her other breast. He laved her with his tongue, then suckled her with an insatiable hunger. She tangled her fingers in his silky hair, writhing beneath him in a drugged stupor of pleasure. She reached for him, but he pushed her back, his hands gentle yet determined, as he fought to ignore the hard ache of his own need.

"We played your game," he said in a husky whisper. "Now we play mine."

His lips trailed across her flushed skin, and he nibbled without mercy at the satiny softness behind her ear, the delicate crease along the inner curve of her elbow, the smooth plane of her abdomen.

Her breathing quickened as he coaxed apart her trembling thighs. His nimble fingers stroked the tight little bud nestled in the silky curls. Prudence pressed herself to his hand, silently begging favors of his fingers she could never have put into words. A dark, secretive pleasure trembled through her veins. Remembering the others so near, she muffled her moans against his shoulder.

For Sebastian, touching her was like touching a woman for the first time. He had forgotten what a delight it was to linger over a woman's body, to explore all the sweet, musky clefts and hollows with his fingers, and then with his lips and tongue. He had never tasted anything so sweet, so infernally intoxicating. There wasn't a pleasure garden in Paris or London to compare to the wonder of Prudence. He wanted to pour the heated whisky over her skin and lick it away, drop by drop. A groan tore from his throat.

He pushed it to the limit for both of them, prolonging the exquisite pleasure until it was almost pain. Prudence felt herself becoming a shameless, wanton creature beneath the shimmering agony of his touch.

She turned her face into her hair and moaned, "Please, oh, please, Sebastian."

He stopped touching her then, completely stopped, and she thought she would die.

"What do you want, Prudence?" he asked hoarsely. "Say it." He knew he was being a bully, but he didn't care. He had waited too long to hear the words.

Her voice broke. "I want you."

With a flick of his fingertip, he shoved her over the precipice of ecstasy. He prepared to follow, but hesitated, knowing he was about to learn the answer to the question that had haunted him since he'd seen her embracing a stranger on an Edinburgh street. Had there been another man? And if there had, was he, Sebastian, strong enough to let his passion for her override his bitter jealousy?

He closed his eyes and pressed himself to her silken sheath. The warm dew of her body eased his passage until he met a faint resistance. He sucked in a breath through clenched teeth, pushing on until the throbbing length of him was gloved in her velvety warmth.

A groan of satisfaction escaped him. Another man might give her diamonds and pearls, but there was one thing only Sebastian Kerr would give her. Her fingernails dug into his back. He opened his eyes to find her cheeks wet with tears.

He brushed them away with his fingertips, ashamed that her pain had given him such exultation. She caught her bottom lip shyly between her teeth.

"I should have warned you," he said raggedly.

"No need. Papa did have anatomy books."

"And what would they recommend to ease the pain?" He fought to hold himself still while his brave beauty pondered the question.

Her eyes brightened. "Practice?"

He gave a surprised grunt as she arched her hips in an elegant circle against him. His voice cracked an octave too high. "I grow fonder of Papa with each passing moment."

He drew his hips back almost to the point of leaving her, then sank his shaft deep into her shuddering body. Prudence closed her eyes, surrendering herself to his sweet, endless filling. Her lips hungrily kissed his neck, catching beads of sweat like nectar on her tongue. Her moans and whispered, wordless pleas sang a counterpart to his throaty groans.

She had never imagined anything like this. She was being possessed, yet gaining a precious gift at the same time. Sebastian rocked hard against her, his tongue stroking the inside of her mouth in flawless rhythm. Waves of delight crested within her, swelling higher and higher until they finally broke over her, flooding her with exquisite pleasure. She gasped against his lips, her hands clinging to him.

As his own body went rigid, she instinctively arched against him, holding him tightly as he thundered to a shuddering climax, filling at last all the empty spaces in her life.

A desperate bellow rang off the lamplit walls of the tiny cavern.

Sebastian awoke and rolled over with a curse, throwing the back of his hand over his eyes and shielding Prudence with the blanket in the same motion. She sat up on her knees, jerking the blanket to her nose. Without Sebastian's warmth to cover her, she felt worse than naked.

The lantern lowered. Tiny's hair billowed around his head like the halo of a crazed Norse god.

Jamie peered around Tiny's shoulder, his hand over his eyes. He moaned as if he were going to be ill. "We ain't too late, are we? Tell me we ain't too late." He peeked between his bony fingers, taking in Prudence's huge eyes and tousled hair above the frayed edge of the blanket. "She looks to be all of a piece, don't she?"

"More than you will be when I get my hands on you," Sebastian growled, wrapping another blanket around his waist. "This had better be good."

"There's somethin' ye got to know, lad," Tiny said in his rumbling voice.

A wing of warning fluttered in Prudence's stomach.

Sebastian swung his legs over the edge of the pallet. "I doubt that. I was doing fine before you barged in."

Tiny swallowed hard. "It's MacKay. I fear we've made a turrible mistake and snatched his bride-to-be."

Prudence eased the blanket upward, planning to pull it over her head if an opportune moment arose.

"MacKay's bride?" Sebastian stood, running a hand through his hair.

The blanket rode dangerously low on his hips. His attempt at pacing was thwarted by the suffocating size of the cavern and Tiny's immense presence. He had to satisfy himself with circling the blankets. Prudence flinched as a lean, muscular calf brushed her back.

To her shock, Sebastian threw back his head and laughed. "All these years and the stubborn old cuss has never married.

I must have underestimated Tricia's charms. We'd best send her back. He'll have the redcoats on us for sure. He's worse than his father when it comes to cozening up to the damnable English."

With Tiny's accusing gaze on her, Prudence swallowed hard, feeling worse than damnable. Jamie's cheeks inflated with a worried breath.

Tiny folded his massive arms across his chest. "That's not the end of it."

"It is fer him." Jamie gripped Tiny's elbow. "Ye heard him. I've changed me mind. Be off with ye."

Tiny shook him away. The lantern threw rocking shadows on the wall. "There's more."

"More?" Sebastian said lightly. "Pray, do tell. My infinite patience is wearing thin."

Tiny pointed at Prudence. Her fingers froze around the blanket.

"That lass told Big Gus to refer all claims fer ransom to her fiancé, Laird Killian MacKay of Strathnaver."

For a long moment, the only sound was the creak of the lantern suspended from Tiny's hand.

Sebastian slowly pivoted to face Prudence. A cold light dawned in his eyes.

She shrank against the wall. Shrugging, she accidentally dislodged the blanket from one bare shoulder. A tremulous smile curved her lips. "I was going to tell you, Sebastian. Truly, I was."

"When?" His voice was deadly soft. "After you and MacKay settled into *my* castle and raised a passel of whey-faced, mealymouthed brats?" His eyes narrowed to silver slits. "First the sheriff. Now MacKay. You lead a very interesting life for such a dour spinster, don't you, dear?"

She felt the color drain from her face. "That's not fair. You don't understand—"

Tiny took a step backward as Sebastian's *r*'s began to roll. "I understand all too well. I sold my soul for Dunkirk and still couldn't win it. All you had to do was waltz in and bat your pretty eyelashes for that miserable lech MacKay."

She stared at the blankets, fighting back tears. Should she confess her engagement was only a ruse to trap him for

MacKay? Sebastian had every reason to distrust her. After all, she had betrayed him to Tugbert. If he believed she was betraying him to yet another enemy, she might never have a chance to make amends. But as she stared up at him, she was no longer sure she wanted to. All of her noble intentions to play angel of mercy, then retreat meekly back to her own life, melted in the condemning heat of his glare.

"Why should you care who I marry?" she asked, her voice rough with bitterness. "You're the one who offered me to your grandfather."

His fingers bit into her chin. "Would you have perferred I had taken you away to Paris that night? Raped you into insensibility to get D'Artan's godforsaken formula?"

She jerked free of his grasp. "I should have shot you," she said icily.

"I wish you had."

"I ought to be worth a pretty fortune to you now. Shall I help you pen the ransom note? Would you like to send MacKay my ear or perhaps a few of my toes?"

His scathing glance took her in, from her tangled mass of hair to her little toes peeping out from beneath the rumpled blankets. "Are you sure he'd even want you now? MacKay's not too fond of used goods."

Jamie's muffled sound of protest was almost her undoing, but she managed to meet his gaze evenly. "Especially goods used by Kerr men."

Sebastian's face went white. His hand twitched, and for a timeless second she thought he would strike her. Instead, he reached down and flicked the blanket back over her shoulder.

A wayward tear trickled down the side of her nose. With a snort of disgust, Sebastian reached under the blankets and tossed a scrap of tartan into her lap. She rubbed the soft wool between thumb and forefinger. It was what was left of Sebastian's plaid, frayed and worn almost bald in spots. She remembered the tender care he had given it, the reverent pride with which he had touched it. It was the Kerr plaid, his only plaid, he had said, and he couldn't afford another.

She lifted her eyes, gazing at him with regret and pity. The brackets around his mouth deepened for an elusive moment, then his face smoothed into the flawless veneer she was coming to hate. He snatched up his breeches and boots.

"Guard her," he commanded Tiny with a dark look at Jamie. "If anyone tries to get to her, fire one shot in the air. If she tries to escape"—his even gaze met Prudence's—"shoot her."

He flung the curtain aside and ducked into the dawn. Tiny followed. Jamie hung behind, his eyes brimming with mute apology until Tiny's hand reappeared to jerk him out by the collar. Prudence hugged her knees and rested her cheek against the coarse blanket.

Her gaze fell on the handbill resting on top of the trunk. The Edinburgh artist had been as much a fool as she. He had captured the warm promise of Sebastian's mouth without revealing any of its sulky threat. For her, the threat had now become a promise.

If his men were goblins, then Sebastian Kerr was no less than their king. She rolled to her side, pressing the scrap of tartan to her mouth to muffle her sobs.

Twenty-five

Sebastian pulled off his mask as he climbed from the dark ring of pines and up the hill, his ankle throbbing in the dawn cold. Tiny dozed beside the cavern, a musket laid across his knees. Sebastian nudged him. Tiny started, blinking guiltily.

"Go prepare their coach for a return to Edinburgh," Sebastian said softly.

Tiny gave his shoulder a brief squeeze before trotting down the hill.

Sebastian leaned against the cavern wall and drew in a deep breath of the bracing mountain air. There had been nights of exile in Paris and London when he would have given all he owned for one whiff of this purity to wash away the sooty miasma of the city.

His talk with Devony had firmed his resolve, but done little to clear his mind. He stared at his rough hands, unable to forget the shattering instant when he had wanted to hit Prudence. To raise his fist and strike the smug accusation right off her lovely face. Being reminded he was Brendan Kerr's son made him want to respond as his father would have done. With his fists.

He lowered his arms with a sigh. Perhaps his father had been right. He was clumsy and silly and not even clever enough to tell the difference between love and pretense.

Prudence had betrayed him to Tugbert and to MacKay. It hadn't been revenge enough to drive him out of England bound like an animal. She sought to imprison him forever in the Highlands, forced to watch as she took her place as MacKay's doting bride and claimed Dunkirk, the only legacy his father had left him, except for a nose that had been broken one too many times.

A scowl creased his brow as he slipped into the cavern.

Prudence sat on the stool, her gloved hands folded primly in her lap. She was clean and flushed ruddy from a brisk scrubbing in the icy water. Her hair was tied back with one of his own frayed satin ribbons. He saw no trace of the woman who had responded to his bittersweet seduction with such eager passion.

His stomach clenched with foreboding. Prudence's composure never augured well for him.

As he approached, she stiffened warily. "If you've come to ravish me, just throw my gown over my head and have done with it."

He eyed the alluring swell of her breasts beneath the redingote and grinned wickedly. "A tempting offer to be sure, but I'd hate to muss your charming new garments. Were they a gift from your fiancé?"

He ran a thumb over the lush fox of her shoulder-cape with the assessing touch of a thief. His knuckles brushed her throat and she jerked her gaze guiltily from his lips. Their eyes met and she flushed, obviously embarrassed that his merest touch could evoke such a wanton response in her.

As the worn linen of his breeches tautened across his groin, Sebastian realized he was in danger of being caught in his own snare. He heeded the warning by crossing to the basin and splashing cold water on his face, whistling jauntily all the while.

Prudence donned her spectacles, deliberately sliding yet another fragile barrier between them. She peered over their rims at Sebastian's tousled hair, the drops of water misting his chest, the breeches riding low on his hips. His sheer male beauty was a primitive thing, both threat and allure.

She hid her turmoil behind clipped tones. "How did Tricia

stand you in the mornings? Cheerful *and* gorgeous. It must have been a daunting combination."

"Simple. Tricia never rose before noon. By then I was bleary-eyed and dissolute."

"As you were last night?"

"Precisely."

Their eyes met, and without warning they both remembered the many other things he had been last night—tender and rough, mischievous and sensitive, patient and daring.

He turned his back to her and pulled on another shirt. By its patched condition, she judged his selection to be very limited.

She resisted the urge to duck as he swung around, pistol in hand. "What are you going to do? Shoot me?"

He tucked the pistol in his breeches as a smile flickered across his face. "Too quick."

He looped a length of rope over his shoulder.

"Hang me?"

"Too merciful."

He started toward her. She swallowed hard. "Beat me?"

He squatted in front of her. "There's only one way to make you truly miserable. I'm going to marry you, Duchess."

His words sang wildly through her mind, then stuck on one discordant note. *Duchess.* He beamed at her as if he expected her to throw her arms around him and smother his face with kisses.

Her fist came out of nowhere, smashing into his jaw with a force that would have quelled Tiny. He fell backward, treating her to the gratifying sight of the soles of his boots.

He sat up, rubbing his chin ruefully. "Are you sure your father wasn't a boxer?"

She stood, her eyes narrowed and her fists still clenched. "You wouldn't marry me for love, but you'll marry me quick enough for a title, won't you? You blackhearted, no-good, grasping, villainous—" She sputtered into incoherence.

"Scoundrel?" he suggested, climbing to his feet. "Rogue? Muzzy-headed lout? You wound me, darling. After the tender moments we shared last night, I had hoped you'd wish to do the honorable thing by me."

"Tender moments, my bustle. You'd tup a goat if it backed up to you."

"Tsk, tsk, tsk. Such language! I dare say you didn't learn that from one of your father's anatomy books."

"It wasn't marriage on your mind last night, was it?"

His jaw tightened. "Unless I'm mistaken, it wasn't marriage on your mind either. It certainly wasn't your impending marriage to Killian MacKay."

Her nostrils flared in impotent rage. She turned her back on him. "What do you think to gain by marrying me? Does lunacy run in your family?"

"Not lunacy. Pragmatism." He rested his hands lightly on her shoulders. "With you as my wife, MacKay won't dare bring the redcoats down on us. If he should be so foolish, they'll have no case. You, my sweet duchess, are going to buy me the time I need to get what I want from both MacKay and my grandfather."

She laughed shakily as she bowed her head. "Such a tender declaration of your affections, my lord. I'm touched."

The nape of her neck was very pale, Sebastian noticed. He hid his pang of regret behind brisk purpose. "Have you any paper?"

She walked over to her trunk without a word. Her face expressionless, she handed him a sheet from the London *Times*. Her betrothal announcement was inked in bold letters at the top of the page. She bent to fish out a quill and a bottle of ink.

"That wasn't the sort of paper I meant," he said angrily.

Prudence shrugged artlessly. The set of his jaw made her wonder how wise she was to bait him.

Before she could hand him a creamy sheet of her stationery, he snatched up the handbill with his likeness and tore it in two. A bereft sound escaped her, but she disguised it as a cough. Using an outcropping of rock as a desk, Sebastian scribbled furiously. She stood on her tiptoes to peer over his shoulder.

He dipped the quill in the ink, wrote something, then scratched it out with furious strokes. "How do you spell 'torture'?" he muttered.

Her lips tightened to a mutinous pout before she sweetly replied, "T-o-r-c-h-e-r."

He frowned. "Looks odd. Oh, well. No matter. D'Artan won't care." He kept writing.

She crept nearer. "What are you doing? Offering to pull out my fingernails so I'll surrender the formula?"

He pursed his lips. "Excellent idea." He scribbled another line, then folded the paper into a packet.

It took Sebastian far longer to write the second note. He hesitated before signing it, knowing he was about to seal not only her fate, but his own as well. The quill hung poised above the paper. Prudence hovered behind him, so near he could feel the soft whisper of her breath against his nape. He gripped the quill tighter, bringing it to bear against the paper in an untidy scrawl.

Sebastian turned so fast that Prudence had to stumble backward so he wouldn't step on her. "Now all I need is something to prove I've got you."

He stroked his chin. His gaze raked her. Her eyes widened as he bent to slip the wicked *skean dhu* out of his boot. Her toes curled deep into her shoes.

She backed away. "A-A-About my toes. I was only joking. I doubt if Laird MacKay would even recognize my toes. He's never seen them."

Sebastian advanced on her, dagger in hand, his expression resolute.

"Or my ears. He's never seen them either. Tricia made me wear those dreadful ear bobs. Why, I'd be willing to bet he wouldn't know my ears from Boris's . . ."

Her voice faded as the stone wall dug into her shoulders. Her knees went weak at Sebastian's intoxicating nearness. She flinched as he reached around and drew away the satin ribbon. Her hair fell in a silky net around her shoulders.

A sob of breathless laughter escaped her. "Oh, my hair. Of course. Take as much as you like. It's quite impossible. I can't do anything clever with it."

His fingers raked her scalp, burrowing deep to free a stray lock from the soft mass. He drew it against her cheek, enchanted by the silky skein, lost in a vision of her astride him, her hair a web of burgundy around his face.

He leaned forward, bracing a knee between hers, his head lowering toward hers. He lifted a hand to stroke her cheek. It was then he remembered the dagger and its grim purpose.

"Ow!" Prudence wailed as his fingers tightened around her hair.

"Sorry," he murmured.

He touched the razor edge of the dagger to the soft strand. The blade pressed, snapping the first of the delicate filaments. His knuckles went white against the hilt.

"For Christ's sake!" he erupted. "*You* cut the blasted stuff. I know nothing about cutting women's hair." He thrust the dagger into her hand, then winced as she cheerfully sawed at the lock he'd chosen. "Not so much, will you? I don't want a bald bride."

"It is *my* hair," she reminded him, thrusting the hair at him. She watched as he divided the hank and tucked half into each note.

"What am I to be, Sebastian?" she asked. "Your hostage or your bride?"

He wet his lips before kissing her hard. "Neither. Both."

He tied on his mask and gathered his meager belongings with icy efficiency, leaving Prudence standing limply against the wall. She fastened the buttons of her shoulder-cape with stiff fingers, knowing the cold outside could not compare to the fearful ice spreading through her heart.

Prudence emerged from the cavern into a dazzling burst of sunlight on frost. The last tendrils of morning mist drifted through the trees. In the clearing below, Sebastian saddled two sturdy horses, his face set in concentration, his old limp more pronounced. His mask shadowed his eyes.

She started down the hill, the stares of the bandits crawling against her skin. As she reached the clearing, Tiny strode through the trees, triumphantly wielding a straggly, dripping mess in one fist. She recoiled, believing for one horrible moment that it was a dead rat, or worse yet, a severed head.

Tiny held his trophy aloft. "That wee countess cleans up real nice once ye wash all that powder and paint off her."

Prudence was even more horrified as she recognized Tricia's wig. Surely only death could separate Tricia from her wig!

Sebastian tightened a cinch with obvious unconcern. "You're a better man than I, Tiny. I never could get her out of all that foolishness."

"She's a feisty devil, she is. She didn't like it none. I had to throw her in the pond."

Sebastian frowned. "I thought the pond was frozen."

"It was. But I chopped a hole in the ice before I tossed her in."

"How thoughtful," Prudence murmured, dodging a spray of water as Tiny fondly shook the wig.

His grin faded as Tricia came charging into the clearing with a furious screech, tattered parasol in hand.

She rammed the parasol into Tiny's rock-hard stomach, spitting at him like an enraged kitten. "Give me my wig, you overgrown barbarian! I'll see you in Newgate for this, if it's the last thing I do!"

Prudence gaped. She had never realized how much Tricia resembled her own papa. Freckles skimmed her aunt's pale cheeks. Strings of auburn hair plastered her face.

Tiny rumbled with laughter and held the wig just out of Tricia's reach. She jumped up and down like a terrier yapping at a bull, then began to flail him with the parasol.

Sebastian could not suppress a snort of laughter. Tricia spun around to see who would dare make sport of her, and glared at the masked highwayman.

Sebastian met her stony gaze without flinching, shocking Prudence with his boldness. This was the moment of truth. Tricia knew her lover's voice groggy with sleep, and had traced his features with her fingertip beneath the half-light of the moon.

The thought gave Prudence a sharp pang in the vicinity of her heart. After all, she reminded herself, Tricia was the wife Sebastian would have chosen. He had once judged Prudence good enough to be his mistress, but not his bride. All of her old feelings of inadequacy came flooding back. Without realizing it, she lifted a hand to smooth her hair into a chignon that wasn't there.

Tricia tilted her nose in the air. "You wicked scoundrel! God take pity on you if my niece's betrothed catches up with you. He is a powerful man, and I can promise you his retribution will be slow and painful."

Prudence felt the tension ease out of Sebastian's body. "Who are you engaged to?" he whispered to her. "God?"

"Why, if my own fiancé were here . . ." Tricia sniffed, mercifully leaving that threat unfinished.

Sebastian turned to Tiny, disguising his voice with a graveled brogue that made Prudence shiver. "Return the countess to her coach. The others are ready and waiting."

"Come, dear," Tricia commanded Prudence, twirling her ragged parasol. "It seems the cretin has taken my warning to heart. Shall we go?"

Prudence inched toward her aunt, wondering what her chances were of slipping away unnoticed.

Sebastian's warm hand closed over her elbow. "The young lady will remain with me."

Both Tricia and Tiny spun around to gape at them. Prudence lifted her chin, determined to salvage some shred of her pride. "You heard the man. I'm staying with him. I'm—I'm bored. I've decided a little jaunt might improve my disposition. They say the Highland air is just the thing for headaches."

"A jaunt?" Tricia echoed. "With a vicious highwayman?"

Prudence pulled off her spectacles. Her hair billowed around her face in a dark cloud. "I'll be fine, Auntie. Truly I will. He won't hurt me." Another lie to add to many, she thought.

Tricia stared at her niece as if seeing her for the first time, fascinated by the resolve in Prudence's violet eyes. "But Laird MacKay? Your engagement? The betrothal papers have been signed. The banns have been posted."

Prudence smiled faintly. "If anyone will understand, Killian will."

Sebastian's hand tightened on her elbow. Glancing at him, she saw his eyes narrowed to stormy slits.

Tiny laced a protective arm through Tricia's. "Come, me wee countess." He gave Sebastian a dark glance over her head. "Ye know how stubborn the young are when they take a notion in their silly noggins."

Tricia gazed up at him, bewilderment softening her features. As he led her away, she clung to his brawny arm without realizing it. "How could the girl be so ungrateful? I finally coaxed some old goat into marrying her and she runs off for a fling with a highwayman. You will watch after her, won't you? She's had her nose buried in a book her whole life. The poor dear hasn't an ounce of common sense."

"Aye, me lady," Tiny said soothingly. "I swear it on me poor mum's grave. I'll watch after the lass like she was me own sweet daughter."

"Stop squirmin', lass, or I'll have to shoot ye." Tiny oomphed as one of Prudence's flailing elbows caught him in the gut.

She clenched her teeth. "Wait until after the vows, won't you? So my husband can inherit." She aimed a kick at Tiny's shin. It was like striking an oak.

Prudence felt as if she had been riding for a lifetime. Every muscle in her body throbbed from the grueling trip up the mountain. She had finally slumped in the saddle, only to be awakened by Tiny snatching her off the horse.

The dirt road was deserted. Somewhere in the small village, a door slammed with a final thump.

Tiny cupped her elbows in his palms and lifted her over the threshold of a narrow house. As she hung in his grasp like an oversized rag doll, a freckled weasel of a man blinked at her curiously. She bared her teeth at him and he sidled away, his long, untidy whiskers aquiver. He could only be Jamie's father, she thought, and shuddered to think of the terrors a tiny Jamie must have inflicted on so timid a sire.

To her bleary eyes, everyone in the room seemed to be animals. Jamie slipped in and out like a sinuous fox, ready to bolt at the merest scent of danger. Jamie's father offered his bony back as a desk so Sebastian could set quill to parchment, signing the document that would bind them as man and wife. The firelight played over the lean planes of Sebastian's face. He was a sandy panther, both compelling and dangerous.

She wondered what sort of animal she might be. As Sebastian handed her the register and forced the quill between her fingers, the answer came to her.

Dinner.

She was a dinner animal.

A bitter viper of disappointment uncurled in her gut. This was hardly the moment of tenderness and celebration she had once dared to dream of. This night she bid farewell to her last hope of affection. She might have been happier at Lindentree as the cherished mistress of her aunt's husband. At least when Sebastian touched her, it would have been out of love at best, tender lust at worst, but never out of greed. Perhaps when this mockery was over, he would send her back to England to salvage some remnant of her dignity. She chewed on her lower lip, terrified she might burst into childish tears before them all.

Jamie's father peevishly asked them to kneel. Tiny lowered Prudence to her knees. The prayer book rustled in the minister's shaking hands. Tiny shuffled his feet while Jamie untucked his father's shirt and honked into the hem.

As Reverend Graham fumbled through a prayer, Sebastian stole a look at his bride, acutely aware of the slight pressure of her thigh against his own. Her chest rose and fell unevenly with each sullen breath. Her eyes were downcast, the lids swollen from weeping. Rather than detracting from her beauty, they gave her face a sultry maturity, stirring against the piquant curve of her cheek and the mutinous tilt of her lips.

He had avoided her all day, deliberately riding behind her, but unable to stop his gaze from drifting to the obstinate set of her slender shoulders. Why did she look so grim now? Was the prospect of marrying him that repugnant? She had once wanted him. But that was before she had entered the polished grace and elegance of society, he reminded himself. Perhaps her time in Edinburgh had opened her eyes to a richer and more opulent world. Perhaps she truly wished to marry MacKay, or a man like him. A man who could lavish her with jewels and wealth and take her anywhere in the world.

But even as he armored his heart with doubts, Sebastian was haunted by the memory of her tenderness when she had dared to fold him in the soft wings of her body, the husky catch in her voice when she had begged him to love her.

His body stiffened with unwanted desire. A fierce wave of possessiveness swept him. Her hand lay in the folds of her skirt. He reached over and took it in his own.

As Prudence stared at his wind-chapped knuckles, the minister's words faded to a buzz. Sebastian's tapered fingers laced around hers. His nails were clean and neatly trimmed. But for their strength and calluses, his hands might have been those of an artist. His thumb stroked the tingling center of her palm in a rhythm she recognized only too well.

"Well, lass, do ye swear it or not?"

She snatched her hand back. The minister was peering down his nose at her with unmistakable annoyance. The hard barrel of Tiny's pistol nudged her shoulders.

"I swear it," she snapped, having no idea if she was vowing to be shot or wed. From the mocking sparkle in Sebastian's eyes, it would hardly matter which.

His smooth, deep voice repeated his vows without faltering.

At last, Jamie's father commanded them to stand. "Is there a ring?"

Jamie opened a grimy burlap sack that jingled with stolen jewelry. Prudence glared at him. He snapped it closed, shrugging sheepishly.

His father wrung the prayer book in his hands. "You may give your bride a wedding kiss if you like."

She turned a cold cheek to Sebastian. He cupped her chin in his fingers and tilted her face to his. Her eyes widened as his tongue parted her teeth and swept her mouth in a feathery caress. She shivered as he drew away. The look he gave her from beneath his smoky lashes marked her as a fool for believing he might allow their marriage to stand in name only.

Prudence shoved a bannock into her mouth, tearing at the biscuit with her teeth like the small, mean-eyed animal she could feel herself becoming.

She huddled against a wall, wrapped in her rumpled redingote, and watched the world through a nest of tangled hair. The scene had the unreality of a dream.

The cracked face of the clock on the mantle told her it was well past midnight. Still the villagers kept pouring in, kegs of ale hoisted on their shoulders, sleepy children clinging to their hands. They had all come to congratulate the bridegroom, the dashing Kirkpatrick, who had kidnapped his bride and wed her at gunpoint. That did not seem to be an uncommon occurrence in this part of the world, and it called for a celebration of the groom's cunning and daring.

Tiny hefted his mug in a toast, spattering ale in Sebastian's hair. Sebastian gave him a mock growl as he swiped at the amber drops. A grizzled old Highlander sprawled on a faded settee tossed a jibe at Sebastian in a thick burr. Sebastian's answering grin reminded Prudence when she least needed it of what a devastatingly handsome man her new husband was.

She jerked her feet back as a sheep trotted into the parlor, his nails clicking on the hardwood floor. He sank down in front of the fire. Tendrils of steam rose from his damp wool.

Jamie's mother flitted in and out of the kitchen, bearing simmering bowls of haggis and dodging teacups tossed by a boisterous and drunken Tiny. She gave Jamie a wide berth and winced each time he called her "mum."

Prudence watched as she slipped her small treasures out from under the greedy eyes of the parlor full of thieves. A pewter thimble sank into a bubbling bowl of haggis. A china cow with no head disappeared beneath her skirts. A silver fork vanished under a chair cushion. Jamie waited until she'd trotted back to the kitchen before extracting the fork, biting it, and tucking it up his sleeve. Feeling Prudence's disapproving gaze, he winked at her. She ducked as a teacup went flying past her nose.

As far as Prudence could tell, being a wife wasn't much different from being a poor relation. No one came over to congratulate her. Sebastian ignored her. She was as invisible as she'd ever been. At least at Lindentree, she could plead a headache and escape to her room. She smothered a yawn with the back of her hand. The sheep gazed reproachfully at her as if she ought to be enjoying herself more. She stared back, musing how soft and inviting his wooly flank looked.

She gave his cheek a tentative scratch. He nuzzled his nose against her palm. Heartened by that overture, she lay back, resting her head against the fleecy underside of his belly and breathing deeply the damp, warm scent of his wool.

Sebastian wiggled his foot. His ankle had gone to sleep along with the rest of him. He rolled onto his back, and his hand plunged off the faded brocade of the settee. His knuckles rapped sharply on the floor. He groaned, stretching lazily as bizarre images flooded his mind: winged teacups; Jamie snuffling into his dad's shirt hem; women tumbling in and out of his blankets like acrobats. Good God, he thought, he'd best trade the traitorous whisky for some good honest Scottish ale! He knuckled his eyes, yawning, then froze, all of his thoughts stripped bare by a vision of Prudence, hair tumbled and legs akimbo, with murder in her eyes and a gun in her hand.

He sat straight up and peered over the back of the settee, and a wave of tenderness washed over him.

Prudence was propped against a pudgy sheep, eyes closed, legs splayed, and chin nestled on her chest. Her hair drooped over her face. Shadows smudged the skin beneath her eyes. Her spectacles hung askew on her nose. She looked like a bedraggled doll, dressed with care, then abandoned, broken and forlorn, by some thoughtless child. The sheep was chewing happily on the fur of her shoulder-cape.

Sebastian rose, stepping over a snoring Jamie. The fire had waned, but the shock of the cool air was nothing compared to the shock of discovering his visions were not dreams, but memories.

He knelt beside her, skirting the carnage of a teacup. Firelight brushed the delicate planes of her face. "My wife," he murmured, cherishing the word he had stolen for such a short time.

He lifted her in his arms. The sheep reluctantly spat out her cape. Prudence laced her hands behind his neck and snuggled deeper in his embrace. Her solid warmth reminded him that she was not a china doll that might shatter in his clumsy embrace, but a woman with the power to bend and glove and mold her lush curves to his own form. Guilt and desire beat sleepy wings in his belly.

As he lay her back on the settee, she blew out a soft breath between pursed lips, stirring his hair with a whisper of movement.

He pressed his mouth against hers.

Prudence stirred as smooth lips brushed across hers, dusting them with the taste of whisky and tobacco. Her eyes fluttered open.

"Good night, Mrs. Kerr," Sebastian whispered.

He climbed back over Jamie and sank down beside the sheep, oblivious to the bewildered wonder that touched her eyes.

Twenty-six

Tiny dumped the large coffer at Sebastian's feet with a grunt of exertion. "There it be. All of it. Jordy done good by ye."

The grizzled bandit behind Tiny flushed at the praise.

Milky sunshine dribbled out of the pale sky, painting the village road a murky gray. Snow melted in muddy patches. Prudence bounced up and down on her toes to warm herself.

They stood in the road in front of the Grahams' narrow cottage. A sleepy-eyed little girl watched from the next stoop, her thin arms protruding from a faded tunic.

Excitement was written in every tense line of Sebastian's body as he knelt beside the coffer.

Prudence nudged it with her toe. "What is it?"

He grinned up at her. "Your dowry."

"My dowry wouldn't be that heavy. I inherited an honorary peerage, not a treasury."

He unfastened the leather straps. "Then consider it a wedding present from my dear grandfather."

He threw back the lid. Prudence gasped. Tiny gave a low whistle of admiration as gold coins spilled from the coffer in a musical stream. Sebastian dug his hands into them. They poured through his fingers in shimmering columns.

Jamie flung himself to his knees and scooped up a handful. "I could buy me a fine pony with a few of these."

Sebastian rumpled his hair. "As far as I'm concerned, you

can buy the finest steed in Scotland. My charming grandfather saw fit to unfreeze all of our accounts."

Tiny scratched his head. "He did it. The old bastard really did it. What did ye do? Promise him yer firstborn son?"

Sebastian's grin faded. His eyes met Prudence's, and a slow flush crept into her cheeks.

Jordy pulled a thick sheaf of parchment from his shirt. "The other one sent this."

Sebastian unfolded the envelope, his hands none too steady.

Prudence adjusted her spectacles, fighting to keep her voice cool as an unexpected desolation swept her. "Have you got what you want? Will you send me back now?"

They all looked at her blankly.

Sebastian scanned the elegant scrawl, frowning. "I just wed you, lass," he said absently. "Why should I send you back?"

"That MacKay was an odd one." Jordy tapped his temple. "A bit teched in the head I believe."

Sebastian's eyes went cool and wary. "Why do you say that?"

"He laughed when he read yer note. Sputtered so hard I thought he was havin' a fit."

Prudence rocked back on her heels. "Perhaps he found your spelling amusing."

Glowering at her, Sebastian snapped the envelope shut. "A pity he wasn't having a fit. A happy MacKay gives me the jitters." He spilled gold into his sporran, then slammed the lid of the coffer. "I'd best pay Big Gus for his hospitality. Then we're going home. To Dunkirk."

"Sebastian?" Prudence said softly.

He swung on his heel, his good cheer dissolving to reveal he was as tense as a cat.

Prudence mustered the tatters of her logic. "Why don't you free me? You have what you want now. You're married to a duchess. You have a fortune in gold and your precious castle. You have no further use for me."

His crooked grin was a haunting echo of his once loving smile. He tilted her chin up with one forefinger. His thumb grazed her lower lip with a delicacy that sent shivers through her. "You'd be amazed at the uses I have for you."

He turned away, striding down the muddy road like he owned it. The others trailed behind. Prudence sank down on the stoop, propping her chin in her hand.

The little girl from the next cottage crept closer. Her adoring gaze followed Sebastian. "He's a bonny one, ain't he?"

Prudence's eyes narrowed. Wind and sun ruffled Sebastian's sandy hair to gilt. "He's bonny all right. And if you're smart, you'll find the ugliest man you know and beg him to marry you."

The child leaned against Prudence's leg, undaunted by her cynicism. "Me mum says he's like Robin Hood. Robbin' from the rich and givin' to them that needs it."

Prudence winced to hear her own innocent words echoed with such childish faith. Men and money. She was beginning to hate the both of them with equal fervor. Even Laird MacKay found her predicament amusing. And Sebastian had always chosen wealth over her. She saw again the gold spilling through his strong, sure fingers. Had he ever touched her with such loving grace?

The child buried her pug nose in the fur of Prudence's cape. Prudence glanced down, ashamed to be so caught up in her bitter musings that she hadn't noticed the girl's bare feet and painfully thin legs.

She hugged her close. She smelled like a child, even beneath the layer of dirt that weighted her hair and dulled her skin. Prudence looked around, really seeing the village perched on the barren shelf of the majestic Cairngorm mountains for the first time. Shutters hung crooked on sooty cottages. Chimneys crumbled into gaping holes where thatched roofs had been blown bare by the harsh winter winds. Spring would come soon, but not soon enough for this village.

Her gaze finally came to rest on the leather-bound coffer sitting at her feet. It was filled with blood money—D'Artan's blood money. Her lips twitched.

She gave the little girl a squeeze. "Tell me more about this Robin Hood of yours, my dear."

. . .

When Sebastian returned, Prudence was sitting on the coffer surrounded by a giggling, tumbling mass of children. He stopped in his tracks, caught unaware by the charm of the sight. Prudence's hair was disheveled, her face flushed with laughter. A wistful smile touched his lips.

How easy it was to imagine her with another child on her knee! A tawny-haired little girl with solemn violet eyes and a husky laugh. Or perhaps a boy with fine dark hair and a penchant for mathematics.

Jamie almost ran over him with the wagon, spurring him into movement, and Sebastian's smile faded. He could ill afford to indulge the wild, selfish hope that the night they had laid together might have borne fruit. As he approached, a towheaded boy threw a staunch arm around Prudence's neck and glared at him with jealous eyes.

Sebastian locked his hands at the small of his back. "Quite a brood you have here, lass. Are they all yours?"

Prudence bounced a plump baby on her knee. "Only the best behaved."

The baby lost his own thumb and tucked Prudence's finger in his mouth.

Jamie climbed down from the wagon, scratching his stomach. "If that don't beat all. Am I to load them up as well?"

Sebastian lifted an eyebrow, as if the decision were Prudence's.

"Of course not," she said, untangling the children from her skirts and handing the baby to an older boy with solemn eyes. "Run along home now, all of you."

They raced away, their laughter echoing on the wind. The last to go was a thin blonde girl. She pressed her lips to Prudence's cheek and whispered passionately, "I'll never ferget ye, Maid Marian. Never. Not even if I live to be twenty."

The girl's awestruck gaze devoured Sebastian from his boots to the crown of his hair. She bobbed a nervous curtsy before scampering away.

Sebastian watched her go, his brow furrowed in a curious frown. "Maid Marian?"

Prudence smoothed her skirts. "Simply a game we were playing."

Jamie was looking at her expectantly. She tucked loose strands of hair back in her queue, dusted off her shoes, and tugged at her redingote.

Jamie rolled his eyes. "If ye'll excuse me, Princess Prudence, I need to load the gold."

"Oh." She stood, stretching like a lazy cat before stepping away from the coffer.

Jamie caught one of the leather handles and tugged. Nothing happened. Prudence quenched a flare of panic.

He fixed Sebastian with a baleful glare. "It's just like Tiny to run off to his own cottage when there's work to be done."

Before Sebastian could reach to help him, Jamie hefted the coffer with both hands. Wiry muscles corded in his arms.

"Damn thing feels like it's full of rocks," he wheezed.

Prudence was seized by a sudden fit of coughing.

Jamie lashed the coffer to the wagon, muttering loudly to himself. "Hadn't even the common decency to ask for pound notes. Had to have a chest of gold like some godforsaken pirate." His voice rose. "Tight as a Scot, ye are, Sebastian Kerr, and always have been!"

Jamie sank down on the coffer, breathing hard. He met Prudence's gaze. "Don't ever forget it, lass. Jamie Graham said it first. Tight as a Scot, that man is."

Prudence dangled her feet off the ledge and watched snow billow out of the mountains in the north. The weather in the Highlands seemed to be as fickle as Sebastian's mood. Who would believe that it was nearly March? As they had traveled through the mountains toward Sebastian's boyhood home, the icy daggers of sleet had shifted to snow, softening the wind with its fluffy white flakes.

Leather boots crunched the frozen earth beside her. "Beautiful, isn't it?" Sebastian propped his foot on a marbled rock.

She sniffed disdainfully. "Tolerable, I suppose."

The sun chose that moment to break through the sky in the west, shattering the dark clouds and tipping the misty peaks with gold. Sunlight and snow spilled across the glen. Snowflakes caught on Prudence's lashes. She blinked them away, fighting the strange exultation that swept her. How easy it would be to fall in love with such a land! As easy as it had been to fall in love with the man who stood surveying the mighty peaks as if he were their master, as well as her own.

Clouds sped across the glen, drowning the sunlight and lengthening the cold shadow of the mountain. Prudence tightened her shoulder-cape around her, suppressing a shiver.

Sebastian sat down cross-legged and unfolded an oilcloth package. A strip of mutton was halfway to his lips when he paused.

His eyes twinkled at Prudence. "You did help Mrs. Graham prepare this. Knowing your fondness for lacing things with laudanum, perhaps you should have the first taste." He held the meat to her lips.

Her eyes crossed as she glared at it. "And if I've given up laudanum for arsenic?"

He shrugged. "Then I shall have to find another duchess to marry. There's always the Duke of Gleicester's widow. She's a bit plump and slovenly, but pliable."

Prudence snapped the meat from his hand with her teeth, nearly taking off two of his fingertips. The mutton stuck in her throat like a rock.

When she didn't fall into foaming convulsions, Sebastian tore into the meager fare with abandon.

Prudence found she had lost her appetite. "I should have let Arlo hang you."

"You're too civilized for that. Too English. Of course, we must never forget it was the civilized English who slit the Scots' throats while they lay wounded on the field of Culloden." He grinned at her. "By the old clan laws, I wouldn't have claimed you as my bride, but as my slave."

His frosty eyes warned her of the myriad of possibilities that word held.

She tucked her reddened nose into her cape. "Then it's fortunate we are now under English law."

"Look again, angel."

He slipped an arm around her shoulders, guiding her gaze

across snow-swept peaks broken by patches of Caledonian pine and the indigo splash of a loch.

His breath was warm against her. "You're under my law now."

A pale moon rose in the twilight sky, and the mountains melted into the velvety gray of impending night. The saddle rocked between Prudence's thighs as she followed Sebastian's horse up the steep path. They rounded a rocky ledge, bringing her her first glimpse of Dunkirk.

Anger swept her, followed by a numbing sense of desolation. How could Sebastian have traded her love for a shattered ruin?

To Prudence, who had lived her entire life among the rolling green hills of England and the misty coast of Northumberland, the stark rock looked as forbidding as a goblin's lair. The moonlight cast a silver wash across its shadow. She shuddered to think how wildly the wind must blow through the castle on its peak.

Their shaggy mounts pawed their way up the rocky slope and into the courtyard. An air of emptiness hung over the small castle, as if it awaited the loving touch of a master who was never coming back. Dead lichen crept up the crumbling stone walls. Jamie's wagon sat in a corner of the courtyard, but there was no sign of Jamie.

Without profaning the eerie silence, Sebastian dismounted and offered her a hand. Prudence flexed her legs while he touched a flint to the wick of a candle stub. The wan light flickered over his handsome face, gone as closed and still as the deserted castle. For the first time, she wondered what he might be thinking, might be remembering. As they passed beneath an oaken door that creaked on broken hinges, she shrank into his side, thankful for his presence.

"Great hall" was too kind a description for this cavernous dwelling. Sickly moonlight crawled through the arrow slits, illuminating the magenta and white of bird droppings spattered across a sea of stone. Gnawed bones and moldy bits of things best left nameless huddled in piles. The twin hearths at each end of the hall were empty of all but heaps of gray ash. Cobwebs shrouded the tarnished bronze of the torch sconces.

A strange emotion seized Prudence. She had a sudden vision of Sebastian dining at Tricia's table, garbed in casual yet elegant splendor. He had not so much as let a crumb fall on his frock coat without brushing it away. Was it any wonder he found civilization a seduction as well as a trap? Who was she to judge him for seeking to escape such squalor forever?

He gently disengaged her fingers, and she realized she had been clinging to his hand. He pressed the candle into her palm and gestured to a set of stone stairs that curved up one wall.

"Go. I'll tend to the horses."

She trailed after him, hesitant to surrender the comfort of his broad shoulders. "I can help."

He shook his head and gently shoved her toward the stairs. "Don't be afraid."

His husky burr gave the words the effect of a charm, a magical incantation that straightened her spine and sharpened her resolve. She wasn't afraid. She was terrified. But she wasn't about to let him know it.

The door opened behind her, and a blast of cold wind deepened the chill of the hall. Then the door closed, and Prudence was left alone in the flickering candlelight. She wondered if another girl had once stood in her place, her hands trembling, her gray eyes brimming with frightened tears, alone in a strange country with a brutal stranger. Prudence shook herself out of her reverie. Sebastian was not his father. And Prudence Walker was made of sterner stuff.

Prudence Kerr, she reminded herself.

The warmth of the candle melted against her palm. If she didn't find a candlestick soon, her hand would be swimming in tallow. She started for the stairs, grimacing as her shoe crunched something small and delicate.

The frail light cast ghosts of shadows on each crumbling step. She stumbled and reached for the wall to steady herself, then jerked her hand back as her fingers sank into damp mold.

There was no corridor at the top of the stairs, only a

narrow landing with a single door. The tower must serve as it had five centuries ago, as sleeping quarters for the entire castle.

A bead of hot tallow spattered on her wrist. Prudence drew in a deep breath and shoved at the splintered door.

Twenty-seven

Prudence held her breath, half expecting to find iron bars on the window and a horde of slavering rats to greet her.

Instead, warmth and light billowed onto the landing. She gaped. Torches set in wall sconces scattered pools of light on the clean-swept stone floor. Crackling tongues of flame licked at a yew log on the hearth. A kettle of herbs simmered over the fire, scenting the air with the pungent aroma of pine. A spray of holly nestled on the windowsill, its red berries gleaming like rubies amid glossy green. Tears came to her eyes when she saw her own night rail draped over the rickety bedstead.

She glided into the tower like a sleepwalker, unable to resist a chamber prepared so artfully for comfort and welcome. Now she knew why Sebastian had sent Jamie ahead. The seductive coziness of the chamber was undeniable. It would be easy to pretend it was not a ruthless mercenary who would come to her bed, but a cherished lover, intent on her delight.

She undressed and slipped the night rail on with trembling hands.

She padded to the window. A sparkling blanket of frost veiled the warped glass. She unlatched the window and pulled it open. Icy wind whipped tears into her eyes. The corner of the chamber jutted over the cliff itself, giving her the curious impression that she was suspended in mid-air. She snatched a breath of the wind, fighting the sensation that she was falling, spinning helplessly into the vale below. Jamie had once told her Dunkirk was perched on the edge of heaven itself. It was easier to believe hell lurked at the bottom of the dark abyss.

She tried to imagine the vale below drenched in the myriad greens of summer. Closing her eyes, she could almost smell the heather, its aroma sweeping through the window on a summer breeze. Then the tower would be a nest for lovers, a comforting haven standing sentinel over the harsh peaks and rolling moors.

She propped her hip on the windowsill, hugging away shivers that had little to do with the cold. Her fear ran deeper than any she had known before. She had fought for control her entire life, swallowing her passions and building an icy shell no man could breach. Until a gray-eyed bandit had tumbled off his horse and into her heart.

What did Sebastian want from her? Was she nothing to him now but a road to respectability? Did he want a wife or a duchess? A hostage or a lover? Was he going to keep her imprisoned in the tower like some triumphant Scottish chieftain of a century ago? Would he come to her in the dark, velvety folds of midnight, weaving his erotic sorcery until she was driven to her knees, helpless to resist and begging for any scrap of affection he might toss her way?

The wind swept her hair from her face. She had known there were risks when she and MacKay had fostered their scheme. But she had felt she had nothing to lose. Nothing but herself.

She leaned farther out the window, drinking in the sustenance of the crisp air, letting it blow through her brain to wash away the stale fog of betrayal and fear.

Sebastian climbed the steps with a weary tread, the triumph of his homecoming marred by a dismal pall of memories. He expected to hear his father's laughter come rolling down the narrow stairwell, echoing with the bite of cruelty.

His breath caught in his throat as he slipped through the door and saw the window across the chamber ajar.

His frantic footsteps had carried him halfway across the tower before his panic shamed him. Prudence lay on the still-made bed, her dark hair rippled across the thin heather tick, her lashes flush against her cheeks. He walked toward her, drawn by the innocent sprawl of her limbs, and gazed down at her. Did he only imagine it or were her lashes damp with tears? The night rail was tangled around her long legs. The soft cotton cupped her breasts and outlined the slender curve of her waist.

She stirred. A gentle fragrance wafted up from the heather tick. He ached to ease himself over her, to mold her body to his own. She was his bride. Not a man in England or Scotland would decry his possession of her. But did having the power to take her give him the right? A cold wind buffeted his back. Prudence curled into herself. He drew the thick quilt up over her and tucked it under her chin. His lips brushed her temple, but she did not stir again.

He turned to latch the window. How long had he dreamed of this moment? he wondered. To stand in the bastion of his own castle. To have Prudence in his bed, her soft hair unhampered by pins, her delectable body free of petticoats and corsets and stays. He craved nothing more than to bury his face in her hair and hold her tight against his pounding heart.

Would she even want him? He had dragged her away from her tidy comforts and brought her to this dirty hole. He had insulted her, embarrassed her, and stolen her precious innocence on a coarse blanket in an animal's den a few feet away from a score of sleeping thieves.

He couldn't promise not to do worse, though, if she pushed him away. If his advances met with anger, or worse yet, a cringe of fright, would he have the courage to take her in his arms and gently allay her fears? Or would he push on, bewitched by a sensual hunger that obliterated both common sense and decency? A fierce urgency rocked him. Time hung over his head like the executioner's noose. How long would he have her? A week? A fortnight? His baser urges goaded him to go to her, to part her smooth thighs and take her like a captive princess on a bed of furs, his to take at his will, as leisurely and as often as he chose.

She's yer wife now, lad. Show her what women are made fer. Make her beg like I made yer mother beg. As Brendan Kerr's voice thundered through his head, Sebastian's knuckles whitened against the windowsill.

He used to sleep under that window, head shoved beneath a moth-eaten blanket to muffle the sounds from the bed. But he could still hear them. Even now.

Without daring another glance at Prudence, he started down the stairs at a brisk pace. Halfway down, his steps faltered. He had come to Dunkirk to banish his demons, only to find them clamoring around his head. With a sigh, he sank down on a dusty step and ran his finger over the scar beneath his chin.

Prudence's nose crinkled, as she was lured to wakefulness by the tantalizing scent of tea wafting to her nostrils. She nestled into the mattress. The heat of her body had warmed it to a cozy nest. She clung to the seductive comfort of sleep, rolling on her back in an attempt to ignore the odd sensation of someone biting her hair. A needle-sharp claw sank into her elbow. She bit back a yelp. Opening her eyes, she was puzzled to find not the starched canopy of her tent-bed, but a sooty expanse of gray stone.

A pair of green-gold eyes filled her vision. She sat up, wiggling her feet to make sure she wasn't dreaming. A ball of gray fluff and muscle teetered down her legs and pounced on her toes with the ferocity of a starving lion.

She laughed and scooped up Sebastian-cat, holding him to her cheek. A paw shot out to bat her hair. She pressed a kiss to the furry swell of his tummy, then looked shyly around the tower. A well-stoked fire crackled on the iron grate.

She sobered, stroking the cat's tousled fur. "It seems our mysterious benefactor wishes to remain anonymous."

She swung her feet to the floor, rubbing her bleary eyes. A cold, gray curtain of rain washed down the windowpane, but the tower was warm and cozy. She traced the irresistible fragrance of the tea to a dented brass kettle hooked on an iron spit over the flames. A chipped porcelain cup warmed on the stones of the hearth. She shook her head at the richness of the bounty.

Beneath the patter of the rain, she slowly became aware of another sound—the steady scrape of metal on earth. She walked over to the window. Her warm breath fogged the glass, and she wiped it clear with two fingers. Still she could see nothing but the cliff below. Only by unlatching the window and leaning out could she glimpse the muddy flat at the back of the castle.

Sebastian was digging furiously, slamming a shovel deep into the earth and hurling chunks of mud and snow over his shoulder. He wore no coat. His rain-soaked shirt was plastered to his shoulders. His hair hung in damp coils around his face. Water flew as he shook it out of his eyes, revealing brows drawn low in a dark scowl.

Prudence's hand flew to her throat when she saw the leather-bound coffer mired beside him. But curiosity overcame her alarm as Sebastian backed up and ran at the coffer. He slipped once, driving his knee into the mud. He set his foot against the small trunk. With a tremendous heave, he shoved the coffer into the gash in the earth.

Prudence slammed the window shut as a hysterical giggle escaped her. He was burying it! Jamie's words echoed through her mind. *Tight as a Scot, he is. Don't ever forget it.*

The steady thunk of iron in mud resumed. That was one less thing to fret about for now, she thought. By the time Sebastian unearthed the trunk from its muddy grave, he would have all he needed from MacKay and would no longer need D'Artan's ill-gotten gold. Or her.

Melancholy lodged like a dull weight in her throat, and she sank down on the hearth. Sebastian-cat bumped his head against her leg. She sighed, glancing at the empty bed. Sebastian had not come to her during the night. Was he still angry at her? Or had the night in the cavern satisfied his curiosity about bedding her? Perhaps he had found her awkward and clumsy. She knew none of the sophisticated tricks Tricia had sworn would keep a man interested for more than one night.

Her fingers curled around the warm porcelain cup. Tricia was in Edinburgh and she was here. Alone at Dunkirk. With Sebastian. And she possessed one talent that all of Tricia's illicit rendezvous had never taught her—making herself indispensable. It had worked on Tricia's doddering husbands and it had worked on Papa. Even at the age of three, she'd been known to toddle up with his misplaced spectacles clenched in her chubby little hands. A simple enough task when she'd been the one to hide them.

A wicked grin teased the corners of Prudence's mouth as she gave the rest of her tea to Sebastian-cat and rose to dress.

Sebastian trudged through the muddy courtyard, his shoulders bent against the weight of the rain. Exertion had warmed him while he dug, but now the dying winter chill sank deep into his bones. He skirted his father's grave without a glance. His gaze drifted to the stone tower, lured by the siren memory of a warm, crackling fire and Prudence nestled deep in the heather tick. Rain trickled into his eyes. He blinked it away. A pillow. He would have to ask Jamie to steal her a pillow.

Shaking off a shiver, he ducked into the damp hall, his hands fumbling to peel off his sodden shirt.

He froze at the sight of a meager flame licking a handful of sticks on the hearth. The wet wood hissed and sputtered.

"God's whiskers!" The genteel oath drew his gaze to a rickety bench.

Prudence stood on tiptoe on its back, swiping down cobwebs with a long stick crowned by a wad of material that looked suspiciously like a satin petticoat. Her old dun dress was festooned with webs. Damp tendrils of hair escaped from her loose chignon. She caught her tongue between her teeth with a puckish grimace.

His hands fell limply to his sides as he was transported from the drafty hall back to a summer morning in an old crofter's hut, a morning redolent with honeysuckle and alive with the lazy hum of bees.

Prudence bounced on her toes to dislodge a recalcitrant web. The bench swayed with a dangerous creak. Jarred out of his reverie, Sebastian crossed the hall in three strides, wrapping his arms around Prudence's waist as the bench collapsed on a splintered leg.

He lowered her slowly, savoring the indolent slide of her warm body down the hard, wet length of his. She still clutched the stick with one hand. Her other hand curled into a fist between them and pushed him away.

"Sorry about the bench," she said, a trifle breathlessly.

Scowling, he kicked it. "Better the bench's leg than your own. How did you start the fire?"

"I caught a dragon and yanked his tail." When Sebastian's scowl didn't lighten, Prudence admitted, "I carried down a stick from my own fire." She tucked a finger between her lips.

He caught her hand and unfolded it. A shiny pink burn marred her knuckle and a blister puckered the smooth web between thumb and forefinger. Her hand was halfway to his own lips when she jerked it back and tucked it in the folds of her skirt.

He glowered at her. "From now on, if you want a fire started, you come to me. Do you understand?"

She bobbed a curtsy, mocking his brogue with devilish skill. "Aye, me laird. Whatever ye wish."

Sebastian bit the inside of his cheek to hide his smile. If only she were sincere! What he wished for was the courage to throw her over his shoulder, carry her back to the bed, and make hot, delicious love to her all morning long.

She dropped her gaze as if she could read his thoughts in his sparkling eyes.

Suddenly her eyes went wild; her lips trembled with rage and a shriek tore from her throat.

Sebastian leaped backward as she swung the stick between them, ramming the end into his chest.

"Out! Out of here right now!"

He backed away, mystified by her sudden passion. Was he

going to be the only Highland laird ever murdered by a petticoat-wielding wife?

She stalked after him. "How dare you? Just look at that! You've the habits of a wild beast. It's a shame, a disgrace, a . . ."

Sputtering into incoherence, she lowered the staff and waved it wildly at his boots.

He looked down, half expecting to find an adder twined around his leg. Mud caked the cracked leather soles, and a perfect trail of goop led back to the door across her newly swept floor.

He threw up his hands in surrender as she backed him into the courtyard. The heavy door slammed in his face.

He reached for the handle, fully intending to storm back in and plant a muddy footprint in a more auspicious place. His boots sucked at the stoop. He glared at them, then bent to jerk them off. The water puddled on the stoop sank into his woolen stockings. He started for the door, heard the warning slosh, and hopped up and down on one foot to peel off his stockings, swearing all the while.

He threw open the door and stood there—a wet, enraged, barefoot Scot.

Prudence didn't even look up.

She had dragged a barrel next to the sagging trestle table and perched on it as if it were a Chippendale chair. Her feet dangled inches off the floor, and he could see that the soles of her white stockings had been stained black by Dunkirk's floors. Even with her hair sprinkled with cobwebs, she looked so cool and composed, she might have been a different woman from the frenzied harridan who had chased him outside. She dipped a feathered quill in an ink pot. Sebastian could think of nothing else to do, so he slammed the door with a satisfying crash.

She lifted one imperious eyebrow and surveyed him over the rim of her glasses. With the faintest shake of her head, she bent back to her task, scratching delicate figures on the back of a tattered envelope.

He opened his mouth to roar a curse, but her soft, cultured tones filled the silence.

"I am working on a list of food and supplies for you to

procure. To begin with, I'd like a churn, a turnspit, a mop, a hoe and spade, some lye, five buckets, two goats, and three chickens." She rose and paced in front of the table. Sebastian stared, transfixed by the graceful sway of her skirts.

She squinted at her list. "I'll also need a detailed accounting of how much land we own and what you intend to do with it. After today, I would prefer we establish a set routine. Breakfast will be served promptly at six, luncheon at two, and dinner at seven o'clock. If you won't be present at any of these meals, send me word at least two hours in advance and I shall prepare a bucket for you. If that suits, of course?" She paused for breath, looking at him sideways to check his response.

Sebastian was at a loss to form one. He had never heard Prudence say so much at one time. He stood there with his mouth open, knowing he looked ridiculous, but unable to pull his gaze away from the enchanting smudge of dirt on the tip of her nose.

She cleared her throat. "Very well then. If you've nothing else to do, you may begin by repairing the bench and table and chopping some firewood. Tomorrow, if it's not raining we can start work on the kitchen roof and mend the fence behind the stable. Then Monday, I thought we would—"

Sebastian threw back his head with a yelp of laughter.

Prudence flushed and tilted her nose in the air. "Have I said something to amuse you?"

"I was picturing the look on Old Fish's puckered puss if he could see his meek little missy right now."

She bowed her head, but not before he saw her reluctant smile.

He curbed his urge to kiss the tip of her grimy nose, and took the list from her.

"I'll ride down to the village and see what I can find."

"Sebastian?" she crooned as he turned away.

He turned back, his eyebrows raised questioningly.

"If you want to be perceived as a respectable laird by your new neighbors, may I offer a suggestion?"

"Oh, please do."

She stood on tiptoe and whispered in his ear, "Pay for the items. Don't steal them."

He doffed an imaginary hat with a sweeping bow that would have done Sir Arlo proud. "Aye, Yer Grace. Whatever ye wish."

Before he could reach the door, Prudence was down on hands and knees, scrubbing the blackened hearth with the hem of her skirt. He closed the door gently and leaned against it, weak with laughter.

He was wiping his streaming eyes as Jamie strutted from the stables toward the castle. Sebastian threw an arm across the door. "I wouldn't if I were you. Not unless you've six months to listen and six more to work."

Jamie scratched his head as Sebastian strode across the muddy courtyard, whistling "Once I Loved A Bonnie Lass." He was well into the third chorus and halfway to the village before he realized he'd forgotten his boots and his horse.

Twenty-eight

The Highland rain yielded to a surprising abundance of early spring sunshine. The northern winds might still blow too briskly for the sluggish, but Prudence gave her new husband little opportunity to feel the chill as together they sought to remedy the neglect of decades.

Beneath Prudence's loving hands, Dunkirk bloomed. She had never before known the pleasure of having her own home. Living in rented London lodgings and then Tricia's overgrown dollhouse had not prepared her for the warm glow of pride Dunkirk stirred in her. Daily, Sebastian brought her new treasures: a tattered mop, an oaken bucket, a cake of precious lye. They were far more dear to her than any diamonds or pearls.

They worked to the music of Jamie's chatter while their own unspoken words hung heavy between them. Sebastian's presence sustained Prudence, brought hope to each day. She basked in the sheer pleasure of watching him chop wood, his skin kissed by a golden sheen of sweat, his cheeks pinkened by the bite of the wind. She ached to press her lips to his throat, to tangle her fingers in his sweat-dampened hair and draw him into her arms. But still he did not climb the stairs to her lonely bed. The thought that he must prefer the stables and Jamie's company haunted her long into her sleepless nights.

The same physical nearness that strengthened Prudence was slowly driving Sebastian mad. As she took to wearing her hair loose or simply pulled back by two combs, baring the delicate curve of her throat, he found his blood boiling with more than exertion. He would stride outside and throw his throbbing body into yet another chore, praying he would tire himself enough to stumble to his blankets and fall into a dreamless sleep. But too often, his dreams were haunted by a throaty laugh and the feel of burgundy hair slipping between his fingers.

One night he sat watching Prudence sew before the fire, his eyes lazy and heavy-lidded. He enjoyed the soothing flow of her work, the graceful flick of the needle through the ragged linen of his shirt.

She glanced up at him. The needle stabbed her finger. As she tucked her finger between her rosy lips, the crumbs of his contentment scattered, leaving in their place a wild unrest, an insatiable desire to know more of her than just her fine-boned profile or the taunting fragrance of her hair.

But he could expect word from MacKay any day. Once Prudence discovered the bargain he had struck with the treacherous devil, he would have no choice but to send her back.

He rose abruptly, leaving Prudence to stare after him, the slam of the door echoing in her ears.

Prudence fidgeted with her hair, twisting a heavy strand into a reluctant curl only to watch it fall straight when she released it. She sighed, wishing desperately for a mirror. For all she could tell from her reflection in the warped window glass, her hair might be a mop of corkscrew curls like Jamie's. She made a face at herself, then pulled the window open for a breath of cooling air. An overcast sky had brooded over the mountains all day, as grim and implacable as Sebastian's most recent mood. The wind was picking up now, and dark clouds banked in the east.

She lifted her skirts and let the teasing wind blow across her thighs. The heat from the kitchen fire lingered against her skin even in the damp tower.

Dropping her skirts, she smoothed the lavender silk with anxious fingers. This was the only fine gown that remained from her days in Edinburgh. She donned her spectacles, then pulled them off and slipped them in her pocket. She adjusted her lace fichu and leaned out the window for the twentieth time. At last she was rewarded by the sight of a lone figure walking through the courtyard, his steps slow, but edged with tension.

Her heart slammed against her ribs. The devil take practicality and efficiency! she thought. Tonight she was determined to use all the charms of home and hearth to find out if Sebastian still wanted her.

She gathered her skirts and was halfway down the stairs before remembering her matching lavender slippers. She raced back after them, and jerked them on as she ran. As she reached the bottom step, she tripped over her petticoat and nearly collided with Sebastian as he entered the hall.

He caught her by the elbows as she skidded past. "Ho there, lass. What's the bloody rush?"

She bobbed an awkward curtsy. "Pardon me. I must tend to something in the kitchen."

She darted past, squinting in misery. Was nothing to go right today? What was Jamie still doing there? The insolent moppet had his feet on her table. But she *had* promised him a slice of her treat. She couldn't scold him, could she? He had been nice enough to procure the tender kidney for her, despite his interminable jokes about *who* he had gotten it from.

She returned to the hall with two brass goblets polished to a high sheen and filled with sparkling ale. Sebastian still stood by the door as if he were an unwanted guest.

He glanced at her, then surveyed the well-stoked fire and satin-draped table, his eyes unreadable. "I'm really not hungry. I thought you'd be asleep by now."

Prudence gave all of her attention to placing the goblets on the table, struggling to hide how deeply his honesty stung. "I waited up for you. You didn't take dinner. I thought you'd be famished." She managed a warm smile.

He grunted, obviously unwilling to take his rudeness into more verbal territory.

As she fled back to the kitchen, Jamie stopped picking his teeth with one of the knives, jumped up, and pulled out Sebastian's chair with a flourish. "A throne for the laird of the manor."

Sebastian sank heavily into the chair. "Playing Cupid again, Jamie?"

Jamie smiled cryptically. " 'Tis wiser than playin' the fool."

A wail of dismay rang out from the kitchen. Sebastian rose, but Jamie placed a hand on his arm, giving him the same warning Sebastian had once given him. "I wouldn't if I were ye."

Prudence did not reappear for several minutes. When she did, she bore a chipped earthenware plate and a look of grim determination. She slid the plate in front of Sebastian.

He stared down at the black shriveled lump, then cleared his throat before softly asking, "What is it?"

"Suet pudding," she replied.

Jamie peered at it. "Looks to be more soot than pudding."

Sebastian gave him a dark look. He poked the miserable morsel with his knife, hoping to cut into it to reveal a steaming core. It shot away, bouncing off his plate and across the table.

Prudence clenched her jaw in an agony of embarrassment. "Would you care for some black buns?"

Over her head, Sebastian caught Jamie's violent wave of warning.

"No, thank you." But she looked so crestfallen, he added, "Well, perhaps just one."

Jamie rolled his eyes and drew his finger across his throat. "I'd best be goin'," he said, clapping on his beaten hat. "I promised this sweet lass in the village I'd stop by and give her a good-night kiss or perhaps somethin' more if she'll allow—"

"Good night, Jamie," Sebastian interrupted.

Jamie glanced at Prudence as if he would have liked to say something kind. The hectic color in her cheeks warned him to silence.

"I'll fetch the bread," Prudence said as Jamie ducked into the night. Her lips trembled. She did not dare meet Sebastian's eyes.

Sebastian rescued his pudding and sawed at it with his

knife. He *was* famished, but not as Prudence thought. He was starving for a taste of her lips, a sip of the tender ecstasy they had shared in the cavern. That one sweet morsel had only whet his appetite for more.

The scent of cedar wafted to his nose. Prudence had hung fragrant boughs over each doorway. He looked around, really seeing the castle for the first time since his return.

The hall was unrecognizable from the cobweb-festooned horror it had been only a week ago. The floor was clean-swept. A braided rug lay in front of the hearth. Two chairs sat cozily on it, as if whispering secrets. Prudence's tender polishing had revealed the ancient beauty of the heavy oak and cherry furniture. She had found the grace beneath the ugly gouges from his father's boots, the careless scars of his own boyhood. The touch of her loving hands was every where.

Except on him.

He dug his knife into the pudding, piercing the charred crust to find the inside burnt to crisp, black flakes.

If she were still there when spring came, he mused, she would fill his hall with flowers—jasmine and honeysuckle and bluebells—until the thought of living without their fragrance would be unbearable. As if in answer to his dark thoughts, the sky lowered its threatening boom with a rumble of thunder.

Prudence returned carrying a platter heaped with salted venison and charred bread. He waved away the venison and swallowed a bite of the pudding.

"Sebastian, I don't expect you to eat that."

He chewed grimly. "I like it."

When she started to protest again, his eyes narrowed in such an evil look that she retreated with the platter to her own end of the table. She tried not to stare as he choked down every last bite of the pudding, then followed it with a healthy splash of ale.

Prudence toyed with the cameo that held her fichu to-gether. Sebastian fought to keep his hungry gaze off her, but lost the battle. Candlelight shimmered over her hair, giving it the rich gloss of sherry wine. The lavender silk gown deepened the pale delicacy of her skin. In his muddy breeches and sweat-stained shirt, he felt like the coarse peasant he was.

She lifted her goblet. "Jamie told me there were two Frenchmen in the village today inquiring about you. Do you know why?"

Her question didn't surprise Sebastian. He was only surprised she had taken so long to ask. Perhaps she was as afraid of the answer as he was.

"They're probably D'Artan's bulldogs. The old man has given me two weeks to send him the formula. If MacKay makes good on his promise, we'll need no longer."

"What did Killian promise you?"

Sebastian winced at her use of MacKay's Christian name. There was both tenderness and respect in her voice.

"A pardon," he said gruffly. "MacKay's gone to London to request an audience with the King. He believes His Majesty will be grateful to know what sort of snake he has lurking in his House of Commons."

Prudence's lips twitched. She and Laird MacKay couldn't have thought of a better way to help Sebastian if they had spent months pondering the issue.

She lifted her fork to her lips to hide her smile. "And what did you promise him in return?"

Sebastian drained the rest of the ale. "You."

Her fork stilled.

Sebastian rushed on to fill the silence, studying the burnt crust of his bun with acute interest. "Since we hadn't the written consent of your guardian to wed, an English court should grant you a dissolution of the marriage posthaste. Of course, to avoid a scandal, it would be best for you to convince a judge our union was never consummated."

"What shall I tell him is the reason for that?" Her voice was strangely flat.

Why did she have to be so damn calm about it? he wondered. He felt like breaking something himself. He stuffed half of the bun in his mouth with deliberate crudity. "I don't care. Tell him whatever you like. Tell him I snore too loud. Don't bathe often enough. Fancy men over women."

She slipped on her spectacles.

Oh, hell, he thought. Here it comes. The bun hung like a rock in his throat.

She peered at him over the rim of her spectacles. "Do you?"

He frowned. "Do I what? Snore? Smell?"

"Fancy men over women?"

He gave her a long look from beneath his lashes. He was suddenly spoiling for a fight, desperate for any release from the turmoil that battered him. He had known this feeling before, but in smoky taverns and boisterous alehouses where he could pick a fight without hurting anyone but himself.

He tangled the butt of his knife in the tablecloth, glanced down, and found the fight he was looking for.

He snatched up the edge of the cloth, overturning his empty goblet with a thump. "This was your gown, wasn't it? The pink gown you wore at the Campbells' the night I robbed you."

She gazed at him, every maddening inch the "Duchess of Winter." "Cranberry."

"Cranberry?" he roared.

"The gown was cranberry. Not pink."

He stood and jerked the cloth off the table, revealing the ugly, scarred wood beneath. The plates shattered as they struck the stone floor. "I don't give a damn if it was fuchsia. I don't expect you to cut up all your fine clothes to serve me. Don't think I haven't seen you! Dusting with your petticoat. Straining cream through your stockings. I never asked that of you."

"I don't need those clothes here. They're impractical. My old gowns are sufficient."

He shot around the table and jerked her hands out of her lap, turning them to the candlelight. Calluses toughened the tender pads. Her palms were chapped and reddened.

A muscle in his jaw twitched. "Your old hands were sufficient too. Look at them now! I remember when they were as soft and white as doves."

She stared at the table. A single tear spilled from her brimming eyes and slipped down her cheek.

A wave of self-contempt swept Sebastian, making him

even angrier. His fingers dug into her wrists. "Dammit, woman! I didn't bring you here to be my slave!"

She stood, wrenching free of his grip. "Then what in God's holy name did you bring me here for? It certainly wasn't to be your wife!" She slammed her palms on the table and faced him nose to nose. "What's wrong with these hands? Are they too stained for you? Too hard? Not as soft and lily-white as Tricia's or Devony's?" She held up her hands between them. "I'm proud of these. They've done more than serve tea and open books. They've never been more beautiful. I've earned every blister, every callus, and every splinter working to make this castle some sort of home for you."

He reached for her, dazed by the magnificence of her furious passion, but his hands closed on empty air. She was already backing out of his reach.

"I'll be glad when MacKay comes, you ungrateful wretch," she said. "I wish he'd come tonight. I should have no trouble convincing a judge of your duplicity, since you obviously find your wife so distasteful that you'd prefer to sleep with your alleged coachman. As far as I'm concerned, you and your precious Dunkirk can go straight to the deepest pits of hell!"

With those words, she burst into tears, threw her hands over her face, and ran up the stairs.

Sebastian sank down heavily in her chair. He rested his chin on his steepled hands.

"You stupid bastard," he whispered.

A rumble of thunder rolled through the castle like the taunting echo of his father's voice.

Prudence pummeled her pillow with her fists. Who had ever heard of stuffing a pillow with dried heather? she wondered. If she wanted to sleep on bracken and gorse, she'd go lie on the wet, bleak moor below. She was surprised Sebastian hadn't stuffed it with thorns. The bloody Scots were as uncivilized as everyone said they were, and Sebastian Kerr was the worst of the lot! Everything nasty she'd ever heard about Scots poured through her head in an invective stream.

Lightning flooded the tower. Thunder cracked like the

heart of a massive stone. She dove under the pillow, where the lingering fragrance of heather haunted her.

Who had ever heard of a thunderstorm this early in the year? Even the laws of God went awry in this primitive land. Was there nothing she could depend on? Nothing, it seemed, but the petty treachery of Dunkirk's master. She and MacKay had been daft to believe they could help such a selfish wretch.

The stifling air beneath the pillow smothered her. She flung herself onto her back, kicking at the wool blanket tangled around her legs. How could she expect a beastly Scot to appreciate the civilized charms of candlelight and satin tablecloths? She should have wrapped herself in an animal skin. They could have squatted in front of the fire and eaten raw kidney meat with their fingers. Lightning ripped a jagged streak across the sky. Her fingernails dug tiny crescents into her palms.

A blast of thunder shook the tower. Wind roared at the window, rattling the ancient panes with fists of wrath. The shadows on the wall danced with a life of their own. Prudence pulled the blanket over her head. Storms usually exhilarated her, but tonight she was afraid. It was as if the storm raged around the tower itself, drawn like a magnet to her own anger and misery.

Without wanting to, she felt the presence of that other girl, Sebastian's mother. She imagined her cowering under the same blankets, smoky gray eyes squeezed tightly shut. Prudence felt as if she *were* that girl, and every beat of thunder was the stomp of Brendan Kerr's heavy boots on the stairs. He was coming for her. She shoved her fists against her ears, mumbling in vain the Pythagorean theorem of numbers to drown it out. Thunder boomed again and she sat bolt upright, trembling everywhere, her night rail plastered to her body by a sheen of terrified sweat.

A burst of white light threw substance into shadow and shadow into substance. That dark shape over there by the window. It hadn't been there before, had it? Wasn't that a plaid draped over its hulking shoulders and the flash of silver a claymore lifted in meaty fists?

With a splintering crash, the wind caught the window and flung it open.

Prudence screamed. A deafening crack of thunder drowned out the shrill sound. Rain poured into the tower, pelting the stone floor. She jumped out of bed and ran for the door. In the heartbeat of darkness between one flash of lightning and the next, she lost sight of it. She reeled around, beating at the walls like a trapped bird. When another streak of lightning lit the room, her trembling fingers closed around the iron latch. She fled down the winding stairs, her white night rail billowing behind her. She didn't care if she ran into the devil himself as long as she escaped the echoing nightmare of the tower.

At the bottom of the last step, her foot thudded against something soft and substantial. She tripped and went sprawling.

A pained grunt was followed by a hoarse oath. A metallic click echoed in the sudden silence. Prudence flung her hair out of her eyes to find herself staring straight down the barrel of Sebastian's pistol.

Twenty-nine

Sebastian stood over her, shirtless, his legs braced apart and one eye narrowed down the long black barrel of the pistol.

Prudence threw up her hands. "Don't shoot me. I'll never cook again. I swear it."

Sebastian's smoldering gaze raked her from head to toe. She rested on her elbows, her night rail dipped between splayed knees. Her unbound hair tumbled down her back in soft disarray. He slowly lowered the weapon, although his ragged breathing did not steady as he had hoped.

Sheepishly, he offered her a hand.

She accepted it, her hand as cool and trembling as a captive bird in his palm. He laced his fingers through hers and drew her up. She glanced at the worn blanket laid over the hard stones at the foot of the stairs.

"*This* is where you sleep?" she asked.

"Aye. What of it?" he said brusquely. A light flush burned his cheekbones as he laid the pistol next to a wicked-looking dirk and a blunt-ended cudgel.

Prudence swallowed hard. "What were you going to do? Bludgeon me if I tried to escape?"

He frowned at her. "Just where *were* you going in such haste? You looked as if a banshee was wailing at your heels."

It was Prudence's turn to look sheepish. Away from the heart of the storm, the thunder faded to an angry rumble, and the rain tapered to a peaceful beat against the wooden door. Surrounded by the soft flicker of firelight, with Sebastian's muscular presence so near, she saw her terror as only a childish fright. How could she tell him she had been fleeing a fanciful apparition of his own father?

"I wanted a drink of water," she said defiantly.

"Indeed." He lifted an eyebrow. "You could have opened your window and caught a bucket of it if you so desired."

She looked away to escape his mocking gaze. The remnants of her ruined feast were gone. The floor had been swept clean of broken shards; the cranberry satin was draped neatly over the back of a chair.

"Wouldn't you be more comfortable sleeping by the fire?" she asked.

Sebastian opened his mouth to tell her where he'd be most comfortable sleeping, but closed it again.

He sank down on the third step and ran a hand through his hair. "And if D'Artan's men should come while I'm 'comfortable'? We Scots learned long ago that comfortable men get their throats slit while they sleep."

Prudence's brow puckered. So Sebastian had lain here each night, wrapped in a coarse blanket on the cold stone floor, a one-man arsenal stretched across the bottom of the stairs, while she'd nestled on her heather pillow like a princess. The realization gave her a queer feeling in the pit of her stomach.

She sank down beside him in the shadow of the stairs, close enough for their thighs to brush. As they listened to the patter of the rain, the storm wrapped them in a cozy web of intimacy. Prudence realized this was the first time they had been utterly alone. There was no Old Fish sneering down his nose at them, no bandits snoring in the courtyard, no Jamie to pop out of the wainscoting. She felt like a child left alone at home to bounce on the feather mattresses.

"Do you think D'artan's men will come?" she asked.

"They might. If our portrait of domestic bliss isn't convincing enough."

"They wouldn't have found it very convincing tonight." There was no reproach in her voice, only a musical humor that made Sebastian ache to reach out to her.

He took her hand in his. The shock of his warm fingers against her skin sent a tremor through Prudence.

He rubbed his thumb over her knuckles. "Have you come to tell me I behaved like a barbarous Highlander?"

She laughed lightly, trying to hide the shattering effect his touch had on her. "I preferred the barbarous Highlander to the brooding Scot. At least you looked *at* me instead of through me."

He was looking at her now, though shadows veiled his expression. "Oh, I look at you." He unfolded her hand and brought it to his lips. With each breath, he pressed a tender kiss to her tingling palm. "I look at you every night while you sleep. With your long legs tangled in the blankets, your lips parted, your face flushed like a babe's." He rubbed his nose against the very calluses he had denounced earlier that night.

Prudence pressed her eyes shut, stirred again by the power of words not printed on a page, but whispered in a husky burr as soft as morning mist against her skin. They sang like a hymn through her lonely soul.

"You could sleep with me." She blurted out the words before she realized she was going to say them. A slow heat burned in her cheeks. She drew her hand from his grasp, knotting it into a protective fist, unable to bear his steady scrutiny. "I am your wife. At least for now. I'm not oblivious to the fact that husbands have certain . . . needs," she finished lamely.

Sebastian rose and paced to the hearth. She closed her eyes again, then opened them, fortified by the overwhelming need to say what she must, even if it came out all wrong. Even if he laughed.

He spread his palms against the stones of the hearth and braced his weight against them. "I fear it's not as simple as your father's books or Tricia's lurid lectures," he said, a desperate humor tinging his words. "We've already taken one too many chances. Most judges would have difficulty believing your marriage unconsummated if you waddled into the courtroom plump with some thieving Scot's babe."

"You once told me you knew of ways to prevent that," she whispered.

He pivoted slowly, his eyes wide with fearful wonder. "Do you know what you're saying, Prudence?"

She leaned her elbows on the step behind her and parted her knees, fully aware of the provocative way her night rail clung to the curves and hollows of her body. "What's wrong, Sebastian? Would making love to your own wife be too tame for a rogue like you?"

Sebastian's mouth went dry and his palms wet. Could this enticing creature with the throaty purr be his shy, demure Prudence? He drifted toward her like a sleepwalker dazed by a brilliant light. Surely at any moment he would roll over on his pistol and be jolted awake, finding himself alone and shivering on the cold, hard floor. He reached for her, expecting her to melt at his touch. His fingers closed like a golden bracelet around her slim ankle, and he cherished the substance of the delicate bone beneath. She shuddered at his touch.

His shadow covered her on the stairs. "I've never made love to a wife before. At least not one that was mine."

His mouth brushed hers, and Prudence moaned. Why did he have to be so beautiful? Words that would have sounded crass from any other man emerged from his sculpted lips like scripture from the mouth of a fallen angel.

Her palms kneaded his chest with kittenish delight. "I thought you didn't want me," she whispered.

Her shy confession sent an arrow of shame deep into Sebastian's heart. He should have realized how Prudence would misconstrue his silences, his brooding tensions. She'd had years of Tricia's diligent tutoring to assure her no man would want her. If only he had a lifetime to prove her wrong! But all he might have was tonight.

He buried his hands in the rich velvet of her hair. "I thought I'd die for wanting you."

A shuddering sigh escaped her. Her thumbs stroked his hardened nipples, then swept lower, tracing the line of tawny hair to the waistband of his breeches. He gazed at the shimmering crown of her head, bewitched by her sweetness, her generosity, the helpless murmurs of need that caught at the back of her throat. As her seeking lips flowered against his belly, he caught her hand and pressed it hard to the cradle of his thighs.

He tilted her face to his and gazed deep into her eyes. "Let me be a part of you."

His hoarse plea sent a shiver of longing through Prudence. He would always be a part of her. She knew that now. If MacKay came tomorrow and Sebastian sent her away forever, he would still be as much a part of her as the whisper of her own breath or the swing of her hair against her shoulders. She would never marry another man. She couldn't settle for an empty shell of what she knew love could be.

She adored Sebastian. She had adored him from the first. Even as she blushed at the swollen heat of his arousal against her palm, she knew neither shyness nor pride would stop her from proving it tonight.

He caressed her temple with his lips. "You've nothing to be ashamed of, lass. Before both God and the law, I'm your husband."

His gaze sought out the shadows at the top of the stairs, then he turned. She trembled with relief as he led her across the hall to the warmth of the hearth. Neither of them was quite prepared to face the ghosts of the tower. He spread out his own blankets, then laid across them the length of cranberry satin. Prudence sank to her knees in the shimmering pool.

As Sebastian drew off his breeches, the leaping flames bathed his skin in bronze. She had never seen him look quite so shy. Here in the ruins of his boyhood, he was stripped of all the masks he'd spent his life crafting. He was neither highwayman nor gentleman nor rogue. He was only a man, rendered both potent and vulnerable by his blatant need for her.

And for tonight—he was her man. As he lowered his body to her own, she reached for him, drank of him, hungered to draw him deep inside her. Her fingers trailed the throbbing length of him like cool ribbons of silk.

Sebastian was helpless to resist her whimpered pleas. All of his determination to go slow, to seek her pleasure before his own, melted as her slender thighs fell apart in dark and feminine invitation, tempting him to tumble her with no more grace than a green lad faced with the shattering miracle of his first woman. He pushed her night rail up with shaking hands.

"You're so damned pretty." His guttural words were both prayer and confession as he reached for her breasts beneath the night rail and entered her, plundering her sleek core with his savage heat.

Sebastian's possession of her was a storm all its own—a magical thunder and lightning roaring out of control. Tonight Prudence would ride the storm, unfettered by shame or fear of the future. She would draw its wildness into her without trying to trap or tame. Her hips moved in rhythm to his, sheathing him deep in the most loving, most private corner of her life, as she was lost completely in the miracle of holding him inside her. She dared to run her hands down his back, savoring the way his muscles bunched, his body tautened, as his thrusts deepened and quickened. Her moans were lost in the rumble of his thunder.

Sebastian felt his pleasure building to intolerable levels too quickly. Some rational part of his mind hesitated, knowing what he was about to do wasn't as safe as he had promised. But it was too late to stop. So little he had done in his life had been free of the stain of guilt. Why should loving Prudence be any different? A gleeful voice in his head urged him to stay deep inside her, to spill his seed in her and bind her forever with his child. But a child had not bound his mother. The sun had caressed the curve of her swollen belly as she stepped off that ledge and disappeared from his life forever.

With a hoarse cry of agony and pleasure, he shoved himself away from Prudence. She reached for him as he collapsed against her, her fragrant strands of hair catching like silken chains on his lips.

Sebastian propped himself on one elbow and watched Prudence sleep. She lay half on her stomach, the lithe curve of her back pressed to his belly, her hands folded like wings beneath her chin. Even in sleep she was irresistible.

He reached around and drew her hair away from her face.

A light flush bathed her cheekbones. Dark lashes fanned against the faint shadows beneath her eyes. Lips still full from his kisses were parted against the blankets.

She slept the enchanted sleep of a woman sated and exhausted by lovemaking. His body gave a wicked stir at the thought. His greediness was an untamed beast when it came to her. He pressed himself to the warm, unsuspecting curves of her rump, savoring a moment of selfish pleasure. She stirred, moaning softly. Was she dreaming of him? He wished he could possess her thoughts, her dreams, all of her. But for now he would have to settle for what was within reach.

Like the natural born thief he was, he came at her from behind, touching and exploring until she began to make small noises deep in her throat. With a delicacy he had never used picking pockets or slipping rings from ladies' fingers, he eased himself into her. Being a thief had never held such joy. This gem was more precious than any he had stolen— succulent and infinitely sweeter. He lay still for a long moment, bathed in the miracle of her quivering warmth. Her fingers kneaded the blanket. She arched against him with a muted whimper.

He pressed his lips to her ear. "Hush, lass," he whispered. " 'Tis only the Dreadful Scot Bandit Kirkpatrick ravishin' ye."

He held himself in check with a control he would have once thought impossible. Reaching around her, he tenderly stroked her until her body was racked with delicate shudders. A tremendous sigh escaped him as he withdrew. He hoped she would awaken wondering if this was real or yet another bewitching dream.

As the deepening chill of the hall sank into his fuzzy brain, he tucked a blanket around her shoulders. With Tricia, he had used any excuse to bolt after their practiced liaisons. The thought of leaving Prudence was like a hand clawing at his heart.

He half hoped MacKay would be denied his pardon. Then he would have an excuse for keeping her at Dunkirk. But without a pardon, what kind of life could he offer her? His face was plastered all over Edinburgh and Glasgow. There was nowhere they could run, nowhere to hide. Even burrowed in the wilderness of Strathnaver, it was only a matter of time before the law caught up with him. Or D'Artan. Jamie had reported that his grandfather's men grew more restless with each passing day.

Prudence nuzzled against his hip in a search for warmth. He should never have taken her to his bed, he thought. He should have sent her back to England and left her to the homely wooing of Arlo Tugbert or some other smitten young man. A man who could offer her a proper home and an honorable name.

A man like Killian MacKay.

He raked his fingers through his hair. Sweet Christ. He was beginning to think like her uncle again.

Sighing, he reached under his blankets for a cheroot. It was the last remnant from his life at Lindentree and he had been saving it for a special occasion. Such as right before he was hanged. He drew the cigar beneath his nose. The aromatic blend of tobacco and fine paper seemed as out of place in this drafty old hall as Prudence.

Settling his shoulders against the hearth, he lit the slender cigar and watched the smoke curl wistfully into the darkness.

Thirty

Killian MacKay trudged up the steep hill, one ear tuned to the whispered promises of an early spring, the other to the jubilant warbling of a mistle thrush. The previous night's storm had washed the sky clean. A fat melon of a sun dodged buoyant clouds against a mat of azure blue. A soft breeze sifted the tips of the swaying conifers in the glen below, carrying to his nostrils the taunting hint of a warming and ripening earth. A hint of green rippled in the brown grasses of the moor.

MacKay ignored the steady pangs of his joints. He had tethered his gelding at the foot of the hill, telling himself his weary bones would enjoy the walk. He knew, though, he was only delaying the moment when he might discover he had made yet another terrible mistake.

He hadn't made the climb to Dunkirk since the sticky summer afternoon when he'd discovered Brendan Kerr had died. He grimaced at the memory of the rocks tumbled over a shallow grave, the hollow tap of his footsteps as he strode through the filthy hall, calling for the boy. His only answer had been the hoarse echo of his own voice and the mocking flutter of the swallows in the rafters.

His hand shook as he slipped it into his plaid and drew forth a sheaf of creamy vellum dripping crimson seals. Dread tightened an icy claw around his heart. If Kerr had hurt Prudence, she had only him to blame. How could he explain to her that he'd had to give the lad a chance? He owed him that much.

The paper rustled as he topped the hill and braced himself for the stark shadow of the castle to fall over him. His dread swelled to amazement as he took in a view of utter domestic charm.

The small castle, once the haunt of only hobgoblins and swallows, looked as if it had been scrubbed clean. The warped door hanging on rusty hinges had been replaced by a new door painted a deep forest green. Two snowy goats nibbled on the grass around the stoop. Three dresses, faded but crisp and clean, flapped on a rope strung between two Caledonian pines.

The rhythmic slap of a trowel on mortar cut a counterpoint to the steady thump of an ax biting wood. MacKay shaded his eyes against the sun. A man worked far down the hill, building up the low stone wall that jutted over the moor. Sunlight gilded his hair. Beside him, a slender woman raked a hoe through the stubborn cords of dead ivy creeping up the gate, her own dark cloud of hair whipping in the wind. In the courtyard, a thin, freckled lad grunted as his ax dug into the roots of a massive stump.

The serpentine roots of the stump gave with a snap. The lad stumbled backward. Despite the cool breeze, he was forced to wipe sweat from his eyes; and then he saw MacKay.

He dropped the ax. "Praise be to the Lord! Swear to me ye're the magistrate. Sweet God, I've been delivered!" He rested his palms on his knees, breathing hard. "Me da always told me I'd be punished for me wicked ways, but I never believed him. I'm turnin' meself in." He strode forward, offering MacKay his upturned wrists. "Ye'll take me back to Edinburgh, won't ye? Maybe they'll ship me off to a work-house where me weary bones can get some rest."

MacKay grinned. "You must be Jamie, the minister's son. The one he fished out of the Glasgow gutter." MacKay looked around. "Where's the other one? The strapping lad he used to run the moors with?"

"Tiny's at his cottage." Jamie's eyes narrowed as he glared at the paper in MacKay's hand. "If ye ain't the magistrate and that ain't a writ of arrest, how do ye know so much about us?"

MacKay smiled enigmatically. "Not a magistrate, my lad. Only an admirer."

Jamie snorted. "Most of me admirers are of the female persuasion." He eyed the hilt of MacKay's claymore. "Ye haven't a daughter, have ye?"

"No. No children."

Jamie looked relieved at MacKay's reply. A husky ripple of laughter drew their gazes to the two figures silhouetted against the azure sky. Sebastian sat on the wall with Prudence nestled in the cradle of his thighs. As they watched, he tilted her face to his and gently kissed her. The knot in MacKay's throat tightened. He slipped the vellum back into his plaid. When his hand emerged, it cupped a gold pocket watch.

Jamie sighed. "I'm warning ye. You'd best go back where ye came from. If they see ye, ye'll never escape. They'll have ye milkin' chickens and polishin' goat eggs quicker than ye can remember yer own name."

MacKay snapped open the engraved cover of his watch, sending a dart of sunlight across Jamie's eyes. "Look at the time, will you? I've an important engagement in the village. I fear I shall have to call on your master another day."

With a jaunty swing of his sporran, he started back down the hill, his claymore clanking against his boots.

"Wait," Jamie yelled after him. "Who shall I tell him called?"

MacKay's cheery whistle floated back to him on a burst of wind. Shaking his head, Jamie hefted the ax and made a halfhearted swing at the stump. Sunlight splintered against the blade as it had flashed against the inscription on the stranger's watch. The ax slipped, sinking into the ground dangerously near Jamie's toes.

His head jerked up. "Why, MacKay, ye canny old bastard!"

The old man was gone. Sun warmed the empty path.

Jamie glanced down the slope. Sebastian had plucked a vine out of Prudence's hair and was tickling her under the chin with it.

Jamie eyed the shade of a pine longingly. "Me da always said I should learn to mind me own business," he muttered.

Creeping beneath the tree, he pulled his cap over his eyes and settled down for a long afternoon nap.

Sebastian lowered the bucket of mortar and stood with hands on hips, surveying his handiwork. When he looked over at Prudence, his expression softened. Her hair hung in snaky tendrils, half up and half down. A fierce scowl furrowed her brow as she clawed at the ivy on the gate like a vengeful lioness.

He wanted to laugh at his own arrogance. He had repaired the stone wall to separate her from the vast emptiness below, knowing deep in his heart that even a mighty fortress would be powerless against it. Whether basking in the deep greens of summer or drenched in the purple of coming autumn, the moor's heathered breath would be carried by wind and mist to breach any barriers he could build. The wind stung his eyes. It wasn't the moor that had killed his mother. It was his father's mercurial temper and unrelenting fear of betrayal.

Sebastian was surprised to find that the rending grief that always accompanied memories of his mother was gone, leaving an odd peace in its place. The early afternoon sun warmed his back. Shadows of clouds chased each other across the dappled grasses. It was too easy to pretend the moment, like the promise of spring, would last forever.

He walked over to Prudence and folded her cool fingers in the warm cup of his hand. "Come with me."

He gave her no time to protest or question as he pulled her through the gate and away from Dunkirk. A narrow footpath materialized from the sheer drop of the cliff. He clambered down the rocks with the confidence of a mountain goat.

Prudence clung to his hand, bracing her weight against him when she would have stumbled. The wind battered them, snatching her breath away. She fixed her gaze on the whipping halo of Sebastian's hair, for without the wall to shelter them, the height was dizzying. Down, down, they climbed into the waiting glen. By the time they reached the bottom, she was gasping for breath.

Sebastian caught her around the waist. "What ails ye, wee English lass? Ha'e ye nae spirit in yer puir pitiful frame?"

She shoved against his chest, hiding her smile behind a black scowl. "Spirit eno' to keep up with a barbarous Highlander, methinks."

With a dazzling grin, he pulled her into a pelting run, away from the shadow of the cliff and into the sunny arms of the moors. They ran hand in hand like children, parting the rustling grasses, freeing the scent of the coming spring from the spongy turf. Prudence laughed, throwing back her head to drink in great gulps of air. Sebastian spun her around, his eyes gleaming with mischief.

As he drew her into the sparkling gloom of a pine forest, she collapsed in a heap on the ground. The ripple of water against rock drew her attention. She crawled forward on her elbows, parting a curtain of needles to peer below.

She was surprised to discover they lay atop a mossy brae overlooking the village. The river twined beside the sleepy cottages, shimmering silver in the sunlight. Smoke drifted from the stone chimneys.

"Sebastian!" she exclaimed as his deft hands worked their way beneath her skirt.

"Aye, dear?" His tongue flicked against the sensitive skin behind her knee.

"You musn't do that. The village is right below."

"We have complete privacy here. Just try not to scream as loud as you did last night when I . . ." His words were mercifully muffled against her thigh.

Heat pricked the back of her neck. "Why, I believe you have a predilection for making love in public places!"

"Nonsense. Of course, there was the time in the sunken bandstand at Vauxhall Gardens . . ."

Her foot came up, catching him neatly in the ribs.

He slipped behind her and nuzzled her nape. "Ha'e ye nae mercy on a puir ravishin' bandit?"

His words evoked a hazy memory in her, like a dream sweetened around the edges by erotic tension. Her head fell back, swayed by the persuasive heat of his lips, the artful press of his fingertips against silken drawers dampened by longing.

Rhythmic hoofbeats thudded on the road below. Prudence

thought it the mad beat of her pulse until Sebastian straightened and lifted a branch.

She felt an agonizing tug at her heart as they saw Laird Killian MacKay ride into the village below, dressed in the full resplendence of plaid and kilt. His broad shoulders were painfully straight. She wondered what the effort must cost his gnarled joints. Stealing a wary look at Sebastian, she saw his mouth was twisted, his eyes dimmed with an unreadable emotion.

They watched the village spring to life. Cottage doors flew open. Sacking flapped in open windows. Piping laughter rang in the air as from every cottage, every yard, every corner of the village, poured children in a ceaseless stream. They danced around MacKay's dappled gelding, faces turned upward, little hands brushing his horse's satiny flank. Not a single hand came away empty. The children ducked their heads, shy eyes glowing, grubby fingers clutching handfuls of sugared walnuts. These children did not look like the children of Jamie's village. Their cheeks were chubby, their feet encased in sturdy brogues. Prudence wondered how much of that had to do with their laird's benevolence.

MacKay leaned forward with a mighty groan and swept a blond boy into his saddle. The boy clutched the pommel, beaming a toothless grin at his envious friends.

Sebastian let the branch fall, enclosing them again in the muted world of green. He rolled to his back, staring up at the creaking canopy. "Twenty years ago he would have lifted the boy to his shoulders. The bastard's getting old." He tucked a pine needle between his lips with painful nonchalance, but the tautness of his jaw betrayed him. "I used to come here and watch him when I was a boy. I thought he might be the king of all Scotland. I think I started to hate him even then."

"For what, Sebastian? Being kind to children?"

He rose without answering, brushing dry needles from his shirt. His eyes were as cold as flints. "We'd best get back. I have a visit to make."

She caught his hand. "Tomorrow will be soon enough." She rubbed her lips lightly over his knuckles, tasting the warm spice of his skin. "Sebastian?"

He gazed at their interlaced fingers as if hypnotized. "Mmm?"

"Are there other ways to make love without making babies?"

Sebastian's breath caught in his throat as he stared down at her, lost in the curious brilliance of her eyes. "Aye."

She eased the tip of his thumb between her lips. "Show me."

His resistance melted beneath the sleek, wet heat of her mouth. Groaning hoarsely, he tangled his hand in her hair, forgetting MacKay, forgetting everything but the temptation to play with abandon at the game they had created.

Rosy shafts of late-afternoon sunlight pierced the arrow slits in the hall. Holding her breath, Prudence eased herself from beneath the weight of Sebastian's thigh.

His long fingers wound in her hair. "Going somewhere, Duchess?"

She winced. Didn't the man ever sleep? She rested her fingertips lightly on his chest. "I'm parched. Would you care for some ale?"

He twirled a strand of hair around his finger. "We shouldn't have sent Jamie away. He could have fetched ale and dropped grapes in our mouths."

"He already believes himself a slave. We mustn't humor his delusions." She wiggled out of his grasp, tucking a blanket under her arms.

Sebastian's gaze swept her from head to toe as she rescued the flagon of ale they had left warming on the hearth. His lazy grin disarmed her. "Decadence becomes you, Miss Walker."

She curtsied, holding the blanket high enough to show off her shapely calves. "Thank you, my lord. I've been practicing."

She twirled away from him and knelt by the hearth, her motions hidden by the folds of the blanket. Her hands were oddly steady, she noticed, as she splashed ale in a goblet, then twisted the lid off the tiny vial she had slipped from her trunk earlier. She dared a glance over her shoulder. Sebastian sprawled on the blankets like a contented satyr, a swath of wool riding low on his hips. A flush of satiation touched his cheekbones. Decadence also became him, she thought. Too well for her peace of mind.

Five. Ten. Fifteen drops. She paused, then tilted in two extra drops of the laudanum. Sebastian's frame was much larger than Tricia's.

Her hands did not falter until she knelt beside him and pressed the goblet into his hand. It swayed, dribbling ale in the sandy hair scattered across his chest. She inclined her head to hide her burning cheeks and dabbed at his chest with a strand of her hair.

He drank deeply. "Mmm. Hot and sweet." His eyes studied her with smoky intensity. "Like you." He cupped her nape and drew her down for a long, wet, open-mouthed kiss.

Prudence wanted to weep. Not sweet, she thought. Bittersweet. She slid down, resting her cheek against the fleecy warmth of his chest. His hand stroked her hair, then fell still. His fingers uncurled against her cheek. When she had measured the rise and fall of his chest for several heartbeats, she rose, dressed quickly, and slipped out into the misty Highland gloaming.

The sinking sun had streaked the sky with pink. As Prudence left the path, her skirt caught on the thorny spines of a hawthorn bush. She jerked it free, ripping a jagged swath from the faded velvet. She had no way of knowing how long Sebastian would sleep. If he awoke before she returned, she would have more than explaining to do.

The sky deepened to lavender as she plunged through a burn swollen from the melting snows. Icy water plastered her skirts to her ankles. A chill nipped the air, drying the sweat at the nape of her neck. She climbed the rocks on the opposite bank, tearing her fingernails on their jagged faces.

She paused to catch her breath. Bowls of mist melted over the glen. The trembling boughs of the birches seemed to mock her. She pulled her shawl up over her hair and darted into the waiting arms of the forest.

A strand of pines streamed past in a blur. She pounded the rich earth beneath her slippers, stumbling only when the rocks bruised her tender soles. A hot blade of pain stabbed beneath her ribs, and she bent double, grasping her side. The agony slowly abated. Her vision cleared. She blinked, believing her bleary eyes deceived her. She wished she had thought to bring her spectacles.

Silhouetted against the darkening sky was a castle of legendary splendor. As she crept nearer, she expected to hear the skirl of bagpipes or see kilted men-at-arms rush out to raise the drawbridge. Only the neatly clipped topiary and mullioned windows assured her she hadn't stumbled through some portal in time. She hastened her steps. This was no time for dallying. She had to reach MacKay before Sebastian did, to warn him that she hadn't yet been able to soften Sebastian's heart toward him.

She pounded on the iron-bound door with her fist, bracing herself to meet the shocked gaze of a proper English butler. The door was snatched open and a strong hand jerked her into the shadowy entrance hall. She gasped as brutal fingers tore the shawl from her hair.

She gazed upward into a face alight with some unnamed emotion. As MacKay's gaze traveled her features, the brilliance in his slate-colored eyes slowly dimmed. He let her go. His color was pasty in the candlelight and sweat tinged his brow. She could smell the staleness of whisky on his breath.

"Sweet Lord, child, I'm sorry. For a moment I thought . . ." He passed a trembling hand over his face.

"That I was her?" she asked softly. "That I was Sebastian's mother?"

MacKay would not look at her.

But Prudence's curiosity was unrelenting. "She came to you, didn't she? Out of the night. Out of the mist."

MacKay ran a hand through his hair. His broad shoulders were stooped as he ushered Prudence through a doorway beamed with crude timber into a study in cozy disarray. A fire crackled on the stone hearth, holding the darkness at bay. Oil lamps scattered pools of light across the polished wood floors. A virginal sat in one corner, its keys furred with dust.

MacKay sank down in an overstuffed chair, hugging his plaid around his shoulders like a shawl. A plump white cat

twined between his ankles. He absently scratched behind
her ears with his gnarled knuckles. Prudence sat on the edge
of the settee, sensing MacKay needed her silence more than
her questions.

He poured himself a tumbler of Scotch and lifted it to his
lips with a shaking hand. "Seeing you and the lad together
today brought back so many memories."

"You saw us?"

"Briefly. I've never been so close to him. It was as if I could
just walk up and . . ." He fixed his eyes on her. The whisky
had burned some of the sharpness back into them. "Sebastian's mother did come to me. Much as you did tonight."

"To beg for your help?"

His even tone shamed her. "If she had asked for my help,
do you think I would have denied her?"

Prudence stared into her lap.

MacKay continued, his words dispassionate. "Ours was an
arranged marriage. D'Artan sent her here a few months
before the ceremony so she could get to know me and my
family. She was little more than a child—huge eyes in a
gamin face. My father was already ailing, but my mother
adored her."

"As did you." It was not a question.

MacKay gazed into his glass. "She fought so hard to hide
her fear. She was sweet and brave and funny. And, oh, so
tempting. I thought it best to put some distance between us
before the wedding. I was in Greece when she was abducted.
It took them months to find me."

"Why didn't the law do anything?"

The look in his eyes chilled Prudence. "With my father ill,
I was the law. I was in this very room loading my pistols to go
after her when she came pounding at the door. To tell me she
had fallen in love with Brendan Kerr. To beg me not to
intervene. To show me she was already with child—*his*
child."

"What did you do?"

"What could I do? I went a little mad inside. Then I let her
go. I let her walk right back into that misty night. Oh, I saw
her after that. On the mountain. In the village. But I always
cut her coldly, turned away. I also saw the way she wore her

shawl pulled up over her face, the bruises on her ankles, the welts on her wrists . . ."

Prudence poured herself a shot of Scotch and downed it in one swig, welcoming the raw path it burned along her throat.

The cat jumped into MacKay's lap and began to knead his kilt with her claws. "But even then my poor wounded pride wouldn't admit that she had lied to me." He lifted his tumbler in a bleak toast. "My godforsaken pride."

Prudence knelt beside him and put a gentle hand on his knee. "Come with me to Dunkirk. Tell Sebastian what you just told me. He believes you abandoned his mother. That you never even tried to help her. Perhaps if you tell him, he'll understand."

MacKay's red-rimmed eyes focused on her. "How can I make him understand when I don't?" He shook his head. "No, lass. 'Tis far too late for me. But not for you."

He stood and shuffled over to a large desk, his steps weighted by the liquor. He pulled a sheaf of vellum from one of the cubbyholes and held it out to her. "The lad's pardon. He'll be expected in London in two weeks to testify against his grandfather before the House of Lords."

She touched the rich paper as if it might burn her. "I wanted you to hide it," she confessed. "But Sebastian's been a prisoner long enough. Tonight I'll give him his pardon. Even if he chooses to be rid of me, at least he'll be free."

MacKay cupped her cheek with a trembling hand. Prudence hadn't seen a mirror since she'd left Edinburgh. She had no inkling of her own transformation beneath the wild, loving caress of both Sebastian and the Highlands. Her hair hung soft and loose down her back. Misty air and hard work had flushed her fair skin with good health. The wind had put a new sparkle in her violet eyes.

MacKay's fingers steadied. "He's a lucky man. You've finally become as beautiful as your aunt always feared you would be."

Prudence plucked a cat hair from his plaid. She despised leaving him alone steeped in guilt and solitude. She wanted to share with him the hope beating in her heart, the joy stirring despite her fear. Beneath his questioning gaze, she went to the desk, uncapped an inkwell, and scribbled some-thing on a card. She pressed it into his hand, then stood on her tiptoes to whisper in his ear.

His weathered face cracked in a smile. "An excellent suggestion. I shall send for my seamstress tonight."

Prudence tucked the pardon in her shawl. MacKay draped the cat over one arm and followed her to the door. She paused. "Tell me, Laird MacKay," she said solemnly, "did you offer for my hand just to save Sebastian, or were you really willing to marry me?"

The cat's gray-green eyes surveyed Prudence unblinkingly. MacKay inclined his head. "Bella and I could have found a place for you in our hearts, had you chosen to stay."

She gave his hand a hard squeeze, then started across the lawn at a run. MacKay watched until she was only a shadowy wraith among the trees, then buried his face in Bella's fur.

Prudence pelted through the trees, praying she would not lose her way. Moonlight dappled the forest floor, sheening off rocks and ferns. A blinking vole scurried out of her path as she rushed on, afraid but unable to squelch the hope that sang with each shuddering breath. She clutched Sebastian's pardon to her breast. Even when she tripped and fell flat, she kept her palm curled around it. As she scrambled to her feet, her shawl caught on a branch and fell away.

She burst out of the woods into a meadow. The swollen moon laved the grasses with silver. A red deer lifted his head from a gurgling stream, his brown eyes knowing and pas-sive, as if wild-eyed English girls plunged through his meadow every night.

Stars winked to life like icy shards against an inky pelt. They looked so near, Prudence would have sworn she could reach out and capture a handful. The land shifted, steepen-ing beneath her feet. The mist curled damp fingers around her skin. Even it seemed welcoming now, like cool clouds banked at the peaks of heaven. She was going home. Home to Dunkirk. Home to Sebastian.

She stumbled into the courtyard, then stilled her headlong flight. Dread quickened her pulse and slowed her breathing.

A solitary light burned in the window of the tower.

The light was an ugly flare against the darkness, as piercing and relentless as a blade through the soft under-belly of the night.

She staggered forward, then stopped again, teetering on the brink of the ugly gash in the earth where Sebastian's coffer had once been buried.

Thirty-one

The leather-bound coffer lay on its side like a wounded creature. Shovel marks gouged the hinges and splintered the panels. The crude lock had been shattered as if by one blow of rage. Or one clean pistol shot. Prudence knew if she had any wits left about her, she would turn around and march straight back to England.

Something stopped her, though. Staring up at the tower, she took one step, then another, hypnotized by the paralyzing inevitability of that light. It profaned the darkness, scarred the beauty of the night, burned her hope to ashes. The main door was partly ajar. She slipped through the crack, holding her breath.

The signs of their lovemaking were scattered across the hall—the rumpled blankets, the dying embers on the grate, the flagon overturned in a puddle of ale. Those warm, rosy hours might have been a lifetime ago. Sebastian-cat was draped across the warm stones of the hearth. He lifted his head in drowsy curiosity.

Prudence's gaze traveled upward to the spill of light on the landing. It beckoned her forward, melted the stairs beneath her feet.

She stepped into the light, crumpling the pardon in her hand.

Sebastian sat with his hip propped against the windowsill,

his back to her. He swung around as she stepped through the doorway. For an instant, the eerie reflection of another man shaded the planes of his face. Then it was gone, nothing more than a trick of the light.

He held out his hand with a mocking smile. River rock streamed through his fingers, crumbling to dust as it struck the floor. "Our future together, my dear."

Prudence steadied her voice with effort. "A future should be built on more than rocks . . . or gold."

"Spoken like a true optimist." He stood, wiping off his hands. "It all comes to the same end, doesn't it? As do we."

"Spoken like a true fatalist."

"Or a realist."

The torchlight brushed his tousled hair with gold. He walked toward her with lazy grace, his movements slowed but efficient. The laudanum, she thought. His gray eyes were as piercing as the light.

"That's right, dear," he said, seeming to read her mind. "I fear you miscalculated. Such a minute amount of laudanum only makes me tipsy. When we lived in Paris, my grandfather used to feed me opium as if it were candy."

She quailed before the knowledge of such decadence, such heartless corruption, and kept her eyes lowered, knowing her sympathy would only bait him.

He reached around her and pushed the door shut. "Where have you been, my Prudence? Were you off having tea with your fiancé?" He stood directly in front of her, his breath a whisper of warmth against her temple.

"I'm sorry," she mumbled. "I shouldn't have drugged you. It was wrong."

"*Au contraire, ma cherie.*" His voice was musing, almost gentle. "It was brilliant. Have I ever told you how very much I admire your mind?" His hands twined through her hair, cupping her skull. She closed her eyes against the power restrained in his elegant fingers. "Even when you betrayed me to Tugbert, a tiny part of me stood back and cried, 'Bravo! What a canny lass she is! What wit! What courage! She sees what must be done and she does it.'"

Her eyes flew open. She tried to twist out of his grasp, but his fingers tightened in her hair. "Stop making sport of me!"

He blinked in childish innocence. "I haven't the wit. You must remember I'm only an ignorant Highlander. I didn't even learn to read or write until I was almost twenty. And I've never learned to spell." He pressed his lips to her hair and whispered, "I find your brilliance exotic . . . and erotic." His tongue flicked across her ear, scorching her like a live flame. "The gold, Prudence. Where is it? Did you give it to MacKay? Or have you another swain in the wings? Prime Minister Pitt, perhaps? The governor general?"

She stared at his chest, her wit working sluggishly at best with his mouth so sweet against her hair, his thigh flexed so casually between her legs. He might still be harboring the idea that she had hidden the gold to spite him. What would he do to her when he discovered it was lost forever?

"Gold?" she said brightly. "What gold?"

Sebastian did not dignify that with an answer. His lips grazed the fluttering pulse at the hollow of her throat. She could not abide his fraudulent tenderness when she could feel the raw anger boiling through him, the relentless nudge of his knee between her thighs.

She shoved at his chest. "Oh, for God's sake, stop torturing me! I gave your precious gold to the poor children in Jamie's village. I was sick of you using me to further your greedy ambitions. I gave it away and I'm glad I did. I'd do it again if I had the chance."

She faced him, her chin tilted in defiance. Her nose betrayed her with a nervous sniff.

Sebastian went utterly still. A muffled snort escaped him, then another. She stepped forward in alarm, fearful his rage might be choking him. He waved her away as a raw whoop of laughter burst from his throat. He stumbled over to lean against the bedpost, clutching his stomach. Tears streamed down his cheeks.

She backed against the door. Had the laudanum unhinged him? She had read of such things. Perhaps the shock had been too great.

"How rich," he gasped. "How very fitting. All the spoils of years of highway robbery given to the needy. I'd be willing to bet you and MacKay had a good laugh over that one." He swiped a hand over his face. "It seems I'm back where I began. At Dunkirk. With nothing but the clothes on my back."

And me. She longed to say the words aloud. But if he started laughing again, she knew the tears stinging at the back of her eyes would spill over. Her fingers knotted. Paper crinkled. She stared down at her hand, remembering the pardon for the first time.

She crossed the tower and thrust the creamy sheaf against his chest. "Not just the clothes on your back. You have far more than that now. You have your freedom."

The last traces of mirth vanished from his face. He took the paper from her hand and gazed at the royal seal without unfolding it.

"My freedom?" He cocked a mocking eyebrow. "You mean your freedom, don't you, Duchess?"

A cry caught in her throat as he tore the pardon in two. "With the gold gone, I'm worth far more dead than alive. Surely you and your precious *Killian* have figured that out."

She backed away from him, knowing she did not want to be alone in the tower with this man. She wasn't even sure who he was.

He stalked her, his eyes sparkling. His smile would have shamed an angel. "You owe me thirty thousand pounds, darling."

"You can't be serious."

Her knees trembled with relief as he strode around her to the trunk. He pulled out an ink and quill and carried them to the windowsill. "What's your yearly pension?"

"Ten thousand pounds."

"Mathematics always suited me better than spelling." He scribbled on the back of the pardon, then held it up, grinning cheerfully. "In three years, you'll be free and clear of me. I'm sure MacKay will wait. He's proved to be a very patient man. If he lives that long."

She cocked her head. "You've gone quite insane, haven't you?"

"We musn't forget your other skills—bookkeeping, embroidery, dusting." He arched one eyebrow in a diabolical leer. "There might even be a hastier way of paying me off. Just how much do you think you're worth per night, my dear?"

He jotted down another figure. "So many choices. Should we make this per night or per event? No doubt you'll expect me to pay you back wages." He gave a beleaguered sigh. "I could be generous and throw in a few extra pounds for the first time. Most gentlemen would."

She circled him, her eyes wide, her mouth a circle of shock. She couldn't believe what she was hearing, could not comprehend the sheer audacity of the man. He was only too eager to reduce each tender moment they'd shared to pound notes and cold shillings.

He tucked the quill between his lips. "I'm not sure about this afternoon. Should I pay half for that?" He cast her a provocative look. "Or double?"

Heat flooded her cheeks. Her first instinct was to box his ears so hard he would suck the quill straight down his smug throat. A deeper intuition stopped her. Sebastian was furious. But the madder he got, the more cheerful he got. How many times had he been forced to swallow his anger? How many tantrums had his brutal father denied him in this very room? She might not be a faro player, but she knew how to call a man's bluff. She unclenched her fists and lifted her hands to the buttons of her bodice.

His smile faded. "What are you doing?"

She slipped a button from its loop, her eyebrows lifted in elegant surprise. "Isn't this how it's done in London? Surely a sophisticated man like you has frequented enough bawdy houses to know the routine."

Sebastian's ferocious good cheer vanished, dispelled by desperation and something dangerously near self-loathing. Prudence nudged off her slippers and propped her foot on a stool, hiking up her skirts to reveal one long leg. With graceful languor, she slid her garter down the silky contours of her calf and peeled off her stocking.

"Prudence." His voice was choked.

She bared her other leg without looking at him, then lifted her arms to draw her gown over her head. She wore no petticoat, only a silk chemise worn to transparency by too many washings in rough lye.

"Don't do this," he whispered hoarsely. "This isn't what I want."

Even as he said it, though, he was moving toward her like a spellbound man, beguiled by the dusky pout of her nipples against the silk, the delicate shading at the juncture of her thighs.

Sebastian wanted to weep. He wanted to fall to his knees at her feet and worship her. He wanted to beg her forgiveness for a myriad of sins, some his own, some his father's, some committed by other men over the centuries.

"No," he breathed even as he reached for her.

She stepped back from his touch. "How much am I worth tonight, Sebastian? A hundred pounds? A thousand?" She tossed her hair over her shoulders. His gaze wavered, drawn to the rippling motion. "I'll tell you how much I'm worth tonight—thirty thousand pounds. If you lay so much as one finger, one pretty eyelash on me, we're even. No debts. No regrets."

He gazed at her sideways for a long moment. "No regrets?"

She shook her head, her eyes luminous.

He came for her then, bearing her back against the wall with a guttural growl. Like the starving boy he'd once been, he devoured her with his mouth, his hands. She was the only one with the power to fill him, to nourish him, to take him to the place where the hunger pangs could not follow. Now all he wanted to do was fill her until she cried out with the wonder of it. He felt her thigh angle upward and caught her long, silky leg, wrapping it around his waist.

Prudence was not nearly as composed as she'd pretended to be. She was shaking, trembling with the same fever that possessed him.

He shoved up her chemise, crushing her breasts against his palms. He tore open his shirt and freed his straining arousal from his breeches, desperate to feel every inch of her skin against his own. He cupped one arm around her buttocks, lifting her, opening her. She was hot, so very hot. He remembered the long winters at Dunkirk when he'd thought he would never be warm again—when he couldn't remember what the sun felt like against his skin or how the summer smelled. Prudence's skin was the sun, her delicate scent the fragrance of endless summer.

He buried his face in her hair and drove himself into her.

They sprawled against the wall in a tangle of hair, limbs, and pleasure. He took her with long, deep strokes, cradling her to him when she might have slammed against the wall. She clung to him like a child, arms and legs wrapping him in a cocoon of melting delight. He groaned, sliding dangerously near to a place where only his own selfish pleasure existed.

Bracing her weight with his own, he reached between them and gently touched her, marveling anew at the delicacy and grace of her femininity. Her shuddering response came fast and hard. He felt it to the very core of his being, felt his own release coming too quickly on its heels. Panic gripped him.

Prudence tightened her legs at the small of his back and softly moaned his name. It was like touching the trigger on a primed pistol. A rolling thunder of ecstasy shot through his loins and poured into her. He lowered his face to her throat, biting back tears, knowing he would have to let her go before she discovered just how low he would sink to make her stay.

Prudence awoke sprawled on her stomach in a tangle of blankets. She opened her eyes, then closed them again, content to nestle deeper into the heather pillow. Her hands balled into fists as she stretched. Sebastian-cat was curled at her feet. The bed beside her was cool and empty. She slid her hand over the faint indentation where Sebastian had slept, assuring herself it hadn't been a dream.

"Slept" was too generous a word. No one could accuse Sebastian Kerr of not getting his money's worth. She sat up, delighting in the faint throb of her muscles, the odd twinges in the nether regions of her body.

The door swung open. She hugged the blanket over her knees, fighting a sudden wave of shyness.

A wicker basket was draped over Sebastian's arm. She recognized it as the one she used to gather eggs. As he gave the bed the barest of glances, her heart faltered a beat.

She watched, perplexed, as he folded his only other shirt and tucked it inside the basket. "Sebastian-cat should be comfortable traveling in here," he said without looking at her. "You musn't risk him running away again. The wee fellow's luck might not hold this time."

She stared at the dusty spot where her trunk had sat only last night. A clean gown and her redingote were folded neatly over the stool. Suddenly she understood the fierce desperation of Sebastian's lovemaking, the agonized hunger of his touch. He intended never to touch her again. Never.

"I won't go."

He went on as if she hadn't spoken. "You can take the wagon to MacKay's. I'll send Jamie for it tomorrow. I've written this statement swearing our marriage was invalid and agreeing to a dissolution." He slipped the paper in the pocket of her redingote, ducking his head. "I wasn't sure if dissolution had two *l*s' or one."

"One," she whispered.

He reached for the cat, obviously intending to tuck him into the basket, but she snatched the puzzled animal to her breast and glared at Sebastian. "Is that what you're going to do to me? Fold me up and tuck me away?"

He ran a hand through his hair, finally meeting her gaze. His eyes were filled with such despair and quiet determination, she wished he hadn't. Sebastian-cat squirmed. His claws raked her arm, but she didn't feel it. Sebastian reached over and gently took him from her.

He set the cat in the basket. His hands stroked the animal's soft fur as he spoke, each word as precise and deliberate as a blade. "MacKay kept his word. I shall keep mine. I haven't much else, but I've still got my word. I want you to go back to England where you belong. Forget about me. I don't need you in my life. I don't *want* you in my life." Ignoring Sebastian-cat's piteous mew, he closed the lid and reached for the latch.

"You don't love me?"

Sebastian's hands faltered. How many times, he wondered, had this brave, sweet woman choked back that very question when faced with her father's absentminded fondness or Tricia's halfhearted affections? He hadn't the eloquence to make her understand how glorious and terrible love was. Brendan Kerr had loved his mother. He had abducted her for revenge, but had kept her for his own dark

obsession. Sebastian still remembered his father's desperate
pleas as he had begged the proud, broken girl for some scrap
of love in return. It was the one thing she had the power to
withhold from him. So he had used his fists to try to beat the
words out of her.

Sebastian latched the basket, plastering on his most
rakish smile. "No. I don't love you."

Prudence's face went white.

He shrugged. "I found your innocence intriguing. Had I
married Tricia, you would have made a convenient mistress.
I wouldn't have had to leave the house to seek my pleasures.
And I've certainly found you a quite pleasant diversion in the
past week. I'm sure you understand. Entertainments are
scarce in this part of the country." He dragged a chair in
front of the window and sat down, his back to her, desperate
to escape her stricken gaze.

"You're lying," she said. "To me and to yourself. What are
you so afraid of, Sebastian Kerr? Why are you hiding
behind—"

"Don't." He cut her off coldly. "We made a bargain last
night. No debts. No regrets. You swore."

He could hear her behind him, dressing with quick, angry
movements. The basket creaked as she paused in the doorway. He felt her stillness and knew it was the last time she
would ever swallow her pride for him.

"Did you ever think of making a real life together?" she
asked, her voice husky. "A roaring fire? Babes playing
around the hearth?"

"No," he lied. "Never."

When he turned around, the doorway was empty. Prudence
was gone.

Sebastian propped his boots on the windowsill as the misty
shadows of twilight painted the tower dark. He had left the
chair only once during the day. A loaded pistol sat at his feet.
He would have need of it when D'Artan's men discovered he
had let Prudence go. He did not stir to light the torches,
though the fire had dwindled to embers. A cool wind drifted
through the window, caressing his face with mocking fin-

gers. There was no need to close the window now. He had nothing left to fear from it. Neither the wind nor the heathered abyss beneath the window was his enemy. All he had to fear now was the silence.

He remembered the sunny day he had buried his father. The silence had been a chiming gift then, the cessation of cannon fire after a long and bloody war.

He stared into the gathering darkness. It was as if Prudence had taken all the sounds of the castle with her, leaving him deaf as well as blind. There was no bright tap of her slippers on the stairs, no whisky-soft ripple of laughter, no purring rumble from Sebastian-cat. He had sent her away, leaving himself to grope through the barren halls of Dunkirk without even the charred stench of her black buns to guide him.

Men don't cry.

An ugly bellow, a bright flash of pain, and a warm spurt of blood from his chin. Even at the age of five, Sebastian had known it to be a lie. He had come upon his father in the twilight that same day, kneeling in the fresh dirt of his mother's grave, his burly shoulders hunched, his florid face twisted with grief. *Men don't cry.*

Downstairs, a door crashed open. A jarring bump was followed by an emphatic curse.

Sebastian closed his eyes. *Not now, Jamie. Please, dear God, not now.* Jamie's grumbling cheerfulness might well be his undoing, like rubbing salt in the wound of a dying man.

Sebastian's prayer went unanswered.

Jamie thumped up the stairs, mumbling to himself. "Doesn't anyone know it's the bloody eighteenth century? You'd think we was livin' in the Dark Ages. Hasn't anyone in this dungeon ever heard of oil lamps? Candles? A man could get hisself killed . . ." His voice rose to a nasal whinny. "Sebastian? If ye've got Pru's clothes off, you'd best get 'em on 'cause I'm comin' up."

Sebastian buried his forehead in his hand, groaning. Why couldn't God be merciful and just let Jamie shoot him?

Jamie stumbled into the tower, throwing down a fat parcel in a rustling heap. "Christ's blood! I suppose ye were waitin' for me to come back and stoke the fire. Bloody slave, ye think

I am." He stomped around, feeding the fire and lighting torches.

Sebastian flinched at the sudden blaze of light.

"Where's Pru?" Jamie's brow furrowed in alarm. "If ye've let her in the kitchen again, I'm marchin' straight back to the village."

Sebastian stood and opened his mouth, but nothing came out. He could not face the questions, the accusations, the recriminations he knew he would read on Jamie's face. He closed his mouth. How odd, he thought. For the first time in his life, he had been struck dumb. Had Prudence left him nothing?

"What is it?" Jamie asked. "Sebastian-cat got yer tongue?" He scooped up the parcel. "My seamstress lady friend said I was to deliver this to ye. I can't imagine why. Changin' clothes every day is a vain and sinful habit. Me mum always said so."

He tossed the parcel at him. Sebastian lifted his hands too late, and the package hit his chest. The fragile tissue split, spilling out yard upon yard of soft wool in alternating squares of green and black—the Kerr plaid in all of its brilliance and splendor. Sebastian stared numbly at the sea of tartan.

The edge of an ivory-colored card peeped out of the fleecy mound. He knelt, holding the card up to the light.

It was inscribed in a delicate script: *Sebastian Kerr, Laird of Dunkirk, Always. Your Loving Prudence.*

Jamie squinted over his shoulder. "What's it say? Ye know I don't read so good."

Sebastian rested his elbow on his knee, his eyes distant. "It says I'm a fool, Jamie. A complete and utter fool."

Thirty-two

Sebastian tossed his new plaid over his shoulders as he led the horses from the stable. "Stop squalling, Jamie. I don't have any choice. I have to go after her."

A light mist drifted over the courtyard, chilling the air without obscuring the moon or stars. Jamie trotted behind Sebastian, peppering his entreaties with curses. Sebastian tossed a saddle on the horse's back and Jamie pulled it off the other side.

"Ye can't do it. D'Artan's men are still in the village. How long do ye think it'll be before they find out ye let her go? Ye'll be dodgin' lead balls all the way to England."

Sebastian's voice was deadly soft. "Jamie, give me the saddle."

Jamie backed away, the saddle held like a shield in front of him. "Let me go for ye. I'll catch up to her. I'll tell her yer a bumblin' fool who loves her. Hell, I'll even kiss her if ye want. I can be as charmin' as the next lad when I set me mind to it."

Sebastian circled the horse, stalking Jamie with all the grace, but none of the shyness, of a Highland wildcat. His gray eyes burned with determination.

Jamie's legs came up against the water trough. "It's not just D'Artan ye've got to worry about. That bonny puss of yers is plastered all over Scotland. Don't ye remember what that stiff-necked sheriff promised? If ye go anywhere near the border, ye'll be hanged fer sure."

Sebastian stretched out his hand, speaking as if to a child. "The saddle, Jamie."

Jamie briefly considered bursting into tears. His wailing had never failed to break his mum. He doubted it would work with Sebastian, though, and hurled the saddle at him with a particularly imaginative epithet.

"Thank you," Sebastian said calmly, striding back to the patient horse.

Jamie drove a hand through his hair, snaring his fingers in the tangles. Sebastian mounted, securing his bedroll in front of him.

Jamie bounded across the courtyard and caught the reins. "Take me with ye then. Ye musn't go alone."

Sebastian attempted to pry Jamie's fingers off the reins, but his bony strength held. "I have to go alone. You said it yourself. It's too dangerous."

"Then ye'll be goin' with me danglin' off yer reins all the way to England."

Sebastian continued to tug at Jamie's fingers as his other hand eased his pistol out of his waistband. "I can't ask you to risk your neck because of my own foolishness."

Jamie gazed up at him, his eyes wide and guileless. "Ye've asked me to risk it fer less."

"So I have." Sebastian smiled—a sweet, tender smile. Then the butt of his pistol came down against Jamie's neck, dropping him like a sack of potatoes.

"You haven't learned your lessons, Jamie Graham," he murmured, shoving his pistol back into his breeches. "A fallen man is a noose for the next man. And I've fallen hard this time."

Jamie looked even younger sprawled in the grass, his lashes spiked over his freckled cheeks.

Sighing, Sebastian undid his bedroll and tossed the blanket over Jamie. "Sweet dreams, my lad," he whispered.

He guided the horse in a prancing circle and thundered through the gate of the courtyard. He dared one look over his shoulder only to discover that Jamie and Dunkirk had been swallowed by the mist.

•   •   •

A lone figure crept through the alley. Fog swirled around his ankles. Light spilled from the bloated moon, caressing his silk mask, shading the set planes of his face with silver. Excitement stirred his blood, quickened his breath. A hint of the old thrill touched him as he slipped into the shadows, moving as one with the darkness, once again lord of the night, prince of thieves. But at the end of this journey, he hoped to steal not watch fobs or pound notes easily crumbled to dust, but a woman's heart, as true and precious as gold refined by fire.

He eased himself into the tavern without a sound. Hazy moonlight drifted through a flyspecked window, staining his hair to gold. At such a late hour in such a sleepy, little village, the tavern was nearly deserted.

A toothless old man polished mugs behind the bar. Two men were engaged in a heated game of piquet at one table. A buxom whore straddled the lap of the younger one. The man's hand crept past her dimpled knee and under her skirt, emerging with a new card. He tossed it on the table, winning the trick. As he gleefully swept the shillings into the woman's lap, the other man swore in rapid French.

Sebastian smiled.

The barkeep glanced up, and his gaze was instantly transfixed by the mask, the swirl of the plaid around Sebastian's shoulders, the wry smile on his mouth. Sebastian touched a finger to his lips and winked. The barkeep gummed a smile and went back to polishing his mugs.

The whore deftly shuffled the cards as the young Frenchman nuzzled her neck.

Before any of them could react, Sebastian swung one leg over the back of a chair and straddled it. "Deal me in, lass."

The Frenchman dumped the woman out of his lap. She sprawled in the floor, scattering the coins. The other man fumbled for his pistol. Sebastian caught both of their heads and slammed them together. They slumped across the table like marionettes with cut strings.

Sebastian smiled at the whore and offered her his hand. "And deal them out."

She could not help smiling back, even as her own hands scurried to gather the shillings.

Jamie blinked up at a sky washed with pearly light. A bird twittered nearby. Where the hell was he? He'd met more dawns than one with that question on his lips, but this morn there was no warm female wedged against his side, no fuzziness of his tongue to warn of a lost battle with demon ale. He lifted his head experimentally. His neck was stiff, his shirt and breeches damp with dew, but the rest of him seemed intact, even rested.

He laid his head on laced hands, content to watch pink wisps of clouds drift across the fading stars. His sharp chin nuzzled into the blanket on his chest.

An image abruptly filled his mind. *Sebastian.* The smile of an angel, the glint of moonlight on a raised pistol butt.

Ignoring his reeling head, Jamie leaped to his feet and sprinted toward the stable. He emerged with one leg thrown over a sleek dun mare, the other leg still dragging on the ground. He righted himself by gripping the mane with both hands. As he plunged down the slope, barefoot and bareback, his mad Highland cry would have chilled the blood of any Englishman.

The burn tinkled a merry welcome as Sebastian walked his horse into the clearing. The crofter's hut crouched in the moonlight as he remembered it. He uncurled his stiff fingers from the reins and slumped in the saddle, too exhausted to move. For two days and two nights, he had ridden with little sleep and less food. He had even followed MacKay's party for an hour yesterday, close enough to call out Prudence's name. But he hadn't. MacKay's guards looked to be the type to shoot first and ask questions later. He didn't intend to risk Prudence getting caught in the crossfire. When they stopped to spend the night in Edinburgh, he had changed horses and ridden on ahead.

If he could catch her before she crossed the border, he would. If not, he would march straight up to the door of

Lindentree, MacKay and Tricia be damned, and demand to see his wife. Then all that would remain was convincing Prudence that she still wanted a stubborn, jealous, greedy Highland rogue for a husband. He sighed and dragged himself off the horse. Perhaps things would look better in the light of morning.

He tended to the mare with weary hands, rubbing down her heaving sides. She had been built for speed, not stamina, and he had pushed her hard.

He left her tethered to a tree and pushed open the hut door, hugging the plaid around him at a rush of chill air.

"Your predictability was always your downfall, my boy."

Sebastian held up his hands in a silent plea as the pistol in his grandfather's hand exploded into a searing ball of pain.

Prudence sat stiff in the sidesaddle, looking neither right or left, her navy skirt draped in military precision over her legs. Sebastian-cat rode at her side, strapped into the wicker basket. Not even the teasing touch of the spring breeze could stir the severe wings of hair framing her pale cheeks. Her eyes were dry, so dry they burned at the prick of the wind. She hadn't shed a single tear since two mornings ago when she'd pounded on Laird MacKay's door. She'd fallen into the haven of his arms and sobbed against his plaid until there were no tears left and her body lay broken and exhausted, seeking only the solace of sleep.

She stole a glance at the man riding beside her. MacKay seemed to have aged since that night. The crags in his face cut deeper; his shoulders slumped. It was as if the flame in his eyes had been extinguished by her bitter tears.

As they rode past a sun-dappled forest, MacKay's armed guards drew in around them. Their faces were set. The burly hands resting on their pistol butts warned they'd be no easy target for any highwayman.

The road flattened into a meadow. Prudence knew they must be nearing the Northumberland border. The tender trilling of a lark jarred her into opening her eyes to the aching beauty of the morning. Tender sprouts of new heather crept over the hills. The rich smell of the loamy earth tickled her nose. A dazzling orb of sunlight hung in a sky too blue to be anything less than a figment of some artist's fevered imagination.

The breeze whispered through the swaying grasses and she imagined she heard her name, carried by the wind on a rich, plaintive note of longing. Her gloved fingers tightened on the reins. Never again would she be ensorceled by a soft burr as bewitching and treacherous as this heartbreaking land. Soon she would cross the border into sane, predictable England where she would once again become sane, predictable Prudence. A pang of grief drove a searing wedge through her heart.

She heard it then, a wild keening like the distant skirl of bagpipes that set the hair at the nape of her neck standing on end. Two men thundered over the ridge, the first bent so low to his mount's neck that he might have been a sinewy limb of the horse itself

The guards drew their pistols. MacKay's gelding pawed the air as he reeled it around, forcing it between Prudence and the approaching riders. Sebastian-cat gave a dismal yowl from the confines of his basket.

Prudence heard her name again, carried not by wind, but bawled in the unmistakable cadences of Jamie's voice.

"Wait!" she cried. "Don't fire. They mean us no harm."

MacKay gave her a doubtful glance, but trusted her enough to call off his guards. His men lowered their weapons with obvious reluctance, no doubt unnerved by the towering stature of the man on the second horse. The sun tinted his blond hair to white. He looked as if he could snap their necks with one hand, armed or unarmed.

Prudence's chin jutted out, a first wild beat of hope smothered by an overwhelming anger. Was she never to be left in peace?

Jamie drew his horse to a halt, his fists crunched in the mare's tangled mane. MacKay's men gaped. They had never seen a man ride a horse like that, with no bridle, no saddle, no reins. And barefoot to boot.

For once, Jamie's eyes were devoid of any humor. "Sebastian needs ye."

Prudence met his gaze evenly, and her words were tinged

with ice. "I fear you're mistaken. He made it very clear to me that he doesn't need me. Those were his exact words."

Tiny spoke up. "Ye don't understand, lass. He left Dunkirk over a day ago. He was goin' to meet ye at the border. So we traveled all our old roads between here and there and saw not a hair of him."

"Perhaps you should check the Blake estate," she said. "He might have stopped at Devony's for tea or other amusements."

With a disgusted snort, Jamie jerked his head at Tiny.

Tiny dragged open the letter flap of his saddlebag. "We found this in the old hollow tree where he used to leave messages fer us."

Prudence unrolled the tiny scroll. Squinting at the elaborate script, she read it aloud, her voice dispassionate. "'Duchess, your husband is my guest. Meet me at the old crofter's hut. Alone.'" It was signed with nothing but a flourished D.

Prudence heard MacKay draw an agonized breath. She handed the note back to Jamie. "I have no husband. I have only a paper in my reticule signed by Sebastian Kerr, denying the validity of our marriage."

Jamie went white. His freckles blazed. He pawed through Tiny's saddlebag, then thrust his hand at her. "D'Artan left this for us as well."

The green and black plaid dangled from his fingers. A muddy hoofprint scarred the soft wool. MacKay paled.

Prudence's mouth compressed to a thin line. "I'm sorry. I cannot help you. Sebastian made it more than clear to me that I was no longer to interfere in his life."

Jamie's lip curled in a snarl of contempt.

Tiny laid a hand on his companion's shoulder. "I tried to tell ye she wouldn't help. She doesn't give a damn about him. Never has."

Jamie hurled the plaid into her lap. "I hope it keeps ye warm at night, Mrs. Kerr, fer it's all ye'll have left of Sebastian once D'Artan gets through with him."

With a piercing cry, Jamie steered his horse in a circle, shoving his way heedlessly through the guards. Tiny cast Prudence a last condemning look before following. The steady beat of their mounts' hooves rocked the turf as they pounded toward the horizon.

Prudence ran a hand over the soft wool in her lap, unable to meet MacKay's searching gaze. Her meticulous fingers caressed the rich material until they caught in the jagged, blackened hole near the hem.

Prudence and Laird MacKay rode in silence, their guards a wary phalanx around them. Sebastian's plaid still lay across her lap. When MacKay glanced at her, she could feel the measuring heat of his concern, but carefully kept her expression stony.

He cleared his throat. "You know, lass, if you wanted, I could ride back and—"

She swayed in her saddle, and he quickly caught her elbow. She pressed her fingertips to her temple, knowing her pallor was convincing, for it was genuine.

She leaned against him. "My head . . . it just began to pound. It must be the sun."

MacKay fumbled for his canteen. She clutched his arm, gazing at him with quiet despair. "The Blake estate is just ahead. Could we stop for a rest? I'm not quite ready to face my aunt. She'll have so many questions . . ."

He patted her hand. "Of course, my dear."

Without asking her leave, he tossed her reins to one of the guards and lifted her into the saddle in front of him. He tucked Sebastian's tartan around her shoulders. She buried her face in it, as he urged the gelding forward, blessing the sheltering folds for hiding the sudden heat in her cheeks.

A row of servants gaped as the Blakes' butler led Prudence and MacKay into the dim coolness of the entranceway. Prudence clung to MacKay, her head bowed, and stumbled as they reached the foot of the stairs.

The loquacious young butler informed them that Miss Blake was in London for the season and the squire had ridden over to visit the countess at Lindentree.

But, of course, he would be more than happy to provide

rooms for Miss Walker and her guest to refresh themselves. After he had shown Laird MacKay to the room next to hers, he even dared to touch Prudence's hand. He was quite sympathetic to her plight. He had read about it in all of the newspapers. Prudence had no inkling that she had become such a celebrity while she was gone.

"Would you care for some chocolate?" he asked. "Or perhaps some piping hot scones with clotted cream and kippers with—"

She smiled wanly. "A flask of brandy and a cigar, please. Immediately." She closed the door in his face.

It was a long moment before his footsteps moved away down the corridor. Prudence darted to the window. No trellis. She grimaced at the sight of the thorny rosebushes below. The room overlooked the back of the rambling Tudor house. She could see MacKay's guards smoking and leaning against the stable wall. A lazy furl of pipe smoke uncurled on the morning breeze. The sun glinted off their pistols.

A shy tap sent her scurrying back to the door. The earnest butler stood there, brandy and cheroot in hand.

"I've heard the Scots are an unpredictable, savage lot," he whispered, gazing at her as if he expected her to throw off her clothes and break into a wild Highland jig. Prudence was half tempted to oblige him just so he'd go away.

The excited hunger in his eyes gave her a better idea, though. She caught his forearm and jerked him into the room. "You're quite right. The Scots are a mad race. And that man in the next room is the maddest of them all."

"The pleasant gentleman with the white hair?" He frowned at the connecting door.

Prudence snorted. "A clever disguise. He is the savage who abducted me. He's returning me to my aunt's estate in the hope of extracting a ransom from the poor dear." She dragged the butler to the window, peering around the drapes with theatrical stealth. "See those men out there? Those are his henchmen. Skilled assassins, every one of them."

"Oh, my. Oh, my!" His voice sank to a whisper. "You don't mean he is . . . he can't be . . . not the—"

Her smile was deadly sweet. "The Dreadful Scot Bandit Kirkpatrick. In the flesh."

A shuddering wail escaped the butler. "What shall I do? I'm new to this post. I wouldn't have gotten the position at all if Devony—I mean Miss Blake—hadn't recommended me. Only a week on the job and I've let a vicious felon into the house." He stared at her hopefully. "Do you think he'd leave if I offered him the silver?"

Prudence lowered her voice, using its husky timbre to contemptuous advantage. "Leave? How would it look on your record if you let the most notorious highwayman since Black Jack Jones escape from your grasp?"

He tugged at one of his wig curls, obviously torn between the fear of murder and the temptation of being a hero.

Prudence toyed with his sleeve. "There is the reward to consider."

A wealthy hero.

"And think of how impressed Miss Blake will be by your bravery."

A wealthy adored hero.

He grasped Prudence's hands in his sweaty palms. "What shall I do?"

She leaned forward and whispered, "Bring me guns. Lots of guns."

Thirty-three

Sebastian's nose crinkled as an acrid stench wafted toward him. Prudence must be cooking breakfast, he thought. He would have to ride down to the village and hire her a cook. He'd much rather have her snuggled beside him, her head nestled in the crook of his arm, than struggling over an ancient hearth. Why, if she were next to him, he could nuzzle her throat, stroke her until she was purring like a kitten beneath him, and . . .

He sniffed. Eggs? Where had Jamie pilfered such ill-smelling eggs? From a bloody dragon? Over the reek of sulfur came a pungent whiff of ammonia that brought tears stinging against his heavy lids.

He struggled to lift them. A fractured eddy of sunlight swirled before his eyes.

Broken images assailed him. A rough-hewn window. Slats of azure blue between bud-laden branches. A breeze drifted through the open window, rife with the promise of spring. Sebastian knew where he was. The old crofter's hut. Pain shot through his ankle. Perhaps the last year had been but a dream, he mused. If he closed his eyes, a girl might kneel next to him, her fragrant hair swinging close enough to brush his chest, her cool fingers touching his brow with loving concern. If she did, he would carry her far away with him and never once be fool enough to look back.

Metal clinked against earthenware. Sebastian's vision sharpened. He muffled a groan at the sight of D'Artan hunched over a brass scale that sat on the scarred table. His grandfather measured out a paper cone of metal shavings, then bent to the hearth to stir them into the bubbling contents of a small iron kettle. Sebastian hoped it wasn't breakfast.

He wiggled his fingers. A stabbing tingle shot up his arm. With his returning awareness came a myriad of other discomforts. His hands were bound at the small of his back, his bad ankle bent at an awkward slant. His shoulder hurt like hell, and that might have something to do with the blackened bloodstains spilled down his shirt. A bitter taste lingered at the back of his throat. He knew that taste only too well. Just how much opium had D'Artan forced on him?

He still felt a bit giddy and almost laughed as he watched his grandfather scamper between hearth and bench like a frenzied monkey. D'Artan muttered something under his breath. A French monkey, Sebastian amended.

He'd never seen his grandfather so ruffled. D'Artan's gray hair clung to his head in wisps, as if he'd combed it with agitated fingers. The heat from the fire flushed his smooth cheeks to pink. Sweat stained his long apron.

Sebastian watched with detached interest as D'Artan carried the small vat from hearth to table with gloved hands. He dipped a silver spoon into the mixture. It hissed and bubbled. When he lifted the dripping spoon, it was nothing but a twisted, smoking mass. Sebastian swallowed.

"I'd prefer kippers and eggs if you don't mind," he said.

D'Artan jerked at the sound of his rusty voice, almost overturning the acid. He steadied it, his hands trembling with annoyance.

With alarming speed, a sunny smile replaced his frown. "You don't have to choose the menu. We're expecting company for breakfast."

Sebastian lifted an eyebrow, studying the table. It was spread with gunpowder, two pistols, a knife, and the vat of bubbling acid. "Who? Lucretia Borgia? Your old card-playing friend, the Marquis de Sade?"

"Wrong again. Your own loving wife. I sent her an engraved invitation."

A lusty roar of laughter burst from Sebastian. D'Artan's smile faded.

"My *wife* won't come. After the way I treated her at our last meeting, she wouldn't spit on me if I were ablaze."

D'Artan stood up and advanced on him. Sebastian held himself rigid, refusing to betray so much as a flinch. "Perhaps you underestimate your charm." His grandfather swiped a lock of hair from his brow with a tender hand. "And your prowess."

"Perhaps I overestimate it. As my father did when he abducted your daughter and expected her to fall in love with him."

A dark red suffused D'Artan's face. His snarl drew his skin taut over aristocratic cheekbones. "Make no mention of that savage to me. The past is done. I care only for the future."

Sebastian closed his eyes in mock boredom. "And a long dull future it will be if it's just you and I sitting here for all eternity, awaiting a lady with a formula."

D'Artan leaned close to him. "If she does not come, only my future will be long and dull. Yours will be very short indeed."

D'Artan's eyes glittered like shards of flint. Sebastian's hope that misplaced sentiment might stop his grandfather from killing him died on a stale and fruity breath.

D'Artan flitted back to the table, rubbing his palms together. Drops of spittle caught on his lips. He held a glass vial up to the sunlight. "I never did see what attraction our proud Miss Walker held for you. I can't wait for the severe little creature to stumble in, weeping and wringing her hands, babbling her precious formula to save your life. How I shall delight in her histrionics!"

"You coldhearted son-of-a—"

Sebastian's oath was cut off by a deafening pistol blast. The thunder of hoofbeats shook the hut.

The vial slipped from D'Artan's hand and shattered on the hard-packed floor. "If that pinched little chit has dared to bring the law . . ." He drew a German pocket pistol from his apron. His boots crunched the broken shards of glass as he went to open the door a furtive crack.

Sebastian had to know what was going on. He shifted more weight onto the leg folded beneath him. The devil dug a bony claw of pain into his shoulder. Sweat beaded his brow. He had to do this quick or he would lose the courage to do it at all. His teeth sank into his lower lip as he flung himself up and around onto his knees, slamming his injured shoulder against the windowsill. Sunlight and agony blinded him. He tasted the metallic tang of blood on his tongue.

As D'Artan bit off a profane curse, Sebastian gazed out the window. Smoke from the pistol blast drifted through the trees. He blinked, seeing the vision before him through a fractured prism of pain, then gave his head a hard shake. Perhaps so much blood had trickled out of his shoulder that there was none left to feed his brain.

But Prudence was still there, armed and straddling MacKay's gelding as if she'd been born to the saddle.

Her voice rang out in a singing brogue that would have done Jamie proud. "Open the door, ye bloody bastard, before I blow yer French arse from here to kingdom come."

Sebastian slumped against the windowsill, banging his head and wondering if it would hurt more to laugh or cry.

Thirty-four

Prudence gave the muzzle of her pistol a dainty blow before shoving it into the sash of her skirt. The butt of another pistol protruded beside it.

Sebastian marveled at the knotting of his gut, the slow, steady beat of desire in his groin. He supposed he'd have to have no pulse at all before his heart stopped shoving blood into all the wrong places whenever Prudence was near. She was angel fire and demon ice perched on MacKay's horse like a Highland princess, his own plaid draped carelessly over one shoulder. She had pulled her skirt between her legs and anchored it at her waist in makeshift breeches. Only the bandit's mask was absent, replaced by an incongruous pair of spectacles. She had come garbed not for a costume ball, but for a deadly masquerade where the players were no less dangerous for being known.

Her horse pawed the ground. She tossed her hair over her shoulder. "Halloo? Monsieur D'Artan, are you home?" Her cultured tones struck Sebastian like a blow.

He hooked his arms over the windowsill to keep from sliding back down. "Get the hell away from here, you daft lass, before you get yourself killed!"

"Quiet," D'Artan snarled, jerking him back by the hair. He had crossed the hut without a sound. An urbane smile replaced his sneer. "Good morning, Your Grace. So delighted you could drop in. Would you mind tossing your pistols on the ground and joining us?"

She smiled ingenuously. "But why, Viscount? I'm really a terrible shot."

In reply, D'Artan shoved the pocket pistol against Sebastian's temple and raked the hammer back. Prudence shrugged, refusing to meet Sebastian's furious gaze, and tossed her weapons down. She dismounted, landing on the balls of her feet with an arrogant bounce.

Sebastian felt D'Artan's nervous jerk as Prudence thrust open the door, sending it crashing against the wall. She swaggered in and sank onto a chair, then pulled a cheroot out of her plaid and leaned forward to light it with the flame of the lantern. D'Artan gaped at her as if she'd just escaped from Bedlam. Sebastian's eyes narrowed. Christ, the lass was magnificent! he thought. But what in the hell was she trying to do?

She wielded the cheroot between two eloquent fingers and propped her boots on the table. "Good morning, gentlemen. I believe we have some business to conduct."

D'Artan's grip on Sebastian's hair slowly eased. Sebastian could almost read his grandfather's methodical mind. D'Artan despised unknowns. If he was going to have to deal with a madwoman, he wanted it over and done with.

He slipped the pistol back into his apron pocket. "I've booked myself passage for France. I must have your father's formula before I go. I have all the components ready to test it. Give it to me. Now."

"I didn't dare write it down." She tapped her temple with one finger. "I keep it in here." She fished a silver flask from the plaid, uncorked it, and took a deep swig. Her eyes sparkled for an elusive instant, then cleared. She swiped her mouth with the back of her hand. "You must remember that it's a dangerous formula. My father died for it."

D'Artan planted both palms on the table and leaned over her. "And I am willing to kill for it."

She took a long draw from the cheroot, betrayed by nothing but a slight pinkening of her cheeks. Pursing her lips, she deliberately blew a cloud of smoke in D'Artan's face.

He sputtered. Tears ran from his rheumy eyes. He jerked Prudence up by her plaid, twisting it tight at her throat.

A moment earlier, Sebastian would have sworn it impossible to stand. But before he realized it, he was lurching up and away from the window, his only desire to wrap his fingers around D'Artan's throat and squeeze the life out of him. A spear of agony shot through his shoulder. His head spun. Oddly enough, it was Prudence who caught him, her hands a gentle vise against his forearms. D'Artan hovered behind her, his eyes bright and wary.

"There now, darling," Prudence said soothingly, guiding him back to the wall. "You mustn't blame your grandfather for being a bit impatient. He's waited a long time for this. Sit in the window, won't you, and block the sun for me. Many of these components are delicate and very sensitive to sunlight." Her hair brushed his chin.

He closed his eyes, aching to draw her against him. "Don't give him the formula, Prudence. He'll only kill you once he's got it."

Her tinkling laugh would have made Tricia swoon with envy. "Of course he won't, you silly dear." She smiled at D'Artan over her shoulder. "Your grandfather is a respectable man."

Sunlight slanted across her hair, warming it to cinnamon. Her eyes glowed with a strange fervor.

D'Artan gestured to the table. "The revolution waits for no man. Shall we begin?"

Sebastian wanted to snatch her back, but it was too late. Prudence was already sauntering toward D'Artan, her shapely rump hugged by the taut curve of her skirt.

He eased his hip onto the windowsill. Balance was tricky if not impossible with his hands bound and his head still reeling from the effects of the opium. Sunlight warmed his back.

D'Artan fussed over his pots and vials with childish glee. "I have determined that your father's foolish accident was caused by using a mercury-based fulminate. I have taken the liberty of substituting silver for mercury."

"How very clever," Prudence murmured. She turned up the lantern to dispel the shadows. Her smoking cigar sat near its base. "There. Add just a touch of that ammonia, won't you?"

"Ah!" D'Artan complied, looking absurdly pleased with himself. "I had guessed as much." A cloud of steam rose from the table.

Prudence pointed. "Now dissolve your silver in your nitric acid."

He beamed. "Already done."

"Why, Viscount! I don't think you need me at all. You've figured it out all by yourself."

"I told you once that I was a bit of an amateur chemist."

"And a professional bastard," Sebastian murmured.

D'Artan smirked at him. "You'd know more about that occupation, wouldn't you? You've been practicing it since birth."

Turning back to the table, D'Artan mixed his ingredients with fussy precision. Prudence smothered a yawn. D'Artan looked up, his face expectant and feverish in the lantern light.

Prudence stretched and took a few steps toward Sebastian. "One final ingredient, Viscount."

D'Artan hovered over the bench, his eyes glazed, his hands twitching in their impatience.

She gestured toward the flask on the table. An angelic smile curved her lips. "A hooker of brandy."

A hooker of brandy.

The husky words resonated through Sebastian's mind as Prudence inched back toward the window. D'Artan jerked up the flask, fumbling in his excitement.

He lifted it to pour. A shaft of sunlight gilded the brandy to a glittering amber stream.

Such a waste of fine brandy.

Squire Blake's words thundered through Sebastian's brain as Prudence hurled herself at him, tumbling them both out the window just before the crofter's hut exploded in a roaring ball of flame.

Thirty-five

Prudence's cheek nuzzled against something hard and familiar. She pulled off her shattered spectacles to discover it was Sebastian's chest. They were sprawled in the grass in front of the crofter's hut, thrown clear by the blast.

What had been the crofter's hut, Prudence corrected herself. Only a smoldering shell of rubble and twisted boards remained. She glanced at Sebastian and saw he'd opened his eyes. Their smoky clarity unnerved her.

She dropped her head back down. She felt as if she was going to be ill. "Oh, dear. I hope you're not angry. I'm afraid I blew up your grandfather."

It hurt like hell, but Sebastian still managed a shrug. "A socially reprehensible, but morally sound decision." His lips touched her hair. She winced as they found a shallow gash on her temple. "You're quite the little actress, you know. You should hire a manager and take to the stage posthaste."

"Can I have a bath first?" she mumbled against his chest. "I thought the cigar was going to be the end of me. Dreadfully nasty, aren't they?"

"Terrible habit. I've been thinking of giving them up myself."

Pillars of black smoke stained the azure sky, sifting sparks and ash high above the pines. MacKay's gelding grazed placidly in the trees across the stream.

Sebastian was very still. "You came for me. Why?"

Their gazes met across his chest. She drew his plaid from her shoulders, folding it with reverent hands. "To give you this."

"Are you sure it wasn't to give me this?" He touched his lips to hers, not caring that they both tasted of blood, sweat, and smoke. Prudence moved against him with a small moan.

He laughed breathlessly. "Although this position has some very intriguing possibilities, would you mind untying my hands?"

He sat up with a grunt of pain as she crawled behind him. "I don't know, laddie," she teased. "Can ye make it worth me while?"

"That I can, lass. That I can."

She dug at the knot with her cracked fingernails. Blood trickled down her cheek, and she swiped it away.

A spasm jerked through Sebastian's body. His arms went rigid. "Stay behind me, Prudence. Stay behind me and close your eyes."

But Prudence Walker Kerr had never averted her eyes from anything. A raw scream tore from her throat as D'Artan lurched out of the ruins of the crofter's hut.

His apron and breeches hung in rags. The flesh of his face had melted and blackened against the bones. But out of that monstrous visage glinted the steely clarity of one eye. A hoarse bellow escaped his throat. He waved the pocket pistol wildly in the air.

Sebastian felt Prudence move, and scooted his body around as a shield. "Dammit, Prudence, stay behind me!"

With his hands bound, though, Sebastian was helpless, a living target for D'Artan's twisted rage. Prudence's own pistols lay in the grass a few feet away, and her knee crunched her shattered spectacles as she lunged for them, ignoring Sebastian's savage oath. D'Artan waved the pistol in her direction and she was forced to freeze, stretched out on her stomach in the grass.

The viscount's eye focused on Sebastian and narrowed. He staggered toward his grandson, the pistol dangling from his charred fingertips.

"You little bastard," he said, his raspy voice low and

vicious. "I wish I'd never laid eyes on you. You've been nothing but a failure all your life—a failure as a highwayman, a failure as a spy, a failure as a man. You make me ill. You're just like your father."

With an effort betrayed only by the skin pinching tight over his cheekbones, Sebastian heaved himself to his feet. "You've always hated me, haven't you? Your loving grandfather ploy was never very convincing."

D'Artan threw back his head with a cackle. "I despised you. I loathed you. Every time I looked at you, all I saw was him. Brendan Kerr. The dirty Scot who broke my daughter—my only little girl . . ." His voice cracked.

Prudence swallowed against a welling of pity even as her fingers curled around the cool butt of a pistol. *Dear God, let it be the pistol I haven't fired,* she prayed, and eased it up.

D'Artan's head lolled. "My precious Micheline, the one fine thing I ever made in my life. You!" His voice rose to a shriek as his last scrap of sanity broke away. Prudence realized with swelling horror that he believed Sebastian *was* Brendan Kerr. "You filthy monster. You stole and raped my daughter and that coward MacKay let you get away with it."

D'Artan lifted the pistol and pointed it straight at Sebastian's heart, determined to take the vengeance that had been denied him for thirty years. "I'll blow all the Scots to hell before I'm done. All the English too."

Sebastian tossed a lock of hair from his eyes and faced his crazed accuser with a courage that tore at Prudence's heart. "We'll be there to greet them at the gates," he said to his grandfather, "you and I."

Prudence steadied the gun against her wrist.

D'Artan pulled back the hammer on his own pistol. "You'll never steal another man's child."

Prudence's finger tightened on the trigger. As she squinted and aimed, blood trickled into her eyes. D'Artan's form ran into a faceless blob.

He lurched forward. "You'll never steal another man's bride like you stole that weakling MacKay's bride."

A voice as sharp as a double-edged sword rang out from the pines. "My pregnant bride, you son-of-a-bitch."

A pistol exploded. A red stain blossomed over D'Artan's

heart. He gave his chest a baffled glance, then staggered backward, crumpling into the stream with a final splash. For a long moment, the only sound was the cheerful chortling of flowing water.

Prudence's gun slipped from her fingers as Sebastian slowly turned. MacKay stood behind him, smoking pistol in hand. Prudence's gaze traveled between them as the two men came face to face for the first time. Broad shoulders, stiffened with pride. Lashes long enough to embarrass even the staunchest male. Brackets around their mouths, carved by laughter and too many tears.

How could they all have been so blind? Prudence wondered, as Sebastian's gray eyes widened with dawning realization. Not his mother's eyes after all. His father's eyes.

Her fingers knotted in the grass. At last she understood the strange bond she had felt from her first meeting with MacKay, the haunting recognition, the tender empathy. It was not her own papa he reminded her of. It was Sebastian. Tears spilled down her cheeks.

MacKay's voice was matter-of-fact as he began to undo Sebastian's bonds. "I've had my suspicions for years, you know. I adored your mother. I fled to Greece because I was ashamed of seducing her before the vows. I planned on returning in the fall when I could make her my wife in every way."

"You were a bit late, weren't you?"

Prudence winced at the bite of contempt in Sebastian's voice.

MacKay took a step back, the ropes dangling from his gnarled hands. "When I returned, your mother came to me. She swore she loved Kerr, that you were his child, not my own."

"And you believed her?"

"I've searched my heart for thirty years trying to find her reason for lying. Why would she tell me such a thing? To protect me? To protect us all?"

Sebastian bowed his head, massaging the circlet of bruises on his wrists. Oddly enough, it was Prudence he studied beneath his lashes, not MacKay. The words he spoke came straight from his heart. "No. Because she felt ashamed.

Because she felt dirty. After the things he did to her, she could never feel worthy of someone as fine as you."

MacKay's mouth twisted. "As fine as me . . ." He shook his head as he walked over to D'Artan's corpse, his shoulders hunched beneath his plaid.

Sebastian's hands clenched into fists. He could not help MacKay now. He had too much of his own pain to deal with. Prudence sat in the grass, hugging herself. Grimy tear tracks stained her face. He sank down beside her, ignoring the throb of his shoulder, and gently gathered her into his arms. She melted against him. He buried his face in her hair as if its gentle fragrance might clear away the smoke of his life once and for all. He nuzzled her throat, tasting her tears on his tongue.

Healing sunlight caressed Prudence's back. They clung to each other, too lost in the comfort of their embrace to hear the crash of the underbrush, the rising voices.

A cold wet snout nuzzled Prudence's forehead. A sloppy tongue lapped her cheek. She opened one eye, peering over Sebastian's shoulder.

All she could see were yellow teeth bared in a canine grin. Her mouth fell open. There was only one dog that dumb and ugly in all of Great Britain.

Prudence tried to speak, but nothing came out except a croak. Sebastian slowly became aware of her stillness. He lifted his head, following her gaze upward from beribboned slippers to satin-flounced petticoats to amber eyes narrowed in avenging slits.

Thirty-six

As Sebastian met the venomous gaze of his former mistress and fiancée, his hands lifted instinctively to adjust a mask that wasn't there. Boris's ears perked up with interest.

"My, my," Tricia purred. "If it's not my dear sweet niece."

Squire Blake leaned over Tricia's shoulder, peering at Prudence through his quizzing glass as if it were a microscope and she a bug. "By God, it is her, isn't it? What do you think of that?"

Prudence stood and clasped her hands in front of her. Under her aunt's avid scrutiny, she felt nine years old again, her cheeks streaked with graphite, her clothes reeking of sulfur. Sebastian rose too. His hands curled over her shoulders in a possessive gesture, warming her with courage.

"How did you find us?" Prudence asked.

"An anonymous note," Tricia snapped.

"D'Artan," Sebastian whispered. "He no doubt intended them to discover us in a fatal lovers' embrace."

"I can explain," Prudence said softly.

Tricia's hands fluttered out to encompass them both. "Why bother? This explains so many things." She began to count off items on her fingers. "You seduced my fiancé. You disguised him as an infamous criminal."

"I fear it was no disguise, Countess. The man *is* an

infamous criminal." Sir Arlo strode out of the trees, flanked by three deputies. His men fanned out, poking the hut's rubble with their walking sticks. Sebastian backed away from Prudence and leaned heavily against a gnarled oak.

"Quiet," Tricia spat at Arlo. "How dare you interrupt me? Where was I? Oh, yes, you ran away with him under the pretense of being kidnapped."

"Quite a grand adventure!" Squire Blake interjected.

"But I *was* kidnapped," Prudence protested.

Tricia arched her eyebrows. "I suppose the rogue has kept you chained to his bed ever since?"

Color stained Prudence's cheeks.

Tricia stepped around her niece as if she'd gone invisible and trailed a crimson fingernail down Sebastian's shirt. "If I'd been wiser, I'd have kept the rogue chained to my own bed."

Sebastian crossed his arms. His lips twisted in a petulant smile. "That's the only way you would have kept me there, darling."

Tricia shrieked.

Sir Arlo held out some iron fetters, his face set in a pleasant smile. "These are the only chains the gentleman shall wear until he's brought to trial for his dastardly deeds as the Dreadful Scot Bandit Kirkpatrick. For robbery. For kidnapping—"

"You can add murder to that, sir," one of the deputies called from where he squatted beside D'Artan's corpse.

MacKay strode across the clearing. "You cannot arrest that man. I forbid it."

"Why arrest him?" Tricia stamped her tiny foot. "Can't we just hang him now?"

Squire Blake rubbed his fat palms together. "Oh, this is quite interesting. Much better than a fox hunt."

Sebastian smiled at Tricia. "Too bad we're not in France, dear. You could have me beheaded."

"With pleasure," she hissed.

"And who might you be, sir?" Tugbert demanded of MacKay.

MacKay slipped a comforting arm around Prudence's shoulders. "I am this young lass's fiancé."

"But I'm her husband," Sebastian added.

Sir Arlo again held out the fetters.

"You cannot arrest that man," MacKay repeated. "He has been granted a full pardon from the King."

The sheriff's smile slipped a notch. "Let's have a look at it then, shall we?"

MacKay looked at Prudence. Prudence looked at Sebastian. His jaw tightened, but he refused to return her gaze. Slowly he lifted his arms, offering his wrists to Sir Arlo.

"No!" Prudence gave an agonized cry. They all stared at her. "Laird MacKay's right. You can't arrest him."

"Why?" Sir Arlo asked coolly.

Her mind raced. Her hands twisted in her skirt, then her head flew up in sudden hope. "Because he's not the Dreadful Scot Bandit Kirkpatrick. I am."

Sebastian groaned. Sir Arlo's mouth fell open. Squire Blake sputtered, his face scarlet, unable to find a fitting adjective for this thrilling new development. Tricia fished a handkerchief out of her bodice and handed it to him.

"That's right." Prudence paced the clearing in long strides, thinking furiously. One of the deputies dogged her steps, shackles clanking in his hands. "I've been the bandit all these years. Why do you think the robberies always occurred along the border? Auntie Tricia would tuck me into my little bed, then I'd shimmy down my trellis and off I'd go, galloping across the moonlit meadows on my stallion—"

"You don't have a stallion," Sebastian gently reminded her.

She paced past him, deliberately stepping hard on his toes. "Perhaps it was a mare then. It's hard to tell in the dark. My only concern was preying upon the rich, robbing the innocent—"

"What an absurd tale!" MacKay interrupted.

Sebastian sighed. "At last, a voice of sanity."

MacKay drew himself to his full height and proudly tightened his plaid over his shoulders. "I meself am the Dreadful Scot Bandit Kirkpatrick."

Sebastian buried his face in his hands with a snort of despair.

"The butler at the Blake estate will be more than happy to confirm my identity," MacKay went on. "His staff made quite a daring attempt to capture me before I escaped. Even the maids were armed." He shot Prudence a narrowed glance. "I'd have probably been killed had not someone had the foresight to inform them I was worth more alive than dead."

For the first time, Prudence noticed the dark smudge of a bruise on his cheekbone. Shrugging guiltily, she bit off one of her fingernails.

The clearing erupted into chaos. Sir Arlo tossed his fetters to the ground with a very ungentlemanly curse. His deputy scratched his head, looking doubtfully between Prudence and MacKay. Tricia began screeching for justice, demanding that Sir Arlo hang them all. Boris danced around Squire Blake, barking furiously.

A shrill Highland battle cry threw the clearing into silence. Boris whimpered and slunk behind Tricia's skirts. Two horses burst from the bracken, their riders pulling up at the last moment to keep from trampling the crowd.

Sir Arlo faced them, hands on hips. "Let me guess. You must be the Dreadful Scot Bandit Kirkpatrick."

Jamie swept off his cap. "At yer service, sir."

Relief softened Jamie's sharp features as his gaze found Prudence and Sebastian, grimy but alive. Tricia paled at the sight of Tiny. She slipped behind Squire Blake, but not even his bulk was enough to hide both her and Boris.

Tiny beamed and nudged his horse forward. "Why, Jamie, there's me wee countess! Hullo, luv. Do ye remember me?"

"Enough!" Sir Arlo bellowed. Prudence almost smiled. Arlo really was quite a commanding figure when irked. "I'd like nothing more than to take the countess's suggestion and hang all of you, but my devotion to the law of England prohibits me. So I'm going to arrest the one man I believe can give me the answers I seek."

MacKay strode forward, but Sebastian stepped in front of him. This time when he held out his wrists, Sir Arlo slipped the fetters over them with a final click.

As the sheriff stepped back from Sebastian, Prudence drew an uneven breath. Her measured steps closed the distance between them. She brushed away a tear with the heel of her hand, leaving a sooty streak. Oblivious to Tricia, oblivious to all of them, she leaned forward and touched her lips to

Sebastian's in a melting caress. Not even the heavy metal chains between them could stop her from pressing her body to his in loving surrender.

He pulled away, lingering only long enough to press his lips to her ear. She held her breath, wanting to savor any tender confession he might make until they could be together again.

"Goodbye, my darling duchess," he whispered.

Her hands clenched into fists as one of the deputies led him away. MacKay strode after them, determined at last to stand by his only son. Sebastian glanced over his shoulder, throwing her a wink. Prudence knew she would carry the image with her forever: his crooked grin, the smudge of soot on his brow, the sunlight streaking his tousled hair. Dashing until the bitter end.

Tricia's fingernails dug like tiny knives into Prudence's forearm. "Come with me, you wicked, ungrateful girl. You're a disgrace to your papa and all of my poor dead husbands. I can't believe the thanks you've shown me for all I've done—"

Prudence jerked her arm out of her aunt's grip. Straightening her shoulders, she took a step forward, using the full advantage of her height to look down her nose at her aunt.

Tricia took a hasty step backward, stumbling over Boris. Squire Blake caught her before she fell. She clutched at her ruffled bosom. "Well, I never . . . The sheer arrogance . . ."

Squire Blake led her away, murmuring sympathetically even as he cast a glance of grudging admiration over his shoulder at Prudence. A whimpering Boris trailed after them. Prudence stood alone. Strangely enough, it was Tiny who laid his big hands on her shoulders. "C'mon, lass. Ye're a bonny brave girl, but we'd best get ye home."

She walked forward dazedly, wishing she could remember where home was.

Thirty-seven

Rain drummed against the roof of the ramshackle building, but not even the downpour could keep the curious away from the courthouse in the heart of Elsdon. It was packed shoulder to shoulder with the assorted denizens of Northumberland and the surrounding counties. Steam rose from damp cloaks. Earls rubbed elbows with farmers, satin vied with wool, as they flocked in, all determined to witness the dissolution of the marriage of the notorious Duchess of Winton.

Reporters from both the *London Observer* and the *Times* shoved their way through the crowd, collecting opinions and gossip. Sympathies were divided. An old farm woman with a face shriveled like a dried apple pronounced the duchess a poor unfortunate girl, carried off by a scoundrel and forced to marry at gunpoint. The young Miss Devony Blake would later be quoted as accusing Prudence Walker of being a "nefarious hedonist" who "dared to abscond" with her own aunt's fiancé. Her honorable father gleefully pronounced the entire affair as "simply rife with intrigue," then struck a noble pose and asked if they might include a sketch of him with their article.

The murmuring of the crowd rose to a low roar as the door of the courthouse swung open, admitting in a blast of rain the object of their fascination. Women lifted fans to muffle their whispers. The men nudged each other, leering.

The *Times* reporter hid his disappointment as one of the local gentry explained to him that the duchess was not the flamboyant creature in the towering wig and dipping dress, but the bespectacled woman behind her.

There was certainly nothing in the young duchess's appearance to invite criticism, the reporter mused. She was dressed in simple black, her dark hair caught in a chignon at the nape of her neck. He cursed himself for not bringing his inkpot. God, how he wanted to sketch her! Lines etched with such clarity were always fuzzed by time and memory.

Thunder rumbled through the courthouse as Prudence walked forward and took her seat in the front. Tricia left Old Fish at the door to shake out her umbrella on the grumbling few who had arrived too late to find seats. Tricia's new beau marched after her with a swirl of his cape—a Corsican count, his pristine frock coat dripping with ribbons and medals.

Prudence folded her hands in her lap. The noise of the crowd seemed to her only the roar of a distant ocean. She could not feel the lash of their whispers, the sting of their leers. She could not feel anything. A terrible numbness washed through her, dulling everything in its path.

One month. Thirty days and no word. Not one note. Not one message. Nothing to indicate Sebastian didn't want her to go through with the dissolution she had allowed Tricia to schedule. Prudence didn't need to hear the buzz of gossip around her to know that Sebastian had been released from a London jail almost a week ago. Old Fish had been pleased enough to inform her of that.

Sir Arlo had wisely decided that he would have a difficult, if not impossible, task convicting Sebastian Kerr, since the scene of his arrest had been crawling with Dreadful Scot Bandits, including a Scottish lord, a duchess, and a carrot-topped minister's son. There was also the matter of a mysterious disappearing pardon and the fact that Killian MacKay, one of the most powerful dukes in Scotland, had publicly claimed Sebastian as his son, illegitimate or not. To save face and stifle questions, it was announced the Dreadful Bandit had perished in the blast that had destroyed the crofter's hut. D'Artan's corpse was buried with suitable aplomb.

Prudence pulled off her gloves, wadding them into a ball. Sebastian was probably on his way back to the Highlands by now, she thought. He was the heir to one of the richest estates in Scotland. He could have his Dunkirk and anything else he was willing to accept from his father. He no longer required a plain duchess of moderate means to buy his respectability.

She stiffened as the judge entered the courtroom. His robes were dusty and his wig looked as if something had been nesting in it. Surveying the crowd, he heaved a tremendous sigh. He wasn't accustomed to such scenes. His most important judgment last year had involved the theft of a pregnant sow.

He pounded on his bench, dulling the murmurs to whispers. Prudence stared into her lap, letting Tricia answer his questions in her tinkling falsetto. Perhaps now Sebastian could escape the battered legacy of Brendan Kerr, she mused. He would always bear the scars, but in time the wounds might heal. She wished she could believe the same for herself.

"Your Grace!" The words boomed out like thunder.

Prudence started in her chair to discover the judge glowering at her. The nervous titters of the crowd faded to silence. "Yes, sir?"

"Your guardian has been kind enough to answer my questions about your abduction. I would appreciate the same courtesy from you. I will repeat my question again. Was this travesty of a marriage consummated?"

Travesty? Pelting hand in hand through a sun-drenched meadow. Quibbling over who would name the goat. Sharing a kiss at dawn, clothed only in the morning's first rays of sunlight. She opened her mouth to lie, fighting to speak past the hard knot in her throat.

A voice rang out from the back of the courtroom. "Aye, sir, that it was."

Prudence stood, gripping the banister for support. Turning, she saw a man standing in the doorway of the court-house.

His lips curved in a naughty grin. "And with great pleasure, I might add."

Prudence went scarlet, then white. The court exploded with cries of shock. The judge hammered on his bench.

Sebastian Kerr stood with his father behind him, both garbed in full Highland splendor. Killian MacKay beamed proudly. Tiny and Jamie flanked them, each wearing crisp new garments. A fat cigar hung from Jamie's lips.

As Sebastian strode down the aisle toward her, Prudence sank back down, her knuckles ashen against the banister. She couldn't look at him. It hurt too much. It was like looking into the sun.

The crowd held its collective breath as Sebastian knelt beside her. He drew an engraved box from his plaid and handed it to her. "I thought to buy you a ring, but Jamie suggested you might appreciate this more."

She opened the box with trembling fingers. A tiny gold matchlock pistol nestled in folds of velvet.

Sebastian stood back, a resigned expression on his handsome face. "Do your worst. I deserve it."

The crowd gasped as she leveled the tiny pistol straight at his heart and pulled the trigger.

A jeweled bird burst from the muzzle, tinkling the first chiming notes of Bach's "Sleepers, Wake." Prudence moved to stifle her laugh, but Sebastian caught her hand before she could. Her rich ripples of laughter spilled through the courtroom.

All traces of humor disappeared from Sebastian's eyes. "I was afraid of implicating you. I couldn't come back until I knew I was truly free." He knelt beside her again and folded her hand in his. "I'm still a bastard, you know."

She primly adjusted her spectacles. "You always have been. But that never stopped me from loving you."

The crowd roared as Sebastian scooped her up in his arms. Tricia fell back in a dead swoon, knocking her wig into the count's lap.

As the crowd parted before them, Sebastian's lips brushed her cheek, her nose, her brow. His hand raked through her chignon, scattering the pins until her hair fell soft and loose around her face.

Tiny and Jamie flung open the doors. He carried her into the falling rain, tenderly tucking his plaid over her head.

"Where I come from," she said, her voice husky, "when a man gives a woman his plaid, it means only one thing."

He paused on the steps of the courthouse, smiling tenderly at her. "Show me."

She did. Their lips met as she clung to him. The crowd bellowed its approval. Killian MacKay turned and gave them a proper English bow. Tiny threw back his head with a roar of laughter.

Jamie wiped his streaming eyes and blew his nose on the sleeve of his new coat. "Don't no one dare say Jamie Graham ain't a sentimental, God-fearin' lad," he muttered to himself.

He tucked his smoking cigar between Old Fish's puckered lips before leaping down the steps, bounding after Prudence and Sebastian in the sweet English rain.